The Last of the Tearoom Ladies

The Last of the Tearoom Ladies

and Other Minnesota Tales

By Peg Meier

Neighbors Publishing
P.O. Box 15071
Minneapolis, Minn.
55415

Neighbors Publishing
P.O. Box 15071
Minneapolis, Minn.
55415

Contents

Foreword

By Garrison Keillor

Every journalist attempts to observe the crooked frontier between news and fiction, which is not so much a distinction between observable fact and fantasy as it is the question, "What is important and necessary to write about?"

Fiction writers tend to write about our mothers and fathers, and journalists tend to write about government, which is to say that journalists write about their fathers. When government acts, journalism writes, and when government doesn't act, journalism writes about the lull. Officialdom is never beneath the notice of journalism; the father always sits at the head of the table.

In fiction, the question of what to write about is addressed in solitude, a writer in a room wondering what these scraps of story are leading him toward, but in journalism, there is an editor to be faced, and one does not want to look dumb. In fiction, dumb is not such a big deterrent, but in journalism, dumbness gets you sent to the back of the class, to the poor wretches who write obits and cover the Boy Scouts and interview visiting authors. And in journalism, more so than in fiction, it's men who decide what's dumb.

In the male world of journalism, the crucial matters are politics, crime, business and finance, sport, the real world of struggle and competition, and the heroes are men who do combat with worthy adversaries, investigate them with cunning, wrest information from them, best them in public encounters, hurl them into ignominy or prison. The heroes of journalism are men who have challenged the official version of events, stood up to politicians, investigated them, shouted at them, abused them, brought the empire down.

In the men's locker room of journalism, the daily question is, "What is happening in this city that I don't know about and that people are trying to keep secret from me?"

There is an older tradition in journalism, however, and that is story-telling, which asks, "What is life like in this city today? What is life like for the others?"

This is the question that moved Chekhov and Stephen Crane, and it is what motivates Peg Meier's writing at the Star Tribune, collected in this book. These beautiful and brilliant pieces about ordinary people are journalism at its most humane and most invisible, the writer putting herself at the service of other people's stories. In the ethic of this writer, everyone has a story, no story is unworthy and the journalist's first duty is to be a passionate listener.

Perhaps their beauty is more evident to a reader who lives outside the city. I live in New York and I miss Minnesota, so my relatives send me pounds of the hometown paper to keep me up to date, and Peg Meier is the only reporter who writes about exactly what I miss in Minnesota. The rest of the paper is about big events that don't matter to me and gossip I can't appreciate because I don't know who's Important anymore, and about the hipness of the reporters, but Peg Meier's stories are about the essential Minnesota, the Minnesota that is utterly unlike New York or Los Angeles, the Minnesota that hasn't changed so very much from when I was a kid. The Minnesota of the hometown, the old classmates, the relatives, the old neighborhood.

The people are as humorous and private and the language as plain and refractive as ever, and that is what makes Peg Meier's stories so brilliant. They are free of media cant and self-conscious "sensitivity" and psychobabble, they are written in a clear Minnesota voice that allows the characters to emerge in their own right.

The work of Peg Meier is very close to fiction, in that she chooses to write stories of fabulous simplicity about people who aren't particularly Important, and she writes about them in language like their own, not as an authority on their lives, but as a journalist, a keeper of their record. This is writing that, at its best, lets you forget that the writer is there, and it probably is going to win no prizes. The Pulitzer in feature writing tends to go to the sort of genre kitsch and soapy melodramas that can be made into TV movies. But the moment you pick this book up, you are back in Minnesota, listening to people talk the way people talk in cafes, taverns, kitchens, church basements and the back seats of cars.

Peg Meier is a journalist of the permanence of Minnesota, the essential Minnesota that is distinctive and remarkable. She is a stubborn original who has stuck to her own lights and refused to write like anybody else. Her style is pure Minnesota, and for that reason she isn't as highly regarded there as she should be, but years from now, when the front pages of 1990 seem only quaint and all the columnists are unreadable, these plain portraits of Minnesota people will be a permanent treasure, a piece of folklore.

Preface

I remember a pleasant few hours sitting with Jay Zachary on his front porch. He was 104½ and living pretty darn well in St. Paul when I had a chance to interview him in 1976. He told me about his health, his pre-breakfast habits (a talk with his Creator and a shot of Old Granddad) and his family. He spoke of his son Ben out on Louisiana Av. and his daughter toward Hastings and another son. . . .

"Whoa," I interrupted. "Just how many children do you have?"

"Ain't got no children," he answered, confusing me considerably.

I persevered. "Well, do your kids come to visit often?"

"Ain't got no kids," he insisted. I began to wonder about this interview.

After a well-timed pause, he said it again. "Ain't got no kids. Got old people. You get this old and your kids is old people."

Nicely put.

I never know what to expect from the people I get to write about. Rarely do the conversations or events go the way I might have imagined. After nearly 20 years of writing about Minnesotans for the Star Tribune, I've learned not to expect. I ask, they tell me. When I'm too dumb to ask, they fill me in. When we're winding down an interview and I ask what else I should know about them, they tell me marvelous things. They're direct and honest and funny and lovely.

For this collection, I've chosen warm, wonderful, real-life Minnesotans who are full of stories. Few are famous. That's because I especially enjoy meeting and writing about "ordinary" Minnesotans who are somehow extraordinary. They have something worthwhile to tell about themselves and are willing to pass it on to others. They know that life is brief and fragile, and they're pushing to do what makes them happy.

These people have had their trials, their fears. Most have affirmed life, rather than despaired. Some have done both.

Your heart will go out to some. Others have humor and persistence you'll admire. And some you may want to give a kick in the behind.

I can't predict which is which. One of the interesting aspects of reporting is getting reactions from readers. I can't guess which subjects will delight my colleague across the desk or my next-door neighbor or my friends. Nor my editors, for that matter.

But I think you'll like many of the people in these stories.

For one reason or another, I like them all.

Peg Meier
Minneapolis
May 1990

Judy Krasselt

Minneapolis' Rosiest Merchant

March 16, 1986

❧

You're familiar with March gloom, right? You know, that kind of gray day when every radio station is playing the blues, and there's as much grit as snow in the snowbanks, and you're sorta hoping some turkey will say something outrageous so you'll be justified in punching that ugly little face.

There's a cheap remedy for Minneapolis March madness: Stop at the Chicago Lake Florist.

For the price of a rose, you can meet Judy Krasselt, one of the friendliest and givingest merchants in town.

Some people walk out with a Sweetheart rose without bothering to pay — they talk her out of one — but we're assuming that you, dear reader, are not that cheap. Besides, her son Old Ern (he was called that even before he had a son, Little Ern) has taken upon himself the responsibility of weeding down the requests for free flowers. His heart is not as soft as his mom's.

But anyway, visit their shop at 717 E. Lake St. for a whiff of the roses and a talk with Judy Krasselt.

She's known for her good spirits as much as her award-winning bouquets. Darrell Ansel, owner of the Chicago-Lake Liquor Store in the next block, said she has the ability to make everybody feel important.

He said, "When I moved to this neighborhood around 10 years ago, she sent flowers. It wasn't something she was doing to get my business." But, of course, she has gotten his business. "She's been our florist all these years. I stop in every once in a while, which according to my wife is not often enough." Sometimes he doesn't get the bill. Ansel remembers the time he ran a newspaper ad announcing an anniversary sale of his liquor, and a bouquet was delivered to his door saying, "Happy anniversary, compliments of Chicago Lake Florist."

Lois Allen, administrative officer of the Marquette Lake Bank, said that Krasselt can't stand to let flowers go past their peak, so she's constantly sending free flowers around the neighborhood. "It can be a dreary, rainy day and her driver will show up at the bank with bud vases full of carnations or roses." When the supply of empty bud vases has built up, Krasselt will send someone around to collect them and they'll start coming back, refilled.

Jan Steinert, a customer who found Krasselt years ago because she frequents the beauty parlor next door, told about ordering flowers for her husband's funeral last July. Steinert was pleased with the blue carnations and red roses Krasselt prepared for the casket, and she wept when she saw that Krasselt also sent a huge bouquet of roses from herself. "She's such an inspirational person," Steinert said of Krasselt. "You know, she could be sitting at home in a wheelchair, feeling sorry for herself."

True.

Krasselt has been in two car accidents that nearly killed her. Vertebrae in her neck are fused, and she wears a neck brace. She has severe headaches. Unable to turn her head, she never crosses a busy street — like Lake St. — alone. She shouldn't lift much of anything, but somehow she thinks that rule doesn't apply to flowers. Or flowerpots. Or sacks of dirt.

Her injuries changed her life in more than one direction, she said. The pain she's learned to live with. What's more important is that she has realized that life is precious.

"I can't imagine anyone being bored," she proclaimed one day to a reporter who didn't have the nerve to admit to her a recent struggle with boredom.

"Look at all these beautiful flowers. There's so much I want to do. I can't imagine a better field to be in. I could spend hours and hours and hours with the plants. The beauty! And the fragrance! Mine is a labor of love. You're never going to be rich in this business; you're dealing with a perishable, and you have to give away a lot of flowers."

That's why customers who send a wire order get a free flower to take home. That's why her customers are remembered in the hospital. That's why the "Dear little ladies from the Augustana home" walk away with flowers in hand. That's why Midwest Challenge gets free bouquets. That's why a child who wanders in with a fistful of pennies and nickels will walk out with a rose. "I want them to have lovely flowers when they're little kids. They're my future customers."

Said her son, Old Ern, "She'll probably die a pauper. And I'll probably die before her, because I'll starve to death."

"Oh, honey," she responded, with a poke at his midsection. "It doesn't look like you're starving."

"No, really," he said. "Every character in the world is calling here for free stuff. I pick who she should talk to. I'm generous, but I think it over."

The other day a boy stopped by and charmed Judy Krasselt with his opening line: "Can I speak to you confidentially?" A good salesman, he got her to buy his goods. Ern Krasselt growled, "But he didn't bathe much."

"Oh, Ern."

"I can pick out a scam pretty fast. When I'm 62 and I have it all behind me, then I'll be nice to everybody."

His mother was born 63 years ago this week (send flowers) in Keewatin, on Minnesota's Iron Range. Her dad was a miner and with 10 children they were very poor, but somehow her mother always had the money and time for petunias and nasturtiums. Judy (actually Catherine; she looked like Judy Garland and picked up the nickname) always loved the plants and wildflowers.

She moved to Minneapolis to go to business school and met Orville Krasselt. They were married 43 years ago, on Halloween. She calls him the most talented man ever put on the Earth — he oil paints, he's a good tailor, he scuba dives, he fishes, he's a metal sculptor, he worked on every space shot before he retired from Rosemount Engineering. She said, "Now I've got him working harder than he ever did."

They raised three sons and a daughter. When he was home in the evenings she worked as a waitress, a caterer, a computer operator, a diamond salesperson, a cake decorator, a cake-decorating instructor. She claims to have done everything that's legal.

Then the car accidents came. On a Sunday night in 1967 she was driving home from a nephew's graduation in South Dakota when a passing semitrailer truck forced her car off the road. She lay in a ditch for almost five hours before help came. Hospitalized for six months, she came home with fractured vertebrae, an injured bladder and burns.

Fairly well rehabilitated three years later, she drove again and "a young fellow was exiting the freeway with no brakes, and you know who got it. He hit me broadside. I thought, 'Oh, no, not again!' " More back and neck surgery. She said she thinks the second accident was worse than the first.

"After those kinds of experiences, you thank God every day you can stand on your two feet. You just take every day as it comes."

That's when she decided to open a flower shop. Time was precious and she wanted to do what she wanted to do. She ran a store at 29th and Chicago for a year and has rented the present building on Lake near Columbus Av. S. for 13 years. "We've got a sauna on one side and a dirty-book store on the other, and rotten parking, but we survive," she said. There are a few parking spots with meters in front of the shop that are very well patrolled by the police. Old Ern is always running out to the meters with quarters from the cash register. When he misses, his mother pays the parking tickets.

The shop has four full-time people (Judy, Orv, Old Ern and designer Karen Tadych) and some part-time people and some part-time-part-time people, and some once-in-a-while part-time people.

They run the flower cooler at Mount Sinai hospital, which gave them a problem last week because somebody ran into the cooler with a cart and smashed the glass. Judy ordered glass from New York and asked Orv to fix it between runs with the delivery truck.

She gets a steady stream of compliments for her bouquets. An example: her mixed spring bouquet (roughly 40 bucks) has pink and white roses plus such blossoms as freesia, heather, eucalyptus, variegated pittoasporum, white snapdragons and leptosperm. "Not your usual stuff, huh?" she said proudly. "I go to bed at night with a good clear conscience. I did the best I could."

In the mail one day last week was a letter from a satisfied customer who included photos. "I hope you can tell from the pictures — I just loved them, especially my bouquet. I received many compliments. Hope all is well with you."

Judy Krasselt has friends in high places. In the governor's mansion, to name one. Lola Perpich grew up in the same town as Krasselt and they've renewed their friendship. Said Perpich, "Judy is one of the warmest, most generous persons I know. She's been very kind to us, and we always get compliments on her bouquets." Translate that to say Krasselt donates more bouquets than she gets paid for, and every spring she's on her hands and knees planting annuals at the governor's mansion.

Another fan is Charlie Boone of WCCO radio. They met years ago in the checkout line of the Richfield Lunds. Boone reached for his money and came up with none. He was apologizing and hoping for credit when Krasselt recognized his voice and bailed him out. What could he do but inquire about her life? And once he knew, what could he do but become a regular at the Chicago Lake Florist? For his wife, he buys Krasselt's Sonia roses (light pink). "I like Judy," he said. "I like to give her my business."

Judy Krasselt is fine, but her husband, Orville, had a massive stroke in 1987 that left him weak and confused. She and her son have kept the florist shop going through it all.

Peter Grise, John Warling

Feeding the State Fair Stars

August 31, 1989

❧

Right smack in the middle of the Minnesota State Fairgrounds is a restaurant graced by linen tablecloths, Blue Danube china, sterling silver candleholders and fresh mums. The chef is top-notch. Entrees include scrumptious Norwegian salmon, New York steaks, Nassau grouper with pureed raspberry sauce, homemade vegetable soup, chocolate death torte. Diners never get billed.

Fat chance you'll ever get invited.

The place is only for the big stars performing at the grandstand, plus their band members and technical crews. Security is incredibly tight. You can't get anywhere near the restaurant — in the middle of the grandstand grounds, behind the stage — unless you have clearance and the right color badges and a personal, mushy note from somebody like Tammy Wynette or Charlie Pride.

This is the third year that the food operation has been run by the Blue Horse restaurant in St. Paul. John Warling, Blue Horse owner, and Peter Grise, executive chef, say they take on the arduous task of catering to the whims of the pampered because, well, it's fun.

"It's a hoot. It's another world," said Warling, who has run the elegant, pricey Blue Horse for 14 years. "All of a sudden we're bigwigs. Our kids can brag, 'My dad works at the State Fair.' "

Warling and Grise genuinely like the performers, at least most of them. Willie Nelson is a swell guy who can put away big platters of beef and shrimp stir-fry. The Oak Ridge Boys are super friendly. The Judds are warm and wonderful.

Grise remembers a pleasant guy coming up to thank him for a terrific breakfast. They chatted a while and Grise thought, "You look awfully familiar." The chef faked it and finally got enough clues to realize he was hanging out with Peter of Peter, Paul and Mary. They spent half an hour in a serious discussion about what they feel is U.S. interference in Nicaragua. Grise later saw a huge line of fans three-wide, hoping for a quick autograph, and he felt especially lucky to have leisurely traded thoughts with the stars.

Diplomats that they are, the Blue Horse people won't specify which performers they haven't liked. Grise does say that while the country groups are nice, the pop stars "have more ego problems. Some think they're quite wonderful." Some performers are just too busy to talk. The Pointer Sisters, for example, disappeared into their dressing rooms and didn't come out except for sound checks and performances. "It takes them three hours to get made up and ready to go," Grise said.

There's a legendary story, from before the time that the Blue Horse had the fair job, about Eddie Van Halen making the food staff pick red M&Ms out of the candy bowl in his dressing room. (Probable explanation: red dye scare.)

Sometimes there are false expectations. Grise remembers an encounter with members of a heavy metal band called Great White. "They had leather jackets, hair, I mean HAIR!, and the women all weighed 80 pounds and they all looked like they'd been on a bus for a long time. I said to myself, 'Here comes trouble.' " But then the lead musician came up to the chef and said in a gentle, tired voice, "We've been on the bus all morning. We know we're scheduled for lunch, but what we'd really like is breakfast, please. Is that possible?" Sure was.

The Blue Horse people say that the performers' often-spoken appreciation is a major motivation for the food crew working hard from 7 a.m. to midnight (or longer) for the 12 days of the fair. Most state fairs, and many other major performance sites, fulfill contractual obligations as inexpensively as possible, including hiring a caterer to bring a pickup full of food to eat off the tailgate or at card tables set up in a field.

That's not the image the Minnesota State Fair likes to present. Nor the Blue Horse. "If you give the performers a comfortable, clean, attractive environment, they really appreciate it," Warling said. "You see them open up and relax."

That's all true, the band and crew members verified the first day of the fair. "Most places, they treat you like you fell off the loading dock at Safeway," said a man who identified himself as Edd Kowalski and who said he has worked for big names like Led Zeppelin. "We may look like slobs, but we like real china, too."

The performers get to specify what they and their crews want to eat. Because road food tends to be poor, they get specific. The Monkees insisted on a certain brand of frozen waffles. The Blue Horse chef had them on hand but prepared a good breakfast, too. The Monkees ate the real food. Stuck with packages of frozen waffles, Grise did destruction tests. He soaked them in water for a half hour; they wouldn't fall apart. He hit them with a meat mallet and threw them frisbee-style against the wall; they survived intact. Warling summed up, "The only way to destroy them was to eat them."

At the Blue Horse, there are 50 people on staff and the restaurant is open as usual during fair time. At their fairgrounds restaurant (only five minutes away in the best of times, meaning, not during the fair) there are eight, including dishwashers and floor sweepers. There's a complete kitchen, plus food trailers parked outside. The produce cooler, for example, has a 24-foot bed with box after box of romaine, corn on the cob ("This is, after all, the state fair," Grise said), pea pods, kiwi fruit (for Four Guys Standing Around Singing), 12 kinds of cheese, etc., etc.

The Blue Horse's fair crew does almost nothing during fair time but work and sleep — about four hours a night. "By the time the fair is over, we're usually speaking in tongues," Grise said. Sometimes the crew gets to wander the fair a bit. The chef admits to picking up fair food, such as brownies or ice cream.

"But I've never eaten a Pronto Pup in my life and never will. I'm not a food snob — at home I love peanut-butter toast — but I just don't appreciate fried food."

Getatchew Haile

A Prized Ethiopian Scholar
July 19, 1988

૨

T his is the story of two telephone calls that changed the life of Prof. Getatchew Haile.

૨

Addis Ababa, Ethiopia, Oct. 4, 1975: "We want to talk to you," the caller said ominously.

"Who are you?" asked Getatchew, a linguistics scholar and member of the Ethiopian Parliament.

"We will tell you when we care to."

Getatchew (in Ethiopian tradition, the first name is the more formal) suspected that he was about to be arrested for speaking his mind about the country's revolutionary junta. He put on his suit coat, stuffed his revolver into his pocket and waited in his courtyard for the military police. The wait was short. "You are under arrest," said a man in military uniform.

Getatchew opened the gate of his estate and pulled out his gun. The soldiers ran away. Soon his house was surrounded by 100 soldiers armed with automatic weapons. The shooting was fierce. Neighbors later said they found 4,000 spent shells in the yard. Getatchew tried to slip out of the compound by climbing a fence. A bullet hit his spine, permanently paralyzing his legs. Within weeks, he was exiled from his native land and nearly dead of infection.

૨

Collegeville, Minn., July 14, 1988: Getatchew, in his wheelchair, was celebrating the publishing success of a St. John's University colleague when called to the telephone.

The caller told him he had been chosen as a MacArthur fellow. "Yes?" Getatchew responded. With it comes a stipend of $66,000, the man said. "Yes," was all Getatchew could say. That amount of money is just for this year, the caller continued; in all, the award will be $340,000 over five years, no strings attached. "Yes," said Getatchew, trying to show he was listening. "Are you there?" said the caller. "Yes," said Getatchew. The called continued, "I would like you to please call our representative and verify our biographical information about you." "Yes," said Getatchew. Numbly, he wrote down the telephone number.

Hanging up the phone, he concluded that the call must be a joke. He said to himself, "If this is serious, he'll call back." He went back to his luncheon meeting, not saying a word about the call. Sure enough, someone from the MacArthur Fellowship did call back and impress upon him that his scholastic abilities were being recognized with one of the world's most prestigious and financially rewarding prizes.

❦

Getatchew hadn't applied for the prize money. He didn't know even that he was being considered. He hadn't had the slightest clue that 15 or 20 scholars from institutions around the world had written letters on his behalf. He had no reason to know that for every MacArthur Fellow selected, about 14 nominees are rejected.

His money worries over, Getatchew Haile hopes now to devote his energies to his research and publishing of centuries-old, non-Western theological documents, of vital interest to scholars of Christianity.

Kenneth Hope, the director of the MacArthur Foundation, claims to have the best job in the world. He calls winning scholars, scientists and artists to inform them that they've won the grants. Getatchew Haile, Hope said, seemed to have a hard time letting the good news sink in. "Stunned" would be an accurate description, Hope said.

The MacArthur Foundation nominees are subject to rigorous scrutiny. The result is a list of some of America's most influential persons.

According to Hope, Getatchew's work "is in an area that some people would consider obscure. But it is very important work, bridging traditions, opening fields of knowledge." It is an area, he said delicately, that "does not pay very well." (Neither the university nor Getatchew would reveal his salary, but he said that when he recently lent several thousand dollars to an Ethiopian friend, his bank account plunged to zero.) Each year, Getatchew has worried that St. John's would not be able to renew his contract.

Hope described Getatchew as "extremely dedicated to his work, and a wonderful human being besides — even though that's not a criterion for the fellowship."

Maybe he'll use the fellowship money to get a new car, one that's more convenient for stowing a wheelchair than his 1984 Chevy, Getatchew said, but not until his current car wears out. More immediately he would like a new, lighter wheelchair to replace the one he bought second-hand years ago. Maybe a house would be nice for his family, but he doesn't want to move from their apartment or change their lifestyle too quickly.

What he does want is to do his linguistic research full time.

In any case, he will not leave St. John's. He said that if he had been offered $340,000 but told he had to go away from the college, he would have said, "Take your money and go."

It was Julian Plante, director of the Hill Monastic Manuscript Library at St. John's, who admired his work and came to his side with the offer of a position when he was recovering in England from the shooting. Not only was it work that Getatchew could do from a wheelchair, it was in the scholastic field he loved and in a small, quiet community where he felt comfortable raising his family of six children. He is, he said, "married" to St. John's.

For 12 years, Getatchew Haile has been putting in a full day as the cataloguer of non-Western documents. For theological reasons, many nations over the centuries have destroyed manuscripts and other documents relating to Christianity. Ethiopia, which had an active Christian community in the 4th century, has a wealth of documents about the early church. It is believed, for example, that St. Paul wrote epistles that have been lost.

The library is gathering microfilm of manuscripts penned by hand, before printing presses were abundant in the 1600s. The library preserves the microfilm, catalogues it and makes it available to scholars. Getatchew reads and analyzes books in many languages, writes reports on the contents and describes their significance. His catalogues have made more than 4,000 Ethiopian manuscripts on microfilm available to the world of scholarship.

At 5 p.m. he goes home to his apartment in Waite Park (near St. Cloud), joins his wife and children for dinner and then begins the part of the day dearest to him — his own research. Each year he publishes about five articles and several book reviews.

By evening his legs and back ache so he works from his bed. He uses pain killers constantly when he's working. He paused and asked, "Don't you want to know what kind of pain killers?" Answer — "Concentration." His legs don't burn as much when he's working as when he stops. He doesn't break off work until "Nightline" at 10:35. All weekend, every weekend, he works at home, reading, writing, rewriting, thinking.

Getatchew Haile was born in rural Ethiopia in 1931 to a family in the learned class. His father was a judge in the Ethiopian Orthodox Church, a Coptic Christian group. Getatchew received his college education in Egypt — by day studying religion in Arabic at a theological college; by evening, social sciences at the American University in English.

In college he added Coptic, New Testament Greek and Biblical Hebrew to his arsenal of languages, including Amharic (his native language), Ge'ez (the official language of the church), English, Arabic and Oromo (the tribal language he knew as a child).

Languages do not come easily to him, he said. "I think you can say I have a habit of being stubborn, of staying seated until I learn."

During theological studies he learned yet another language, modern

Hebrew. He realized one day that the words in four languages — Arabic, Ge'ez, Hebrew and Amharic — were often similar. He hadn't realized they are sister languages. For fun, he filled a notebook with word lists to compare the similarities. His Hebrew professor happened upon his work and started asking questions. Getatchew explained he was even more interested in comparing the languages than in his class work.

In graduate school the professor had done similar work comparing Semitic languages. "You ought to go to Tubingen to pursue this," said the professor. Fine, said Getatchew, where is Tubingen? West Germany. That meant learning German. He entered a work program in Germany for just a summer. He hadn't heard enough German to be able to teach himself proper pronunciation, so back in Cairo he went to a German Lutheran Church service. The pastor, a friendly, scholarly man, introduced himself afterward, learned of Getatchew's interest in studying German and helped him get a university scholarship in Germany.

He established an excellent record at the University of Tubingen, received his Ph.D. and began to publish a distinguished series of scholarly papers. He returned to Ethiopia, where he worked for the minister of foreign affairs and quit after a few months because he found the work boring. He wanted to teach and research. He took a university position at Haile Selassie I University and taught languages and literature from 1962 until the Ethiopian revolution in 1973, with breaks for a sabbatical at the University of California at Los Angeles and a year of teaching at Oklahoma State University.

Emperor Haile Selassie himself asked Getatchew to teach languages to his teenage grandsons. Getatchew realized that the job could only lead to trouble. What if the grandsons didn't learn well? What if they needed discipline? He didn't say yes or no to the emperor, but just slipped away and was forgotten.

During the revolution, he became caught up in politics. The emperor was overthrown and the university closed. A junta of Marxist army officers assumed power and held elections. Getatchew represented his district in Parliament and was assured by the revolutionaries that they wanted his true opinions. While he supported the revolution to some extent, he saw inequities and lack of due process. He spoke out in Parliament. It was then that the junta sent soldiers to his home.

Word that he was shot and paralyzed went quickly through the academic world. Scholars and statesmen protested his treatment, and five weeks after the shooting the embarrassed junta allowed Getatchew and his wife, Misrak, to go to England. He said that the Ethiopian military hospital "luckily" had done nothing to treat his spinal injury. Doctors there would have done more harm than good, he said. After St. John's University offered him a position, he worked to get his children exit visas from Ethiopia.

Until last week, he said, the most important award to come his way was his election last October to the British Academy, one of the highest honors the British academic world confers. Getatchew was the first African to receive the award.

He is pleased, of course, but puzzled by the recognition that has come his way in the last year. He is quick to explain the importance of his work, but somewhat shy about his own accomplishments.

"Who am I," he asked, "that they should find me?"

Professor Getatchew is happily doing his research at St. John's University. The MacArthur Fellowship checks have arrived as promised.

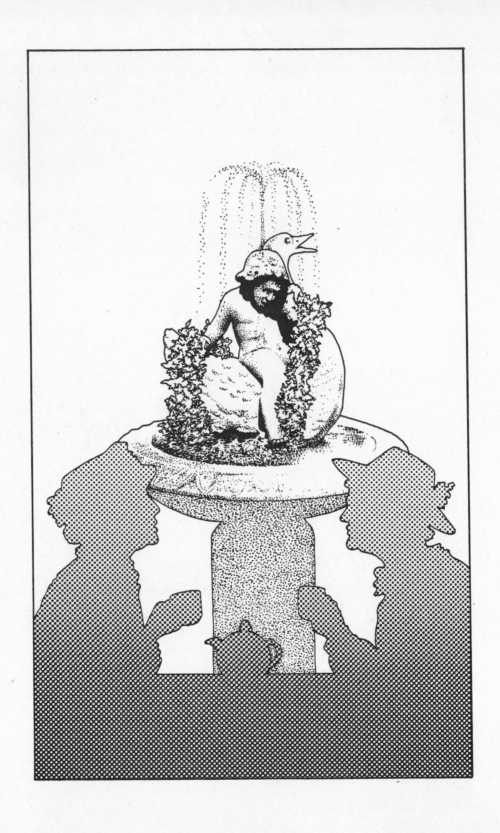

The Last of the Tearoom Ladies

Goodbye to the Fountain Room

February 9, 1985

❦

Look out, Mr. Greenberg. The usually genteel ladies in your tearoom are plotting a revolution.

They're so angry with you that they're taking drastic action. They're signing a *petition!*

"We do not want the dining room closed," they're pleading in the harshest language they know. "We have been coming here for years and think it's an injustice to the patrons and employees to close such a wonderful place." The next sentence reverts to decorum: "Please keep it open."

The Young Quinlan department store downtown is closing at the end of April after 90 years. The current store at 901 Nicollet Mall was built in 1926. Now the store has lost its lease, and close-out sales are under way. The Fountain Room restaurant on the fourth floor, reached by elevators operated by white-gloved women, is to remain open only until the end of February.

The villain, the ladies said, is Robert Greenberg, president of the Minneapolis-based 614 Co., which owns the Young Quinlan building. Speculation is that his company will redevelop the block, perhaps remodeling the building and dividing it into specialty shops and offices.

Greenberg claimed innocence. When called by a reporter, he pointed out that Cluett, Peabody & Co. operates the tearoom and made the decision to close it. Greenberg said, "We have absolutely nothing to do with it. I just go up there and eat."

That did not satisfy the tearoom customers. They want action. Or at least an alternative.

"Can you tell me where we're going to have lunch?" they beg of the waitresses.

Every Monday through Saturday the tearoom is frequented by 200 to

300 proper people who have time for a leisurely lunch. Some come every day. Most are elderly women, with hair the color of snow, hair shaped by their hairdressers into perfect drifts. The women are wearing classic suits. Many are in furs.

Not that the tearoom is terribly expensive. For example, the classic salad of the week, the Chicken Salad with Toasted Slivered Almonds on Pear Halves, with a Strawberry Garnish, is $4.25. The most expensive item is the ever-popular Five French-Fried Butterfly Shrimp on Toast ($5.25). The caramel rolls, known in Minneapolis as "sticky buns," are 55 cents. The drink of choice is coffee (50 cents); the owners didn't renew a liquor license this year so patrons can no longer get their Manhattans and Bacardis ($1.85).

The busiest day is the third of the month, when Social Security checks are deposited. These are customers who split their checks to the penny. ("You had the salmon plate, that's $4.80, and I had the $3.25 tuna/ripe olive sandwich. . . .")

The food is good and easy to digest. The atmosphere is pleasant. As employee Mary Lang, 28, put it, "No dangling plants. No loud music. No young men in purple lipstick to say, 'Hey, can I take your order?' "

It's a doily kind of place. Doilies are under the plates. Doilies are under the glasses of Raspberry Crush (Raspberry Sherbet Smothered in Fresh Frozen Raspberries and Complimented with Ice Cold Milk, $1.30).

Chandeliers hang from the ceiling, and the swan in the fountain spews water over coins. Even the signs are polite: "Powder room." "Kindly signal for elevator."

The building does show signs of aging. The restaurant's green flowered carpet is worn; the paint and wallpaper are peeling. "And they didn't give you a grand tour of the kitchen for good reasons," Mary Lang told a reporter and photographer. Joe Hoff, the Young Quinlan building engineer, had a nice bowl of steaming vegetable soup after he battled a water leak. "I had to shut it all down and climb down a shaft for a story and a half," he said. "It's an old building, you know."

The customers don't mind old and worn. "It's nice here," said Florence Zeis, 85 years old and a long-time customer. She left Minneapolis for California for some 30 years but came back here a year ago after she lost her husband. She was relieved to find the Fountain Tea Room still in existence. She lives in a high-rise at 2700 Park Av., and one day last week, when the temperature was well below zero, she took a bus downtown to have chicken salad at the tearoom. Sitting at one of the tiny tables set up for one customer, she said she would sign the petition. She hopes it will keep the place alive.

So do the other signers, who displayed lovely cursive handwriting, some a bit shaky. Joyce E. Schachar of Minneapolis complimented the staff on "34 years of super service." Jeanne J. Ewing of Hopewell, N.J., noted she has been coming to the tearoom "all my life — and every visit since moving away years ago. To break such a tradition would be very sad, indeed." Kim Kachelmyer wrote, "I love you *all!*"

The place still attracts some new blood. Two people who signed the petition and answered how long they have been Fountain Room customers wrote: "David Carr — 1 hour and 45 minutes" and "Jeff Barge — 2 hours."

And just what are the chances the tearoom will be saved?

"Zero," said Jerry Smale, president of Young Quinlan, who eats in the tearoom three or four times a week. "The Fountain Room is not going to be open without the store. Once we leave here, they can't stay. Our lease is up April 30. That's it."

But isn't it touching that these elderly women are doing their best to save the tearoom?

"It's touching, and I wish to hell I could give them some hope."

This, of course, leaves people out of work, about 35 to 40 of them. Effie Lee, for one. She's "approaching 50" and has been at the tearoom "going on 23 years." Like many of the help, she's done it all at the Fountain Room: smorgasbord preparer, baker, sandwich maker, pots-and-pans person — "everything in the kitchen." Some of her "new" people have been there five years, eight years. The salad girl has been there 20. There was a time when all the waitresses knew the customers; now the waitress with the most longevity has been there a mere six years. Yet they are fond of the patrons, bustling around them and asking, "And what can I do for you today?" and "How about a nice bowl of soup to warm you up?"

One of the retired waitresses, Helga Benson, stopped in last week. "She had lunch," Lee said. "A caramel roll, but I don't know if she had the creamed chicken or the shrimp."

The Fountain Room did close. The Young Quinlan building now has shops and offices. Effie Lee works elsewhere and still mourns the loss of her old tearooom, especially the relaxed pace and the gracious customers.

Bill Richardson

The Neighborhood Barber
November 9, 1985

T he man in Bill the Barber's chair didn't say a whole lot until it was time to reach for his checkbook and to give Bill Richardson the usual speech about how he should raise his prices. Then the customer, Reed Bjork, said to Richardson, "Remember when you cut a kid's hair three times in one day?" Richardson remembered. That kid was Reed Bjork at about age 7.

What happened was that in 1957 or so Bjork's mother sent him to Richardson for a cut. He paid his dollar and went home. Mom didn't like his looks. "Not short enough," she snapped, and sent him back. Richardson took more off, no charge. Mom still wasn't satisfied. She grabbed her scissors and said, "I'll show you what a haircut is!" Unfortunately, she was a lousy barber, and the poor kid's hair was so patchy he had to go back to Richardson. For a crew cut.

Bjork now is a bus driver and has moved away from his childhood neighborhood, but he drives extra miles from Lake Nokomis to have Richardson cut his hair. "You hang onto some of your roots," he said. "It's not hard for me to find Bill."

It's not hard for anyone. Bill Richardson has cut hair on the same corner of south Minneapolis — 38th and Grand — for 50 years. As he puts it, that's four generations of hair.

His wife, Doris, would like him to retire or at least cut back on the 49 hours a week that the shop is open or maybe give up making house calls and nursing-home calls ("Bill, you've been house-calling every night this week"), but he won't. He says, "If you're going to have a business, you have to keep up with it." So a few weeks ago he had the shop ceiling replastered and walls painted and a new hot-water tank put in. No need to quit when you're only 74 and you feel good, he said.

Retirement isn't all it's cracked up to be, Richardson said between customers. He told of a friend who retired and had a hard time adjusting to life at home. One day the man crabbed at his wife, "Edith, turn down the hi-fi," and she crabbed back, "Ebert, put your hat on and get out of here."

Lots of people who stand all day complain of sore feet and legs. Not Richardson. Some barbers say their hands suffer from frequent soakings in water and Pinaud's Special Reserve cologne. Not our Bill. Some small businessmen say theirs is awfully hard work for the buck. No way. Says Richardson about barbering, "It's no problem. It's about as relaxed as you can get. Nothing to get fussed up about."

Sit around his shop awhile and you'll hear customer after customer urging him to raise his prices. He charges $4.50 for adults (mustache trim free), $4 for men over 65 (eyebrow and nose-hair trims no extra charge) and $3.50 for children, except on Saturday, when kids pay $4.

"But I'm not cutting hair for just what the sign says," he tells people. That means his customers tip well. "You'd be surprised how many get out of the chair and give me $10. 'Don't you want change?' I say. 'No, you keep it.' And others give me $6 or $7."

He had an assistant from 1935 to 1969. "That's when the Beatles came to town and it got real popular to have hair, hair, hair. You know, until five years ago they'd say to you, 'Bill, don't cut it too short.' Now it's, 'Can't you cut it a little shorter?' "

Richardson's daughter, Lynne Anderson, tells a story about him that he says he's forgotten: Back in the hippie days, Richardson noticed a young shaggy man hanging around outside the shop. It took several weeks, but finally the man walked in and said to Richardson, "I notice you don't butcher people. I just want a trim."

He's still known for respecting his customers' wishes. The other day he said, "Do you want it to the ear or a little over?"

"Just a quarter-inch from the ear."

"Do you mean a quarter *over* or a quarter *under?*"

"Under."

"A quarter-inch under it is."

Hanging on his wall is a proclamation from Mayor Don Fraser, who stopped by the shop for the 50th anniversary party in September. Said the barber to the mayor, "How do you do, your honor. I'll be with you in just a minute." Richardson was pleased and perhaps a little flustered by all the attention and praise, but he kept working on the hair of the 16-year-old boy who had stopped by for an emergency cut. (Richardson keeps current. He's comfortable with tails in the back and short sides.) The mayor graciously waited.

"I guess you'll have to vote for him now," said a woman who accompanied her husband to the shop. Richardson neither confirmed nor denied his allegiance to Mayor Fraser; he doesn't talk politics in the shop.

Council Member Joan Niemiec came to the party too. So did customers, neighbors and friends. His daughters hung a banner that said, "We're proud of you, Dad" and got him a fancy cake decorated with pictures of a comb and a barber pole.

One of the nicest parts of the 50th anniversary celebration was the gift of kind words from the priest next door at Incarnation Catholic Church. The Rev. Robert Monaghan had announced from the pulpit that "an outstanding member of our community" had been a neighbor for 50 years. The church bulletin had said, "Why not stop by and give a friendly hello or a word of congratulations!" Monaghan's flock does as told, and perfect strangers came by to wish the barber well. Richardson isn't even a member of the parish; he's a Nazarene who goes to church each Sunday morning and evening.

Some of his customers, amazed by his 50 years in the neighborhood, have said to him, "It must have been a cornfield here when you started." It wasn't. Incarnation Church, he said, had four priests and a monsignor, plus 28 sisters living in the convent. (Now there are two priests, no monsignor and two nuns, neither of whom lives in the convent; it's a home for battered women and children.)

Fifty years ago the corner had two drugstores, two filling stations, two tailor shops, a dime store, another barbershop, a bakery. "There, where it says YOGA there was a radio and vacuum-cleaner shop," Richardson said. "And what's now the Vietnamese restaurant was a restaurant run by two sisters, Ann and Jen."

That's when his shop was at 3807 Grand Av. In 1952 he built his own place, around the corner and twice as big, at 313 W. 38th St. "I bought the land in '40, but it took 11 years until I had the money to build it."

Bill's Barber Shop didn't close during World War II, even though he didn't cut much hair. He took the war-effort program at Dunwoody Institute and worked at a defense plant and General Mills' machine shop. The shop kept going, with a 72-year-old barber at work.

Richardson is a gentle type. To an old duffer who made his way blindly across the room after a haircut, the barber said, "Just a minute. I'm letting your forget your glasses." To a customer who was getting his fringe of hair trimmed for a trip, he joked, "Your resistance will be cut down when you fly." About Don Martini of Edina, "He comes back here for every haircut, and I'm real grateful." About the people who run the Saigon restaurant and the Grand Bakery and the dry-cleaning shop and the beauty parlor, "They're real good people."

For his customers, he doesn't bother to think up chatty conversation: "If I don't talk too much, I think they appreciate it. They can sit and relax and get a haircut. People don't confess too much to their barber, no matter what you hear."

He was born in St. Paul and as a boy lived in Fairmont and on farms near Wadena and Hewitt, Minn. At age 17 he studied at the Twin City Barber College and in 1932 bought a country barbershop near Hewitt. It was there he found his fine wife, who was a teacher at the school he had attended as a boy. Tired of small-town barber hours (7 a.m. to midnight on Wednesdays and Fridays; 7 a.m. to 2 p.m. on Sundays, open on Mondays), he moved back to the Twin Cities.

He made enough money to buy a nice house 3 miles from the shop, and to send his three daughters to college.

Time has gone fast, he said, and his wife explained, "You get busy and the first thing you know, it's been 50 years."

Business is good so Bill keeps working. At 79, he is cutting hair from 8 a.m. to 4 p.m. Tuesdays through Saturdays, plus house-calls.

Beth Stiegler Puchtel

Seamstress with Spirit

December 29, 1988

❧

G ee, she would hate to have to leave her bridal-gown shop on the Nicollet Mall. Beth Stiegler Puchtel loves the old place — with its windows that actually open, with sufficient space to spread out fabrics and patterns, with memories stuffed in every part of the 80-year-old building.

And with her late great-aunt's spirit roaming the place and whispering advice.

"Be picky," says Aunt Bessie. "Do it right the first time."

Puchtel, 35, is one of the remaining tenants at 920 Nicollet Mall, which promises to be the heart of the proposed LSGI retail complex. LSGI developers are trying to line up retailers and financing by spring. If the plan goes ahead, the city will buy much of the property between 9th and 11th Sts. and start condemnation proceedings.

So every day when the letter carrier comes around, Puchtel half expects to find the 90-day eviction notice for her and the other renters.

A sentimental sort, Puchtel cringes at the idea. Her late Aunt Bess spent decades working joyfully in this building. Bess Stiegler (Puchtel's grandfather's sister) had been a Minneapolis milliner for some 50 years. For most of those years, she had her shop on the second floor of the Nicollet Arcade, as it was called then.

Aunt Bess's Vogue Hat Shop was just four businesses down the hall from Bridal Vogue, where her niece now produces custom-made gowns for brides and their attendants.

The younger woman can certainly feel the presence of the elder. Even in the women's bathroom. Puchtel was plenty surprised the first time she found Aunt Bess's spirit hanging out there.

Puchtel gets goosebumps when she goes by what was her aunt's shop, now the custodians' room. "It's like she's still here, and I'm supposed to be in this building," she said. She remembers watching Aquatennial parades from those windows. She remembers being 3 years old and sitting at her aunt's Singer sewing machine, learning to make doll clothes. She remembers her aunt's persnicketiness.

Puchtel doesn't want to come off as a wacko, so she doesn't mention Aunt Bess's spirit to just anyone who crosses the threshold. If a particularly nice customer happens to comment on Aunt Bess artifacts — her old sewing machine, her bridal bonnet, the shoe she wore at her wedding — then Puchtel will tell about Bess and how she lived to age 95.

She also tells them of being happy in her work, in her shop. She doesn't have the city's highest-paying position, but as Aunt Bess often says, "If you love what you do, that's the most important thing."

Design and needlework come so easily to Puchtel that she figures Aunt Bess willed her the skills. Puchtel tried all through her early years to find a vocation other than sewing, but she ended up in fashion costume design at the University of Minnesota.

"Get an education," Aunt Bess used to say. "Then make the most of it."

So Beth Puchtel designed for sweater manufacturers in San Francisco and for coat and ski-wear manufacturers in the Twin Cities. Her design business was at Rush's Bridal on the Nicollet Mall for three years.

She kind of expected that she, like her aunt, would never marry, but Scott Puchtel came along — "the one guy I couldn't ignore." They've been married for 10 years and have three sons, ages 3, 5 and 7. "They're the reason I work by appointment only," she said, and they're also the reason she needed to open a shop outside the home.

"I used to do sewing and pattern-making at home until 2 or 3 in the morning, with little kids eating bobby pins and safety pins. I hoped they'd catch on to French seaming and pinning hems for me, but I realized that was not to be."

It was her old business associate, Andy Rush, who took her to the window of his place and pointed across the street. "You should be there," he said, gesturing toward Aunt Bess's old shop. Bess wasn't there anymore; she was in a nursing home.

Bess Stiegler was born in Latvia in 1893 and moved at age 4 to England with her mother, brother and sister. They left to escape pogroms against the Jews. When she was 18, she and her brother moved to New York. Two years later they settled in Minnesota, partly because her sister, a fashion designer, had married and moved to St. Paul.

Bess settled on millinery. She loved the years when a new hat was what a woman bought if she wanted to cheer up, charm a man or have a chic lunch with a girlfriend. She wore hats all her life, summer and winter. In winter she had a fur bonnet with ear flaps.

She hand-sewed all her hats and became known for the quality of her work. It was so good, in fact, that examples are in the collections of the Minnesota Historical Society. "It's nice stuff, with real flair," said Marcia Anderson, museum collections curator. The Twin Cities over the decades has had enough fine dressmakers and milliners that the historical society is doing in-depth research on the industry.

When fashions and hair styles changed in the 1960s, Stiegler turned to making bridal headpieces. Her big dream always was to make a hat for Queen Elizabeth. She did not get the chance, but late in life, when her stories improved upon reality, she sweetly told people at the nursing home, "Do you know I designed a hat for the queen?"

By the time Beth Puchtel decided she couldn't couldn't change destiny and she better work at becoming the best designer she could be, Aunt Bess was old and didn't have the patience to teach her millinery. "So," said Puchtel, "I had to be content with looking at what she made and learning from that."

Aunt Bess helped out in another way. She often said (and still says), "Now be sure you're getting a good price!" Bess hated it when people would call up and say, "How much are your hats?" Nobody would call up Dayton's and say, "How much are your dresses?" People need to be trained that hand labor is desirable, that a fashion sense is valuable, but neither Aunt Bess nor her niece has much inclination to do the training. Says Puchtel, "If they're not as ecstatic as I am about lovely things, why bother?"

And now, as Puchtel is getting more and more letters from property owners in the warehouse district, enticing her to rent, she wonders if Aunt Bess is ready to move across town.

Aunt Bess may be ready to move, but the proposed development fell apart in 1989. Developers are ignoring the corner. "I'm not going to complain," Beth Puchtel said. "I'll be here until the building comes down."

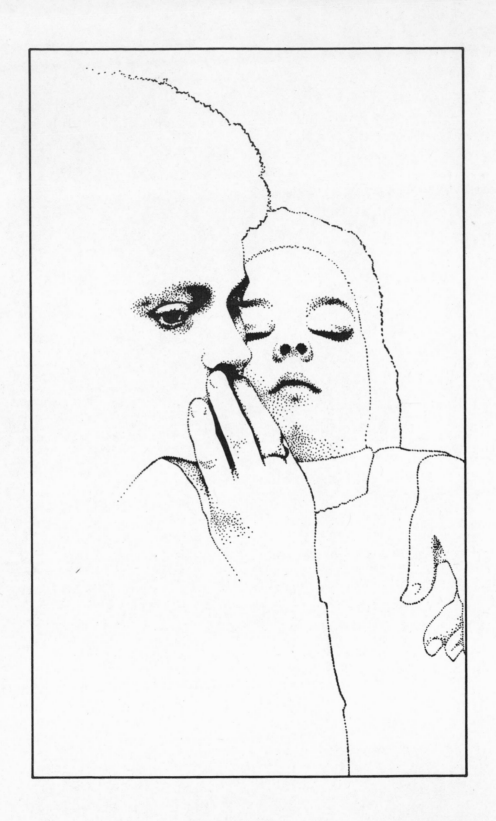

The Baunes of Willmar

"We Sure Will Miss Krissy"
June 30, 1985
ẑ

Their children, say Tom and Ginger Baune, are their joy. Not for all the world would they have preferred a childless marriage. But for them, having children brought tragedy as well as great joy.

The Baunes of Willmar, Minn., had three daughters, the two oldest of whom were afflicted with a rare genetic abnormality called MLD. Victims are crippled and slowly are killed.

Krissy Baune died in January 1985 at age 9, after four years at home in a coma. Leah Baune, four years younger, would have had the same story had it not been for a medical miracle. A year ago this week she had a bone-marrow transplant from her healthy baby sister, Angela, that just may be saving her life. If Leah continues to do well, she will be the first MLD victim to lead a normal life.

After a year of being cautious, her doctor now allows himself optimism. He won't be surprised, he said recently, if Leah graduates from high school and dances at her parents' 50th-anniversary party.

Doctors at the University of Minnesota Hospitals say the Baunes' situation with two very ill children was not as rare as one might think. Many dozen — perhaps several hundred — families in Minnesota alone have two or more children with cystic fibrosis and other severe genetic disorders.

Tom Baune, 32, and Ginger Baune, 31, opened their lives to a reporter for 10 months. They are remarkably outspoken people. In fact, they say what has saved their marriage and their sanity is being able to talk it all out — with each other, with friends and occasionally with counselors. They have been strikingly honest with their daughters. They have pestered doctors for information. In turn they have shared their knowledge and emotions with everyone who has had the nerve to ask. Only rarely did they refuse to answer a reporter's questions.

This, then, is the story of a Minnesota family coping in a formidable situation with dignity, courage and sometimes even humor.

Tom Baune (rhymes with brownie) and Ginger Radel were high school sweethearts. They were married in her hometown of Wabasso, Minn., on Sept. 1, 1973. Married life, Ginger said, was wonderful, for a while. She had a job she liked as a licensed practical nurse at the Christian Rest Home in Willmar. A year after the wedding, Tom began teaching auto-body repair at the Willmar Area Vocational Technical Institute, a position he still holds. They bought a house in Willmar.

They both love children (Tom is the kind of guy who enjoys playing with friends' kids), and they wanted three. Ginger and Tom had no idea that each of them carries one bad gene. We all have a few faulty genes among our 30,000 and we never know it. However, the chance of two people with the same bad gene marrying and having a child together are extremely small. If Tom and Ginger had each married someone else and had children, almost certainly they each would have had children free of the disease. One of their few forbidden topics is how their lives would have gone if they had married others.

Even when two carriers — like Tom and Ginger — have a child, the chance is only one in four in each pregnancy that the baby would be affected. Luck, however, was against the Baunes twice.

Kristina was born Nov. 3, 1975, an apparently healthy child. As a toddler, Krissy was dainty and noble. She didn't like to roughhouse or get dirty. Her hair came in thick and black, her face was lovely, she was a beautiful child. And loving. Krissy aimed to please.

Leah came next, on Sept. 7, 1979. She had lots of personality and an iron will. Even as a little tyke she had a sense of humor.

By May 1980, Krissy, then 4½, was acting somewhat strangely. Both Ginger and Tom noticed small changes.

For a while they didn't dare admit it to themselves, but they noticed that Krissy seemed less outgoing. She was slow at working jigsaw puzzles, and they caught her staring into space. With hindsight, they can see in photographs that Krissy held her baby sister, Leah, in an awkward position; Krissy's hands turned peculiarly inward.

Tom thought Krissy's problem was boredom. He said to Ginger, a meticulous housekeeper, "Let the toys stay on the floor. Leave the house a mess. Shut off the TV and play with the kid. She needs attention."

Grandma Radel was the first to insist, "She walks funny." That same day an adult friend who babysat for Krissy mentioned that she wasn't playing with other kids as much as usual and wasn't running.

Krissy was taken to the pediatrician. He didn't know what the problem was but recommended that the Baunes get her to the University of Minnesota Hospitals in Minneapolis. They went in on May 14, 1980, a Wednesday. By Friday the doctors put a name on her problems — metachromatic leukodystrophy (MLD), a disease that affects the brain, spinal cord and nerves throughout the body. It is progressive and degenerative and fatal, the

Baunes were told. And genetic. Either you've got it or you haven't. Just to reassure everyone the doctors said, let's test little Leah, 8 months old. Bring her in Monday, and we'll all feel better to know she's normal.

Leah wasn't. That Tuesday she was diagnosed as having MLD.

Tom vividly remembers the day of Leah's diagnosis: "They told us, 'You have an appointment in peds.' We knew if the news was good, they'd shout it out to us right there. We walked down that hallway, and I'll never forget it. We didn't say a word. I stopped for a cigarette and then we went to peds. There were six or eight people sitting around a table. We knew."

Tom asked them then, as he did at every subsequent appointment, "Is there anything we can do? Anything at all?"

No. Sorry, no. No, no, no.

"Dumb, the way they handled it," Ginger remembered. "There was no emotional support at all. And nothing medical to do. That first year was hell."

🐿

Krissy's deterioration was rapid.

By August 1980, three months after the MLD was diagnosed, she no longer could walk on her own. Her ability to grasp went next, so she couldn't feed herself. By her fifth birthday on Nov. 3 she could not chew; Ginger took Krissy and four little girlfriends to McDonald's and ordered only a milk shake for the birthday girl, who sat in a wheelchair surrounded by adults dabbing at their eyes. Christmas pictures show Krissy staring at the lights on the tree; she was blind by spring. Speech went fast; in winter she was reduced to a mumbled "Mommy" and "Daddy."

Worst was the pain. Krissy's muscles froze in contracted positions (one Sunday in church her hand got caught behind her head in a spasm), and her body sometimes went hard as a rock. She screamed in terror. She couldn't sleep. Some nights Ginger and Tom got only an hour's rest, and once Ginger lost 20 pounds in two weeks. After a year the doctors tried muscle relaxants for Krissy. They seemed to ease the pain so much that Ginger called them "the most wonderful drugs in the world."

It was almost a relief when Krissy stopped responding to what was going on around her. Ginger said last fall, "Since that first year was over she's basically stayed the same. It's easier to take. No surprises."

A university neurologist once gave the Baunes his description of children in the last phases of MLD: "The house is empty and the lights are out." The Baunes thought that was the cruelest statement in the world. Later when they told people about Krissy, they sometimes used the expression themselves. It got the message across.

Krissy was in a coma. She couldn't see or hear or think or feel. Or so medical tests indicated. Her parents weren't so sure. Sometimes she seemed to hum when they held her. When she snored they would say to her, "Krissy, stop snoring!" and her breathing pattern would change. Was that coincidence? They didn't know.

Ginger insisted on treating Krissy as if she were conscious. She talked to her — "My sweet little Krissy," she would coo, "how are you doing today?" — and stroked her and kept her pretty.

People who saw Krissy for the first time said the experience was not as jolting as they had expected. They had steeled themselves for the worst, and here was this pretty little thing with dark hair and eyelashes a mile long, who looked for all the world as if she were sleeping. Imagine a 9-year-old who's fallen asleep in the back seat of the car and is carried into the house at midnight, limp and floppy and occasionally opening an eye for half a second and then drifting off again. Krissy was like that.

But on the second or third look, visitors realized that those purple corduroy pants covered just skin and bone. No muscle. She weighed less than 50 pounds; at one point she was down to 28. Her eyes opened at random, apparently not in response to sound or action or anything else. Her dad accurately described her as looking peaceful.

Krissy wore diapers. Her mother refused to change her in front of other people's kids, "not that I'm embarrassed, but she would be." She was fed through a tube in her stomach. Four times a day a solution dripped into her body from an IV stand. It took an hour or two. Ginger was never farther than a room away and checked every minute to be sure that the solution was dripping well and that Krissy wasn't throwing up.

Nine-year-old Krissy began to develop breasts. Soon she would menstruate. Her mother hated that. Mother Nature was going through the charade of womanhood for Krissy.

From 8:30 a.m. to 3 p.m. each school day for years, Krissy was at a special school for handicapped children, provided free by the Willmar school system. She was carried or taken by wheelchair to a special bus, also provided without charge. Krissy got some physical therapy at school every day to supplement what her mother could do for her at home. Some of the children at the school could learn, but Krissy's main reason for being there was to give Ginger a break.

After Krissy and Leah were diagnosed in 1980, Ginger quit her nursing work. Krissy was 8 and Leah was 4 when Ginger became pregnant again in 1983. She had amniocentesis to check for signs of genetic problems in the fetus, and the result was negative. Their baby would not have MLD. What if she had? "We don't know," Ginger said. "We didn't get that far." Angela, nicknamed Angie, was born Oct. 18, 1983. She's a happy child; into everything; a sweetie. She's lovable, for more reasons than that she's healthy.

❧

Leah started showing a few symptoms of MLD in the winter of 1983-84. She was a bit shaky and uncoordinated. Her gait became irregular. She was 4, the same age as Krissy had been when Krissy's problems appeared.

At an appointment with university doctors in April 1984, Tom asked his usual questions: "Is there anything yet? Any experiments? We'll try anything."

Well, maybe, the doctors said. There was a new method. It was risky and experimental and expensive. They could try a bone-marrow transplant for Leah. Tom and Ginger, as carriers of the bad gene, could not be donors. Fortunately, and in the nick of time, the Baunes now had a possible donor — baby Angie.

Angie's bone marrow could give Leah the one gene that Leah lacked. It serves as the blueprint for making the enzyme needed to protect the insulation around nerve fibers throughout the body. Without that enzyme, the myelin insulation around the nerve fibers fails, bringing deterioration of the brain, muscles and nervous system.

Doctors were pretty sure that taking bone marrow would do the baby no harm, but they could not guarantee even that. And if the transplant seemed to work for Leah, it might only postpone her agony. Maybe months or years later she would develop the same symptoms, or even worse ones. Maybe the toxic drug treatment necessary to the procedure would leave Leah so vulnerable to other diseases that she would die. Maybe. Everything was maybe.

Doctors counseled with Tom and Ginger for hours and gave them the worst possible scenarios. With the outcome so uncertain, they did not want the family to be confident. On the other hand, they didn't have to explain what would happen to Leah if the transplant were not done; Krissy was the model.

No, Tom and Ginger decided. Forget the transplant. They couldn't do it. They planned to spend a hunk of time in Duluth, which Leah loved. They wanted a nice summer for her while she could enjoy it. They didn't have the energy to subject the family to a transplant. They didn't want to hurt their kids for research to save somebody else's later.

Slowly, slowly, they changed their minds. "We had to look at it from Leah's perspective," Tom said. "She had no chance otherwise."

The Baunes took Angie in for tests to see if her marrow was a match. They had to wait three weeks for results. It was a go. Leah was started on the drug treatment to destroy all of her marrow so that Angie's could be substituted. (The treatment is called chemotherapy and is given to some cancer patients, but MLD is not a form of cancer.)

For eight days in a row Leah had chemo. She rested one day. Then, on June 26, 1984, she had the transplant.

A medical team took a pint of thick bone marrow by needle from 8-month-old Angie's hip. Tom nearly threatened to strangle a clumsy nurse; he was afraid she would trip with the plastic bag of marrow. The magic potion was dripped by intravenous feeding into Leah's bloodstream for two hours. The marrow cells, with an uncanny homing instinct, headed toward Leah's bones.

Vinje Lutheran Church in Willmar was open all day for anyone who wanted to pray for the Baunes.

Donor Angie emerged fine; she stood the next day for the first time in her life. Dr. William Krivit, the university's chief of pediatrics and the man in charge of the Baune cases, breathed a sigh of relief that at least the baby was OK. Krivit said, "Her mother and I were both sweating bullets when that operation was over. We've never lost a donor, but we are talking anesthesia."

Predictions on Leah's chances came further down the road. As her mother put it, "We'll get the news gradual, whether it's good or bad."

Krivit said, "We never promised the Baunes anything."

❦

The family spent most of two months last summer at University Hospitals and the Ronald McDonald House.

Bills were so complicated and came from so many directions that Ginger, the family bookkeeper, lost track, but the transplant totaled somewhere around $100,000. Every time Leah went back to University Hospitals, which has been at least once a month for the past year, the bill jumped another $2,000 or $3,000.

Ginger didn't like the idea of being on the receiving end of fundraisers, but that's where she found herself. And gratefully. Tom said, "This community is absolutely marvelous — what they do and how much they're concerned. It don't happen anymore."

Tom's friend Don Rinke, a counselor at the vo-tech, was chairman of the Leah Baune Fundraiser Committee, which brought in about $35,000. Rinke said most of the money came from individuals' donations, the majority of which were $1 or $5 or $10. Most came from strangers, who tucked in notes with good wishes and prayers.

There were a host of fund-raisers. Regis Hairstylists had a cut-a-thon: proceeds, $500. Elementary-school children from southwest Willmar staged a carnival: $105. Dr. Joe Wange, an oral surgeon, declared July 12 as Leah Baune Day and donated a quarter of the money he took in: $441. Children of Calvary Lutheran Church put quarters and dimes in a plate for Leah: $350. Elderly residents of the Christian Nursing Center sold coffee mugs: $400. The Street Rod Association Rally pitched in cash: $465.

This was not the first time Willmar's 16,000 people helped the Baunes. When Krissy was diagnosed in 1980, about $20,000 was raised — enough for a $15,000 addition to the house to make it better suited for a handicapped child and for two years of medical bills. The big event then was conducted by the local Elks, who sold tickets for a hog roast at $4 each and raised $8,000.

Once the Baunes decided to try the transplant for Leah, they decided to worry about health, not money. University Hospitals, however, said financial considerations could not be pushed aside. When Krivit learned that Blue Cross refused to pay for the transplant, he got on the horn and talked a Blue Cross executive into a corporate "donation" of $15,000.

Krivit, as well as many other medical people on the case, have contributed part of their time on Leah's case.

Blue Cross/Blue Shield did pay for Krissy's medicine and food but not supplies. Ginger pointed out an example: The insurance company ruled that disposable diapers were a luxury and therefore not covered. For years Ginger washed Krissy's cloth diapers. But when Leah was sick after the transplant and Angie was in diapers, Ginger "ruled" that Krissy's disposables were a necessity. The Baunes dipped into "Krissy's diaper fund" for $116 a month.

❧

MLD was identified about 30 years ago, Krivit said. Before that, victims caught pneumonia easily and died so early that the disease wasn't recognized. About 25 babies with MLD are born each year in the United States. Bone-marrow transplants on MLD patients were tried only twice before Leah. Each child had a slightly different enzyme deficiency. One child died. The other, Tommy Renier of Chicago, rejected two transplants from his sisters before a third took when he was 11 months old. Tommy, almost 4 now, is not yet walking and he has trouble putting together sentences, but his mother, who lost two other children to MLD, said he is "doing super."

While the bone-marrow transplant was new for MLD victims, the University of Minnesota has been a leader in bone-marrow transplants for many other diseases, performing the procedure nearly 500 times.

Krivit said some people object to all genetic research, even the kind of procedure performed on Leah. "The abstract is always a lot easier," he said. "But when it comes down to my family or your family or a child named Leah, then we want to give them a chance of life. We're not talking about putting someone on a machine to sustain life. Leah's not on machines. Look at her. She's running and talking and learning."

❧

Leah is an intelligent, engaging child. She also is demanding. Some would say spoiled rotten. Some days she alternates between whining and bossiness. Her parents know it. She was born fiery, they say. And when Krissy was so sick at the beginning of her illness, baby Leah was passed around to friends and relatives, all of whom doted on her. Plus, everyone acknowledges, it's tough to discipline a kid who may be dying. At University Hospitals last summer Leah was a little beast, and perhaps that was a defense mechanism. She wanted to keep people with needles at bay.

There's yet another reason Tom and Ginger let Leah have her way: They're sorry they punished Krissy for behavior she couldn't help. In the early stages of Krissy's disease, Tom and Ginger rebuked her for such infractions as being inattentive or wetting her pants. They had no way of knowing that Krissy's problems were medical. A few times they spanked her, and she just stared at them. Ginger said, "Scold or praise her, and she'd be blank."

Leah was well aware that her big sister was going to die. When a doctor spelled out "D-E-A-T-H" in front of Leah, Ginger protested, "Say it out loud. Leah lives it every day. She knows."

By last fall Leah began to ask, "Will I get crippled like Krissy?" and "Am I going to sleep all the time like my sister?"

Tom told her, "No way. That's why we got you that bone-marrow transplant." Ginger couldn't be so definite. She couldn't lie. She said to Leah, "I hope not."

Ginger sat at her kitchen table last Oct. 15 with a cup of coffee, more than willing to tell her story to a reporter. "It's nice to have someone who's interested. Most everybody is sick of listening to this."

Angie was sleeping in her crib, Krissy was off at "school" and Leah was in front of the television, watching for the umpteenth time a video of the movie "Annie." Leah watched it nearly every day. Some days twice. It drove Ginger nuts.

Death was on Ginger's mind this Monday morning. "I try to imagine what it'll be like, Krissy's funeral," she said. "I sit here during the day and daydream about it. I picture going to see her for the first time and taking Leah and Angie to see her. I imagine them closing the coffin. I don't know why I do that."

People told Ginger that Krissy's dying would be a blessing for the little girl and a relief for the family. "Some people say, 'What difference will it make? Her brain isn't working.' But you don't want to give it up either. It'll be hard for me because I'm so used to taking care of her, day in and day out."

The Baunes tried to include Krissy whenever they could. One time last winter, they took her to the Chanhassen Dinner Theatre. Several years ago they took her sledding; they wrapped her in blankets and took her down the hill a few times. She was the "honorary flower girl" in the wedding of her godmother, Aunt Sherri Radel. Yet outings were rare.

Ginger said that for four years, "I've been sitting here with two kids sick and dying. We ain't had no future as a family. For the first time we had some hope when we got Angela. Then this good news with Leah. The transplant offered us some hope for her life. We had two good things in a year. If it fails, there's nothing we can do. But we have hope now."

Did she believe the transplant was working?

"I kind of think I do," Ginger said, "but I'm afraid to say that. It could turn around so fast. When we got Leah home from the hospital and she was doing so good, it was kind of hard to see Krissy because we couldn't try it with her. (Krissy's condition was too advanced to try a transplant.)

"That made me more determined than ever to take good care of Krissy. I could never put her in a home or a state hospital. It would hurt me if she was gone, and it hurts me while she's here. It slows us up because we can't go places with Krissy. We can't just run out the door like normal families. But I don't think it hurts the kids to have her here. I think she teaches them good things. Leah always remembers to include Krissy, even though she knows Krissy can't participate. Any time little kids come over, they're intrigued with Krissy."

Ginger told about a boy from Willmar, age 5 or 6, who came visiting with his mom. The mother was on best behavior, voice soft, expressions sympathetic. The boy burst into the conversation, "I wanna see that girl that can't talk or walk." The woman was horrified. Ginger was amused. She told the boy, "Come on. Let's go see Krissy."

Ginger admitted that avoidance of guilt was a prime motivation for her. "At least I know I've taken care of her. I would feel bad not doing it. We can hire a nurse, so we're not tied down 100 percent. We have it pretty good, actually."

She said she was not as bitter as she was a few years before, but she still got angry. She and Tom hated to be thought of as "those people with the sick kids."

"People stare," she said. "That's normal. I'd do the same thing. But some people practically drive into a tree when they see us out for a walk. There's Leah with her bald head, on her Big Wheel. Krissy is in a wheelchair, Angie in a stroller. People look at me with my kids and they're thinking, 'My God, how many more like that is that woman going to have?'"

She said she likes to tease Tom by saying she wants to have another baby, "but he about goes crazy." Leah bugs him for a brother named Travis, "like in 'Old Yeller.'"

Sometimes the horrors that haunt Ginger involve Angie. "She don't have MLD, but there are hundreds of other things. Are they going to take my third baby?"

Usually, though, she doesn't worry about Angie. The Baunes don't live safety first. Ginger doesn't rush toward Angie — or even Leah — each time one takes a tumble. But she said, "If anything happens to Angie, I'd just die."

And she added she didn't know how she'd take it if Leah's transplant failed.

Just then, with the tension in the kitchen at the breaking point, came the sweet voice of a 5-year-old. Leah was belting out with the movie's Annie, "To-morrow, to-morrow, I love you to-morrow. It's only a day away!"

That day was good, Ginger concluded that evening.

❦

The next day stank.

In the morning Ginger found Krissy's head in a puddle of blood. Krissy, who routinely ground her teeth, had loosened one. Leah, up half the night with a rotten cold and diarrhea, was weak and raspy. Angie for some reason was clinging; she wouldn't let Ginger alone while she tried to strip sheets off Krissy's and Leah's beds. Tom overslept and was late for a 7 a.m. meeting at school. Ginger made an appointment at the Willmar Medical Center for Leah. An hour and a half later they had good news and bad news — Leah liked the doctor ("He don't give me no shots"), but she had bronchitis. Back to antibiotics.

Then University Hospitals called with results from Leah's examination a week earlier. Three tests were normal; one was worse than two months before, and it's the first to go haywire when MLD makes itself evident, Ginger said. The bone-marrow transplant apparently was not doing what it should, or so she thought. "The news threw us," Ginger said. "It's kind of hard to be optimistic."

As it turned out, the Baunes overreacted. The report was not that bad. They have insisted on learning all they can about their daughters' conditions, and sometimes they don't have the skills or knowledge to make proper sense of the information. The doctors, brilliant as they are, have been far from perfect, Tom said, at "speaking English."

❧

The Baunes have kept a sense of humor, some of it black. Tom has delighted in getting rid of insurance salesmen by saying, "I'd be interested if you can insure the kids. Please, come on in and meet them." One look at a comatose kid in a hospital bed and another bald from chemotherapy has sent the agents flying.

❧

You hear so much about divorce now, Ginger told the reporter one November day. "You've got to work so hard to stay together, and ours is double the amount of work. You get mad and frustrated, and he's the first person you take it out on."

She said she hated Tom some days because he could walk out the door, go to work and forget about sick kids. She couldn't forget for a minute, not when she had to suction Krissy's lungs and bribe Leah into taking her medicine and try to sneak in a 30-second nap as she cuddled Angela. Busy as she was, she was bored. "It's hard to stay home day after day and find some excitement in life."

Tom objected later that his life wasn't a bed of roses either. "No way. The thing is you have the same things on your mind, plus you have the pressures at work and then you come home to a not-pleasant situation. Everybody at work is talking about their kid's basketball game or new bike, and you're going home to a child who can't participate."

Same with women friends, Ginger said. She dropped out of some activities because the women were complaining about having to chase their kids. They should be thankful they have kids to chase; that was her thought.

Sometimes Ginger would harp at Tom to get a second job to pay the bills. Or do what he loves, work on cars in the family's garage and get paid for it. But under that pressure, Tom said, work would not be therapy. It would be just more stress.

Tom did have times when he thought it would be best for the family to move Krissy into a nursing home. Ginger couldn't do it. Too easy, she said. And too hard.

Divorce also would be too easy.

"We made a vow," Tom said. The night Leah was diagnosed, he and Ginger rented a room at Howard Johnson's in Bloomington. He remembered, "We sat on a balcony and decided our kids needed us now more than if they were healthy. We knew 70 percent of the parents of sick kids end up in divorce, and we said that wasn't going to happen to us."

What saved the marriage, Tom maintained, is talking. "The worst thing would be for one person to clam up."

They talk a lot at home. But Ginger added, "I think it takes outside help." They were counseled by Tom's priest. They talked over every aspect of their lives with two couples who are their good friends, Steve and Jan Frank and Kim and Debbie Baker. They saw a child psychologist at the university. They quit going to a counselor who didn't talk about their kids being sick; the counselor kept wanting to know what in their own childhoods kept them from coping well.

Once a year Tom and Ginger hired a nurse to take care of the girls and they went away, just the two of them, for a weekend in a motel room. Don't picture a luxurious weekend with room service and romance. Tom would yell at Ginger. Ginger would yell at Tom. They'd get it all out.

And then they'd joke about which one was going to get the privilege of walking away from home and who'd be the poor slob to get stuck with the kids.

"We've left nothing unsaid," Tom stressed. "Not to each other."

He thought a few seconds and added, "Not to Krissy either. Every day we told her we loved her."

To Tom, one of the most amazing thing about the last five years with his wife has been this: "When one of us got the weakest, the other would get the strongest."

His worst period was a big family gathering on Christmas of 1980. Krissy had failed substantially; she wasn't walking and was barely talking. Leah was a baby, too little to enjoy presents and doomed to end up like her sister. "It was awful," Tom said. "It was hard to watch the healthy nieces and nephews."

Ginger's worst time was right after Angie was born. Krissy had pneumonia. The birth was a Caesarean section so Ginger couldn't lift any of the children. She thought she didn't care anything about this new baby. She blamed Tom. She said she nearly cracked up. Thank God, she said, Angie wormed her way into her heart.

The Baunes' favorite pastime had been fishing, but there's been precious little of that in recent years. You can't leave kids with MLD with a 13-year-old sitter.

Yeh, said Tom. It's been hard. "We kind of grew up too fast."

~

By last December Leah was sluggish. She sat around watching TV. Ginger couldn't get her interested in much. Lack of vigor, Ginger said, is a symptom of bone-marrow rejection. "But maybe she's just bored."

She had good reason to be bored. University doctors prohibited her from being near animals or with children other than her sisters. A bout with chicken pox, measles, strep throat, pneumonia or any of the hundred other illnesses could kill her because the drug treatments had destroyed all her immunities. Before her transplant, Leah said goodbye to a friend with, "Well, I'll see you when my bone marrow grows."

Cold weather kept her inside the house. Ginger sometimes took Leah to the house of their good friend Debbie Baker, where there were no children to infect Leah, and that was the highlight of Leah's week. She was a tad too young to start kindergarten last year, but she did have a visiting teacher an hour a day from the Willmar schools. Leah was permitted to go to the grocery store at midnight, when few people and their germs were present, but that worked for the family only once. Whenever she was around people, she had to wear a mask to reduce the chance of infection.

But Ginger could note some physical progress. The muscles in Leah's legs were stronger, and Ginger attributed that to private ballet lessons every Thursday. ("She's always two beats behind the teacher, but she's doing good.") She was an inch and a half taller than the previous June, before surgery, but three pounds lighter.

Leah, however, was wobbly. Her head bobbed, her hands shook. Overall, her instability had not gotten any worse since before the transplant; some days it was hardly noticeable, on others she shook like a leaf and needed both hands to feed herself. One day she was eating breakfast with her grandfather, and as she tried to eat cereal, her spoon clanked on the inside of her bowl. "Well, Grandpa," Leah observed, "it looks like another shaky day."

She positively would not allow help, though. Ginger said, "Krissy used to let us help, but maybe that was down the road farther."

~

Ginger hadn't gotten far on her 1984 Christmas cards. "We send 100 every year. This year I sent seven. I wasn't in the mood." The ones she sent went to people they had met at University Hospitals. That seemed the priority. The Baunes received cards from people they had met at the hospital, which included news of some of the children.

"Randy died," Leah interjected.

Her mother responded, "Yeh, he did. Petri, too. And another little girl did. About six died when we were there or after we left."

Leah listened to this soberly, then announced, "My daddy learned me skipping." And she proceeded to demonstrate.

One day just before Christmas, Leah hauled out a videotape to play on television. It was of her Lutheran Sunday School class practicing for a children's program.

The teacher, on tape, asked the children, "How many of you remember Leah Baune, who was in our Sunday School class and was real sick and now she's better but she still has to stay home?"

"Hey, I ain't sick," Leah protested to the TV set.

The teacher asked the youngsters to say, "Hi, Leah. Merry Christmas" and requested them to sing the first verse of "Away in a Manger" in their loudest voices. Loud they were.

"They're not singing," Leah objected. "They're hollering."

❦

Krissy died the way her parents had hoped — peacefully, at home, with her family, and only her family, at her side.

It was Friday evening, Jan. 25, 1985. Krissy had been fighting colds and flu, but her condition was not nearly as grave as the winter before, when she had been on the brink of death several times. The Baunes had been told then, "She has 24 or 48 hours." Krissy had pulled through, but it was clear she was worsening. Tom and Ginger braced themselves last fall for the likelihood that a respiratory problem might take Krissy in winter.

The afternoon preceding her death, Ginger called Tom at work and said, "It's different this time." Anticipating that Krissy would linger for a few days, Tom bought groceries for the family and ordered oxygen tanks for Krissy. For distraction he rented five Clint Eastwood movies.

Krissy's breathing slowed. She became pale, and her arms and legs were cold. "This is it," Tom and Ginger told each other. At 7:45 p.m., as Ginger gently rocked Krissy in a rocking chair, the child took two deep breaths and was gone.

Ginger and Tom instructed the girls to kiss their sister goodbye. "Ah, she's not dead, Dad," Leah protested.

To occupy Leah and Angie, Ginger's 19-year-old sister, Wendy Radel, and her boyfriend, Stan Rohlik, and family friends, the Franks, came to the house. Tom and Ginger quietly held Krissy's body for half an hour. Then they called the doctor and Roger Bengtson, the mortician, who, by the way, was having a rough week. He had made funeral arrangements for four of the Galaxy plane crash victims and a baby who had died of Sudden Infant Death Syndrome. He and his wife, Barb, knew the Baunes well (Barb used to baby-sit for Krissy) and mourned with them.

As usual, it was Leah who lightened the load in the Baune family. Jesus might have time to read to Krissy in heaven, Leah said, so she packed some books "for Krissy to take with her," including Leah's favorite on learning numbers. She drew pictures of Krissy in heaven and propped them behind Krissy in the casket. Leah picked out a flock of stuffed animals to be buried with her sister. What surprised Tom and Ginger was that Leah insisted that Krissy take Ewok, one of Leah's favorite toys.

Leah's only memories of Krissy were of an extremely sick child. Yet she grieved. Leah said after a table prayer the day after Krissy died, "Well, it sure is going to be pretty in heaven, but we *sure* will miss Krissy."

Angie, at 15 months, of course didn't understand the death. Krissy in her coffin looked the same as Krissy in her bed, and when Angie was taken to the funeral home to say goodbye, she tried to wiggle down from her mom's arms to sit on Krissy's stomach, like always.

Ginger Baune's care and planning of Krissy's funeral showed. Ginger wanted the day to be memorable, to be a celebration of her eldest daughter's life, of Krissy's struggles.

Krissy's Sunday School class filed by the open coffin and up to the choir loft of Vinje Lutheran Church. During the service they sang "This Little Light of Mine," "He's Got the Whole World in His Hands" and "Jesus Loves Me." It was obvious they had been told of Ginger's wish that they sing happily. They belted out, "Lit-tle ones to Him belong, They are weak but He is strong . . . " Smiles came to the teary faces below.

Officiating were the family's clergymen, Ginger's Lutheran pastor and Tom's Catholic priest. However, it was Krissy's nurse who gave the eulogy. Arita Malam's specialty is working with dying children, and she had been with the Baunes on and off at their home since Krissy was diagnosed in 1980. She started her eulogy with, "I will not promise you that I shall not shed tears while I talk about her." As she spoke, she cried several times. She laughed, too, at happy memories: How Krissy always called her dad "Thomas." How Krissy in the early stages of MLD called her wheelchair her throne and played princess in it. How Krissy was soothed by music played by her school-bus driver.

Arita Malam told about "this little girl who never went a day without being properly dressed, including jewelry and her own special perfume, Love's Baby Soft." About how Ginger was on the telephone one day and heard a commotion: Leah had put roller skates on Krissy and was trying to pull her out of her wheelchair to skate. About how Leah told people that next summer when the weather would be nice, she'd teach Krissy to walk again.

Arita said Tom and Ginger wanted her to stress that they were proud to care for this daughter, that they were proud of Krissy and all she meant, that there was not one hour they regretted spending with her. They had had 5½ years of "hard, hard work every day, every night" that left them "probably more weary than you and I will ever be," Arita said. "But Krissy was not ever, *ever* a burden. Ginger said they would have kept her another 20 years if they could."

She stopped for air. "They want to make sure that you know God gave them the strength to do what they did for these many years . . . Sure, they got impatient at times, upset with God."

But, Arita said, they could remember Krissy one particular day, after she lost the use of her legs but while she still could speak. She took her dad's face in her hands and told him, "Thomas, some day when I'm big and you're little, then I'm going to carry you."

᠎᠎

Late one February evening Leah and her dad went shopping for Valentine gifts. It was the first time the child, now 5, had been to a store in months. They roamed through Herberger's department store in Willmar, and Leah was thrilled with everything she saw. She wanted to get her mom a pair of slacks that Tom reported to Ginger later were an atrocious color and wider than a house. She picked out pajamas for Angie, earrings for herself. From the bra department to the toy department, she wandered the store in ecstasy, saying over and over, "Ain't that boooo-ti-ful!!!!"

Much to her surprise, Ginger said, adjusting to Krissy's death had not been hard: "Maybe we did our grieving for five years. The tension is off, the stress. Now comes the missing."

She and Tom acknowledged that life had improved for them in many ways. He removed the hospital bed a week after Krissy died; her sick room was again their dining room. For the first time in five years they were sleeping through the night. They were no longer shut-ins. Ginger got to take Leah and Angie to the park. She didn't have to check sidewalks to see if she could maneuver a wheelchair. The family went ice fishing.

Sometimes on a weekend drive Tom stopped the car in the cemetery for a few minutes. Even seeing Krissy's grave wasn't mind-wrenching, he said. Leah liked to leave notes for her sister, and Leah and Angie played tag around the tombstones.

Tom said, "I never thought I'd be the kind to go to a cemetery. I thought that was morbid, sick. But we take a ride and end up there."

With the weariness diminished, Ginger had the chance to feel grateful. "I used to be bitter," she said, "but now I feel so good we got to take care of her and didn't give up."

She hates it when people say, "God gives sick children only to strong people." Are they stronger than most people, as their friends and relatives speculate?

"No. We had no choice," Ginger said.

At least in retrospect, they could see that help came from many directions. They've lost some friends, but the people who emerged the closest to them are stuck like glue.

What's really important, Tom said, is they had their Krissy for a while.

"Look at the impact she's made," he said. "She's done more than any basketball star or college graduate. She left so much behind. My little girl couldn't walk or talk, but she changed people's lives. They took a closer look at themselves and their families. They appreciated their own kids more because of Krissy.

"Sure, I would have liked to have celebrated her first date or seen her drive a car. We were gypped by time, but not in intensity."

Added Ginger, "But I don't want to do it again. I don't know if I could do it so well again."

Tom said, "We'll do it if we have to. We're rested now and if we have another battle, we can handle it."

"That's what worries me," she said. "I feel we're always on the edge. We're always ready for the next tragedy."

Tom said they realize that the odds are against Leah. "Like the first heart transplant. It worked for a while, but not forever. We've got to realize that."

This summer, he said, may be the calm before the storm.

☙

When Dr. Krivit called the Baunes in May to report good test results and to give Leah more privileges, they decided to celebrate by going to a good restaurant. Leah got to choose. She picked McDonald's. She got to go to church on Mother's Day for the first time in a year. She got to touch a dog. ("A clean dog," she reported.) She was up to 41 pounds, an all-time high. She was being spanked when she was naughty. She could have a friend or two over, and she shyly approached kids in the park. (Krivit still would not permit her to be in crowds. He said, though, she probably can start kindergarten next year.) Leah was learning to pump a swing, to hang by her knees on her gym set, to swim.

The highlight of spring was her ballet recital. She couldn't appear with other children, so she had a private recital. For weeks Ginger found Leah practicing at home. "Step and point and curtsy," Leah would be saying to herself. Fifteen relatives gathered at the Willmar Labor Home to watch her perform in a lavender tutu for all of five minutes. Everybody cried except Ginger; she was too nervous for Leah.

Krivit was, believe it or not, more upbeat than the family late in May. He based his optimism on test results, but he also told of a telephone conversation he recently had had with Leah, whose transplant was then 11 months old.

"Leah spoke to me with clear sentences, like a normal 5-year-old," he said. Think of it: She's talking, thinking, reacting, laughing. "And how was her sister by this point? She was flat in bed and not talking. She was comatose and being fed by a tube."

He said the relevant question is this: Did the bone-marrow transplant do that? It's impossible to say. However, the pattern in families with juvenile-onset MLD is that the victims progress at about the same rate, meaning that Leah probably would have deteriorated as fast as Krissy did. Most children who have signs of MLD at age 4, as Leah did, can't walk by age 5. Dr. Meryl Lipton said, "Leah certainly is not severely handicapped." The doctors' best hope is that the illness's progression has been stopped. They have little hope that Leah's shakiness will end.

Krivit said his doctor colleagues ask, "Are you only lengthening the process? Is that a gain? Did you do the right thing?" Of course, he said, there's a chance the disease will get Leah eventually. It may take 25 years. Who knows?

But there's hope now, he said: "If you could tell a parent that the child would graduate from high school and dance at your 50th wedding anniversary, they'd kiss your hem."

So Leah will live to maturity and beyond?

Krivit said, "I think she will. There's a hope she will."

As to the costs, including monetary, Krivit said, "If we are successful and she does not deteriorate further, the cost . . . will be less than what they've put into Krissy — emotionally, financially and psycho-socially."

If the procedure works for Leah, the goal is to do bone-marrow transplants for other victims before MLD has done its damage. Testing has become more sophisticated, and transplants could be done for children before instability sets in.

༊

And where does that leave the Baunes? Fishing, that's where. Picnicking. Golfing. Tom is taking the summer off work: "I'm not going to be obligated to nobody." Except maybe to his wife, who wants him to finish building a back-yard fence and remodel the upstairs of their house so they can move back into second-floor bedrooms. They planted rose bushes in the back yard for the kids this spring — yellow for Leah, pink for Angie and red in memory of Krissy.

They decided to enjoy the summer. Leah was doing well and Angie was precious, they told each other, "so let's enjoy them while we have them." But never did they let unmitigated optimism escape their lips. Tom and Ginger Baune insist on taking life one day at a time.

Leah will be the flower girl in her Aunt Wendy Radel's wedding July 13. She is excited about wearing a long white dress and a ring of flowers on her head, but she refuses to get her hair trimmed. She's afraid she'll end up bald again.

As for herself, Ginger said she has hung around home long enough. She wants to get a part-time job in the fall — maybe in nursing; maybe not. "It might be kind of nice to see healthy people."

She said she and Tom are trying to forget the worst of the last five years: "Thinking about that dang hospital sometimes gives you nightmares."

Tom said they are thankful that Leah has made it a year since the transplant. "Frankly, that's a lot better than we had expected."

Five years later, the Baunes are doing well. Leah, now 10, is chipper and hard-working. She has braces on her legs and sometimes uses a walker. Because her handwriting is shaky, she produces her homework on a computer. She's getting A's in math. Angie is 6 and "just super," her dad reports. Ginger is working as, of all things, an aide to handicapped students in a Willmar school. She loves it. Tom continues to teach auto-body repair. "Life has calmed down, thank goodness," he said.

Patty Williams

Chief of the Grammar Police
October 1, 1989
ᴈ

Patty Williams of Excelsior is to grammar what Miss Manners is to social graces.

Mind your subject/verb agreements and your implied antecedents or you risk getting a reprimand from Williams. She sends out forms that she developed, sternly labeled "GRAMMAR POLICE CITATION."

Take the deplorable example of Charlie Gibson, host of the "Good Morning, America" TV show. On the air, he referred to Jesse Jackson as "Reverend Jackson." Wrong, wrong, wrong, Williams wrote.

She let him know that "reverend" is an adjective used to describe a person: "It is not correct to say 'Thank you, Reverend Davis' any more than you would say 'Thank you, Honorable Humphrey' or 'Thank you, Adorable Gibson.' One would say 'THE Honorable Sen. Humphrey' or 'THE Adorable Charlie Gibson.' " She signed her letter "THE Frustrated Patty Williams."

Gibson took the slap on the wrist better than some. He addressed an envelope to "The Frustrated Patty Williams" and started his letter with, "Right you are! And wrong am I. Not only am I wrong, but I have been making the same mistake for years." He related that he checked with a friend who's an Episcopal minister and a stickler for grammar, who told him that, yes, technically, he had sinned against the rules of grammar.

"Just one other thing," Gibson concluded in his letter to Williams. "If anyone ever calls me The Adorable Charlie Gibson, I'll belt him."

Williams doesn't mind being called The Persnickety Patty Williams but says she tries not to be difficult: "It's just that I view poor use of the language as a form of air pollution, or ear pollution, or something. It grates on me. I'm not a terrible stickler. If an ordinary person uses the language incorrectly, I bite my tongue. But people in public life should know better."

She picks on public speakers, radio and TV stars, newspaper writers. (Gulp.)

It's when people are trying to be proper and elegant, she said, that they get into trouble with the Grammar Police. (Williams is the only cop on her force.) Her pet peeve is someone saying something along the lines of: "The governor invited my husband and I to the dinner." Wrong, she said, waving her arms for emphasis. You wouldn't say, "The governor invited I to lunch." So don't let that little "and" get you bollixed up.

Williams, 61, said she had trouble with grammar as a kid, until she started on her three or four years of high-school Latin. All of a sudden, she understood. She understood that subjects and verbs must agree. She understood that "unique" is an absolute; it means "one of a kind" and there is no such thing as "very unique" or "somewhat unique." She understood that "appendectomy surgery" and "free gift" are redundant.

She not only understood. She reacted strongly when someone broke the rules. She is the administrative assistant for Trinity Episcopal Church in Excelsior, where the rector catches her cringing and crossing her eyes whenever someone commits a grammatical error.

Fearing that she'll come across as a rigid know-it-all, Williams usually signs her citations with something friendly, such as, "In the spirit of good fun but in the interest of better language."

Lois Van Hoef

The Orange Julius Lady
September 16, 1985

ʅ

Lois Van Hoef used to say she's seen it all at her Orange Julius franchise in City Center in downtown Minneapolis. Now she says she's seen a lot, but, "Who knows what I'll see tomorrow."

Take an example from a few weeks ago, she said.

A teenage punk rocker came along, his hair dyed in pastels. Hunks of hair stretched up straight, nearly brushing the ceiling. (Only a slight exaggeration, she claims.) He asked to buy an egg from her.

"Hard-boiled for a snack?" she asked.

"No, raw."

"Blended into your Orange Julius?"

"No. Just a raw egg."

"What will you do with it?" she said, suspicious.

"If you will just please take the yolk out and put the white in a cup, I'll show you," he said, ever so nicely.

So she sold him an egg for a quarter, the same price as hard-boiled or mixed into an Orange Julius. The punker took a comb from his pocket, beat the egg white with it, poured it over his head and combed up his hair into rigid spikes. The egg white is better than hair spray for firmness' sake, he announced. Van Hoef and the punker giggled over the absurdity — "They've got good senses of humor, some of them," she said — and the young man went happily on his way.

She thinks of him often, she said. "I can't imagine what he smelled like at the end of the day." Not that she hopes to find out.

More than eggs, Van Hoef sells Orange Julius drinks. On a good Saturday, her City Center franchise sells 500 or 600. It's a frothy drink, mixed in a blender with crushed ice and secret Orange Julius powder. The orange flavor is still the most popular (65 percent of sales), with strawberry and raspberry in the next spots. Pina colada, banana, etc., trail behind, but have their fervent devotees.

Van Hoef, 59, and her husband, Robert, a St. Paul developer, own two of the 10 Twin Cities Orange Julius franchises; their other is in St. Paul's Town Square. He wanted a small business to run in their retirement years, but she said, "I've yet to see the whites of his eyes down here."

Lois Van Hoef is a graduate of the 10-day Orange Julius School in Denver. Don't laugh, she said, it wasn't a snap. "I'm no math major, and I thought I'd never pass." She struggled through bookkeeping and food costs and was offered a franchise. Her business, Family Venture, Inc., opened five years ago in Town Square. Town Square is a lot different from City Center, she said; more inviting, warmer with its flowing water, its trees and vines. City Center is more — more — well, it has bright lights and seems more like a carnival, she said.

She opened the City Center stand two years ago and manages it most weekdays for about five hours: "just right." In St. Paul, several women in their 50s work at the stand. In Minneapolis, she gets young employees by calling churches and asking for good kids.

Orange Julius has franchises around the world, and she's visited them on family trips from Florida to Michigan to London. She just got back from Greece and Turkey but didn't bother to look for them there. She's not nuts, she said; Orange Julius is not her entire life.

The possibility exists that someday her three grown children may buy her out, and she'll retire. "But how many books can you read? You can't go out to lunch every day. I enjoy my workers and my customers."

She's not getting rich overnight, but the business can't be doing too poorly. She carries a Gucci bag.

At first, she said, she wasn't nuts about the Orange Julius idea. "All three of our children had gotten out of college, and I looked forward to staying home and reading books." But she has ended up loving the work: "It's lots of fun. I love people, and believe me, this means lots of people and lots of kinds of people."

There was the woman who insisted that Van Hoef charge an Orange Julius on her Dayton's credit card, even after Van Hoef patiently explained Dayton's didn't have a thing to do with her Orange Julius stand. "She must think Dayton's owns the world."

There's the lonely factory worker in his 50s or 60s who stops by nearly every day to tell Van Hoef, "I think I'll retire next week," and each time she says, "Oh, why would you do that? You'd be bored."

There's "Jack the UPS Man" who stops by every day for a regular hot dog and a large Pepsi, and the gray-haired gent who three or four times a week orders the same thing — a large hot dog with cheese and a small diet pop.

Each day in City Center, Van Hoef sees businessmen in spiffy suits playing video games in the arcade. She sees retail people in their fashion wars, intent on out-dressing each other. She sees 14- and 15-year-old girls in their Madonna imitations, wearing big cotton sweaters hanging off their shoulders and Lucy Ricardo bows in their hair and lace socks on their feet. She sees hard-core punks in leather pants and ripped shirts.

She gets lots of nice people telling her their life stories. She also gets crabby people, like the woman who was furious that Van Hoef would not give her change for a dollar one busy Friday afternoon. The woman fussed and fumed, and eventually got an "I've-got-it" look in her eyes. She ordered a bag of potato chips, paid the 37 cents, got 63 cents change and pitched the chips over the counter at Van Hoef. "There!" the woman exclaimed, jubilantly, and marched off, victory hers. Van Hoef was irritated, but struggled to regain her composure.

The variety of people is so good at City Center, she said, that whenever her 82-year-old mother comes to visit from Grand Haven, Mich., she brings her downtown to observe. "Lois, I've never seen anything like it," is the way her mother always begins her report at the end of the day. She was especially mystified by the punkers, who she thought were from very poor families. (Holes in the clothes.)

Why in the world would punkers hang around the antiseptic City Center, clearly a better environment for yuppies?

"Ask them," Van Hoef said, nodding toward a picturesque group marching past her stand.

"Well," explained Marnee Resnikoff, a champion in the punk hair division, "put it this way. I'm the only one out in New Hope like this." But City Center? "I don't know why, but this is where everyone gathers. This is where you see all your friends."

You see people like Dave Copeland, a 16-year-old student at Minneapolis's Southwest High. He was wearing a black T-shirt and ripped black shorts, his father's black polyester shirt and a black cape on the back. Dangling from his ear were two earrings: one in the shape of a bat and the other, he explained, "a dead Nazi."

And much to Van Hoef's excitement, along came the young man who had used the egg-white treatment.

"I used to buy eggs here," Lester Williams, 17, of Minneapolis, said by way of reintroduction to her. She didn't recognize him because his hair was almost short enough to quality for a crew cut and his clothes weren't torn. He said, "Before, I was revolting against the repression in the world. I'm just a skateboarder now. I've been accepted into junior college." Van Hoef enthusiastically congratulated him.

Lois Van Hoef still owns the Orange Julius business, but she no longer sells eggs to spike-heads. They don't hang out at City Center any more.

Garrison Keillor

A Tender, Bittersweet Farewell
March 22, 1987
❦

Sometimes when Garrison Keillor is stuck on his writing, he studies an old black-and-white photograph hanging in his office at Minnesota Public Radio. Shot in 1947, it shows the members of his boyhood church in south Minneapolis during a fundamentalist conference. He's related to half the people.

The picture will be among the first things he unpacks when he moves to Denmark a few days after his last "A Prairie Home Companion" show on June 13.

"To me," he says, "that's my life — my life in a frame. My treasure. I think as long as I have this picture, I'll still be able to tell stories about Lake Wobegon. I can just pick out one face in the crowd, look at it long enough and I'll remember something. This is my future as a writer."

He lovingly points out the faces. Here's his mom; his dad is missing from the picture and probably was on the road for the Railway Mail Service. Great Uncle Alfred over there must have been about 80 when the photo was taken, and lived to be 93. Cousin Bob Anderson, who was pretty good on a baseball diamond, still looks this youthful. That woman married Keillor's uncle and later went crazy. These two — Aunt Elsie and Uncle Don — were some of his favorite relatives when he was a kid and now have been recast as Earl and Myrna of Lake Wobegon; he puts them in the monologues because they love being there.

In a voice no different from the one millions hear on the radio each week, Keillor talks about the photograph: "It's such an old, trite thing to say, but it's a picture I looked at so many times as a kid and never thought much of. You get into your mid-40s and these things start to become terrifically important. You have etched all the details in your memory. You cling to them."

❦

Until a few years ago, Garrison Keillor says, he was a writer, not an object of curiosity. He could walk the streets of St. Paul on a Friday or a Saturday morning — eavesdropping, chatting, asking questions, mostly listening, in search of monologue ideas for his Saturday evening variety show.

He remembers, "I always thought that one of the most wonderful things about the show was that I didn't know many people who listened to it, and they would tell me about their kids and talk about walleye fishing and complain about work and compare automobiles and discuss gas mileage. From this and my memories, I derived a town and populated it. I didn't invent anything. I simply took what I saw around me and put it in another form and came up with fiction.

"I would take a small thing and make it stand for something. To me, that's what a writer does. I think that I was put here on Earth to do that, to write in extravagant praise of common things."

Now, though, he is a celebrity, and he says it is not nearly so wonderful as being a writer.

"Then, you see, you lose your ability to gather material. Suddenly people don't talk to you about all these interesting things. They talk about, 'Isn't this interesting what's happening to you?' I don't know that it is so interesting, actually."

Actually, what it is, he says, is rude. He says he is treated in St. Paul the way Elizabeth Taylor is treated in Hollywood.

True, autograph hunters don't lay traps for him, he admits under questioning. Thrill-seekers don't storm his house. He doesn't have bodyguards. But Twin Cities newspapers have crossed the line of privacy, he maintains. It's the newspapers that are forcing him away, he says over and over. What makes him angriest is that the papers printed his address when he bought a new house a winter ago. He complains they view him as a symbol of excess and unearned wealth, as a distant figure without morals.

Distant? He, Garrison Keillor, who has never lived anywhere but Minnesota? He who likes to recite the counties of Minnesota and the streets of Minneapolis? He who was born in Anoka, reared in Brooklyn Park, schooled at the University of Minnesota, who has lived in St. Cloud and on a farm near Freeport and in St. Paul's Crocus Hill and St. Anthony Park? A distant figure? Outraged, he says he's the local boy whose privacy and dignity have been violated.

"You walk down the aisle of Rainbow Foods and a couple comes towards you and he's 8 feet away. He doesn't even turn to his wife. He's looking straight at you, saying to her, 'Look, there's the man in the newspaper. Isn't that the guy we saw on the front page of the newspaper?' It's like you're a display of creamed corn, you know."

So Keillor is packing it in, letting Minnesota Public Radio fend for itself and moving to Copenhagen with Ulla Skaerved, the Danish woman he married in August 1985. He's not sure his 17-year-old son will join them; her three children will.

Keillor believes that in Denmark he will be able to write and talk with people and be himself again, unburdened by the press. Each time he has visited Denmark he has been reminded of Lake Wobegon. His knowledge of the Danish language is limited, so he'll have to resort to reading panto-mime, and that will be good for him, he says. He can retreat to a corner and watch people again.

He won't have to be funny. In Denmark, he says drolly, he is seen as a tall, sweet man who sings and is remarkable for his knowledge of Ameri-can popular music of the 1950s and early 1960s.

He'll be writing. His first task is a piece for the New Yorker about a stranger's view of Denmark. After that, he doubts he'll write much about Denmark. He intends to write about Lake Wobegon. "These people are still alive for me, and I want to take them into another book and I want to take them into a movie." He hopes that his screenplay will be filmed in Minnesota.

❧

The old photograph he cherishes was taken outside his family's church when Keillor was 4 years old. In some ways, he says, he grew up to be a preacher. He maintains that his religious views are basically un-changed from the Plymouth Brethren faith in which he was raised — "the belief in God, the belief that God's love was given generously to man-kind, that the love was shown most generously in the life and death of Christ, that the promise of eternal life comes from the acceptance of that love. To me, that's not ever been in doubt."

The people he grew up among, he says, extrapolate from those views and have definite ideas of how anyone who shares the faith ought to live.

"I don't live like that. I have habits they would not accept. I've never hidden them." Like what? "I enjoy Scotch. I enjoy beer. I enjoy wine. I stopped smoking two years ago, but I didn't stop because it was a problem for my faith; I stopped because it made me feel bad. Also, I am a writer, a line of work of which they are suspicious. They believe that you really only need one book — the Bible — and perhaps some commentaries on it, and beyond that, fiction, and nonfiction, is the pride of man shown forth in print."

His people, he says, preach that the gift of God's grace leads a person to renounce earthly ambition and to turn away from things of the world — things they find pale and gray and unappetizing.

"But it doesn't seem to work this way for me," Keillor says. "This world seems to me so, so lovely. Its people are good. The great beauty of the life that I've led is that I've had a chance to see so much and meet so many people."

His parents, now living in Florida, are not as strict as some of his relatives, he says. They listen to his show and enjoy the Lake Wobegon stories. He has cut down the references to his parents in the monologues "because it was hard for them to see how a person could stand up and talk about your mother and your father, and it would be based on experience but it really wasn't meant to be based on the literal truth."

Not to worry; he has lots of other relatives with stories. Some of the most memorable events of his childhood, he explains, he has never told on the radio. They're too vivid. He doesn't trust himself not to break down. "I have this terrible dread of weeping in the public view, and I've come so close, so often. It doesn't have to do with being a man. It has to do with being a performer."

❦

No, he says, it doesn't scare him that people think Lake Wobegon is a real place "because if they ever came looking for it in Minnesota, they'd find a lot of places better than Lake Wobegon. I think Lake Wobegon is a pale shadow of what really is here." And maybe across the country, for all he knows.

"I sure will miss St. Paul, Minn.," he says. "Minneapolis, too. I will feel lost, I'm sure, for the next 10 years of my life." He wonders what it will be like to be celebrating his 45th birthday in Denmark on Aug. 7 and be serenaded with songs he doesn't understand.

He says Minnesota people have been good to him, from the string of English teachers who hovered over him with encouragement; to superb college teachers such as John Berryman and Allen Tate; to Bill Kling, president of Minnesota Public Radio, who gave him chance after chance. His meeting Kling, he says, has the charm and unreality of a fairy tale. "The king saw me walking down the street and said, 'That one there, give him the bag of coins.' "

Most of all, he says, he values the Minnesota people who have been his following: "The audience that I really treasured was here." Minnesotans have written to him, praising him when he was on target, correcting him when he was not, offering ideas and telling him stories about what happened to Uncle Harry on a car trip out to Montana in 1938.

"They knew that what I was dealing with was not a fill-in-the-blanks sort of nostalgia. They knew that I was trying to describe lives that are real."

❦

The power of radio never ceases to amaze Keillor. He gets evidence of it each day in the mail, letters written to a stranger regarded as a friend. In a batch last week, he got a letter from an 87-year-old Ohio woman who crocheted an afghan for him. A representative of a Congregational church in St. Paul is hoping he will lead a hymn sing. A Hopkins woman sent him the missing verse of "Tell Me Why the Stars Do Shine."

Then there are the invitations to write and speak: The Academy of American Poets would like him to guest-edit an issue of its newsletter, choosing four to six of his favorite poems and writing a short, critical introduction. Columbia University wants to use his Lake Wobegon stories to help teach English as a second language. Somebody in Hutchinson,

Kan., would appreciate his penning a few words on the question, "When do you take time to read?" A public radio station in Washington auctioned off the chance to have Garrison Keillor make a tape for the high bidder's answering machine. The state of Minnesota would like him to be the honorary chairperson for Arbor Day, the theme of which will be "Trees: Our Prairie Home Companions."

Some of it he will be happy to do. He says he tries to be generous with his talents and his money, as he was taught, but he can't do everything that people want. Nothing now that involves travel. "I'm not going anyplace but Denmark."

He will decline an offer to write a column for U.S. News & World Report. "I think I could write a good column of a sort, but I can't really write a column that they would want. They think I could be James Reston or someone standing on a mountaintop, and I really can't. They would want me to write about American culture from the perspective of the heartland or small-town America or something. I don't know anything about small-town America!

"I'm a fiction writer. I'm a storyteller. I'm a journalist. I'm better off the more particular and specific I am, and when I get away from that, I feel it, I feel it. People ask me questions about mid-America and I break into a sweat. I was brought up to be polite and answer these things, but I don't dare."

Keillor said the invitations to speak make him frightened for the world because they give him far too much credit for knowing things: "If you can piece together a 15- or 20-minute story with some little trail of narration that — as all good stories do — hints at far more than it says, then a lot of people will come to think that you have the answer to life's many problems. If they could get to know you better!"

❧

He is trying to decide what to do with the people of Lake Wobegon.

"That is my urgent problem right now. I'm inclined to just sort of while away the weeks and sort of talk about their flu and have the fishing season start and the school year end. Flag Day will be June 14. They could celebrate Flag Day a couple of days early for my sake, I would think. I could have them all line up as the Living Flag and go out on that.

"Some people tell me that I ought to resolve it all in some way, but I don't know what they mean by that. I don't know what's to be resolved."

Garrison Keillor's experience as an American in Denmark was short. Life there was not as he had envisioned. Within a few months, he moved back to the United States — to Manhattan, not Minnesota.

Marion Weisler

Mother of a Most Honorable Son

May 26, 1986

❧

It will be horrible, and it will be wonderful. She expects to blubber like a baby. This Memorial Day Marion Weisler of Roseville gets to rub her fingers over the Vietnam War Memorial and to see her son's name on it.

For two years, she has tried to get "James R. Weisler" added to the monument. He was killed in 1969 in Thailand, considered a noncombat zone. Marion Weisler didn't care what it was considered. He died in a war effort, she protested over and over. Explanations and regulations were worthless to her. She wouldn't be satisfied until she forced the powers-that-be to see things her way.

She won. "I loved him dearly," she said. "That's why this was important."

Jimmy, she said, had a lot of responsibility when he was young. She and his father were divorced when he was 15, and he cared for Laurie, who was five years younger, and Elliot, seven years younger. Two years after the divorce she opened a restaurant — the original Mamalu's, a rib joint on Lexington Av. in St. Paul. Seven times a week, Jimmy would drive her to work at 2 p.m. and pick her up at 3 a.m.

His sister described him as "a very funny, popular, very social kind of guy." He graduated from St. Louis Park High School in 1965 and studied auto mechanics at Dunwoody Institute. Rather than risk being drafted into the Army, he enlisted in the Air Force. He wore his uniform when he married his sweetheart, Melanie. They had a baby girl and named her Felicia. He was stationed in Thailand, a noncombat zone, and was about to be transferred to Germany, where his wife and daughter could join him.

Neither he nor his mother were political people. She can't remember his views on the Vietnam War. And she never stewed about his safety. So when an Air Force lieutenant in uniform came into her restaurant early one evening in October 1969, she assumed he was a customer.

"He told me right in the restaurant," she remembers. "It didn't connect with me. It can't be, not my son, he wasn't in a combat zone. I ran into the back room and stuffed a towel in my mouth to keep from screaming. There were customers out there. To me, it was a callous way of telling me."

What he told her was that Jimmy was part of a crew hit by a crippled plane attempting a landing at a Thailand air base. The plane went out of control and crashed. Jimmy died of a head injury. Others also were killed. Marion Weisler doesn't know how many; the Air Force wouldn't tell her.

Jimmy was buried at Fort Snelling. His mother was so devastated that she couldn't set foot in her restaurant for 18 days. She eventually got a letter "from a general or somebody big," she said, about "what a good boy he was, what a good job he had done, and 'Sorry about that.' That's all you get — regrets. You don't get much else."

Months and even years later, she found herself leafing through the sympathy cards and pages of the funeral register. "The pain stays forever. Forever."

Years passed. The Vietnam Memorial was finished in 1982. Marion Weisler's brother went to Washington in 1984 and visited the memorial. He expected to find the name of James R. Weisler. He saw 58,022 other names, but not Jimmy's. How come?, he asked Weisler. She didn't know. When she knew, she didn't accept the reason.

She set into action. Her first try was Sen. Rudy Boschwitz's office. She wrote, "I hope you can help ease the anguish of a mother's heart. . . . I see no reason to omit his name just because he was killed in Thailand. . . . The Udorn Air Base was where our planes flew to Vietnam and back, and he definitely was killed trying to help our own planes. I have heard of your many kindnesses. I do hope your helping hand will extend out to reach and help me."

Boschwitz tried, Weisler said. But the Pentagon insisted on a narrower definition of killed in action. She persevered. She wrote to Defense Secretary Caspar Weinberger and the Jewish National War Veterans, the Defense Department, the Air Force. A niece is a bank vice president in Washington, D.C., and she tried to get the ear of important people she knew. Nothing worked for Marion Weisler.

"I got form letters. 'They were trying.' 'They were trying.' I thought it was down the tubes, all the work I did."

What finally worked was the intervention of Leo Broadhead, a retired Air Force lieutenant colonel who had flown in the Vietnam War. So had his son, who was killed shortly after takeoff on Guam, not an official combat zone. Eventually Broadhead got the government to agree to adding 108 names to the memorial. One was Larry Broadhead. Another was Jimmy Weisler.

In mid-April of this year, Marion Weisler got a form letter from Jan C. Scruggs, president of the Vietnam Veterans Memorial Fund, saying, "It is truly an honor to have this opportunity to invite you to a Memorial Day ceremony in our Nation's Capital that will, I believe, have special meaning for you and your family."

An understatement, Weisler says.

So today is the day. She has never seen the memorial. "I'm dreading the confrontation, but I'm glad it's happening." Her son, 32-year-old Elliot, her niece, her brother and sister-in-law will be with her today. A friend of her niece is providing a chauffeur and limousine so they won't have to be troubled by finding a parking place.

Jimmy's widow and daughter can't be there. The girl whose father died when she was 16 months old is graduating from high school in Oregon next week.

Marion Weisler is 68 and retired now. She still thinks about Jimmy every day. She wonders if she'll be able to hold herself together today. "I cry at 'Taps.' I'm a good crier. I'll be crying during the ceremony, I'll tell you that much." To this day she can't stand funerals. They bring back the awful day Jimmy was buried. "They've had to carry me out. I've thought I was going to die."

But now she's mostly recovered, she said. "You look around, and it's 17 years already. I'm fine now. Life goes on. There's another generation. I have three lovely granddaughters. But it's a heartbreak when a mother loses a child. He was my first born, you know."

Jimmy Weisler's name was engraved on the memorial, just as his mother was promised.

The Bra Fitters

Ogres No More
April 4, 1985
❧

"**N**ow bend over and shake, honey."
Those were among the most obnoxious words facing an adolescent girl in the late 1950s. They came from an ogre known as the Bra Fitter.

What got us thinking about her was a big Dayton's ad announcing this is Bra Fitting Week. The ad was scary: "7 out of 10 women wear the wrong size bra. We'd like to change those figures. Do the straps slip from your shoulders? Or do they leave ridges? Are the cups less than smooth? Does your bra ride up? Are you often adjusting it?"

They've been peeking!

This week Dayton's brought in all sorts of hot-shot bra fitters from around the country. We'll introduce you to one in a minute.

But first, back to those humiliating days of yesteryear....

❧

When enough of your girlfriends were flaunting bras and you would beg hard enough, your mom would take you downtown for the big event, A Fitting. She'd find a chair in the foundations department and abandon you. This was a big day in your life, and what would she do? Turn you over to a perfect stranger, a professional fitter.

Ask around. See if it isn't true. The fitter invariably was an elderly woman with big breasts, wiggly upper arms and cold hands. Her job description called for an outdated hairdo and a foreign accent. Never was there a fitter over 5-foot-1. Never was there a fitter who didn't try to sell padded bras to 13-year-olds.

Your fitter would take you into a tiny room with mirrors everywhere and hand you a bunch of bras. She'd disappear. She'd be gone long enough to make you think you were on your own. You'd strip, even past the undershirt. You'd be trying to figure out how to get the darn thing on, trying to remember how your sister did it. Whamm, you'd hear the monster coming and you'd see her ugly old hand grip the edge of the curtain and you knew she was going to fling it open. There was *nothing* you could do to prevent her from coming in uninvited! And there you were with the bra caught around one ear. You'd instinctively wrap your arms around your body, wishing you had more arms.

It was her profession, she did this every day, so she had no compunctions about being blunt. She'd "tsk-tsk-tsk" and make some rude remark about boniness. She'd order you to bend over and scoop your "bosom" into the 32AA bra, noting there wasn't much to scoop but who knows there might be some day so you'd better get used to doing it right. She'd pinch and grope, saying, "Well, dear, you want it to fit right, now don't you?" Not especially.

She'd stare. She'd touch you in places even your mom didn't dare.

You'd never put on a bra before in your entire life, of course, so bending over and scooping and hooking infinitesimally small snaps at the back was a challenge.

(Out of orneriness, some of us for months afterward fastened our bras on backwards and then swung the bras around, until the wiser, more agile girls in gym class made nasty comments. Those were the days when one's social status was determined by the number of hooks on the bra. "One-hookers" were wimps and wore the equivalent of today's training bras. "Four-hookers" were cheerleaders. The boys could tell who was who. At first we thought the reason they were sensually rubbing our backs as we danced slow at the Y was that they were getting romantic. Then we realized they were counting hooks by Braille.)

But anyway, eventually the Bra Ogre would find a bra that fit fairly well, after some tucks, and she'd let you escape. So much for the glories of womanhood. Only when you got home could you pretend your first bra was a thing of beauty, knowing full well, of course, that an undershirt was far more comfortable.

Friends of mine report other tragic moments with bra fitters: One fitter quoted the pencil test ("If you put a pencil under your breast and it stays, then you should wear a bra.") and refused to sell her one; my friend has never recovered. Then there's the woman whose first bra was the shape of two flat washcloths who is shocked that the industry now sells "prostitute underwear" to 13-year-olds. And the large-breasted woman who reached puberty when skinny Twiggie was in style but whose first real bra in seventh grade was a B-cup with concentric circles, "like Rosie the Riveter would have worn. I felt like a walking army tank."

A male friend reports that the object of his lust in seventh grade had bra-fitting problems. One day, on the steps of their Catholic school, wads of Kleenex fell from the bottom of her jumper.

❧

With all this in mind, we strolled over to Dayton's downtown store to get a look at the modern bra fitter. We guessed the profession now attracted young, svelte things with good uplift.

We found Fran Musante of Hamden, Conn., an "education director" for the Smoothie line of bras. She's not like the old-fashioned fitters. She's far younger (43) and taller (5-foot-6) and classier and funnier. She doesn't stand around with her arms under her breasts for support. Her shoes aren't scuffed orthopedics, her sexy blue nylons aren't snagged. In one respect, though, she's like her predecessors. She's a 36D. "Full figured" is her preferred description. She said, "In the good old days, I was a 34D. When you go on the road, you go to seed."

She, too, remembers the woman who fitted her first bra: "She looked about 7 feet tall and she wore a white starched uniform and she scared the heck out of me. I didn't salute her, but I almost did."

Musante doesn't bark orders, but she does give a severe message: *Every* woman should be measured for bras *every* year. Even without a weight gain, bra sizes change "because gravity takes its course. The sands shift." Which is to say that as a woman ages, her breasts get longer and her hips get wider. She told of a Dayton's customer who walked in with a 36B bra and left with four new 34Ds, one on her body. The satisfied customer came back a few hours later, her niece in tow for a fitting. And then there was a young woman, about 19, who had lost 50 or 60 pounds and her bra fit "like a vest."

Bras, Musante continued, are engineered — her word — to anchor and fit a specific body size. Men used to do all the engineering; now more and more women are involved, which Musante calls progress. When she was younger and a perfect 34D, she was a model for the industry. "That means bras were built on me."

She has done everything for the bra-body industry ("foundations" and "brassieres" are obsolete words) that there is to do, except be a sales representative for a company. She has managed a specialty shop. ("Consumers are tired of self-service. Just as you want shoes fitted, you want bras fitted.") Now she travels the country for Smoothie, training clerks how to fit and sell bras.

Dayton's trains many of its bra sales consultants at fitting seminars at least once a year and it has a continuous training program in bra fitting that is run by a woman with the interesting name of Betty Stringfellow. Fitters have to watch videotapes and read booklets and even pass tests.

"Obviously, you don't teach this entirely out of a book," said Mary Bruckman, the bra buyer for Dayton's. "It's by experience." When a woman with an unusual problem comes in, she can serve as a learning experience for fitters. This has to be nicely done. Bruckman said, "We can't have 10 people staring at a customer and saying, *'My,* you're peculiar.' "

And, yes, she said, she certainly hopes fitters are nice to first-bra buyers.

In addition to having local experts, Dayton's sometimes likes to have manufacturers send specialists to work directly with consumers.

That's why the people who make Smoothies — The Strouse, Adler Co. of New Haven, Conn. — sent Fran Musante to Dayton's for a few days. Rarely does she work with customers anymore, but she said she likes short spells of it. Mostly she likes the chance to get women fitted right. She can't stand to see women pulling at their bras.

Many other bra companies — Olga and Vassarette, Vanity Fair and Maidenform, for example — sent representatives to the Twin Cities this week for Dayton's Bra Fitting Week at the downtown stores and the Dales. Things went well. "I'm a new woman," said a customer, happy with her new 34D. A clerk said to another woman at the cash register, "I like that on you."

So if you see the streets and homes of Greater Minneapolis-St. Paul dotted with the self-satisfied smiles of women whose bras fit well, you'll know why.

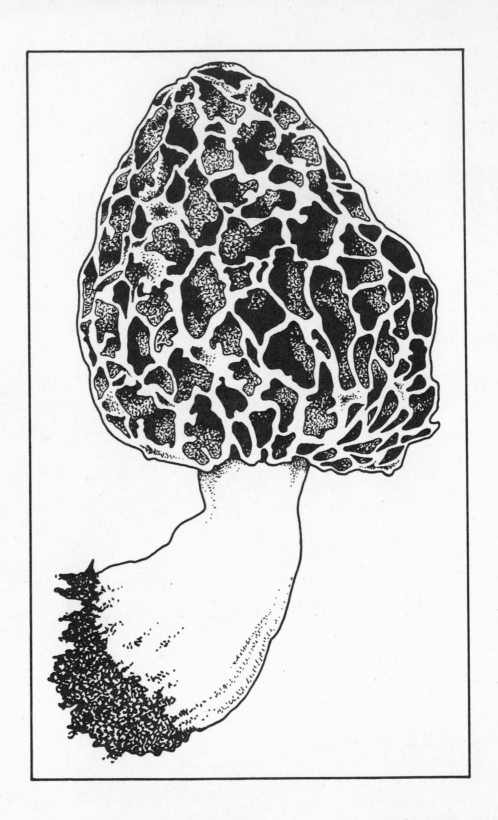

John Ratzloff

The Mushroom Man

May 25, 1986

❧

"**B**ring junky clothes that you don't mind getting wet and muddy," he told me on the telephone. "I'll bring the blindfolds."

Jeez! These morel hunters are protective of their territories. Blindfolds of his guests in place, John Ratzloff drove us somewhere west of the Twin Cities — at least we think it was toward St. Cloud, although he denied that and pretended we were in Iowa — and let us see again when we were far off the beaten track. So no matter if you threaten to pull out my fingernails or make me dunk my morels in ketchup, I can't tell you where we picked 20 pounds of them in an hour 'cuz I don't know.

And, yes, I know Lunds sells fresh morels for $8.99 a pound and Surdyk's sells six or eight dried ones for $4.49. But you can't have mine for $50 a pound, because we ate them on the spot — cooked up in omelets, and, for dessert, sauteed in butter and lemon juice. Those that were left over are only happy memories now, so don't bug me.

Ratzloff coerced his buddy, Jerry Petermeier, to lead the hunt. It was Petermeier who taught Ratzloff about mushrooms and life five years ago. Ratzloff had dropped out of the wing-tip life (his description of leaving the advertising world) to live in the woods near Annandale. He had no job, no plans, no car, no television. What he did that winter was read, including Petermeier's entire collection of books about mushrooms.

When spring finally came, he searched the woods every day for hours and came up with not one morel. He announced to the visiting Petermeier that the morels had succumbed to winter kill. Petermeier went out to check and came back in 15 minutes with a hat full of morels. Ratzloff ran out the cabin door swearing. He told himself he wouldn't come back without a find. Four hours later, he returned — with one morel.

"It's been easy going ever since," Ratzloff said. "I arrange my life around morels. There's no job I wouldn't quit if they wanted me to work in May."

Part of his living now comes from morels. He, Petermeier and Paul

Chelgren put together and published a book called "Roon: A Tribute to Morel Mushrooms." They made up the word roon and gave it a primary definition of "a person possessed by extreme or insatiable desires for morel mushrooms." Another definition is "one who is given to luxury and sensual pleasures."

These guys are kind of strange on the subject of mushrooms. Petermeier carries a walking stick with a head shaped like a morel, and he uses a knife that looks like a morel. They daydream about making a million on a perfume with the nutty smell of morels.

One day a week ago when the rains held off for most of the day, Ratzloff gave himself the day off to take me morel hunting. With us was his friend Maureen O'Kane. She had gone morel hunting twice this spring and had gotten skunked both times. She pleaded for the experts to show her the way. The first thing they did was insist she change out of her boots. Petermeier called them "mall boots," the kind you'd wear at Southdale, not in the forest.

Petermeier led us toward the morels, pointing out the flora along the way: columbine, catnip, jack-in-the-pulpit, wild geraniums in bloom, showy orchis (which I thought was the finest smell ever invented, even beating morels, an opinion not shared by my hosts). We allayed our hunger with wild leeks and the curled-up tips of bracken ferns, which are served in some gourmet restaurants. Petermeier also recommended the violets, but we skipped that course.

"Over there is one of the most important plants in the woods," Petermeier said. "It's mullein, the softest leaf around. Good if you run out of toilet paper." Not to be confused with burdock, which he calls "nature's Velcro."

We got to a briskly flowing stream and got across by gingerly stepping along two felled tree branches and using another branch as a pole to steady ourselves. We three klutzes said later we were surprised Petermeier could get us to attempt the balancing act. He used elementary psychology: "The morels are on the other side."

Then he yelled the golden worlds: "Morel time!" Standing there was the prettiest thing — a 6-inch golden morel. "Can we pick it?" O'Kane asked. "Go to it. They're your lunch." They? Plural? Sure enough, there were morels all around us! We novices had walked right by a bunch. O'Kane picked dozens and celebrated by sticking her nose into her bag and sniffing. Petermeier and Ratzloff were pleased but not overjoyed: "We haven't found the mother lode yet."

Sometimes near the end of the season, they said, the morels are so thick and fragrant that you can smell them before you see them. A bit later, O'Kane thought that happened to her but it turned out she was smelling the morels in her backpack.

We tripped over a patch that O'Kane and I called a mother lode, but the men said no way, you need two or three times as many morels to qualify as a mother lode. But we picked and picked and were ever so pleased with ourselves, realizing later the men had led us to the spot and practically pushed our noses into the dirt before we caught on.

And then came the sweetest moment of all. Eating them. Ratzloff and Petermeier had talked about a morel lunch, but I didn't realize it was going to be out in the woods, next to a morel patch. "Come up here and bring some wood," Petermeier shouted to us. Right there on the edge of a farmer's plowed field, he built a fire. He pulled two little frying pans from his backpack and plopped in a hunk of butter. O'Kane cleaned morels. We passed a bottle of Beaujolais, taking glugs out of the bottle. Petermeier the magician produced fresh lemons, hot sauce, freshly ground pepper, a dozen eggs. Soon he had the world's best omelets going.

Just who is this Petermeier anyway? Turns out he's a professional chef, just about to begin working at the University Club. He sure knows food. Like the joy of dipping French bread into the juice produced by sauteed mushrooms. And he used to be a priest who outfitted and guided teenagers on wilderness canoe trips, thereby explaining his adroitness at getting us to ford the stream.

For dessert, Ratzloff cooked us some — what else? — morels. Just morels, lemon juice, butter. One morel was so big it filled the whole frying pan. Tastes better than filet mignon, Petermeier said. I think he's right.

We discussed life and death (no, silly, not death by mushroom poisoning). We pulled wood ticks off our bodies and displayed our badges of honor, deep scratches. Petermeier warned us that in some weak moment, O'Kane and I will be likely to say, "I know where we can find morels." "Damn lie," I said. "I have no idea where we are." "Lucky for you," he said. "You'll have to stay ethical."

Ratzloff started stewing about having to go to New York the next day on business. He's the founder and partner of click!, which makes and markets photo peripherals. He realized that people are shooting enormous numbers of photographs, but unfortunately the images are too often stored in shoe boxes. Frames and albums barely accommodate the photographs. click! is making calendars and books to hold amateurs' photos.

The company is doing well. Ratzloff wants to quit though. He gains weight and gets a spot on his hand when he's not happy. See the spot? Not even a whole day of morel hunting made it go away. Time to quit again. This time around he has a wife and son and can't hide in the woods for a winter, but life is too short to fret and break out in spots.

Ratzloff quit that job, and another one. He's trying to support his family, which now includes a daughter too, by being a full-time morel photographer. Many a month, that doesn't work out perfectly, so he's willing to shoot almost anything and anybody.

Alpha Lundeen

Whatever Happened to Baby Alpha?

September 24, 1989

❧

If you're really into family planning, you may want to start thinking about when to conceive the first child born in your community in the 21st century.

We can't guarantee fabulous gifts and great press for the first baby born after midnight on Jan. 1, 2001. But we can point out the historic precedent from a century earlier.

The Charles Lundeen family of 427 Knox Av. N. made news with the birth of a girl, the first 20th-century baby born in Minneapolis. "WHAT SHALL WE NAME THE BABY?" blared the front-page headline in the Minneapolis Journal the evening of Jan. 1, 1901. The newspaper invited readers to submit names for "the little stranger." (The little stranger, by the way, weighed 12 pounds at birth.)

The newspaper offered no prizes for the perfect name — "it's just a little matter of civic pride" — but it did offer some guidelines: "The name must trip well from the tongue and it must . . . fit the girl and the occasion. It may be that some already established appellation may be found or adapted to suit the case or it may be that some clever word-smith may make a name that will be just right. In any event, 200,000 heads are better than the two of the Lundeens."

The Journal's readers loved the idea and started submitting names: Henriette Centurette; Twencentriella; Alpha (meaning "first"); Vini Minnie; Nova Centuria; Una; Prima Adonno; Minnie Firsta. Dr. Henry B. Fay wrote to say he thought that "Socia" would be a good name because "it is the Latin derivative of socialism, which Baby Lundeen will see before she reaches three score and ten."

Other newspapers spread the word on the contest. Soon people from all over the country were tossing in names. The Journal said that the Lundeen baby is "about as famous as any young lady of her age in the United States."

Local people donated gifts. Charles J. Alexander, 1014 Hennepin Av., offered to make a dozen photographs of the Lundeen baby "as soon as she was old enough to hold up her chin and look pleasant."

The naming decision was announced in the Journal on Jan. 9. "THE BABY IS NAMED: She Will Go Through Life as Alpha Twencentia Minnea Lundeen." The name may sound dreadful to us, but at the time it was wholeheartedly approved. The Journal said the family so appreciated all the interest in the baby that "as soon as the little one is a week or ten days older, she and mother will be glad to receive visitors to their home."

Glad? Can you believe it? Especially considering that Alpha had six big brothers and sisters, and their house was likely modest, because their dad was a laborer for the railroad.

Alpha granted an interview to a Journal reporter on her 4th birthday. She was described as happy, healthy and hearty and possessed of delightful manners; when introduced to the reporter, "she held out her chubby hand and remarked with a little bow of courtly grace, 'I am happy to see you.' "

We can find no trace of her after that. Alpha, if you're out there, please let us know.

December 15, 1989

❧

We learned what became of Alpha Lundeen, the first baby born in Minneapolis in the 20th century, and it's a tragic story. Over the love of a man, she killed herself.

Alpha's tragedy came when she was 23 years old. A graduate of Minneapolis' North High, she worked as a secretary for the Woolworth Co. Depressed over an entanglement with a man, she committed suicide at the downtown YWCA by swallowing carbolic acid, a particularly painful way to die.

Friends and family agree on that much. But to this day, two stories are told about Alpha's relationship with the man. One is that she loved him dearly, but he no longer wished to see her. She lived with her family at 427 Knox Av. N., growing more and more depressed. One morning she took the streetcar downtown and swallowed poison over her lunch break. Her family, humiliated by the suicide, held a private funeral the next day and buried her at Lakewood Cemetery.

Another version is that her boss — a married man — was pursuing her. Today we'd call the situation sexual harassment. He was older, maybe 29. She couldn't fight him off and ended her life.

One of Alpha's best friends in high school called us to say that Alpha is still on her mind, 65 years later. The friend, 88 years old, vehemently denied a rumor of the time that Alpha was pregnant when she died. In fact, the friend explained, if Alpha would have died in our times, the death would be attributed partly to Premenstrual Syndrome.

Mizinokamigok

Knitter of Ojibway Ways
June 1, 1985

❦

"I am Mizinokamigok," she wrote in her letter to the newspaper, trying to get us interested in her needlework. "The American name placed on me is Elizabeth Gonier."

"Placed on me" may sound militant, but she isn't. She says that her role for much of her life has been to be a bridge between her Ojibway people and white society. "I may sound like I'm being stubborn when I say, 'Don't call me Indian. I have nothing to do with India. I'm Ojibway.' But if people are going to know, I have to explain."

She has worked as a translator and a teacher of Ojibway language and culture. Now her health is poor. She has had to figure out some way to stay at home in Crystal and support herself and her 17-year-old son. So, as in every other crisis in her life, she taught herself a way out of a tight spot.

She learned to knit.

Five years ago she didn't know what to do with a knitting needle. She figured it out on her own. Now sweaters bearing the label "Mizinokamigok Original" are selling for $75 to $100. Buyers with that kind of money are white and well-off, completely unlike her, she points out. But no problem. People who buy her sweaters and dresses and coats, she says, are given a subtle lesson in Ojibway color and form. Some buyers tell her the handwork looks European. She knows otherwise.

"The patterns and colors I learned not from a school, but from *us,* the way we live and the way we view things," she said.

Miz, as she calls herself, was born in northern Minnesota on the Nett Lake Reservation some 40 years ago. (Age, she says, is a white hangup. "For us, age is no consideration. Who you are, what you're doing and how you feel about yourself are more important. How can the year you were born be significant?") The name Mizinokamigok, meaning "Island on earth, island in infinity," was given her before birth by an elder on the reservation.

As a young child, she was educated in the Native American manner.

Adults taught her how to cut bark, how to dig roots for baskets, how to harvest and cook wild rice. Never was the instruction formal, Miz said. Children observed. When they asked questions, then adults explained.

"But I realized that no matter how much I knew of that, it wouldn't help me with others," she said. White-culture schools bored her. She quit school after ninth grade. "It was so stupid and repetitive and didn't teach me anything I needed to know. I was so dumb and naive that I quit."

Determined to understand more of the world ("I've come as far as I can here," she told herself), she moved to Minneapolis as a teenager. She had heard about the University of Minnesota, where, she says, "I set to educate myself." One small problem emerged: "No one told me I needed to go to high school first. No wonder it seemed a bit difficult at times! Well, no matter."

Did she learn anything useful at the university?

"Boy, did I learn! I learned how to stand in line. I learned how to react when you stand in line for hours and they slam the window down in your face. I'm *serious*. I didn't know someone could treat you that way."

At one point she had a scholarship, she said, "just for being a real live Indian. I did more than that. I used my 'native intelligence' to be an ambassador for our people. It was fun."

But to complicate things, she became ill her last quarter at the university with a tumor in the pituitary gland and had surgery.

She stuck it out ("Somebody has to know how to interpret our culture to the greater society"), and in 1961 she graduated from the university in sociology and anthropology. Eventually she taught there. On and off from 1970 to 1975 she was a lecturer in American Indian Studies. (These dates come from the university. Her culture doesn't encourage specificity about such things as dates and numbers.) She also taught at Macalester College, the College of St. Catherine and the College of St. Thomas. She taught the children of the Robbinsdale School District and adults in the Anoka community education program.

Miz said she didn't teach by rote. "I explained." She said the students responded well to her. Sometimes they stayed around far into the night. "Can you imagine anyone at the university *wanting* to stay until 11:30?"

Jack Dean, who teaches social studies at Blake Middle School, was one of Miz's students. He calls her a powerful teacher, able to interest people in a variety of subjects they continue to study outside class. "For example," he said, "I'll never view nature with the indifference I did before. . . . She helps people cross over and meet Native American culture on at least neutral ground."

Most of her teaching is oral, he said. "The idea is to make use of the things in your head because if you write them down, you can lose them."

Miz was married but her husband has left her and their son. She's grateful she has that son. She had ignored advice from doctors that her health was fragile and that it would be a mistake to have children. "I always said I would have a child and I did. He's strong and healthy and beautiful." She named her boy Eni mi bi nes. That's a name given him by an elder. Miz would not interpret it. That is her son's privilege. He chose not to. He prefers his other name, Dean Edward Gonier. Dean was 2 when she started teaching at the university, and he spent hours in her Ojibway language classes. Sometimes when the adults were stymied, the little guy would pipe up with the right answer.

When a malfunctioning endocrine system forced Miz to give up teaching, she turned to another part of her brain, she said — designing, creating, watching. She said she can spend hours watching anthill activity. "Creating," she said, "gives me happiness. Euphoria even!"

Decades ago a white woman whom Miz calls "a benevolent old lady" wanted to give her money to study at the Traphagen School for Design in New York City. Miz turned her down. "I don't need to, I already know how to design." She's glad she made the decision to go to the university instead. "I might have been tempted into strange ways of thinking in the big city of New York."

Like what?

"Like thinking money is the important thing. That having fine clothes is *the* way to live. I didn't want to have to deal with that. The old lady thought I was ungrateful and stupid. These things were wrong for me."

Still, she wanted to go to New York and look. She saw "different cultural stuff — the art galleries, the Statue of Liberty." She also traveled to Colorado, California and Boston.

When her health failed years later and she found herself spending hours in her favorite chair knitting, she said one day to her son, "Dean, this is what I think. Being as I do this all the time, let's try to make this our livelihood."

Dean jumped into action. As his mother knits, he is the business's bookkeeper, chauffeur, delivery man, letter writer, fashion photographer. He also does the cooking and housework. And back before his shoulders grew so big, he sometimes was forced to try on sweaters for her.

Miz said, "I'm starting to make a living this way. I don't see another thing for me to do. This has got to work. Mainly I'm a designer and things come from inside my head."

She knits at least three or four pieces a week. Many have bold stripes. In others, the colors flow together. The colors — heather next to plum, greens and blues woven together — are a good part of the beauty. Her house in Crystal is strewn with works in progress. There's a coat here, a sweater with a leaf pattern started over there, another sweater with ribbon woven in, draped over a chair. About a slinky black dress she said, "This doesn't look like anything on a hanger, but you should see it on." She invited over a friend, Giesela Keys, who's a part-time model, to prove her point.

Miz doesn't regard as special that she figured out knitting on her own: "You do what you have to. I could build a bridge if I had to."

Because money is scarce, she buys lots of remnants. She can eyeball how much yarn she'll need. One of her favorite sweaters has a yoke made from a dollar's worth of yarn she picked up on sale. She's frugal; she spent only $1,200 on yarn last year. She talks on the phone and knits. She watches TV and knits. She knits in times of joy, she knits in time of upheaval. "This fits my personality and my freedom."

She used to sell through retailers but ran into problems, including insurance. Right now she's selling only out of her home. She's in the telephone book under Mizinokamigok. She said she will be glad to go to people's houses if four or more people are interested, and she hopes to have showings several times a year at an Edina building.

Miz also has written books for elementary-school children, with her theme of Native Americans in suburbia. They were about little Hope going to school, turning 6 years old, etc. She said the books "were lavishly illustrated by a Polish lady friend." Unfortunately for both of them, the books project got bogged down in the state Indian Education office, she said, and were not published.

One other thing: She hopes she doesn't come across in this article as haughty. "As one who strives for humility, that is the last thing I need. Honest and forthright maybe. But not braggy."

Miz said she would like this article to end the way her conversations and letters do. "Me gwetch, me gwetch." That's Ojibway for "Thanks, thanks."

Miz's health has not been wonderful but her knitting is. She would be pleased to make a special sweater for you.

Dan Witkowski

A Super Magic Man
March 27, 1988

❧

Dan Witkowski was up against the giants. He was the eighth to present his proposal for producing the half-time entertainment at next year's Super Bowl. The first seven were big outfits, including Disney and Radio City Music Hall. In came Witkowski — a 30-year-old magician from Minneapolis, cherubic, chubby, kind of bumbling.

He put his briefcase on the table and gave what seemed to be a rambling little talk — actually very well-rehearsed — to Pete Rozelle and other National Football League big-shots. Witkowski's approach was based on the idea that in order to produce an impressive half-time show you have to pull a lot of magic out of a limited space. To illustrate, he reached into his 3-inch-thick briefcase and pulled out a bowling ball. A real bowling ball. He heard a cynic whisper, "It's a balloon." Witkowski dropped it — supposedly accidentally — onto the conference table.

It thudded. Ka-boom!

Witkowski commanded attention. The committee loved his multi-million-dollar proposal. He walked away with the biggest entertainment production of the television year. It has the highest Nielsen ratings and the biggest advertising expenditures.

This is the kid from Northeast Minneapolis who started doing magic shows at age 5. The most frequently spoken words in the Witkowski household were, "Go away, Danny; we don't want to see any more card tricks." During his years at De La Salle High School, he was getting paid for magic on the convention and banquet circuit all over the Midwest, with audiences as large as 900. He was good, really good, and was the only student in his school to own a tuxedo. (It was denim.) He quit the University of Minnesota his senior year to produce big shows for Valleyfair, started his own company at age 20 and hasn't slacked off since.

Now at the ripe old age of 31, he is becoming internationally known. His company, MagicCom, Inc., is doing less magic and more producing of extravaganzas.

Witkowski is known for creativity and for meticulous planning and presentation, a rare combination. Back to the Super Bowl proposal, for example. He and his team worked up an elaborate, high-tech half-time show calling for 3,000 performers and crew members, plus 26 Royal Lippizaner horses from Vienna and 200 members of the Southern Cal band marching out of a huge Trojan horse. MagicCom accounted for every detail, down to the fact that the setting sun will be shining into the eyes of fans in sections L, M, N and P. (Not that Witkowski is taking advantage of that to create illusions.)

NFL rules state that entertainment concepts be submitted in advance, in detail, in writing. Witkowski figured his proposal would be thumbed through and tossed aside unless he could personally explain its brilliance as he proceeded.

So his company printed it into a nice little book, added intriguing illustrations, bound it in fancy blue leather, printed "Dan Witkowski" and "Super Bowl XXII Sorcery Spectacular" in flashy silver letters on the cover and sent it to the NFL in plenty of time to meet the regulations.

Here's the gimmick: In the lower-right corner of each book was drilled a quarter-inch hole. Through the hole was a heavy brass padlock. Witkowski didn't send keys with the books. He waited to hand them out at the meeting.

❧

Want to know how successful Witkowski's business has gotten?

His company is No. 3 in magic, measured in dollar volume. It's behind David Copperfield and Siegfried and Roy of Las Vegas. MagicCom's business increased 10-fold in 1987 over the year before; this year he estimates it will increase 23-fold over last year, and then stabilize. He has a full-time staff of five, a few others on contract and lots of specialists on the coasts — choreographers, scenic designers, wardrobe designers, special-effects people. He's been featured on the Today show and has performed three times at the White House.

He did a 1988 Super Bowl pregame show that was a tribute to Bob Hope; Hope's manager said that Hope was "very, very, very happy" with Witkowski. He has photos of himself with George Burns, Lucille Ball, Orson Welles. He will be on 180 million boxes of General Mills cereal. Pamphlets with his magic tricks are inside millions of cereal boxes. Scads of kids are sending in $9.95 and two box tops for a video in which Witkowski explains 12 magic tricks to Trix Rabbit, Count Chocula and other General Mills celebrities.

Witkowski is doing well — very well.

He doesn't brag; all his accomplishments are phrased in terms of "we." He wiggles nervously during discussions of money, and he lives relatively modestly. He has fixed up his townhouse on the near north side of Minneapolis to suit him — a big mirror etched with his monogram in the living room; marble-like columns and swags in the bedroom, befitting an unmarried showman — but the place isn't big and it's not high rent. His company recently moved from an office with peeling wallpaper to niftier quarters on Hwy. 55 that feature a "magic" coffee service. (His illusion makes it seem that the hands pouring the coffee are not attached to a human body.)

If he had some time, he might think of looking for a Rolls Royce, but meanwhile his black Chrysler convertible (with "PRESTO" license plates) is plenty good enough. He's almost apologetic for not displaying conspicuous consumption. He says that he's as materialistic as the next guy, but, really, he's been busy. Maybe someday he'll buy some horses. Honest, he'll start spending soon.

He used to pray that he would have a show every night and wouldn't have to get a real job. Now he doesn't have to take everything offered him, and is concentrating on producing. Some of his productions have nothing to do with magic.

He'd like to be to magic what Jim Henson is to puppets: He wants to use magic in merchandising, education, network television, cable, video, records, toys. He says, "In magic, we're selling a form of fantasy. It's not so limited as being a magician cutting someone in half."

His friends and colleagues say that Witkowski hasn't outgrown his britches. (Except maybe literally. He says he has to lose 60 pounds before he's the magician for the Super Bowl.) Eileen Noble, who has known Witkowski six years and married his best friend, Jim Noble, reports he's the same Dan — unassuming, funny, charming, constantly creative, great with kids, ethical, direct and Minneapolis' most eligible bachelor. She said, "He's so neat I can't figure out why some woman hasn't grabbed him. Maybe because he's married to his job."

He puts in 60 or 70 hours a week for the business but says he "works" only two or three; the rest of the time is fun. That's his goal — fun; profitability will take care of itself. If he wanted to get richer quicker, he could do a magic show in Las Vegas for two years. The same show, night after night. No thanks.

He doesn't consider leaving Minneapolis. ("L.A. is so heartless. Northeast Minneapolis isn't.") He doesn't consider changing his name to something less Polish. He doesn't want his company to be on the New York Stock Exchange. He doesn't consider slacking off on charity shows because he's busy. He's still a nice guy.

❧

Danny Witkowski grew up in a working-class family in Northeast Minneapolis, the youngest of five children. His dad, the late Joseph Witkowski, worked weekdays in the bottling department of Grain Belt Brewery, weekends as a butcher. His mother, Olga Witkowski, sewed for various companies.

At age 5, he found magic on the back of cereal boxes (he regrets they weren't General Mills) in the form of tricks by magician Mark Wilson.

Little Danny showed his stuff to Mrs. Haskell's kindergarten class. In elementary school, he performed at birthday parties and on the banquet circuit, already earning real money and developing a stage persona. He tried not to come off as a smart aleck, but as a vulnerable, clumsy, apologetic type whom the audience would feel for. His magic would appear to backfire and people would think, "The poor little guy!" Then, of course, everything would work and he'd pretend to be surprised. He still uses that approach, and it's still winning hearts.

Marge Johnson, Dan's sister who's eight years older, remembers that as a kid he never wanted anything for birthdays or Christmas unless it was from Eagle Magic Shop. Rosie Witkowski, another sister, says Danny drove his siblings crazy with his stupid tricks. He'd usually flub them. On purpose? "No," said Rosie, "I don't think so." She claims to have a scar from the time Danny tried to saw her in half. She's kidding.

Then there was the time Danny talked his mom into letting him practice an illusion that made it look like he was putting swords through her head. To make the trick more realistic, he instructed her to scream at the right time. Unfortunately, the scream came just when Olga Witkowski's two little granddaughters, about 4 and 5, walked into the house. They thought Uncle Danny was doing in Grandma.

Dan remembers putting his dog into a laundry basket and putting arrows "through" it. The puppy's name? "He didn't live long enough to get a name." He's kidding.

When he was in high school, magician Mark Wilson came to town. Determined to meet Wilson, Witkowski got the editor of his high-school paper to assign him the story, and he talked his way into lunch to ask Wilson how he did his illusions. Tad Ware, who was representing Wilson's sponsor, Pillsbury, said the kid was "not boorish, but gutsy. Still is."

The Witkowski family got tired of doves boarding upstairs and rabbits running here and there, especially because Dan is allergic to rabbits. His mom got annoyed with him because he talked her into hauling him and his props all over the Twin Cities for magic shows, and invariably he'd get the directions wrong. She worried when he got more and more into magic: "I used to tell him, 'Don't you ever think you can make a living at this nonsense!'"

Danny somehow always knew he could. He was determined to become famous and he worked hard at it. When his Ukrainian Grandma Chas used to tease him, he would tease right back: "OK, Grandma. But when I'm famous you'll sit in the balcony. I won't get you a front-row seat."

One of the few jobs he has had outside of magic was as a tour guide for WCCO-TV when he was in college. He thought of writing his memoirs and calling them "TV Guide."

To this day, his family and friends enjoy giving him a hard time. Says sister Marge: "He can't balance his checkbook, and here he is doing these super productions." His mother adds, "I don't always tell people I have a famous son. I just say I have a son in show business. If they push, I say he's a magician. 'A musician?' they say. 'What does he play?' "

But behind his back, they brag about him. Like how the Disney guys said his research was so solid that he found out stuff about Mickey Mouse that they didn't know. Like how he's one of the few fortunate people on earth who wandered into something that makes him happy and pays big bucks. They beg to be included. Marge pleads with him, "Danny, I want to be in the half-time show. I'll diet. You can cut me in half. You can do anything. I'd be nice to you."

Witkowski says no matter how big he gets, he'll never get the respect in Northeast that he would if he'd become a priest. His brother Jim came the closest: He trained as a mortician.

❧

Dan Witkowski is a born merchandiser.

He says his 14-minute half-time show for next year's Super Bowl show has the potential to be the highest-rated television show of all time. He has a promotion in mind to make that happen. We can't give away his secret, but try to visualize two products, a soft drink and a fast food that are advertised lots on TV. After Christmas people who buy them will get little envelopes with their purchases. They'll rub a coin on the outside to see if they get a prize immediately, but they'll be told to keep the envelope sealed until Super Bowl Sunday and open it when the magician (Witkowski) says. If they do what he says, the TV screen will cause something magical to happen to the game card inside. And, of course, something magic will happen to Witkowski's wallet, too.

He's also a dreamer. Here's an illusion he wants to perform someday:

He gets two people up from the audience — a skinny man and his hefty wife.

He drapes them with a fabric banner. He's going to make them disappear. Abracadabra! Darn. The people are still there. Try again. Abracadabra! The man and woman have switched places, but they're not invisible. Again. Abracadabra! The man is still there, but the woman has turned into a walrus.

Wow!! How would you do that, Dan?

"Can you keep a secret?"

Sure.

"So can I."

Critics panned the Super Bowl show. Witkowski defended himself by saying it was better in real life than on television. He has not yet turned a woman into a walrus, but this summer he is turning his girlfriend into his wife.

Ned Waldman

Memories of a Boyhood Love
December 17, 1987
❦

People ask Ned Waldman, who's Jewish, why he gets all foggy-eyed about Christmas, why he busts his butt to promote a book about a fictional old lady at Christmastime.

Usually he doesn't explain. Memories hurt. He lets people presume he's just another publisher after a buck.

But catch him in a sappy mood in December, and maybe he'll tell about Adele Molitor and the book he published in her honor, "A Cup of Christmas Tea."

The story starts with a Jewish family in Minneapolis in 1933, the Depression. Ned Waldman's mother had suffered from rheumatic fever as a child and her weakened heart became infected shortly after the birth of Ned, her second son. She died when he was two months old. Her husband — grief-stricken, unemployed, hopeless — soon abandoned the boys and left for California. Grandma Waldman took in Ned's brother, who was 3. Other relatives had health and money problems themselves, and Ned was put in the care of the family's housekeeper, Adele Molitor.

The family had found her through a want-ad, and she had tended the baby since the day he was born. She pleaded with the child's grandmother to be allowed to keep him. Temporarily, it was allowed.

Adele loved him greatly, and he has more than memories to prove it. There's the little cardboard box she filled with his clipped curls and on which she wrote, "Ned haircut May 17, 1937, 3 years and 9 months old. Some baby boy."

She was Roman Catholic, childless and divorced after a marriage of several months. During the day, she worked as a piece-rate ironer for a clothing manufacturer and she put Ned with other children in an early form of day care. Otherwise, she took him everywhere with her, including church. Not that she forced her religion on him, he says, but she seemed glad for his company during mass.

The Last of the Tearoom Ladies ❦ 81

The two of them lived in an apartment a couple of blocks from the Minneapolis Basilica. They had one room and a closet. The bathroom was down the hall.

She had him call her "Adele." Recently, though, he ran across a Mother's Day card he had inscribed, "For Adele (Mom)."

Christmas was their favorite time together. Each year they put up a tree next to the window overlooking the alley and decorated it with bubbling lights and ornaments special to them, such as the miniature teddy bear he still hauls out on bad days. They sent out 100 or more Christmas cards. They listened to Kate Smith on the radio; her "Silent Night" is still his most precious song. He can almost smell the Christmas tea she steeped, and the cinnamon and spices that wafted through their home. He can recall every detail of his toy soldiers all in a row. "Everything was from Woolworth's, but it was all beautiful," he said. He doesn't remember a whit about kindergarten, but every memory of those early Christmases is sharp.

All that Waldman remembers of his boyhood with Adele is tinged with love and joy.

But when he was 5, they were pulled apart. "I was — I don't want to make it sound terrible — I was taken from her," he said. "Evidently, my family thought I should be among them and raised in my Jewish heritage." His father's brother came to pack him up. Adele told Ned decades later that it happened two weeks before Christmas. He went to live with his mother's sister for a year, and then with another aunt on his mother's side, Millie Stillman, and her family in south Minneapolis.

"That woman, my Aunt Millie, now there's another incredible woman," he said. "I was doubly blessed." She and her husband, Norman, had two sons and a daughter and Ned to raise. She puts it like this: "I have four children."

Adele asked to be able to see Ned regularly. He says now, "A lesser woman would have left and been done with me." His Aunt Millie, knowing full well how important Adele and Ned were to each other, encouraged them to continue their relationship.

Waldman says, "Instead of giving up on me, this beautiful person, my Adele, visited me every week. Until I could drive, and get to her place, she came to see me. On every important occasion, she was there." Eventually, Waldman's son and daughter also came to know Adele.

And every Christmas, except the two he was in the Army, Adele and Ned were together at her home. He, of course, didn't have a Christmas tree at his house, but he would put one up in hers. The older they got, the more artistic he strove to make it.

Fiercely independent, Adele never was any good at accepting things from Ned, even after he was a successful businessman. Gifts could not be ostentatious. He connived and wheedled to get her to accept things. She did like the rosary he had blessed for her in Rome.

For 46 years Adele lived with a man — Waldman thinks they didn't marry because of the church's stand on her divorce — and he died a month before her. She was 87 when cancer took her in 1984.

Meanwhile, Minneapolis teacher and actor Tom Hegg wrote a poem in 1981 called "A Cup of Christmas Tea." It's about a man who reluctantly goes to visit a great aunt, elderly and frail, and how the visit turns out to be a blessing for both.

Hegg and the book's illustrator, Warren Hanson, published it out of Hegg's house. Both did it as a tribute to older women in their families. It sold nicely, and the two went after a national publisher.

In New York, Hegg was told: Poetry doesn't sell, Christmas books have too short a shelf life and you're an unknown author. He got it sold to a Minneapolis publisher, but after a while she wanted out. She approached Waldman.

Waldman knew vaguely of the book — he is co-owner with his cousin, Norton Stillman (Millie's son), of The Bookmen, Inc., one of the state's largest book distributing firms — but hadn't read it. Hegg invited him over to his house one summer afternoon, and in the gazebo Hegg read the story to Waldman. There was Waldman, all dressed up in his power suit, blubbering, remembering Adele.

Quickly, he bought the book's rights for $25,000. This is the third Christmas that his little publishing company, Waldman House Press, has handled it. He hopes that this year total sales will top 100,000 copies. He claims not to know how much profit the book has brought him — maybe $10,000 or $25,000, he says, when pressed — but "I wouldn't sell that book today for half a million dollars, cash. I've read about successful people, and when asked why they did something, the answer is never money. The money will take care of itself."

Besides, someday "A Cup of Christmas Tea" will be a national bestseller, he's sure. It's a word-of-mouth book, and the word is spreading.

Last year it was reprinted in Woman's Day. Charles Kuralt compared it to "A Christmas Carol" and "other Christmas stories read around crackling fires this time of year." Helen Hayes wrote to say she loves it. Hundreds of radio stations, including WCCO, an early supporter of the book, will broadcast the 8-minute tape this Christmas Eve. A reader wrote to Waldman to complain that one quick read of the book ruined her makeup. A 94-year-old woman wrote that the book moved her to visit her 102-year-old friend.

"These aren't isolated instances," Waldman says. "In my view, this book either passes a person by or moves him or her greatly."

Because Hanson's illustrations tell the story without showing the characters, Waldman says "you can imagine your own relative, any color, any age, any parts of beauty." Guess who he thinks about.

"I have a hard time, I think, showing love," Waldman says, "reaching out and showing people. But it's easier during Christmastime. All that comes back, Adele's love and her pride and her dignity. You know, she could put on inexpensive clothing and it would look good, because she was proud. And independent. She shoveled her walk until she was 86 — dynamic lady."

He's so lucky, he says, to have a book to help keep her in his memory. What's best, it's a Christmas book. As he says, "Christmas is an extra excuse to care."

"Moonlight" Graham

Chisholm and a Field of Dreams
June 6, 1989
❧

One summer day maybe 10 or 12 years ago, two dapper men walked into the Chisholm newspaper office and started asking the publisher about old Doc Graham, major-league baseball player turned small-town physician.

What fiction writers W.P. Kinsella and J.D. Salinger learned about Graham became a subplot of Kinsella's book, "Shoeless Joe." The book became this summer's surprise hit movie, "Field of Dreams."

The book and film involve an Iowa farmer who builds a baseball diamond in his cornfield with hopes that Shoeless Joe Jackson will return from the dead to play there. In the course of the story, Graham gets a chance to stare down a pitcher.

It's high fantasy, but the details about Graham's life are the real, honest-to-goodness truth. Almost all of them, anyway.

Archibald (Moonlight) Graham really did have the dubious honor of the shortest baseball career in history. His entire stint in the major leagues consisted of playing a single inning for the New York Giants in 1905. He never did get to bat. He didn't want to be sent to the minors, so instead he really did go back to medical school.

Graham settled in Chisholm and practiced medicine there for more than 50 years. He was just as sweet and kind and beloved as the movie portrays him.

Probably even more so. What the movie doesn't get into is that Graham was called a Pied Piper because he handed out dimes and lemon drops to the kids.

He had 10 bucks for any Iron Ranger pinched for cash. He gave away more free eyeglasses than any other Minnesotan. He was Chisholm's best booster of high school athletics. He monitored the blood pressure of every school child for decades and he stressed preventive dentistry, practices far ahead of his time.

Dead for 24 years now, Doc Graham still is revered in Chisholm. The worst that natives say about him is that his diphtheria inoculations stung and that he didn't socialize much or take a drink.

Although he's a local legend, not a darned thing in town was named for Graham until the last few weeks — not until Hollywood spread his name, not until Chisholm people streamed into Hibbing to see the film, not until a trickle of tourists began inquiring if a ballplayer named "Moonlight" Graham actually lived here.

Town leaders voted last week to pay $550 for a banner to fly over main street proclaiming Chisholm as Graham's home. And the new $40,000 playground that the children had voted months ago to name "Paradise City" has been renamed "Paradise City: A Field of Dreams." Sunday it was dedicated to the memory of Doc Graham.

ɤ

Veda Ponikvar knows as much about Graham as anyone alive in Chisholm. She's the 70-year-old editor and publisher of two weekly newspapers, and she was a close friend of Graham and his wife. She wrote about him when he was the school doctor; she wrote his obituary and his eulogy, and she's writing articles about him now that he has, in a way, come back to life.

"Field of Dreams" producers offered her $100 to permit them to portray her in the film. She signed the papers (and donated the money to the playground project) but hasn't seen the film yet. Too busy. Judy Regan spoke for many in Chisholm when she said, "Veda could have played herself better than Anne Seymour did; she's better looking and has a better voice."

Ponikvar's part in the movie is summarizing Graham's life. The real-life Ponikvar says that Graham was born in North Carolina; the film inaccurately gives his birthplace as Chisholm. He earned his medical degree from the University of Maryland in 1905, the same year he played for the Giants. Then he did post-graduate work in pathology at Johns Hopkins University in Baltimore and interned in New York City. (His brother went on to be president of the University of North Carolina.)

He came to Minnesota in 1909. The story is that he walked into Chisholm's Rood Hospital (now torn down) and asked for a job. How he picked Chisholm is a mystery. It was the year after a fire had burned the mining town to the ground. Almost every brick store on the main street today was built the year Graham arrived. He became the school system's physician in 1917; for two months every summer, he did post-graduate work in New York hospitals. He retired in 1961, at age 82.

From 1915 to his death he was married to a woman he adored. Alicia was from Rochester, Minn. Most of her clothes were blue, and people still talk about how shopkeepers would put blue dresses and hats in their windows, knowing Doc Graham couldn't resist buying them for her. Though they both loved children, they never had any of their own and lavished affection on generations of Chisholm children.

Graham died in 1965 (the movie portrays him as still alive in 1972) and was buried in Rochester (that accounts for disappointed tourists not finding his gravestone in the Chisholm cemetery).

What irks Ponikvar is that there's only a brief glimpse of Chisholm in "Field of Dreams." Most of the Chisholm scenes were shot in Galena, Ill.

Bill Loushine, Chisholm High School's swim and baseball coach when Graham was still practicing medicine there, can point to two small inaccuracies in the movie: Graham never had the moustache that actor Burt Lancaster sports in the role, and Graham didn't have an office on the street. (He practiced out of the elementary school.) But it's true, Loushine said, that Chisholm people didn't know much about his baseball days: "We heard he was supposed to have been a big-league player but he never talked about it." Never was Graham called "Moonlight" in Chisholm. Nor Archibald or Archie. Doc was the name.

Paul Perkovich, 78, and Albert Gornick, 72, wish the movie had told of Graham's generosity. They remember going to state tournaments in the 1930s with $2 or $3 in their pockets, knowing full well that Doc Graham would be there too and would be willing to buy the kids enough White Castles to fill them up.

Michael Valentini at age 37 is one of the younger people in Chisholm to have Graham as his doctor. When he and his girlfriend, Kathy Bangs, saw the movie the day after it opened in the Twin Cities, they were mesmerized. The movie ended, the credits rolled and there they sat, staring at the curtain. The movie hit him hard partly because of its theme — "I consider myself a dreamer and this movie is about dreams more than baseball" — and because his town is Doc Graham's town. Valentini went back to Chisholm, where he manages his family's Italian restaurant, and he prodded civic groups to start recognizing their deceased doctor.

❧

Doc Graham became a figure in literature and film because author Kinsella was poking around in the Official Baseball Encyclopedia one day. He ran across an entry mentioning Moonlight Graham. Kinsella was fascinated with the name, which came from Graham's bout with insomnia as a ballplayer.

"The more I found out about Doc Graham, the more I realized he was better than anything I could invent," Kinsella said later.

The encyclopedia said Graham died in Chisholm, so Kinsella and another man came here to check out the story. Supposedly Kinsella now denies even knowing Salinger, but Ponikvar is positive the visitor was Salinger. That's how he was introduced and that's who he looked like. "I never questioned it," she said. (In the film, Salinger's character was changed to a fictional author named Terence Mann. Salinger reportedly didn't much like being a fictional character, and out of respect for his wishes the story line was changed.)

In Chisholm, the two authors spotted a photo of Graham on a file cabinet in the newspaper office. They asked for it. Publisher Ponikvar said no. They offered to pay for it. She said no. They said they'd pay anything she wanted for it. She said no. They insisted. The fourth and final time, she said no. Graham's widow had given the photo to Ponikvar many years before. "Mrs. Graham walked in one day wearing her very beautiful blue hat and gave me the photograph," Ponikvar explained. "She told me, 'I don't know anybody who would appreciate this more than you.' "

Kinsella and Salinger hung around Chisholm about three days, Ponikvar remembers, and couldn't come up with any dirt on Doc Graham. Kinsella wrote later in "Shoeless Joe" that "all (they) uncovered is all good: no paramours, no drunken binges, no opium habit, no illegitimate children, no crazy wife locked in the attic, no shady financial dealings, no evicting orphans or midnight abortions. . . . It's a sad time when the world won't listen to stories about good men."

And that, says Ponikvar, is the honest-to-goodness truth about Chisholm's Doc Graham.

❦

WARNING: Do not continue reading unless you have seen the film or read the book.

Sam Nenadich of Chisholm, a former municipal judge and U.S. Steel supervisor, said the film hit him like a ton of bricks. He wishes he, like the characters in the film, could go back in time and again see Graham walking the streets of Chisholm, umbrella in hand, overcoat flapping. Or that Graham could visit present-day Chisholm.

But, Nenadich said, "If he has come back, it hasn't been to Chisholm. We're waiting for him."

Jan Haugen

The Senator's Gatekeeper

May 23, 1989

❦

The first thing one Monday morning, Jan Haugen opened a registered letter from a Minnesota woman pleading to have her new husband, an Egyptian citizen, admitted to the United States.

It was a letter designed to pluck the heart strings. But Haugen's job in Sen. Rudy Boschwitz's St. Paul office is to handle hundreds of touching, sappy, frantic, weepy and angry letters from people separated from loved ones. In a typical day, she might field 40 distraught phone callers, receive 30 plaintive letters and write 10 official letters of her own. To stay sane, Haugen needs to keep her heart strings stuffed down deep, where they're not easily plucked.

She reviewed the facts of the latest case: A Twin Cities woman had gotten to know an Egyptian man here. They went to Egypt to be married. She came back to the United States in a week, without him. Her girlfriend who accompanied her on the quick trip also married an Egyptian there. U.S. immigration officials had informed the first woman that they didn't believe she had married for love and that they intended to refuse her husband an immigrant visa. He would not be permitted to live in this country.

You see, for years immigration officials had been appalled that aliens got a foot in the door here by paying U.S. citizens to marry them. It wasn't at all unusual for aliens (usually men) to pay $5,000 and more to Americans to enter a sham marriage. After these aliens became permanent residents, they were divorced. Immigration authorities put the lid on that in 1986. They now have tough guidelines on what is true love, and they ask some pretty intimate questions. This particular marriage was for convenience, they decided.

So the woman wrote to Boschwitz, asking that he twist some arms and get her man into the country. The letter was assigned to Haugen, who spends 75 percent of her time on immigration matters.

She is not expected to make Solomon-like decisions. "You can't make a judgment call," said Haugen, who has worked on immigration matters for two of the five years she's been with the Boschwitz staff. "You're supposed to say, 'Here is a constituent who's having a problem and wants our help.'"

But if she had to make a judgment call, she continued, she would be skeptical about this case. Here's a Lutheran woman marrying a devout Moslem man, and she told immigration authorities she would not live with him in Egypt or in any country other than the United States. "Hmmmm," Haugen summed up suspiciously. Cupid was conspicuous by his absence.

Other cases on which she has worked have made her heart sing. She's persuaded immigration officials to allow a mother-of-the-bride to come here from Venezuela to witness a wedding. (It's rough to get some aliens admitted even as tourists, even for a few weeks.) She worked her tail off to get the Iranian mother of a constituent into this country for medical treatment; unfortunately the woman died before Haugen could persuade immigration officials. She helped get a Minnesota woman, falsely accused of running drugs, out of a French prison. She got a Mexican couple a tourist visa to attend their granddaughter's first birthday party.

Staffers who previously had Haugen's job got too involved, she said. They went nuts worrying about the cases. She doesn't: "I make it a point that when I leave the office, I leave the office — unless I have to call some embassy at 2 a.m. to straighten out something."

Tim Droogsma, Boschwitz's press secretary, said Haugen's job is tough. "Being on the phone eight hours a day with bureaucrats in various agencies isn't fun. Jan is the persistent type who doesn't give up easily. She's very, very good."

Immigrants identify with Boschwitz, who was born in Germany and remembers steaming past the Statue of Liberty at age 5, Droogsma said. The word has gotten out, especially among southeast Asians, that Boschwitz's staff cares about unraveling immigration problems. His office does as much immigration work as the offices of the other nine Minnesota congressional members combined, according to Droogsma.

Haugen keeps a file of thank-you letters from people she has helped, just in case the senator ever gets angry and wants to dump her. (Doubtful, his aides say.) The writers praise the senator's office — and occasionally Haugen by name — for the extra effort exerted. They mention Haugen's "can-do" attitude.

Helping people and working for a politician she respects are more important to Haugen than making big money, she said. She brings in $17,800 for her full-time job in Boschwitz's office and another $2,400 for her evening job as mayor of Shorewood.

"Rudy is so tight-fisted with money. As a taxpayer, I love it. As a worker, I hate it. But at age 61, I figure what the heck. I'm here to help people. Makes me feel good. If I make enough to eat as much as I want," she said with a pat, pat, pat on her stomach, "then I'm OK."

Her proudest moment, she said, was the case of a Minneapolis woman who was on welfare until she married a man from Nigeria. He was working and studying at the University of Minnesota Hospital. He supported her and her two children from a previous marriage and helped her to get an education. They had two more children, the second of whom was born with a serious heart defect requiring several operations.

Because the man had received U.S. money to support his education, he had pledged to go home to Nigeria to pass on his knowledge. But he and his wife were fearful of taking the sick infant there because the nation lacked the medical treatment she needed. She would die there, the parents contended. Immigration officials didn't buy that argument. The man would have to leave, they decided.

Haugen went into action. Previously she had told immigration officials, "Look, I won't push you. I know your rules and why you're doing what you're doing. I won't push unless it's really, really important." This was the time to push, she decided.

She begged, she pleaded, she cajoled, she got letters of support, she got doctors' statements, she got proof that the baby couldn't get adequate care in Nigeria. Finally, immigration people said wearily, "You've worn us down. We're going to issue a waiver." He could stay. Victory!

Some months later, Haugen looked up from her desk to see the couple standing outside her office with a little handful of spring flowers for her. The teary couple thanked her and hugged her close.

It was such an emotional moment, said the stoic Haugen, that she actually got a lump in her throat.

Deb Davis,
Lillie Gibbs LeVesconte

A Tale of Two Mothers
May 14, 1989
❧

It seems Deb Davis has it all.

Deb is 35 years old, naturally pleasant, optimistic, nurturing and well organized. She has a devoted husband and two healthy, exuberant preschool children. She earns $42,000 a year in a responsible full-time job at an insurance company. Her husband, Phil, makes $56,000 a year. They helped design their new house in St. Paul; it's so perfect for them that they call it their "Leave It To Beaver" house. Deb's husband not only ungrudgingly does half the work with the children and the house, he actually sees when a kitchen counter or kid's nose needs wiping. Both sets of grandparents live in the Twin Cities and come to the rescue on 30 minutes' notice. The Davises have a cleaning service every two weeks, and on most Saturday nights they hire an adult baby sitter so they can go out on a date, just the two of them. They do volunteer work. They alternate attendance at aerobics class, and she weighs a steady 115.

Her friends call her "Super Woman." She said "Basket Case" would be more accurate many days.

So why the frustration? Why has Deb been so rattled some mornings that she has sobbed in her car in the company lot? Why did she start seeing a therapist and refuse to go away quietly when told she was undergoing the "normal" strains of a woman with small children? Why does she flop into bed exhausted, some evenings right after the kids are down at 8:15? Why has she dreaded long holiday weekends, with no breaks from the family? Why, until the last few months, did she not step out of the house with the two children for errands or fun unless another adult was along? Why does she feel she has to work at keeping not only the romance in her marriage but the sex too?

"Why can't I enjoy my life?" she asks herself. "Why am I so overwhelmed?"

Deb doesn't ask for pity or praise. She recognizes that her blessings are numerous; often she says out loud that she has everything a modern woman could want. Her heart goes out to those who haven't — single parents, families with sick kids, people who can't afford a baby sitter for relief, young parents without family or friends nearby.

If she, who's so lucky, sometimes has trouble coping, she can readily imagine the frustrations that others have in child-rearing.

And she knows her life will be easier in a few years. Just in the past few months — after Andy turned 4 and Michelle 1 — home life has smoothed out. But still sometimes she's frantic.

One evening, as she was trying to sort laundry and as both children were trying to crawl up her legs, Deb asked, "Have women always been this busy?"

❧

Yes. Historians reading the letters and diaries of generations of American women find a common thread — they worked hard, both in and out of the home, and they were worn out.

With the possible exception of Deb's mother's generation — many of whom were full-time homemakers and child-rearers and did not have to grow food or make clothes — women for centuries have been desperately juggling duties and hoping for enough strength to get through the day.

Consider Lillie Gibbs LeVesconte, who grew up in St. Paul less than five miles from where Deb Davis lives. (Her parents' home is now the Gibbs Farm Museum at Larpenteur and Cleveland Avs. in Falcon Heights.) Lillie and her husband, John, raised their family in several houses near Prior Lake. The family was middle-class, but struggling. She wrote detailed letters to her sister, hundreds of which from the period 1893 to 1914 are preserved at the Ramsey County Historical Society. Lillie and her husband, John, reared four children. Most of her letters quoted here are from around the turn of the century, when she had two youngsters.

Often, she noted, she was trying to write a letter and rock the cradle at the same time. "I'm so busy I've hardly breathing time," was one of her favorite lines.

On an October day in 1899, when Lillie was 33 and her two children were 5 years and 6 months, she lugged 59 bushels of potatoes into the cellar and put up part of the cabbage, carrots, onions, beans and beets she grew. Then she wrote:

"I've always done my letter writing in the evening, but since I weaned the lassie she has squalled & squalled about going to sleep and just tired herself and everybody else out every evening. By the time she was asleep I would be so sleepy I would have to retire (to bed). She does a little better now but still has a cry. I wish somebody would tell me how to help out of doors and get the house cleaned and the winter sewing done all at the same time."

One January day Lillie apologized for her tardiness in correspond-

ing: "You will think I am dead or keeping boarders. I haven't written because I was rushed with all sorts of business every day and evening. . . . I had an extra big washing Monday & left most of it on the line, and a nasty sleet came and I've been drying them around in the house ever since."

Her letters tended to conclude: "Well, I've written enough of my troubles" or "Written in haste, Love, Lill."

❦

What Deb Davis does for a living is training and development. That means she teaches such skills as how to be a good communicator and motivator and how to accomplish many tasks without letting important ones fall through the cracks. She carries those skills home with her. When she talks with her children, she leans forward in rapt attention. She dishes them heaps of praise. She insists on positive behavior: "I'm not going to do anything if you crab at me like that, Andy Davis. We talk nicely to each other at our house."

Because the children are in day care from before 8 a.m. to 5 p.m. each weekday, she tries to give them her full attention at home. Bedtime, for example, is a routine of storybooks, at least two choruses of "We're Gonna Win, Twins," hugs and kisses galore, lots of loving words and many refrains of "sweet dreams." Deb is absorbed with her children's welfare. Maybe too absorbed, she decided.

Last fall Deb found herself fantasizing about running away from home. Some payday, she told herself, she just might drive to the airport, buy a one-way ticket to someplace or another that's featured on a travel poster, change her name and get a schlock job in a new town.

In reality, of course, she came nowhere near deserting her family.

She said, "I knew that the whole idea of Supermom is nuts because most Supermoms out there are scrambling just to get through the day." Her friends with preschoolers reassured her that they too wonder, "Can I get through supper? Can I get past the kids' bedtime? Hey, I didn't get married to live like this."

Accustomed to feeling talented and competent, Deb found it hard to realize she was barely coping. She felt like a servant to the children. She agonized over everything. She got exactly 10 children's books on every library visit so she wouldn't have to figure out how many to return. She refused to even consider getting the kids a pet. She struggled to limit her cleaning to sucking up Cheerios under the highchair with a Dustbuster, pushing aside fond memories of the spotless house in which she grew up. She felt drained and dried up.

She did what she always has done when she needed answers; she got library books. The experts had lots of advice: Get out of the house more, hire housekeeping help, be more relaxed, hang in there until the youngest child is 3, develop a sense of humor, stop trying to be Supermom, recognize that marital satisfaction is low when the children are young.

That advice added to Deb's frustration because "I felt we were trying to do all the things the books said to make life less stressful."

Next step, see a shrink. The counselor proposed the same solutions. After a few sessions, the counselor concluded that the Davises were a thriving family and that Deb and Phil were doing an outstanding job rearing children.

End of counseling, goodbye.

Deb exploded. "Dammit, I'm too competent to qualify for counseling? Well I'll tell you something — I'm not feeling competent." She half joked, half cried to her girlfriends that she was fired from counseling.

She would survive, she knew. That wasn't enough. She wanted her life to be joyful, as it was before she was a mom. She had to know how to stop associating her beloved children with stress. She begged the counselor to take her back and teach her how to enjoy her time with the children.

A combination of ideas from the counselor, husband, friends and books began to help. She realized she had been putting her children's needs way ahead of hers and her husband's. She had responded every time Michelle whined, thereby training Michelle to be a whiner. She had carried Andy to bed every night, even when her back was out of whack and she had a nasty cold. She had to teach herself to tell him, "I love holding you, but right now I can't carry you."

She concluded the only reasonable thing: She had been making herself crazy. "I think a lot of moms do this, working too hard at being a good parent. I asked my counselor, 'Am I incredibly inadequate?'" No, the counselor answered; people just don't like to talk about how incredibly hard parenting is. Especially for those who make it top priority.

🦌

Lillie LeVesconte wrote 90 years ago, "Before Harold's and before Amy's birth, I would have spells of the blues and be just positive that my hours were numbered."

After the births, her nerves were shattered. Her husband managed a feed mill, and, as was usual then, the family had a big garden and some livestock. The family's cow wasn't producing milk and had to be sold. Lillie was inconsolable. "I long for milk — so does Amy. Harold has drank hot water all winter but Amy didn't take kindly to it but hasn't grown thin. I have. I am getting so thin & wrinkled it scares me to see myself in the glass. I don't work hard either but the disorder & quarrels & bawling every hour of the day wears on me more than a little bit."

🦌

Deb and Phil Davis were married in 1981. In two or three years they decided it was time for the children they wanted. She had trouble conceiving, and they applied to adopt. As they waited, she became pregnant and miscarried early. Andy came to them from Korea when he was 4 months old. The videotape of generations of new relatives greeting his arrival at the Twin Cities airport — a tape he now happily watches a dozen times a week if permitted — shows that he was one of the most welcomed children ever to join a family. An enthusiastic mother, Deb no longer pulled out her briefcase full of office work when she was home.

Andy was 2 years old when Deb became pregnant with Michelle. Deb thought she wanted full-time motherhood and quit her job as a training manager at United HealthCare three months into the pregnancy. She yearned for a good stretch of time with Andy before he had reason to be jealous.

Things backfired. She had a difficult, uncomfortable pregnancy. Premature labor sent her to bed for five weeks. After Michelle's birth, Deb was overwhelmed. She sent Andy to her parents for a week and gave up the notion of breast-feeding Michelle when she was 10 days old.

"I went bonkers. I walked around the house carrying Michelle and crying. I was exhausted from being up a few times every night, and I thought I'd never be happy again."

Not only was Deb Davis hit by post-partum depression, she was astounded at how much time and energy her first brand-new infant took. It didn't help that the Davises were squished into an apartment while their new house in St. Paul's Highland Park was being built. One room was living room, dining room, Michelle's nursery and office for Deb, who had been teaching a business course at the College of St. Thomas. Every time Deb or Phil talked to the builder and they added such niceties as brass doorknobs and marble tiles, the price went up, from about $130,000 to eventually $165,000.

She was nervous but bored — "How many hours can you spend building things with Legos? I watched the clock until Phil came home at night" — and felt cut off from the world — "I realized how many of my social needs had been met at work." She remembers desperately calling her cousin to watch the kids, just to give her a break to walk a few blocks to return a video. She cried all the way to the shop and all the way back.

Full-time motherhood, she decided, may be great for other women but not for her. Michelle was 2 days old when Deb debated going back to work. By the time the baby was 6 weeks old, Deb was job-hunting. When Michelle reached the 3-month mark, Deb traded her jeans for a business suit. She took a deep breath and walked into her new office at MSI Insurance in Arden Hills to begin work as a training specialist.

Never regretting the decision to work, Deb said she feels no guilt for putting her children into day care — "and no guilt is pretty good for someone raised Catholic," she added with a laugh. "I was irritable and angry at home. I felt like a slave. Not being with my children full time makes me a much better mother." To her, day care for her two children at two centers definitely was worth $1,100 a month.

❦

At the heart of Lillie's letters are her frustrations with housework,

The Last of the Tearoom Ladies ❦ 97

garden and family: "Sewing and mending is always piled high, and the weeds grow so fast."

Her house was, for the times, big and comfortable. But the times were different from now. The toilet, of course, was outside. The woodstoves couldn't keep up with the winter cold; she wrote that the frost on the dining room window was so thick that the room was dark and sometimes even the inside walls were frosty. She did have a foot-pedaled sewing machine and a wood-burning cookstove, but no vacuum cleaner, no car, most likely no electricity or telephone or running water. Occasionally she had a hired girl, but she crabbed at how lazy they were and how much they stole.

One day her wash included "68 diapers and a good share of them were more than dirty as Amy had the summer complaint (diarrhea) in the winter. . . . My washing generally took me all day." A full day of washing was followed by a full day of ironing and then a full day of cleaning.

Only rarely did she entertain other than her family or her husband's, but at one point she had her sewing society of 10 women and three children: "Of course I wanted to have every inch of the house clean and as big a dinner as the rest of them serve. . . . For dinner I had roast beef, mashed potatoes, boiled onions, creamed cabbage, pickles, canned apples, two kinds of cake and blackberry pies."

In 1901 she wrote, "Please don't expect many letters from me this fall. Don't think that I am working hard. I go to bed very early and have to rest while nursing the baby. But we have two (hired) men just now and had 3 last Friday & Saturday and it makes lots of cooking & trying to can apples & make pickles at the same time."

The worst times for the LeVescontes and the Davises alike were when there was illness:

Four-year-old Harold in 1899 "has 4 very decayed double teeth and the last two days can hardly eat — one of them aches so. We have had an awful time with him tonight. When it aches, he doubles up his fists and fights and kicks and shrieks like a maniac. John was in for shutting him up in the dark til he behaved. But I took him in my lap and got him quieted. We are trying to get something from Hastings that will kill the nerve."

Lillie wrote the next year that she had been very sick with a bowel obstruction. The doctor prescribed seven tablespoons of castor oil: "It seemed tuff to have to give him $8.00 for the little while he was here. But I might have died. I wouldn't have dared to take such a dose without medical advice. It was the same thing Lud DuBois died with. I was in great pain and didn't know what the matter was as I never had any stomach trouble before. I don't know what caused it as I had only eaten what the rest had. I'm well now. Of course, I didn't get much work done this week."

Despite the workload, she tried to take time to enjoy the children and to build happy memories for them:

"Harold is interested in the story in the Youth's Companion about

Lion Ranch — he turns the chairs down all around Amy and calls her his lion. He will tell me, 'Give me something to feed her, she's a-roaring.' But a few evenings ago, his lion surprised us by taking hold of the top of one of the turned down chairs and raising herself on her feet. Now she can stand by a chair quite well so I suppose she will soon be what mother calls a 'toddle toad.'"

When Harold was old enough to read to himself, Lillie wrote, "He has been very happy to-day over a little paper covered book, 'How to Trap Wild Animals.' It is so exciting to him, he tries his best to read it all. We are all quite well altho I have been through a harrowing experience. I had four teeth pulled by a traveling dentist. I guess he did as well as any, but the teeth were all gone but the roots, so he couldn't help but hurt. That was last Tuesday, and I've been living on spoon victuals ever since."

Delighted by her children's language and observations, she observed, "She (Amy) never creeps now. I wish you could see her taking stub steps with her feet very far apart & her arms out like wings to balance herself. . . . Amy said of the fog, 'Oh my — clouds fell down.'"

ℰ

Reading for fun went out the window when the number of Davis children went from one to two. Now Deb reads such books as "It's Your Baby and Child" and "Siblings Without Rivalry." And, of course, "Curious George" and "Green Eggs and Ham," read out loud, many, many times.

Her goal is to raise two well-adjusted, creative, happy, assertive human beings. She sees big differences from the way she and her brother were raised. Deb's mother, 54-year-old Joyce Meyer, agrees with Deb that control was the major objective a generation ago.

"I always said you had two choices — either you have control or the kids do," Joyce said over a roast beef dinner at Deb and Phil's one Sunday evening. Joyce enjoyed her kids, she said; she appreciated the opportunity to stay home full time with them, and she had no doubts that raising them strictly was the way to go, she said. It made sense that when her husband, Les, worked two jobs and wanted peace and quiet at suppertime, he got it. Joyce said they had no problems with her children, except Deb got a little smarty-mouthed when she was in her late teens. "But there was never any lack of respect, just different values from ours."

As she spoke, her grandson provided an impromptu lesson in how discipline has changed over the generations. Andy spilled his milk at the dinner table. Deb wiped up the floor as she comforted him, "It's OK, honey," and then gave him a big smooch. Joyce said that when she was little, her mother would have hollered, "If you weren't fooling around, you wouldn't have knocked that over." Deb said when she spilled milk as a child, she was told quietly that careful children don't do that.

ℰ

Clearly, Lillie believed in discipline: "Harold makes lots of work yet.

He still wets his clothes — from laziness — when out of doors. He has been whipped so much he is getting used to it. Lately I have whipped him awful hard. And he behaves better. He don't care a bit if he is tied up or shut up. . . . A few of the things I had to whip Harold for, he pulled a handful of Amy's hair out & scratched her arm till the blood run & kicked her in the mouth, made her lip bleed, etc."

❦

Patience is one of Deb Davis's strong suits. At her angriest with the children, she yanks an arm or puts her hands heavily on a kid's shoulders while giving a strong talking-to. She and Phil don't spank. They don't yell. Even when a furious Andy took a hard swat at his baby sister, Deb managed to grab him and pull him into the next room for a time-out without whomping him, as she was tempted to do.

One winter evening Deb got a last-minute invitation from a friend to go to the ballet. She was trying to get dressed up and out the door; Andy, feeling abandoned, was a cranky terror. He begged her not to go. Trying to calm him, she asked, "Do you know what ballet is?" He whirled on his toes to show he did. They had a three-minute discussion of dance and art and love. Andy reverted to his sweet disposition. Deb put on her coat, kissed Phil and the kids goodbye and walked out. Andy wailed. She didn't look back.

Rarely does Deb ignore a chance to teach as she goes. With the sing-song voice of a kindergarten teacher, she explains and reinforces. One evening when home life was great, she said, "My goodness, you children are mellow tonight. Andy, do you know what mellow is? No? It means kind of relaxed, quiet, peaceful. Like Mom is most of the time." That was a joke, and Andy got it.

Humor doesn't come easily to serious Deb, who said she works at lightening up. Phil is the one who worries about family finances and other big issues, but he's better at day-to-day enjoyment. (Deb, holding a raw potato: "Does this look kinda green to you?" Phil: "Maybe it's not ripe yet.") (Phil: "Did you wash your hands?" Andy: "Yep." Phil: "Which week?")

When the Davises learned that Andy needed glasses for astigmatism, Phil jovially told Andy, "Now you'll be like Mom and Dad. I suppose Michelle will want glasses too." Deb took another tack. She spent the day crying. She called her best friend long-distance and tried to break the news of the glasses gently. Her friend, Michele Hoch in North Carolina, said, shocked, "Deb, that dramatic build-up! I thought you were going to say he needs a heart transplant or something."

Phil and Deb try to spend an hour after supper every evening playing with the kids. Often the play is in earnest. Andy loves practicing with his Sesame Street flash cards. He may see "school" and guess "spider," but he gets enough encouragement that even when he's wrong he wants to continue. Michelle, meanwhile, is put through a routine of "Where are

Michelle's toes?" and "Where is Daddy's nose?" Deb said they don't push the children, that they just enjoy learning. Phil jokes that they have Andy working hard to prepare for his law-school boards.

❧

In the months when relatives stayed with her family or she was work-ing outside the home, Lillie's problems were compounded. Her husband was a rural mail carrier for some years, and she sometimes took his route so he could tend to other business. Lillie complained to her sister that she had no time for afternoon coffee or card-playing or shopping. Her letters were litanies of her labors.

"I have today cleaned the sewing room and that was a dirty task as the carpet had been down 1½ years. The tacks were so rusted and I was digging at them with an old knife, blistering my hand badly."

"I have been making some new underwear for myself for summer."

"There's lots of mud tracked in. It seems as if I have the broom in my hands from morning til night, as I can't get used to working over dirt."

Her husband helped out a good deal. Sometimes she noted that he wasn't as fussy as she. When she got back from a trip to St. Paul with the children to see her family, she wrote: "John thought he had cleaned up some but the rooms were frightfully dusty and I did have to pitch in to get the house in any kind of shape yesterday. I got the trunk emptied and everything in its place." And, "When I came in John had his sleeves rolled up washing dishes with might. They had all been piled up since Sunday afternoon. But we had supper all ready at 8 o'clock."

She longed for new technology. "Some women around here are greatly taken with a new washing machine called the NonSuch. It's a small affair — all but the price, that is $5.00. They say it takes the dirt out of anything and is no work at all. It's sold somewhere in Minneapo-lis and can be had on trial." (Her sister took the hint and bought it for her.)

"I've just been cleaning the cellar out. We have had such a host of rats in there. They ate up all the carrots and nearly all the squash."

"The few American neighbors around here have been a little more sociable this winter and we have been invited to oyster suppers, etc. But can't go as I do not want to take the children or leave them. There's one tonight. That makes five that I have missed."

❧

Deb Davis doesn't believe in sacrifice as a builder of moral character.

She tapes "All My Children," the soap opera she's faithfully watched since high school, and tries to catch up on episodes after the kids are in bed and on weekends.

She feels no need to kill herself preparing meals. She can't imagine life without her microwave. Even corn on the cob at her house is the kind made in the microwave. "What's for supper?" are the harshest words ever mouthed, she said. "Don't tell Grandma that the sauce is made from Prego," she warned Andy at the supper table.

Phil is just as likely as she to make the tuna casserole — and to load the Maytag, deliver the kids to day care, pick up toys and change diapers. He has a high-pressure job — he's the director of the state's Law Enforcement Training Center — but can't imagine not pulling his fair share of family responsibilities: "I don't think a two-career couple with kids can function well if one isn't fully engaged in the responsibilities."

His wife, he said, continues to amaze him after eight years of marriage. She has to be an active parent, an active employee, an active spouse. He said, "I can't think of many people with more energy. She's one of the most intense people I know. That's not always good; it has its benefits and pitfalls. The benefits accrue to the kids. She goes and goes and eventually she realizes she's exhausted. That's just the way she is."

Deb and Phil say that they work at keeping their love for each other alive. She said, "I don't want our kids to go off to college and realize I barely know this man." They had a good laugh about Andy announcing gravely one morning at 5:45, "Mommy, it's not nice to lock the bedroom door." The Davises think their love will survive; the only time they fleetingly considered divorce was one nasty day when they wallpapered Michelle's room.

One of Deb's worst fears is getting pregnant again. She said, "Parenting is the hardest thing I'll ever do, and the most rewarding. It's not just the busyness. What I didn't anticipate was how hard it is emotionally, and the stress of never being off duty." Two kids may be manageable someday soon; three would be disaster, she said.

Even though she had a tubal ligation immediately after Michelle was born, she feared her tubes would reconnect, an extremely rare but possible occurrence. She fretted about an unwanted pregnancy and sent Phil to his doctor to ask about a vasectomy. His doctor couldn't believe Phil needed the surgery and sent him home to ask Deb to talk to her doctor. Deb's doctor reassured her, "Deb, I know how strongly you feel about this. I fried your tubes. Don't worry."

❧

Lillie would have sympathized with Deb. After giving birth to her third child, Lillie wrote, "Dear Sister — Your welcome letter found us all well. I try to look after the children but three is 'too many.' Harold & Amy sneak out without their wraps and the baby snuggles around in her nightgown too long so they keep catching colds."

Keeping romance alive was not Lillie's priority: "Tomorrow will be our seventh anniversary. I expect to go to the sewing society in the afternoon."

❧

Despite the exhaustion, despite the tribulations, Deb wouldn't go back to her childless days. "Being a mother is much more intense than I thought it would be. Some days I feel so consumed there's nothing left of me. I didn't anticipate how intense the love and protectiveness is. There's no feeling like loving a child, your child, taking pleasure at all the dumb little things, the hugs, the games, the words. Nothing has ever been so emotional for me as being a mother. It's powerful. It's different from the love of a spouse. I'm responsible for that life. It's amazing."

❦

One of Lillie's four children survives today. Lester LeVesconte, 85, of Lombard, Ill., said he remembers her as a good, loving mother doing the best she could under less than ideal conditions. Her children did well: Harold became a patent attorney; Amy, a chemistry professor; Lillian, a missionary to Formosa, and Lester, an electrical engineer.

But in her letters as a young mother, she left no message that motherhood was worth all the trouble. When a friend of the family landed herself a rich husband, Lillie brooded about women luckier than she. "They get the good man & fine home and plenty of children to pet and will never have to be up nights with colicky babies or have any of the trials that the young wives live with." That was in 1903, after 10 years of marriage. Her nerves, she wrote, were "all used up."

She summarized her life with this closing of a letter: "It is late & we stand up early, so good night, with love from Lill."

❦

Two days ago Deb Davis lost her job. Her position and at least five others were eliminated by MSI Insurance as part of a general cost reduction. As one who's prone to fretting, Deb took the news calmly. She said she's never had a problem finding a good job. Meanwhile, she's looking forward to spending time with her kids. Not too much time, though. She wants to start a new job in a month.

Deb found employment at Lutheran Brotherhood as a trainer. She reports that she and Phil and the children are doing well, partly because the household no longer has a baby. Andy is 5 and Michelle is 2.

Browns Valley Man

Those Old, Old Bones

January 15, 1989

❦

Not many families hope to find a skeleton in the closet, but this one did.

The Jensens, you have to understand, were pack rats. They jammed their big old house in Browns Valley, Minn., with arrowheads, antique dishes, Indian headdresses, stamp collections, stacks of yellowed newspapers and old radio parts.

So when William H. Jensen, amateur archaeologist and historian, hid a box of scientifically important old bones, he lost track of it. The last time he saw his famous prehistoric skeleton, called the Browns Valley Man, was in 1950, when Jensen and his wife left home for a few days to enroll their younger daughter in college. Jensen feared that someone would steal his prized possession, so he hid it.

He hid it so well that it wasn't found for 37 years.

The bones lost for so long in the Jensens' home are important because they may make up the oldest, most complete human skeleton ever found in North America. If the Browns Valley Man is 9,000 to 11,000 years old, as several Minnesota archaeologists believe is possible, the skeleton will become a national treasure and play a key role in understanding the first migration of humans into the Western Hemisphere. The bones are at the center of a controversy involving the scientific interest in studying them and the religious obligation of the Indian community to rebury them.

Jensen rummaged through attic and basement and storage buildings for years before he died in 1960. His wife continued the search until her death in 1984. Sure that the skeleton was somewhere in the house, the Jensens' daughters and sons-in-law didn't toss out a single thing without checking twice that it didn't hold the precious bones.

At one point a few years ago, they thought they had them. In the back of a china cabinet stored on the porch, they found a human skull. Unfortunately, it wasn't the right human skull. It was only a measly 100 or 200 years old.

They finally came across Browns Valley Man in 1987. Roger Weeks —
the husband of the Jensens' elder daughter, Eloise — was cleaning out
what the family calls the "vegetable room," which other people might call
a fruit cellar. There, in a pile of boxes on a table, was the right box of
bones.

Weeks hauled it upstairs and announced, "I think I found something
good." Gingerly, his wife and her sister, Janet Jensen Presley, went
through the tissue-wrapped packages. Although they half expected the
bones to have disintegrated into powder, the skeleton was in as good
shape as it had been when unearthed in the 1930s. Spring floods that
soaked the basement hadn't reached the vegetable room, and the temperature had stayed between 50 and 65 degrees — just right for old bones.

That afternoon, the family sat on the front porch of the Browns Valley
house and talked over what should be done with the skeleton. William
Jensen may have liked keeping the bones at home — he welcomed visits
and letters from scientists from around the world — but his daughters
wanted the skeleton in safe keeping. They got on the telephone and started talking with historians and scientists. After months of conferences, they
decided their best option was to give the bones and lend the artifacts to
the Science Museum of Minnesota. Whether the museum ultimately re-
ceives the bones is open to question.

"The important thing," Eloise Weeks said, "is that people who are
studying these things should have access to them."

❧

William Jensen happened upon the skeleton in 1933. He was the
owner of a grain elevator at Browns Valley, on the South Dakota border.
On the afternoon of Oct. 9, he was having some gravel hauled to surface
the elevator driveway. A friend, Matthew Granoski, dropped by to chat and
noticed a small piece of bone in the new gravel. He picked it up and
handed it to Jensen. "Here, you geologist," he said. "What kind of bone is
this?"

Jensen said it looked like human bone, but he couldn't be sure. He
and Granoski walked up and down the driveway, looking for more bone.
They found several pieces, all small, and then happened upon a short
piece of femur, unmistakably human. Almost immediately afterward, a
worker raking the gravel in the driveway found a brown flint spearhead,
beautifully chipped by an ancient worker.

Ecstatic, Jensen drove to the village gravel pit and searched for the
source of the load of gravel. An employee had a wagonload of gravel and
said he hadn't seen any bones or arrowheads. All he was interested in, he
said, was getting this gravel hauled. Jensen started pawing through the
load and found a gray stone knife, stained with the same brown encrusta-
tion as the flint found in the driveway. From the gravel pit, Granoski
picked up another gray stone point. Nearby were fragments of a human
skull.

Glancing up the face of the gravel pit, Jensen located the spot where the bone and flints had been uncovered. About 4½ feet from the top of the pit was a U-shaped streak of brick-colored gravel and on top of the gravel were 8 or 10 inches of black soil. The black soil seemed undisturbed; it was not mixed with the gravel. Clearly, this was the site of a prehistoric burial pit.

The body apparently had been placed in a hole scooped out of clean gravel. The pit had been lined with red ochre, as are some other prehistoric gravesites.

Jensen and the others found more bones and artifacts. The next few days he photographed the site (the still photos and home movies he shot still exist) and wrote a detailed description of the find.

In January 1934 Jensen wrote to Albert Jenks, then chairman of the University of Minnesota's Department of Archaeology. Jenks was the professor who rather prophetically had written to the state Highway Department in 1931, asking workers to be on the watch for bones and artifacts uncovered during road construction. Less than two months later a grader working near Pelican Rapids turned up a skeleton that came to be known as Minnesota Man. Actually it's the skeleton of a teenage girl and is considered to be about 5,000 years old. While that is old, it isn't old enough to rank as one of the earliest humans in North America.

Jenks visited Browns Valley later in 1933 and confirmed Jensen's discovery. University scientists studied, reassembled and measured the finds.

But Jensen insisted they be returned to him. Family archives contain letters from respected scientists from all parts of the world, and some came to visit Jensen on his quiet, shaded street in little Browns Valley. Jensen also enjoyed visits from ordinary people who came to congratulate him and get a peek at the old bones. Sometimes he and his wife, Martha, talked over the idea of donating the skeleton and artifacts to a museum, but always the answer was no. "He just liked to keep them here at home," she said in the 1960s. He kept the bones in a cardboard box.

Yet through it all, he was haunted by the fear that someone would still steal them.

❧

The Jensens didn't discover for a while in the 1950s that Browns Valley Man was missing; William Jensen had gotten involved with his other hobbies. His mind was far-reaching, and his collections were diverse. Coins and radios and books took over when the bones were out of his sight.

The house had an "old smell" to it, the daughters say. Their mother found that annoying and would say, "Let's get these windows open." But she, too, loved Sunday afternoon expeditions to look for arrowheads and to visit with Sioux Indians.

For four years, the Jensen daughters — Eloise Weeks of Anoka and Janet Jensen Presley of Edina — have sorted through their late parents' possessions. Part of the reason it's taking so long is that they, too, like the old stuff.

Presley said, "We keep finding interesting things we'll look at later."

Now that the bones and other valuable collectibles have been removed from the Browns Valley house, the thrill of the hunt is over. But, the daughters said, going through the possessions of their packrat parents has been fascinating.

"They were interested in everything," Presley said. "My dad would be interested in what's happening to the bones now."

The bones are in the hands of scientists, who are trying to determine their age.

Mike Osterholm

Would-have-been Channel Swimmer
August 15, 1986
❧

Minnesota's Mike Osterholm battled severe abdominal cramps for an hour before dawn Thursday, and then had to be pulled unconscious from the English Channel.

He lasted only three hours in the water, the first two swimming strongly and the last doubled over in pain. Osterholm, state epidemiologist, had hoped to swim the channel in 14 or 15 hours and be the first Minnesotan among the 300 names in the channel record book.

Up to the last minutes he begged to stay in the water and to try to work through the cramps that ran from his rib cage to his groin. After he was hauled out he kept saying, "I just want to swim."

He may get a second chance. Favorable tides run through Sunday. They don't start again for another two weeks. If he recovers as quickly as he and his coach hope, he may try the channel this weekend. He plans to take a practice swim this morning to see how it feels. Osterholm has trained for the swim since Christmas, full time for three months, and figures he'll never have the chance again to train so intensively.

He had been scheduled to start swimming at Dover about dawn yesterday morning. Bad weather, however, was moving in, and it seemed that the swim would be canceled. But then Reg Brickell, a fisherman who has escorted swimmers across the channel for 19 years, suggested moving up the swim five hours. To catch the current correctly, Brickell wanted Osterholm to swim from France to England, rather than England to France. Three hours after the decision was made, Osterholm was on Brickell's boat, chugging to France.

When the boat was a mile off the French shore, Osterholm, his coach and a boatman rode a dinghy to shore. At 1:15 a.m. the boatman radioed, "He's on his way."

"Good," said his wife, Peggy Osterholm. "It's probably good he can go tonight. He was too keyed up to sleep."

The water was about 60 degrees, a temperature frigid to most people but one that Osterholm has been able to stand easily. The water was relatively calm. Some channel swimmers have gotten freaked by the things, living and dead, that bump against them in the dark. Not Osterholm. He's a night person and loves to swim at night.

This night he plodded on, next to the fishing boat, doing a regular 58 strokes a minute, thinking of victory. His coach, Kris MacDonald, was on a high, too. "He's really in the water," she said with a giggle. "We really did it."

After Osterholm was in the water for an hour, MacDonald lowered a rope with his dinner, a plastic bottle of warm chocolate instant breakfast. She said, "Your stroke looks good."

Peggy Osterholm went to the tiny galley behind the pilot and made peanut butter and jelly sandwiches for the people on board. Jokes began to fly: "Are we almost there yet?" The official swim observer, Sandi Gill, hired by the Channel Swimming Association to be sure all the rules were followed, began working a crossword puzzle while keeping one eye on the swimmer. Osterholm's father-in-law and a friend went below deck to play cribbage.

"Two hours down," MacDonald told Osterholm at 3:15 a.m. He had done 4 miles, just 28 to go. He chugged down one of his favorite swimming meals, a hunk of chocolate and warmed-up Pepsi-Cola with extra glucose.

"Your stroke looks good, Mike. Are you cold?" MacDonald asked.

"Yeh," he said. "Until the sun comes up."

At 3:45 a.m. the cramping began. He put himself in a fetal position and tried to work out the pain. "Go easy and you'll be O.K.," said his coach. "Take your time, Mike. Nice and slow. O.K.?"

The pains got worse. He would swim a few strokes, then stop and curl up. MacDonald told him he probably had a cramp in his diaphragm. "Not to worry," she said. She told him over and over — slow down, relax, we've got all night, we can make up the time later, you're tough, you can do it.

His voice got weaker. "Oh, Kris, I don't know what this is."

"Are you O.K?" she asked.

"I don't know."

"Is it the stomach or diaphragm?" He didn't know. "I gotta swim." He took off with a few crawl strokes, then collapsed again.

MacDonald asked the two boatmen, "If we need to, we can get him out pretty easy, right?" Right.

She told Osterholm, "We can ride this out." But no position she suggested — resting on his back, doing a few backstrokes, sidestroking — eased the cramps even a bit. He couldn't straighten out. "I just can't breathe," he said.

"You've got to swim slow and see if you can work it out. I know you can. That's it. Relax. Go nice and slow. It'll be getting light soon. I think you just got anxious and cramped up."

Osterholm's father-in-law, Dick Johnston, couldn't watch any more and searched for dawn on the other side of the boat.

"I'm O.K., I'm gonna get it," said the voice from the water. After two strokes, though, he said, "I just can't."

The official observer said softly, "It's a shame. When this happens, it's usually when they're just a mile from finishing." That close to the end, a swimmer may be able to wait out the cramps, or try to paddle in.

"I've never had this before," Osterholm said.

He saw the boatmen pull a dinghy close to him. "Don't take me out," he begged. They took the dinghy out of his eyesight. MacDonald told him, "You're at three hours. The sun will be coming up soon and you'll get warm."

But he hadn't swum for an hour, and the cold was beginning to get him. He drifted close to the boat. To touch it is to be disqualified. "Away from the boat!" the observer yelled to him. A boatman said, "Ah, he won't hurt the boat."

After another 10 minutes the dinghy with boatman Ray Brickell aboard was moved closer to the swimmer. "I just want Ray here near you," MacDonald said. Osterholm started choking in the water. MacDonald said, "I don't know how much longer I can let you in there like that." Peggy Osterholm, pale, went below deck.

The official observer said, "It's been an hour since he's had these pains."

Osterholm said slowly and quietly, "I'm beginning to feel like I'm going to faint." He slumped. His face was in the water.

"Get him out right now. Right now!" the coach commanded. The crewmen grabbed him and put an old sheet under his arms and dragged him into the dinghy at 4:32 a.m. "I'm O.K.," he said. Later he didn't remember being pulled from the water.

They laid him on the deck and covered him with blankets, coats, rags, anything they could find. He lay with his head on his coach's lap, shivering violently. "You stuck with that an awfully long time, Mike," she said. "You did the best you could." For the next hour he lay writhing on the deck, his body still cramping. At one point MacDonald asked him, "Do you know where you are?" He opened his eyes to the awful realization and groaned.

The observer told his relatives that the pains he fought for an hour would have defeated most channel swimmers in 10 minutes. She told Osterholm, "You'll have to come back next year."

Then came the apologies and the shame. He buried his head in the blankets. People around him tried to figure out what had gone wrong. Nerves, maybe. He wasn't sick to his stomach, so it probably wasn't the huge spaghetti dinner the night before or the food during the swim. ("Pepsi-Cola would turn your guts awfully, wouldn't it?" Reg Brickell said.)

By 6 a.m., when the sun was a big orange blob, Osterholm could stand on the boat deck with help. He looked rough. "This channel has claimed so many victims," the official observer told him. "You mustn't feel bad."

Osterholm tried the channel again four days later. He swam nine hours from England and could see the French cliffs when abdominal cramps stopped him. Two years later, in 1988, a wrist injury forced him to quit after three hours in the water.

Scout Troop 100

Their Dear and Dark Stories
July 27, 1989
🦌

Xeng Lor's story came spilling out one day. He was sitting around with Dave Moore, the scoutmaster of a Hmong Boy Scout troop in Minneapolis, and began to describe what had happened to him in Southeast Asia.

When he was 4, Xeng and his people were evacuated by helicopter from the top of a burned-over mountain. As a teenager he swam and floated across the Mekong River, his youngest brother clinging to his back. A few years later he decided to try to get to America, even though his father would stay behind, unable to try adjusting to strange ways in a new land.

Moore was transfixed. He had heard the adventures of his other Hmong scouts over the years, but he found Xeng's particularly gripping.

"You have to write down your story so Americans can read it," Moore told the young man.

"Yes," Xeng said. "When my English is better, then I'll write my story."

Moore was firm. "No. Now."

Xeng kept talking. Moore started taking notes.

🦌

As far back as Xeng's memory goes, there were airplanes overhead and distant bombing. He was 4 years old in 1965, when his family and about 100 other villagers left home one night because they thought the Vietnamese were too close. Again and again they had to move on.

Sometimes they were reduced to eating the leaves and roots of wild plants. Other times the Americans dropped 100-pound bags of rice from airplanes. One bag nearly hit Xeng. When Xeng was older, his mother died, leaving him to care for his 4-month-old brother. There was no milk for the baby, so Xeng fed him rice-water soup. Xeng worked every day in the fields and cared for chickens, ducks, pigs and three water buffalo.

*Whenever he saw a banana tree that his mother had planted, he missed
her and he cried.*

❧

Dave Moore had been a scout leader for 15 years when he started
meeting the Hmong. He taught social studies at Minneapolis' Edison
High School, which in 1980 became the hub of the English as a Second
Language program for hundreds of Hmong students. He didn't teach the
Hmong in his mainstream classes, but scout and school officials, seeing
an opportunity to help the boys adjust to America through scouting, asked
him to reserve a classroom and hold an information session.

Moore had a better idea: He would reserve the school gym and hold
as close as he could to a real scout meeting for the Hmong boys and girls,
right down to the flag salute and a sweaty game of Prisoner's Base. It was
impossible for Moore to explain the rules of the complicated tag game so
that the boys would understand, but he started the game anyway. They
didn't get it. Everybody stood around, stymied. Then, bingo, a few of the
boys, including Xe Vang, caught on. They taught the others. Soon everyone was playing. Later some of the boys said it had been the first time they
had relaxed in America.

❧

*Xe Vang was born in about 1963; he does not remember a time when
there was no war in Laos. He and other boys were caught trying to escape
to Thailand and sent to a re-education camp for 500 "juvenile delinquents." A bamboo fence surrounded the camp; anyone who got within
15 yards of the fence was shot. Conversations between two people were
not permitted; when three people talked, they had to shout so that the
guards would know what they were saying.*

*After six months in the camp, a friend of Xe tried to escape. He was
caught. Xe was among the prisoners ordered by guards to kill the escapee.
The usual method was that guards would pummel a prisoner with rifle
butts or sticks and then make the prisoners finish him off by kicking him.
Xe's friend knelt before the fellow prisoners and implored them to be
merciful.*

"It is too hard to die," he said. "Don't kick me. Just cut my throat."

*But the prisoners began to kick him. Xe and an old Laotian man
hung back at the edge of the crowd. It took the condemned boy two or
three hours to die. Xe held his head down so no one would see his tears.*

❧

Moore thought he had done his bit for the Hmong and scouting. He
was busy with his teaching and with Troop 33, his mostly white scout
troop based at Westminster Presbyterian Church. But every once in a
while a Hmong boy would stop him in the halls of Edison High and ask in
fledgling English,"Are we going to have scout?" So he held another meet-

ing or two in the spring of 1981. Then an overnight camping trip seemed a good way to draw boys into scouting.

After Moore gave a little talk on good nutrition and how to eat in the great out-of-doors, the boys nodded politely and sat down to plan their menus. The finished sheets showed the same items for two breakfasts, a lunch and a dinner — chicken, rice and noodles. Moore started to protest, but the Hmong bilingual teacher laughed and said, "It's OK. That's how we eat."

There was a food variation at the scout camp. "Can we fish?" Xe Vang asked. Yes, of course, Moore said, but he wouldn't catch much in the Rum River. Xe ran off. He came back in an hour or so, with two heavily laden strings of fish, enough for a meal for the whole troop. He had rigged up a reel from a rock and a pop can.

Campfires, Moore found, were ideal places for Hmong kids to tell about their lives.

❦

Days passed with Yee Chang and his family running and hiding, snatching a little rest when they could, surviving on roots and leaves, running all night when the country was too open to hide. They crossed pine-covered mountains and descended into jungle and crossed mountains again. They passed caves where there lay the skeletons of Hmong soldiers, dead at their guns. They ran through deserted Hmong villages. There were always stories and rumors about those who fell behind to be butchered by the communists. The people kept silent, speaking only in whispers. Babies were not permitted to cry, and if they did they were given opium to make them sleep. The opium killed some of them.

❦

The Hmong boys warmed quickly to scouting. Moore figures it was because they liked the discipline, the structure, the leadership. Plus, they could get together, speak Hmong, have some fun and learn about the United States. Moore found himself with dozens of eager Hmong scouts. They bounced around from meeting place to meeting place for a while until Moore persuaded leaders at Westminster Church to sponsor a second troop.

Troop 100 was formed of Southeast Asian boys — mostly Hmong, occasionally a Lao, Vietnamese or Cambodian. (It was open to any boy interested in Hmong culture, but white kids didn't join, partly because so many of the activities revolved around learning English.) The boys chose their troop insignia — the three elephants that are the symbol for Laos. They started winning scout skill events and Camporee competitions.

"They were winning everything in sight," Moore remembers.

The boys progressed remarkably, he said. Yee Chang, for example, became the troop's senior patrol leader, then advanced to Eagle Scout. As one of his projects, he taught a class in the Hmong language to Ameri-

The Last of the Tearoom Ladies ❦ 115

cans. By February of 1986, Yee stood before the Westminster congregation and briefly told his story. No one would have guessed, Moore said later, that five years before Yee could not understand English.

In the nine years of Troop 100's history, about 300 boys joined and 13 reached Eagle rank, the highest in Boy Scouting. Fewer than 1 percent of all Boy Scouts achieve Eagle rank.

The troop still exists, and Moore still is the scoutmaster. The kids have changed, though, he said. "Now they're more Americanized, more sophisticated in such things as popular culture. In that way, they're more American than I am."

❧

With morning light coming on fast, Vang Yang, his mother and sisters and about 30 others went to hide in the bushes back from the river. Vang's baby niece was hungry so his mother gathered wood and began to build a fire to cook rice. Just then a communist patrol came walking along the path. Without hesitating the soldiers began shooting. Vang's mother fell over dead. Vang and his sisters ran, choking and sobbing. They ran and ran. When at last they threw themselves down in the forest to catch their breath, one of his sisters was missing. The others didn't know what to do. Vang could not imagine going on living without his mother. He was just a young boy, maybe 7. He and his sisters couldn't survive in the forest. So they turned back and gave themselves up. Vang got a last look at his mother, still lying in her own blood.

❧

Whenever Moore and a scout would be alone — hiking, gathering firewood, killing time in a classroom after school, driving to a scout camp — Moore asked about the old country.

"That's how I got to know them," he said, "learning their stories. It's as if they needed to tell. Some needed to rehash the stories, over and over."

In 1986 Moore had to interview an immigrant, any immigrant, for a history course he was taking at the University of Minnesota. He had plenty to choose from and decided on Yee Chang. Yee's was a clear, action-packed narrative. Moore wrote it and showed it around to friends, who said, "This is good stuff. You should send it to a magazine."

Moore's life was so busy that he couldn't carve out the time to rewrite the story and submit it, so he asked his school district for a two-week leave. It was denied but he was told that if he would work on a book he might be eligible to take a sabbatical at half pay. Good deal, he said.

So he spent the 1987-88 school year taping the scouts' stories by night, writing and editing by day. He had regular contact with the boys and whenever they would casually tell him something worth adding, he'd rush home to his word processor.

The result is "Dark Sky, Dark Land: Stories of the Hmong Boy Scouts of Troop 100," a collection of stories Moore wrote about 17 of his scouts and including the full versions of the narratives included here. The book will be published this fall by Tessera Publishing Co., 9561 Woodridge Circle, Eden Prairie, and will sell in bookstores across the country for $14.95.

❧

Each family had to contribute at least one soldier for the defense of the settlement. Chao Lee was only 8, but he was the only male in the family so he became a soldier. He was assigned an M-16 rifle and five hand grenades and was sent on regular tours of guard duty at the edge of the village. One day he was caught in a barrage of shooting. A bazooka shell slammed into a tree above him. It tore off a branch that crashed down onto Chao's leg. He crawled downhill to a stream so he would have water. For two weeks he lived there, groping under rocks for crabs and crayfish. When he found one, he would eat it raw. Slowly, his leg healed and he could make his way back to his village. Years later, safe in Minneapolis, he said, "I don't think about the past. If you think about the past, it'll drive you crazy."

❧

Moore said that the Hmong boys who have become scouts are the cream of the crop. They are the ambitious, outgoing, resourceful kids — not necessarily the best academically; the boys with the best grades don't take time away from their studies for scouting.

"I'd call the scouts the most likely to succeed," Moore said. "You know, I've gotten to know these kids so well. They're like my own sons. It hurts me to know that the (U.S.-born) kids who sit next to them in class have no idea who they are, what they've gone through. Maybe this book will help a little."

Once while picking up Xe Vang for a driving lesson, Moore encountered some American teenage girls who asked, "Are you visiting Chinks?"

"No," he said, "I'm visiting friends."

❧

Yeng Vue would like to get back to Laos some day. Not to farm again. Not to help rebuild or to carry back the knowledge of the Western world. What he wants to do is identify the men who killed his family. He would hunt them down and kill them one by one, like animals.

❧

The original group of scouts, of course, has dispersed. Su Thao is a junior at Augsburg College, Xa Vang is the receptionist at a Vietnamese doctor's office in Minneapolis, Kou Vue is attending Winona State University.

Moore has grown increasingly interested in Southeast Asian history and culture. After a few university courses in the Hmong language (equipping him only to say several rudimentary phrases), he took a trip to Laos in 1987 and told himself, "I have to get back here with one of my scouts."

Last year he took Yee Chang. They spent time with Yee's extended family and friends.

"I had a lump in my throat for three days," Moore said.

The boys, now men, say that scouting helped them tremendously. Yee Chang, an Eagle Scout who will attend St. Olaf College next year, said it gave him a big jump on learning American culture.

Also, he said, "The Hmong troop is important to the Hmong community. It gives them a chance to see what their children have learned in America. It says to everyone that the Hmong can accomplish something in America, as Hmong."

And Su Thao, another Eagle Scout, said, "You feel great about yourself because you're part of a group that can overcome obstacles. You get confidence to go out and meet challenges."

🐦

Chue Vue's family had to flee their village. For days they thought about the blind old grandmother they had left behind to die. It had been a terrible thing to do, a violation of their most sacred values, to leave an old person to die alone. And yet they had done it as a matter of survival. Was she dead by now? Perhaps they might send someone back to check on her. With luck, the communists might not yet have found her. And so a search party consisting of Chue's uncle and some young men was sent out to find her. They found the cave and the grandmother, still alive. She had eaten all the food and had taken the opium, but it had not been enough to kill her. Two men began carrying her, but they were surprised by a communist patrol. In the fire fight that followed, one young man, who had just married, was killed. The others, including the old woman, got away. They never were able to recover the body of the young man.

Northwest Stewardesses

Recalling the 'Glory Days'
June 29, 1989

❧

The glory days for Northwest Airlines stewardesses were 50 years ago. At least, that's what the stewardesses of 50 years ago say.

Standards were high, and only smart, stylish and energetic applicants were chosen. Commercial flight was so novel and exciting that passengers and curiosity-seekers at airports asked for stewardesses' autographs. Before each flight, the stews were dispatched by limousine to Wold Chamberlain Field. They appeared on radio shows to plug their airline and the aviation industry. They were begged to speak to PTA groups and civic organizations; they did, without pay from the company. On flights, they had time to pamper passengers, to sit down and chat, to play a game of cribbage, to get to know repeat customers' names and preferences. They couldn't accept tips, but sometimes rich businessmen sent them gifts.

There were some drawbacks. Most notably, the DC-3s flew low and bumpily. (Cabins weren't pressurized, and planes rarely climbed above 10,000 feet.) Sometimes a stewardess would have a full plane of 21 passengers and all 21 would be airsick. Under each seat was an ice-cream bucket for just that reason.

But all the stewardesses were required to be registered nurses, and nauseated patients were nothing new to them. Besides, the classy uniforms and the $110 a month made up for a lot.

That's how 16 of Northwest Airlines' first stewardesses remember what they call some of the best years of their lives.

They gathered in Bloomington last week for a two-day reunion that was organized by Helen Jacobson Richardson, the third stewardess Northwest hired in 1939. She was promoted to stewardess trainer and then, like the others, had to quit when she married. Many married doctors or pilots; she chose a doctor in 1942 and hasn't worked outside the home since.

Richardson, and the other stewardesses of 50 years ago, feel sorry for today's flight attendants, who, the older women said, are basically high-flying waitresses.

"It was a very prestigious, glamorous job in our day," Richardson said. "Today, well, today I'm really embarrassed when I go to the airport and see how they look and act. They don't operate by the standards we did."

Bruce Retrum disputed that. He's the secretary-treasurer of Teamsters Local 2747, the union representing Northwest flight attendants, and is a former Northwest steward himself. He said the life still is exciting and talked of flight attendants being at home in Minneapolis one day, shopping in Seoul the next and lying on a Hawaii beach the day after that.

"But glamorous? I'm not fond of the word glamorous," he said. "It's hard work, damn hard work. When you've been on duty up to 18 hours on a flight from New York to Tokyo and served two hot meals and a snack to 400 passengers, it's hard to walk off the plane and imagine yourself as glamorous."

And as for standards, he said, one can't compare 1939 with 1989. U.S. airlines have tens of thousands of flights a day and 50,000 flight attendants. Northwest alone has about 60 round-trip flights a week to the Orient. Training and practice for the new kind of flying has to be different from the past, he said.

Just as decades ago, safety and service are the main concerns, Retrum added. Now, however, flight attendants can regard their work as a career, not just a short-term job.

Cathy LaPointe of Eden Prairie has been a Northwest flight attendant for 19 years and still loves the work. She flies primarily the international routes and says Northwest today is trying to get back to the classy service of the past — at least for now in first-class and business classes. Some of that eventually will reach the coach passengers, she predicted.

It's true, Carol Grewing said. She's Northwest's director of customer-service training and is responsible for flight-attendant training. She told the former stewardesses last week that the grace and class they brought to the profession are what the airlines are trying to restore. "You started with elegance in the '30s and we're going back to elegance in the '80s," she said, and then showed slides of the caviar and vodka served to first-class passengers on international flights. The effort to make passengers feel pampered and special is again apparent, she said.

"You carried hot thermoses of coffee for your passengers," she said. "Now we serve sushi on our Oriental flights. The idea is the same — service."

❦

The year Helen Richardson started working for Northwest — 1939 — was 36 years after Orville Wright made his first powered flight, 12 years after Northwest Airlines inaugurated its first passenger service and eight years after the first stewardess began work, for United Airlines, she said.

In the years since she retired, she's wondered what happened to the women she taught to walk tall, to serve passengers graciously, to be hostesses, to gently rebuff the advances of male passengers.

So more than two years ago Richardson started pulling together a reunion list. She had a list of 81 women who flew for Northwest from 1939 through 1941 and tracked them down through their nursing schools, their hometown newspapers and post offices and — because so many married doctors — physician directories. Many former stewardesses knew how to find one more. She learned that 23 had died. Eventually she found 40 living.

Richardson said she wrote to Northwest Airlines President Steve Rothmeier, asking for passes to fly in the women for a reunion. No response. She wrote again, asking Northwest to sponsor a reunion luncheon. The company declined. So she decided to proceed anyway, hoping that some of the group would want to spend their own money to get together.

They did. They came from as far away as Florida and Arizona. Most hadn't seen each other for more than 45 years. They all used the maiden names they had long ago put aside, and they referred to the others as "the girls." There were shrieks when they recognized each other, displays of old photographs when they did not. "I found out I'm not the only one who's changed," said Mary Withrow Davidson, of Kansas City, Mo.

Because two of the stewardesses recently died and another four became ill, those who attended called themselves the survivors. Most were in good health and very capable of having a good time. Not a small percentage still wore high heels, dressed sharply and looked as if they'd have no problem balancing a tray on a turbulent flight. But they hastened to point out that in their day, there were no trays; stewardesses served box lunches of a sandwich and fruit, and no alcohol.

Karmen Egge Seybold of Milwaukee said her flight career was a leisurely one at first. Sometimes there were only five passengers flying out of Minneapolis. She got to know lots about them and they about her.

By September of 1941, though, the planes began filling up with military personnel. "It was still fun, still adventurous, but the coming war brought a different tone," she said.

Richardson remembers some flights being so full that stewardesses couldn't hitch a free ride to the starting points of their flights. Sometimes they had to go by train, which terrified her. She couldn't stand their clanging.

Ruth Beinstadt Brukardt of Menominee, Mich., pointed out that each flight had only one stewardess: "I always tell everybody that there was one of us and two pilots. We didn't have to share." After a five-hour, many-stop flight to Billings, Mont., way back when, she and the rest of the crew were snowbound over Christmas. Each day for a whole week, the flight crew would report in uniform to the airport, only to be told planes couldn't get out. "So we'd go back and party."

Among the stewardesses' duties was handing out chewing gum to help relieve ear pain during takeoffs and landings. Richardson had a fancy silver case to pass gum to passengers. She recently sent a photo of it and a letter to the William Wrigley Jr. Co., in Chicago, and got a personal letter from William Wrigley and 31 pounds of Doublemint to share with the stewardesses.

The former stewardesses hate to think of themselves as old enough to be history, but they're willing to be called pioneers. Richardson is writing their stories to give to the Minnesota Historical Society. And she announced that the Smithsonian Institution is interested in their old uniforms. Amazingly enough, three of the 16 still had theirs and were willing to donate them.

Reunions are meant for trading stories, and that's what the stewardesses spent most of their time doing. They told about being sent to modeling school for instruction in makeup, posture, gait and other social graces. They remembered the rigor of their training. They laughed about the language and suggestions in a 1940s Northwest pamphlet advising passengers to ask stewardesses for help on such matters as:

■ "Weather to order. Accustomed to a cozy 72 degrees? Tell the stewardess — she'll fix it with a flick of her competent wrist. Or if you consider anything over 68 degrees stifling, she'll fix that, too. Too bright outside? Just ask for sunglasses."

■ "Light up! Sure, smoke if you like. But since fellow passengers may not like the heavier smoke of cigar or pipe tobacco, would you mind sticking to cigarettes? Ash try is on seat arm, or on wall just under the window."

■ "For the younger set. Hate to travel with baby? Simple solution: Go by air. The journey's over in one-fourth the time, your registered nurse-stewardess capably relieves you of much care. Crayons and color books help pass the time."

■ "With our compliments. The delicious meal served you aloft may be breakfast, lunch or dinner. In any case, it's sure to be appetizing — and free! A thing to shrewdly remember when comparing costs of ground and air travel."

■ "Ask us another. What town is that? Is that the Mississippi? How high are we? When do we get to Butte? How long is that wing? One of the duties of the stewardess is to know all the answers — or to find someone who does."

From 'stewardess' to 'flight attendant'

The title has changed since 1939, and so have many job requisites, though Northwest still emphasizes poise, tact, maturity, self-control, humor, good grooming and personal appearance. A comparison:

	1939	1989
Marital status	Single	No restrictions
Race/gender	White females	No restrictions
Age	21-25 to start; had to quit at 30	No upper limit; some are in their 60s
Work experience	Registered nurse	Posts involving public contact preferred
Height	5-2 to 5-5	5-2 minimum
Weight	120 pounds maximum	Proportionate to height
Salary	$65/month in training; $110/month for first 6 months; maximum of $150 a month (equal to $1,640 today)	About $1,250 to $3,750 a month ($15,000 to $45,000 per year)
Total number	30	7,000

Steve Keillor

A Writer in His Own Right

April 28, 1988

❧

L et's get the snotty comparisons out of the way.

Garrison Keillor's "Lake Wobegon Days" has sold 5 million copies or so. His brother, Steven J. Keillor, six years younger and six inches shorter, has written a biography of an obscure Minnesota politician/newspaper publisher that has sold 600, maybe 700, copies.

But, hey, does Steve Keillor mind that the subject of his book — a man who was governor for four whole months in 1936 — comes across as fodder for a Garrison Keillor monologue? Does it bug Steve that his big brother is rich and famous while Steve wrote his book on a $3,000 grant and is struggling toward a master's degree in history and is trying to find a teaching job so he can feed his wife and three children?

Steve Keillor presents a convincing argument that he does not mind. "His success is so astonishing that I never take him as a comparison," Steve said of Garrison. "I plow my own furrow."

Yet there is one thing that irritates him. When his book, "Hjalmar Petersen of Minnesota: The Politics of Provincial Independence," (Minnesota Historical Society Press, $14.95) was published last June, B. Dalton Bookseller failed to place a hefty order. Or any order.

"Zero," Steve reports. "I did get sort of perturbed, you know. It wasn't because I was comparing it with Garrison's 'Leaving Home,' which was coming out at the same time. I was comparing it with, say, all those books of lutefisk jokes that were in all the bookstores. I've got this book I worked for six years on, and I can't even get it into the bookstores, and what people want is lutefisk jokes."

Let it be known that Steve Keillor's book has gotten excellent reviews. "A comprehensive and captivating account, . . . eminently readable," proclaimed the Duluth News Tribune & Herald. Jean Brookins of the Minnesota Historical Society Press said Keillor is a publisher's dream: "He's a fine scholar, he writes with grace and clarity, and he is so young and so motivated that we can expect many more fine books from him."

Keillor turned 40 this week and didn't fret: "If I was a baseball player, I'd be having a crisis. Historians get better with age."

No midlife crisis for this man of confidence and quiet humor, who shares his older brother's talent for story-telling. Steve told about the day he turned in the final proofs of his book. Absolutely elated, he was walking across the Wabasha bridge in downtown St. Paul when he heard an altercation between two drivers.

"I turned my head to look, and I walked into a lamp post. I got a huge lump on my forehead. I didn't want to go to the emergency room of the hospital so I went over to Garrison's house to get some ice." Garrison gently ribbed Steve for being so excited about producing 260 pages on a four-month governor, plus another 70 pages of reference notes and bibliography. Garrison ruminated about turning the incident into a "Prairie Home Companion" monologue.

If he did, Steve never heard it. When he and his wife, Margaret, moved to the small town of Askov, north of the Twin Cities, in 1979, they tried pulling in Minnesota Public Radio, "but it didn't come in very well and then we sort of stopped trying."

You see, the Keillors aren't all bent out of shape about Garrison's success. It's not what his five siblings talk about when they get together, Steve said. But it does make for an anecdote now and then. He recalled an incident last summer, when Garrison was in Denmark and various Keillors were minding his stately St. Paul house. The Keillors were amused that people would stare as they jogged by or roll down their car windows.

"Once after our Sunday dinner," Steve said, "this black limousine stopped across the street. This woman got out, ran up to the porch and did something, I don't know what. By the time I got out there, she was running back to her limousine."

If the gawkers could have taken a look at the house-sitting Keillors, he said, they'd have seen "a very normal family.

"My dad was usually out with his T-shirt on and mowing the lawn. My mother, she always cleaned up the house before the cleaning woman came over. My kids are used to living in the country where there's no obstacle to them shouting as much as they want, and they were out all summer, running around the yard, yelling.

"My biggest challenge was trying to figure out the TV. I couldn't even figure out how to turn it on. It has pedals or something on the floor and a little box on top and a hand jobbie."

The point is, Keillor said, "Our lives haven't been changed all that much because of Garrison. We take it in stride."

In fact, when Steve Keillor speaks of "my brother," he tends to mean his identical twin, Stan, an attorney for the Minnesota Court of Appeals. Steve said, "We jokingly say that Garrison developed a love for the spotlight because he was taken out of it so abruptly when he was 6 and we were born."

Steve is kind of quiet and shy and serious, but he did his best to promote his book. Unlike Garrison, who moved to Denmark and then New York City to escape stares and questions, Steve forced himself to seek recognition on a 20-city book tour including such places as International Falls, Willmar, Fergus Falls and Rochester. He talked with any newspaper reporter or radio broadcaster who consented, and he's pleased that they were so gracious to him and said nice things about his book.

Some mentioned his famous brother, some didn't. Either way was fine with Steve. Most people, he said, seem to be more interested in the idea of a writer living in a small town than in who his brother is.

The subject of Steve Keillor's book, Danish-born Hjalmar Petersen (1890-1968), in addition to being a politician, was the newspaper editor and publisher in Askov, which had a population of about 200 when Petersen moved there in 1914. For more than five decades, his Askov American carried pithy editorials and articles that Keillor said tell a great deal about life in Minnesota.

Keillor moved to Askov because land was cheap and he wanted to raise sheep. He had read about Petersen in books about Farmer-Labor politics, but Keillor hadn't remembered that Askov had been Petersen's town.

"When I found out that his widow was still living and that no one had written a book on him, I started to get the idea that maybe I should do it. Also, I had a background in Minnesota income tax, and he had been the author of the first income-tax act in Minnesota."

Working part-time in Askov doing tax and accounting work, Keillor had plenty of time to research Petersen. "Like a lot of people in rural Minnesota, I was underemployed," he said. "I had plenty of time; it was money that was the problem." His wife helped underwrite his research by going back to work for a few years as a Social Security disability examiner.

The more Keillor poked around in the life of Petersen, the more intrigued he became. He didn't decide to do a book until 1981, when Petersen's widow, Medora, celebrated her 85th birthday. At a public celebration in the Askov school gym, a speaker announced in front of about 200 people that Keillor was going to write Petersen's biography. After that, Keillor felt committed. He raised $1,000 from local people to support his research.

Keillor read 50 years of Petersen's editorials that document his travels, opinions, friendships and mistakes, and he pored through 30 boxes of Petersen's political and personal papers, preserved at the Minnesota Historical Society.

He had a definite advantage in researching a subject who had lived in the same town. In his book's introduction, he wrote: "I was fortunate to be able to put down my research cards or cease my writing and go for a walk past my subject's newspaper office, into his living room to talk with Medora, or into his church to sit and ponder. The closeness to scenes of Petersen's life helped to bring a human empathy to my scholarly objectivity."

His own personality, Steve Keillor said, is much closer to Hjalmar Petersen's than to Garrison Keillor's. Like Petersen, he's very independent, has a temper and tends to brood on things too much, he said.

Keillor now is a graduate student in history at the University of Minnesota, Minneapolis campus, where he teaches a night class in Minnesota history. He's sending out his resume, hoping for a job teaching history at a community college or state university. He wants to stay in Minnesota, but he did consider a job in Mason City, Iowa. "It's only 40 miles south of the border so I figured I could commute."

Meanwhile, he's an Askov booster. Keillor is of English and Scottish ancestry, but he likes the fact that in Askov the street signs are in Danish. During interviews, he handed out "Velkommen to Askov" brochures, which he developed when he was Askov city clerk.

And he's an unpaid booster of a friend's bed-and-breakfast in the restored Askov home of Hjalmar Petersen. He offers to serve a fine breakfast of aebleskiver (Danish pancakes) to any guest who has read his book, saying, "There aren't that many readers, so I'm not extending myself that much."

Steve Keillor has a temporary teaching job at Normandale Community College in Bloomington and is working on his doctorate.

Narum's Foursome

40 Years of Togetherness
March 9, 1985
❧

Leave a party when it's still fun, they were taught.

So after 40 years, the owners of Narum's Shoe Store at 810 E. Lake St. are getting out while business is good and they still like their customers and the smell of leather.

Closing up. Selling out. Trying to get down to the last pair of Red Wing boots and Selby shoes. Taking their last trips to nursing homes to deliver corrective shoes. Explaining they no longer can take special orders for AAAA or EEE shoes. Hearing for the last time, "Can you hold the check until Monday?" Watching faithful customers leave teary-eyed.

"It's like they think there isn't another shoe store in all of Minneapolis," said Margaret Saterstrom. "It's the funniest thing."

Poignant, too, she'll admit.

She and her sister Laura Nelson are the daughters of the woman who started the business in 1912. An early women's libber, they call her; she liked to sell more than anything. The girls themselves were working in the store by the time they were 12, and in high school they had dates waiting outside the window when the store closed at 10 o'clock on Saturday nights.

Laura and Margaret married men they met at St. Olaf College about the time of World War II. Both Al Nelson and Stan Saterstrom were offered positions in the store. They thought they would try it for a year or two. Not they, not their wives and not their wives' parents were sure such family togetherness would be healthy in business or at home.

Al Nelson said last week, "This is the only place where wives taught their husbands the business and they're still married. There aren't — make that weren't — many men who could survive that. It won't work again in a hundred years.

"I want to tell you something. It's due to our wives. They have the greatest ability to get along. Married couples associated in business have a tendency to say, '*We* did this and *they* didn't.' You don't hear that here. Not much anyway."

When they married, the women vowed to rarely be in the store. "But we've been here all our lives," Laura said. They worked two or three days a week, even when their four children were young. Laura does accounts receivable, Margaret accounts payable. All four Nelsons and Saterstroms wait on customers, most of whom are the age described as the "mature trade."

They have even more in common than being family and partners. They live together three months a year at their Lake Minnetonka summer home. They all sing in the choir of Our Saviour's Lutheran Church at 24th and Chicago. They raised their kids together. They play golf together.

They've had their differences. But all four agreed on something for the first time in decades: Let's quit while we're ahead. Even though three deals from prospective buyers fell through in the last year, they decided to retire.

"Forty years, and I don't know where the time went. No life can go so fast. We've been blessed with good health and happiness," said Stan Saterstrom.

"We can't push the good Lord any further," added Al Nelson.

Besides, the lease is up the end of March and the gumball machine is empty.

✓

A good friend of theirs, a pastor, has often told them, "You don't run a business. This place is a front for a social-service agency."

The Saterstroms and Nelsons are famous in the Chicago-Cedar neighborhood for taking in strays. They give work to young people they pick up at church or at Twin Cities seminaries. They encourage relatives of homebound people to take along many pairs of shoes, try them on the feet, bring back the rejects and pay when they know how many pairs they will keep. (They've never lost a dime that way.) They extend credit. (They're not fools. They carefully eyeball a person first and maybe make a phone call.) They stand by their employees. (They kept Malcolm Borgendale on after a hip-replacement operation. And after a second. And a third. At last, after his fourth, he decided to hang up his shoe horn.)

One of their best employees has been Florence Haley. She was a customer decades ago who had four boys to keep in shoes. The Narum shoe men gave her all the credit she needed to make ends meet and told her if she ever wanted to work, she could manage the basement shop stocked with bargain shoes. She wasn't so sure she had the skills; she had only a fourth-grade education. They pushed her. She was a wild success and had a following of people who wouldn't let anyone else wait on them.

"She was just the way our mother was, exactly!" Margaret said. "A natural in sales."

Florence Haley is now 77 and has been with Narum's for 22 years. She is nearly blind because of deteriorating retinas. No longer able to read or write or even recognize people from more than a few feet, she uses a magnifying glass to make out the size printed inside a shoe. "But I'll be very thankful to keep what sight I have," she said. She's not too proud to ask, "Will somebody be my eyes?"

With Narum's going under, Haley is going to retire. She's moving to Ebenezer Towers and is ecstatic because a closet is big enough to hold her 52 pairs of shoes.

She'll praise her bosses as long as anyone will listen. Did you know, she asked, "They come every day and take me the 2½ blocks to work and then take me home at the end of the day?" And that sweet Margaret Saterstrom, she said, "She saw me through chemotherapy until she broke her arm."

No better people, Florence Haley proclaims.

"This store doesn't function like the average corporation," Al explained as he put tongue pads inside special-order shoes.

"We've always operated on a cooperative basis. When we were incorporating, my father-in-law's greatest problem was it would cause hard feelings if one (of the sons-in-law) was president and one was treasurer. So Stan said, 'Why don't you be president and I'll be secretary-treasurer?' My father-in-law said, 'Is that all there is to it? I thought there would be a big fight.' "

And the two sons-in-law still are speaking, Stan added.

Maybe because they don't have standard-size feet themselves (Margaret is a 10AAA, Al a 13AA, Stan a 14D and Laura a quite reasonable 8½AA), these shoe people, believe it or not, want to fit shoes. They like to sell shoes that fit. They like it when customers walk out in new shoes or boots, confident they'll fit. They've even bothered to sell mismatched pairs to people whose feet aren't the same size.

"You know," said Al, "63 percent of women have bigger left feet than right feet. I've never had a scientific explanation of that." Did you know that a half-size difference in shoes is only a sixth of an inch? "Three full sizes in an inch! Isn't that interesting?"

It was to customer Mike Adamovitch, 25, the proud owner of a new pair of 13D Red Wings, regularly $80, closed out at $39.88. "How many college kids at shoe stores at the Dales would know stuff like that?" Adamovitch questioned.

Not much astonishes Narum's owners but they do tell this story with relish: During the going-out-of-business sale an elderly woman bought three pairs of shoes, paused and announced, "I'd better get the blue pair, too." Later she said, "I hope I live long enough to wear all these. I've got another three pair at home that I've never worn."

❦

Laura's and Margaret's mother, Marie Thune, was born in 1881 on a farm in Toten, Norway. Always interested in a business career, she ran an embroidery shop as a young woman and was good at handwork, especially tapestries and Hardanger. Her aunt, Laura Dahl, had emigrated to America and persuaded Marie to join her in Minneapolis and work at her husband's shoe store on Cedar Av. Marie didn't know much English but that wasn't a handicap in the center of Minneapolis's Norwegian community. She put her meager savings into the business, which then became the Dahl and Thune Shoe Store. She was the first "shoe lady" of Minneapolis.

In 1914 the partners moved to Lake St. at Chicago Av. That was the suburbs then; the Chicago streetcar line ended a block short, at 29th. They shared space with a men's furnishings store run by a young man named Andrew Narum, also a native of Toten, Norway. Andrew and Marie were married in 1915. The store took his name.

"He let her go wait on people while he did book work, while he did stock work, while he built shelves," Margaret said. "We realize that now. He wouldn't approve of me saying that, but she was the brains behind the business. She was a businesswoman more than any other thing. She loved people and she loved selling and had an innate business sense. Yet she never deprived us at home. We were taken care of, sometimes by live-in help."

Both her parents but especially her father, Margaret said, were very sensitive to those less fortunate. "He kept digging into his pocket. They were good-hearted people. They never wore it on their sleeves. It was just there."

Family was so important to their father that he tried to get to Norway every seven years while his parents were alive, "whether or not he had the money," Margaret said. She was 10 when her dad took her along. Times were so bad the year Laura was 7 and went with her dad to Norway that their mother, at home running the business, had to have cash in hand when she went to St. Paul to buy shoes at the Foot Scholls factory.

Later on, in 1933, a customer came in and said to their father, "Mr. Narum, my grandson should go on to school, but I don't have the $35 a month I need to send him to the university. I have a piece of property and a cabin on Lake Minnetonka. I'd like to sell it to you for $35 a month."

Well, Narum really didn't have $35 a month that he didn't need to plunk back into business, but he did it. The family is glad, not only that he helped out but that it now has a lovely piece of lake frontage.

Business was terrific during World War II; Margaret and Laura remember lines going halfway around the block when people got their shoe ration stamps. When the store had hosiery for sale, customers went nuts. Al and Laura were already married, and Al went off to fight the war. Margaret and Stan got married in 1946.

"When the boys came back from service, Dad went to them and said, 'I'd like to see this store stay in the family. Business is growing and it would be a good livelihood for you. I'd like you to buy into it if you want, but family businesses don't often work. If you want in, though, it's yours.' "

They did and for some reason it worked. Inside speculation is that it helped that Stan Saterstrom is a business conservative and Al Nelson is more likely to take risks. They didn't encourage their children to join the business: "The four of us have gotten along so well and enjoyed it so much, why put stress on it?" Margaret said.

The business moved around a few times in the neighborhood, settling at 810 E. Lake St. in 1952. It grew with each move. The store was open two nights a week, then three, then five, then back to none when suburban people, a bulk of their customers, didn't want to come to the inner city after dark. Margaret said, "I hate people talking about this part of the city going downhill. I mean, nobody will tell me it's going to pot. It hasn't."

Narum's survived a fire in 1979 and a tornado in 1981. It survived the coming and going of trends. (When high-topped women's shoes went out of fashion in 1923, Andrew Narum was stuck with hundreds of pairs. He sent them out to be cut down to oxfords. "I doubt he got rid of them," Laura said.) Narum's survived when the trend in children's shoes went to tennis shoes, and it dropped the children's trade in 1979.

Narum's made it through good times and bad, but it won't survive the owners' retirement. The close-out sale will last another week. The Nelsons and Saterstroms will clear out the place and be out by the end of the month.

"Well," said Al, "it's been fun."

The Nelsons and the Saterstroms are doing well in retirement. "I tell you," Stan Saterstrom said, "if things were any better I couldn't stand it. Life has been good to us."

Tom Washington

Putting Women on the Defensive

April 6, 1985

ere is a man engaged in dangerous work.

Tom Washington teaches self-defense to women. Most of them think they have little strength. They don't believe they could ward off an attacker. Tom Washington knows differently. He teaches them a few moves that are relatively easy: A kick that can shatter a man's knee. A blinding poke to the eyes. A smash to the groin.

In class he plays the part of a mugger. He insults the women and chokes them and pummels them. He teaches them to react with anger, not fear.

The problem is sometimes these whipped-up women don't know their own power. They fight back. He has to remind them — about every other minute actually — not to follow through with the moves or he'll get hurt. "Please be careful. You could hurt a man horribly. That man is *me!*"

He wears a plastic groin guard, but one time a woman gave him an exceedingly good smash to his privates with her elbow. When he woke up several minutes later, there were his students looking down at him, petrified they had lost their instructor.

He wraps his forearm with a towel to soften the women's blows. It's harder to protect his bad shoulder. Years ago a woman stepped deftly aside when he grabbed her arm and, just as he had taught her, she stepped back and pulled away with all her might. His torn shoulder muscles remember the incident well. He has lost some of the function of the arm. Sometimes after a rigorous workout, he paces the room, rubbing his shoulder and muttering.

So tell us the truth, we said to him: Are you afraid of these women?

"Yeh, I'm afraid! I'm afraid in every class," he said in a voice that showed he considered the question ridiculous.

Here's a big man — 6-feet-1 and 180 pounds — afraid of tiny Linda Senty, 27 years old, 5-feet-1, 103 pounds. She says of his classes, "They've given me self-confidence, even though I know I'm small. I've never been attacked, but, like most women, I've had the nightmares."

And he's afraid of older women such as Juna Oberpillar, 67, who said, "I think I'd feel more comfortable walking places now. You feel braver."

He's leery even of little Shanise Lewis, 10, whose mother signed her up for self-defense "because I don't ever want this child to go through what I did." When Washington made a threatening move toward her, Shanise smooth-as-silk stepped aside and pretended to punch him where it hurts. He fell to the ground. She play-acted a kick to his knee and threw in a quick jab toward his eyes for no extra charge. Still acting the part of attacker, Washington yelled, "I'm sorry. Stop, stop!" and the girl giggled with delight.

Washington earned a doctorate from the University of Minnesota's Department of Spanish and Portuguese in 1982 but prefers to teach self-defense these days. His religion is Bahai and he wants to act on the tenet of his faith that men and women are equal. An intimidated woman in this society is not equal, he says.

He wants to get across his idea that it does not take years of study in karate or judo for a woman to know how to protect herself. She doesn't need precise moves. She doesn't have to hit in *exactly* the correct position. Washington says that after a series of his classes (usually eight, each 90 minutes), a woman is more likely to be able to put a look on her face and determination in her stance that together say, "Stay away from me. I could be tough." And if someone should step into her space, as they say in this self-defense business, the woman will wait for the right moment and then pounce.

Washington advocates a good measure of common sense. If a guy with a gun has you alone in the elevator, don't be stupid. Give him your purse. And stay away from bad places, especially at night. Don't ask for trouble. But if you get trouble, don't let anyone get close enough to intimidate you.

His teaching is peppered with his theories: "If you get angry, that's not what he's looking for. He's looking for a victim."

"Do this and he'll let go. I *guarantee!*"

"Do this and he'll say some very unnice things."

"As soon as the man relaxes, he's vulnerable."

"All women in normal physical condition have how many powerful weapons?"

"Five," shouts the class.

"Right. Your mouth; use it to bite and scream. Two powerful, multi-purpose arms, two powerful legs."

To demonstrate that leg power, he has each student snap a broomstick with a sideways kick of the foot. "Remember, it takes three to five times as much pressure to break this broomstick than it does to break a man's knee."

He teaches specifics:

"Keep your eyes up. Women tend to focus on the guy's feet and don't even see it coming."

"Don't kick the cheeks, kick the tailbone."

"No, no! Kick the *closest* knee."

"You can literally break his neck like this. Quadriplegics can live very fulfilling lives. Give him a chance to find out."

What about that? What if a woman decks a guy and it turns out all he really wanted was directions to a gas station?

That's the trouble with women, he said. Men know enough to assume a defensive position and attitude *before* something bad happens. Women spend their time wondering if danger is approaching. Even those trained in self-defense tend to picture a courtroom and charges of beating up an innocent man.

No way. He says you know instinctively if someone is threatening you. There are all sorts of clues. Don't over-intellectualize. If someone is coming too close, yell. Let him know you're not a wimp. "Don't focus on fear. Focus on anger."

He won't take men or boys in these classes. For one reason, males *know* the kinds of simple things he has to teach females: How to make a fist. Not to turn your back on someone threatening you. That if a jerk grabs you by the shirt you don't put your hands to the shirt. Poke the sucker in the eyes.

♥

Tom Washington won't say much on the record about his life. He's single now and has a daughter. He grew up in Rock Island, Ill., and had a brutal father, who Washington says beat up the boys and sexually assaulted the girls. Tom learned to box as a teenager and when he got good enough, his father left him alone, he says.

Washington won't give his age. Sometimes he says, "Just say I'm old enough to appreciate a woman and young enough to do something about it." Other times he says, "Age — that's a white, middle-class hangup."

He taught dance as a graduate student. He began to develop the self-defense course while teaching Spanish at Hamline University. It had become increasingly clear to him that sexual assault problems, women's fear and women's health problems were interrelated. (You should hear him fire off steam about the health afflictions of rape. Closed Fallopian tubes because of venereal disease, for example.)

He figures he has taught self-defense to about 2,000 women. He started teaching it full-time a year ago. He's planning spring sessions in West St. Paul, the College of St. Catherine in St. Paul, Forest Lake, Belle Plaine and other locations. Most courses run about $50, with price breaks for students, families and girls 14 and younger. He can be reached at P.O. Box 10119, Minneapolis, 55440.

Someday he would like to put his thoughts and his moves on videotape so he could reach a larger audience. He wants every woman to feel safe.

Washington tells of a woman who brought her 12-year-old daughter to classes because she didn't have a sitter. Sometime after they finished the course, two men attacked the girl. The kid fought back. She broke a leg of one of the men.

Washington spends no time sympathizing with the man.

"If someone attacks you" he tells the class in a gooey voice, uncharacteristic of him, "have a massive outpouring of love. First, for yourself. Second, for all the people he's attacked before. And third for all the people he'll attack after you unless you stop him now. Go for it!" The goo is gone from his voice.

In each class, he hands out a ton of Xerox copies. Stories of a Chicago woman who fought off a rapist, of a Philadelphia nun quoted as saying, "I was really upset about choking him, but you do what you have to do," of a 78-year-old Arizona woman who slugged a purse snatcher in the groin. Articles called "Rapists: How to Spot Them in Time" and "Get counseling before the wedding, psychologists say."

Washington insists the chances of an attacker having a gun are relatively small in the Twin Cities. Most often women here are abused by men they know, especially men they know intimately. Don't let yourself get caught up in an unhealthy relationship, he stresses.

As the classes progress, Washington gets tougher. First lesson he grabs a woman's arm and says, "Hey, just be nice and you won't get hurt." Eighth class: He gives a hefty choke, and blocks the woman with his body and says, "One word out of you and you're dead!" The voice is nasty, the threats include some words you don't hear in Sunday School. That's to get women used to the language. ("Don't think about the attacker, 'My God, he's so powerful.' No, he just swears a lot.")

Sometimes Washington leaves the class during discussions. "There may be some things women aren't comfortable talking about in front of a man." One of those topics is rape. While most of the students have not been assaulted, those who have can tell stories that make them all more determined than ever to learn to protect themselves.

A woman who was raped told her classmates, "I want to know this stuff so good I won't ever be victimized again. I'd rather be dead."

Someone else enrolled her daughter because the child had been assaulted. The girl was having fun in class one day but the mother wasn't. "Get mad," the mother yelled. "No laughing. Remember . . ." and she yelled the name of her child's attacker. The kid's eyes changed.

Washington not only puts himself on the battle line. He encourages the women to practice their moves on husbands, boyfriends and male friends. A woman told of a man who pooh-poohed the idea of women's self-defense. "I don't think it'll work," he told her. That got her mad. He made a threatening gesture. Poor guy landed on the floor facedown. After that he thought it would work.

Tom Washington still is teaching self-defense in the Twin Cities. He figures that by now he has taught more than 6,000 women.

Muriel Humphrey Brown

It's a Two-party Marriage
November 16, 1986

ह

"This is a whole new life for me. I don't live a life of politics any more. Max and I have so much fun. We have a wonderful companionship that Hubert and I didn't have, couldn't have. We were so busy, and it was so official almost all the time."

— Muriel Humphrey Brown

Fall used to be campaign time for Muriel Humphrey. It meant airplanes, white gloves, perky hats, more smiles than God put inside a person, sore feet and a cramped right hand. She would insist she would campaign for no more than three days, and she would get home exhausted after five.

Now the campaign hats are stowed away in a showcase in her Excelsior home. Fall means football. For seven years she has been, she said, "thoroughly happy" being married to Max Brown of Nebraska, who converted her to the Cornhuskers.

Near their television is a pillow she gave him that reads, "We interrupt this marriage to bring you football season." The Browns live primarily in what had been her house on Lake Minnetonka, but they drive nine hours to Lincoln for every Nebraska home game and stay in their condo there.

Max, she said, has only one failing. He's a Republican.

Luckily for her, he votes in Nebraska. They have a deal: Any time one supports a candidate, the other is told so he or she may match the contribution — for the other candidate, of course. During the 1984 presidential race, they watched separate televisions.

Before their marriage, they had long discussions about politics; they decided not to try to get each other to switch political parties. They talked, too, about Muriel's visibility and what it would be like for Max to have his wife recognized in the grocery store and hear her being told yet another anecdote about Hubert Humphrey as mayor, senator or vice president. Max said he could bear it. If he hadn't had his eye on just one woman, he said last week, "I probably could have looked around and found a Republican."

"Oh, Max," she protested.

The kidding aside, she said, "I think if you've had a good first marriage, you're likely to have a good second one, too. You learn to take things easier. You don't tend to jump at each other. Your tolerance is greater. When you're young, you have babies and new careers and so many stresses that are behind us now. I wouldn't trade either of my marriages. I've had two very, very lovely husbands. Max and I feel we're the luckiest people on earth."

❧

Muriel Brown is 75, or so she says. She really won't be 75 until Feb. 20. "I think 74 is kind of a blah age. You can brag about 75."

For several months this summer and fall, shingles, a painful disease of the skin and nerves that's caused by a virus, had her sidelined. (She's using lots of football metaphors these days.) "I had it on one side of my tongue, and it followed the nerve to my ear. Oh, so painful." Her energy is finally coming back to where it was, she said.

Both the Browns are retired. They spend five months of winter on Sanibel Island in Florida. Muriel gets hardly any political mail any more ("just bills") and no longer has the secretary she hired for a few years after Sen. Humphrey's death. She still serves on two boards — the IDS Mutual Fund Group and Midwest Federal Savings and Loan. Max used to manage radio station KRVN in Lexington, Neb.; now his son is in charge. Max is active with the University of Nebraska's agriculture school, especially in trying to upgrade the veterinary school.

Max Brown and the former Muriel Buck met in sixth grade in their hometown of Huron, S.D. "We didn't date," she said. "I would have flipped if he had asked me out." He went off to Brookings State College, and she stayed in Huron for college. They each married. He could keep track of her because she frequently was in the news.

In 1978, Muriel was in Huron to dedicate the airport to Hubert's memory. Max's sister was there and told her that Max's wife had died. Muriel sent him a sympathy note. Later when she was in the hospital, Max sent her a letter. She said, "He had his phone number on there, so I called him. We had so much fun talking that we decided we'd better have a date, in neutral country."

It would be the first time they would see each other in 50 years. He sent a photo to be sure she would recognize him, and they met for lunch at the Holiday Inn in Willmar, Minn. "I got there first," she said, "and combed my hair and put on a little more lipstick. I wasn't nervous or anything, oh, no." They talked for four-and-a-half hours. "We had a lot in common because we had grown up in the same town, almost the same neighborhood." That was in August. Their second date was a football game a few weeks later. They were married in February.

She won't compare her two husbands: "It isn't fair. I never want to hurt Max's feelings in any way. He's so caring, so understanding. My children and my grandchildren just adore him, too. All my friends, Hubert's friends, like him very much."

He's certainly his own man. She wanted him to dress up in a blue jacket and tie for photographs. He adamantly refused.

❦

The political arena is so far behind her that she's fuzzy on details. Vietnam, for example. It's hard for her to remember just when her husband as vice president sent a memo to President Johnson, expressing fears about Johnson's plans to escalate the war.

She said, "I guess Hubert's name will come up every time Vietnam is rehashed. It was a very difficult period, and I keep thinking I should read more about it and learn more of the background. I don't want to read it, though. Now I'm reading Herman Wouk's 'Winds of War' about World War II. He writes so beautifully. Gosh, I wish he'd write about Hubert."

She doesn't even guess what her late husband would think of President Reagan or Central American conflicts or yuppies. Things have changed too much, and "I never expressed Hubert's opinions very well." One thing she's sure of: "He wouldn't have backtracked in helping people."

Of course she doesn't mind, she said, that people say "Hubert" instead of "the former vice president" or "Sen. Humphrey." In fact, anybody who appeared at his Senate office and asked for him by his childhood nickname of Pinky was given immediate access. She said, "He never insisted on title. He loved being in whatever office brought him the title, but the title itself was insignificant. He loved being the vice president. He loved being senator. He loved being senator more than almost anything else in the world.

"And he would have been a wonderful president for our country. He cared so deeply for it. He was so prepared — educationally, his experience, internationally, the people he knew. He was ready to be a great president. Our country lost a great man."

Her voice quivered. Then she brightened and said, "He would have loved Tuesday night" (election night) when Democrats across the country did well. One success in particular brought her joy and made her nostalgic. Her son, Hubert H. Humphrey III (Skip), was reelected Minnesota's attorney general. That November night, for the first time ever, Max Brown went to an election party.

❦

A certificate testifying to the nine months Muriel Humphrey served in the U.S. Senate after Hubert's death hangs in the Browns' Excelsior home. "That's to remind Max that I used to be somebody," she said. But it's not in the living room; it's on a wall in the basement office.

A few photographs of the old days are in the balcony room where she does her needlepoint. "I took some of the pictures down; it was a little overpowering for Max," she said. One that remains is of her with Lady Bird Johnson and Mamie Eisenhower inside the White House. It's signed, "With love, Lady Bird."

The house is the one she bought and extensively remodeled after Hubert died: "I remember the Monday morning that came and there weren't any trucks that pulled in. No workmen. I felt kind of lost."

For a few years after his death, she couldn't look at the old Humphrey scrapbooks or books. "Now I can. I get quite moody though. I've got letters of Hubert's that are so wonderful. We wrote to each other two or three times a week when we were going together. I've been wanting to go through them, edit them, make copies and put them into small books for the kids. I've been putting if off though. It's hard to go back. I look at some of the things Hubert and I did, and it's hard to believe it all.

"All the campaigning. I don't see how we did it. Not just for Hubert, but for Democrats all over the country. We did it well. It was a tremendous experience, and I wouldn't trade it, but I wouldn't do it again. It was so difficult when the kids were little."

She talked of the years when Hubert Humphrey was just getting into politics. He taught at Macalester College and worked a few part-time jobs on the side. To knock $20 a month off their apartment rent, she scrubbed the hall floors and he put on storm windows. She made her own clothes and was afraid to wear them, for fear they looked homemade. He was gone so much that she looked forward to the political meetings he conducted in their living room; at least she'd have him at home for a few hours.

"We were always broke every time he ran for office, it seems to me. When Hubert ran for mayor in 1943 and lost, we had $7 left at the end of the campaign. We had two babies, and a dog too. We had to have a baby sitter, and we decided she needed it more than we did so we gave her the $7."

He was elected to the U.S. Senate in 1948. She remembered, "We were so naive to begin with about Washington, and we had to learn fast because he was popular his very first year there. I had a baby (Douglas, the youngest of their four children) at home. Everybody else seemed to be living like southern gentlemen, and it was a little difficult to take."

Sometimes it still surprises her that Hubert is gone: "He enjoyed life so much. I always thought he'd outlive me by 20 years. He was so energetic and he was so healthy, until this cancer thing."

❧

Life now is easier to take. Max and Muriel Brown have good friends, many of whom started as his friends. (Read: Republicans.) The Browns have 17 grandchildren: 12 hers, 5 his. When they're in Minnesota, they play Swedish poker with other couples at least once a week ("It doesn't take a lot of skill, thinking or money"). She cooks three meals a day. "Not gourmet; nice, ordinary sorts of things," like fried bluegills he caught in Lake Minnetonka. She's going to put together a little book for her granddaughters of her favorite recipes and her mother's. The Browns live well and try to keep in mind the saying on the pillow that Muriel's daughter, Nancy Solomonson, gave them: "Go first class. Your heirs will."

Said Muriel Humphrey Brown, "I don't have any profound answers any more. I'm so thoroughly happy in my own life."

Mrs. Brown reports that she and her Max are very happy together.

Margaret Yan

Ask Her About Apheresis
April 8, 1989
❧

Two of the day's first official duties for Margaret Yan, R.N., are to rent a video and to make a nose-scratching device, both for the benefit of the man on the couch.

He's John Kelly, a special kind of blood donor. For almost two hours, he has tubes running in and out of his arms, making it impossible to move much, even to turn pages of a book or to scratch. He's not in pain or even uncomfortable, just confined and potentially bored. So the friendly folks at the Memorial Blood Center of Minneapolis have rented "A Fish Called Wanda" and promise to scratch almost anywhere he itches.

Beyond that, they try to make him feel like, in their words, a quiet hero. His platelets will be used for a patient with leukemia or another life-threatening disease. Kelly started donating blood 20 years ago when his cousin had Hodgkin's disease. He's given blood in Minneapolis 36 times, including nine times with this more elaborate procedure. Still, Nurse Yan and the others go out of their way each time to let him know what a swell guy he is.

And does he feel heroic? "Nah," says Kelly. "I come in, watch a movie and eat a fistful of cookies."

Actually, he's the hard-driving type; his 8 a.m. visit to the blood bank was preceded by an aerobics class and a stop at the Minneapolis offices of Ryan Construction, where he manages real estate.

Kelly and about 800 other people are apheresis donors at the blood center. Apheresis is a method of collecting large numbers of platelets and white blood cells from a single donor. (Platelets are rapidly replaced.) In one visit, Kelly can give the number of platelets that it takes six to eight whole-blood donors to provide.

Blood is being taken from Kelly's right arm and collected in a $30,000 processor, which separates the components. Platelets are kept, and the red cells, plasma and extra fluids are returned to Kelly's left arm.

This time his platelets are not specified for a particular person as they sometimes are. The day before, for example, apheresis donors were need-ed for two kids at Children's Hospital — a 14-month-old boy with a kidney tumor and a 9-month-old girl with leukemia. Because platelets were avail-able for them, doctors could give them a more aggressive form of chemo-therapy than would otherwise be possible.

"When Margaret has stories like that, it's very difficult to say no," said Kelly, who has five kids of his own.

So he donates his platelets every two months; some people give every month. To Kelly, the worst side effect of the apheresis procedure is that he leaves the blood bank with wrinkled shirt sleeves. Some donors say their arms are a bit stiff for five minutes after the needles are removed. A few with small veins notice later in the day that their inner arms are bruised. Some donors — women, mostly — feel chilly and are wrapped in blankets.

Most of the people whom Yan begs to be apheresis donors are long-time blood donors. That's only because the procedure looks worse than it is; frequent donors trust the blood-bank workers. So the appeal is made to people who come to give a regular donation of whole blood. After they see the 43rd blood-bank employee wearing a button that says, "Ask me about apheresis," they do.

You can be an apheresis donor if you are between 17 and 66, weigh at least 110 pounds, are in good health, have never had hepatitis, have good veins and have a couple of hours to spare.

Oh yes, one other requirement. No members of the TBA need apply. That's the Tiny Bladder Association. People who need to find a bathroom frequently aren't encouraged to get all hooked up to the equipment, par-ticularly because a pint and a half more fluids are pumped into the donor than are taken out. Occasionally a whimpering donor is disconnected and bolts toward the bathroom.

Apheresis donors make the most of their time at the blood center, Yan says. An ad exec once brought an assistant along, stationed him on a stool next to his couch and held a business meeting. Another harried businessman comes in regularly for apheresis and a nap. Two women in their mid-20s who are best of friends come in together and yak. A man whose seasonal business is slow in winter, calls Yan during the cold months and volunteers; his only wish last time was that she have "Three Men and A Baby" on the VCR. Another donor had been too busy to see "The Drowning Pool" starring Paul Newman, so he rented it and brought it in with him.

Sometimes donors call Yan afterward. "You know that 8-year-old girl with aplastic anemia I donated for? How's she's doing?" Yan gives them a general update if she has one, but for reasons of confidentiality she can't say much. And she'd rather not tell the donor if she knows that the patient hasn't made it.

But she's good at buttering up the donors. "Somebody should be nice to them," she said. "To spend two hours here, a needle in each arm, doesn't sound like the most pleasant thing in the world. Sometimes people take time off work without pay to do this if the evening appointments are filled. These are really wonderful people."

Meanwhile, her current wonderful person is snorting with laughter at the movie scene where the third dog gets squished. Luckily for Kelly, the movie finishes just before the apheresis machine gives a friendly doorbell-like signal at 10:14 a.m. that it's done. Yan makes sure she rents movies that run about 1 hour, 45 minutes, the same as the apheresis procedure. Don't expect to see "Out of Africa" with Margaret Yan at your side.

Kelly pretends to be mortally wounded as Yan gently pulls the adhesive tape from his hairy arm. Then in the blood bank's canteen, the quiet hero has a cup of something (hot water, to be specific; he's given up coffee) and two cookies and heads off to work.

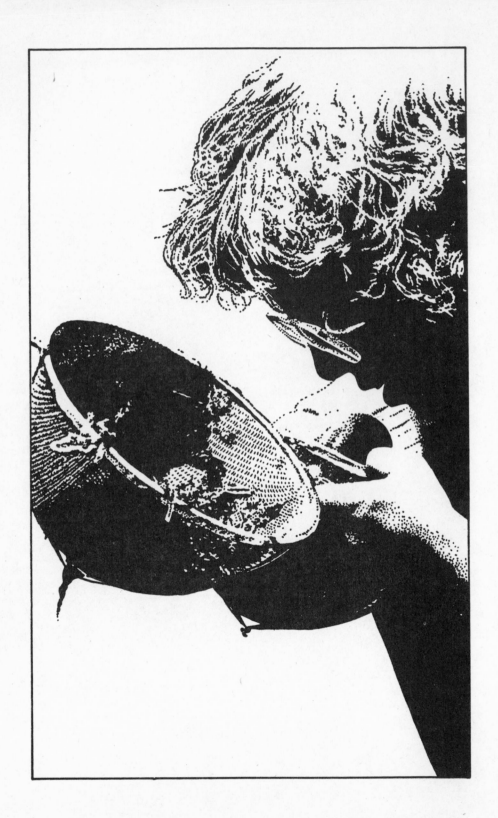

Tadpole Safari

Stalking Spring Peepers

June 29, 1985

❦

Jeepers, creepers,
Where'd you get those peepers?

In the muck, that's where. A dozen people who couldn't resist a "Bring your own waders" party went on an expedition to capture little tree frogs called spring peepers.

Volunteers scooped up hundreds of spring peepers one afternoon last week from swamp water in the Carlos Avery Wildlife Area, a state-owned park in Washington County. The peepers were in their tadpole stage, just before they were to develop legs and hop their way to trees. They were transferred in buckets to two Hennepin County parks where their kind has died out. Hennepin County Park biologists are hoping that the peepers can reestablish themselves at Lake Rebecca and Baker Park reserves.

And why wade around in goop to capture half-inch tadpoles and transport them across county lines?

For the peepers' peep.

"That's what it comes down to," said Donna Compton, a wildlife technician for the Hennepin County Park Reserve District. "The peepers sound nice."

She said it'll be easy to tell if the peepers thrive in their new homes. Just listen.

❦

It was a perfect day for a tadpole safari.

The temperature was in the 80s, a potentially uncomfortable heat for people wearing chest-high rubber waders, but clouds kindly kept away heatstroke. There wasn't a mosquito or fly in the marsh. Even the slime smelled good. Nature was noisy; the birds were whooping it up. The marsh is surrounded by woods, and the oak and aspen leaves rippled in a soft breeze. Sedges (grasslike plants growing in marshes) were available for study if one tired momentarily of tadpoles.

The only difficulty was trudging through water that was waist-high in some spots while trying not to let wader-clad feet get tangled in vegetation.

"I don't know how adept you are at woods and water walking," Compton had said to her crew when they were suiting up on land, "but I'd suggest you leave your wallets and watches behind." In other words, some of you clods may find yourselves with marsh water up the nose and down the britches.

Volunteers moved laboriously, like space-suited men on the moon. If a person stood in the same spot for a few minutes, feet sank in the muck. Then when the body would move ahead, the feet wouldn't. There were bets on who would take the first spill. It was Lynelle Hanson of Hastings.

Few things in life are as uncomfortable as waders full of water and gunk, especially when the wearer has to retreat the distance of a city block to find firm ground in order to remove the waders and drain them.

While the adult humans strained water to their hearts' content, 6-year-old Tiffany Janiak played on the edge of the marsh in her rubber boots. Every once in a while, she would shout to her mother or sister. "Oh dear, I wonder what I'm going to do with this humongous water beetle." "There must be a *school* of tadpoles here." She found a tiny peeper and pronounced it the runt of the litter.

❦

Finding volunteers to hunt tadpoles is a cinch, Compton said. Would-be naturalists sign up for this kind of thing.

Consider Judi Janiak of Fridley. She and her children have done other volunteer work for the county parks — bird banding and searching for nests of hawks and owls. She showed up for the peeper hunt with Tiffany and her other daughter, 14-year-old Audra.

Her son, David, is the family's herpetologist (someone who studies reptiles and amphibians), but he's a teenager now and has a part-time job and had to decline the invitation to the peeper party.

Janet and Carl Fultz of Hastings left their jobs and baby behind for an afternoon in marshdom. Carl, 34, cleans carpets for a living. "Hopefully, I'll be doing this for a living someday," he said, as he performed a masterful scoop with a brand new Ekco kitchen strainer (provided by the county) and came up with six tadpoles and a snail.

It's necessary to weed out the spiders, lizards, salamanders, vegetation, snakes, etc., before the harder task of separating peepers from other tadpoles. Now some of you out there in your easy chairs may think a tadpole is a tadpole. But Compton didn't want the big tadpoles that will become leopard frogs and wood frogs. Hennepin County has plenty. Let them go, she instructed.

She taught the volunteers the peculiarities of the peeper tadpole: an

X on the back and a stripe between the eyes. "Sounds like a punker at Uptown," a voice suggested, which led to a discussion of trying to export peepers to trendy Lake Harriet and have rich people participate in an "Adopt a Peeper" program.

Someone shouted to Compton, "Do peepers have pinkish eyes?"

She answered, "Yeh, but so does everything else. That's no guarantee of a peeper."

"Hey, Donna," someone else yelled, "what has pink legs?"

As she made her way over to investigate, the volunteers offered guesses. The best was, "A ballerina frog in pink tights." The silliness ended when Compton examined the beast and ruled, "I think it's a wood frog that's hemorrhaging."

Stunned silence.

The injury wasn't the finder's fault (the frog must have been sick or chomped upon), but the incident was a reminder of the fragility of life in the marsh. Compton had told volunteers to handle marsh life carefully; not to put insect repellent on their hands because the chemicals could damage the tadpoles; not to squeeze or poke the tiny tadpoles.

❦

More information from Donna Compton about spring peepers, known to biologists as Hyla crucifer: They live in a broad band across the eastern United States; Minnesota is the farthest west. Adults mate in the spring in the water. Eggs are laid over a two-week period in the spring. Unlike some toads and frogs that lay eggs in a big mass protected by a jelly-like substance, the peepers lay eggs singly.

Adults, about 2 inches long, live in trees. Their toes have little suction cups that keep them firmly attached to branches. They spend winters frozen solid under leaf litter — oak leaves and other vegetation. So peepers need not only marshes for egg laying and tadpole days, but also an upland deciduous forest for adult life. Spring peepers can't live in fish ponds. Fish eat peepers in any form they find them: eggs, tadpoles and adults.

It's Compton's guess that peepers were indigenous to many Hennepin County marshlands. But as forests were cleared for farmland, the peepers had to move or die.

The park system has a mandate for restoring the areas to their previous, pre-urban condition. For four years, volunteers have found peepers to transfer. All previous attempts, however, were with adult peepers. Compton hears peepers in the marshes now, so she knows the project worked at least somewhat well. But she can't do accurate counts; capture/recapture and leg banding don't work with frogs. One year she tried to trap peepers, but they hopped right back out of the pit traps.

Not that much else is known about spring peepers, Compton said. She said she pressed a herpetologist for more information, and he said, "You should go to the Bell Museum (at the University of Minnesota) and look at the jars, but most of the jars will be full of unidentified frogs." People have suggested a research project be done on the peepers, and she's all for that. But that's not her job.

For the volunteers' benefit, she carried some written biological information. It was ignored. The volunteers had more fun straining goop and sorting tadpoles than they did perusing "A Key to the Tadpoles of the Continental United States and Canada," from Herpetologica magazine, Vol. 26, No. 2.

Peepers' peeps can still be heard in their new homes.

Makela Scott

A Mother at 16
May 22, 1988
❦

Meet Makela Scott. She started taking birth-control pills at 13, lost her virginity at 14, got pregnant at 15, gave birth to a son at 16, moved herself and her baby into their own apartment in south Minneapolis at 16½ and got really bummed out about life at 17. Now she's 17½. Life, she says, can be tough. "This baby business ain't easy."

❦

It was Sept. 29, 1986, Makela's 16th birthday, and she was five months pregnant. She said she thought her baby was a boy. She wanted a boy. She hated the idea of a daughter. But if it was a girl, Makela said, she'd teach her not to do this stupid thing of having a baby so young.

"Sometimes when I really sit back and think about it, I wish I hadn't gotten pregnant. But I knew what I was doing when I laid down."

No one thought she'd be the type to get pregnant, said Makela (pronounced Ma-KEY-la). She was too quiet, too responsible. She had boys for friends but no one special. Until Bill. She liked his broad shoulders and his smile. He came here from Iowa to look for work. They met when Makela and her girlfriend were sitting on a bench in north Minneapolis, waiting for a bus. Bill and a male friend came by in Bill's big black car. She recognized him; she'd seen him cruising before. "Wanna ride?" he asked. Driving around Lake Calhoun, Makela told Bill she was 17, exaggerating by two years. He was 20.

Months later, her voice was dreamy when she spoke of their early dates. "I got the first rose he gave me. He was walking around the block with me, and he picked someone's flower and gave it to me. Things like that are kind of sentimental. When my baby gets older, I can say, 'This is the first rose your daddy ever gave me.'"

Because she didn't want her girlfriends to steal him, she kept quiet about Bill. Having him was her favorite secret, ever. One day he told her that he would marry the mother of his baby — not that he wanted to get her pregnant, she said, but just to prove he was an honorable man. "Then I got pregnant, and he got scared." Bill asked her if she wanted an abortion. No. He told her he wanted to do whatever she wanted. She wanted his baby.

When his baby was stirring inside her, she fantasized out loud: "The baby probably will look just like him. He's got short hair, wavy." She grinned and touched her upper arm, "Muscular up here. Pretty teeth. A cute smile. I have a feeling the baby is going to look exactly like him."

Is this love, Makela?

"When I see him, something comes over me. I can be mad at him and when I see him, the mad goes away. I never cared about anyone else like I care about him." Marriage? "If we got married at this young age, we'd just get divorced. I don't know what I want to do, and he don't know what he want to do."

Her mom, she said, didn't like Bill: "He's not around as much as he should be, and she don't like that. I just hope that eventually we be together and everything be's OK."

❧

She's weary in October. Besides going to high school, she's working as an aide in a nursing home—eight hours on weekends, four or five or six hours during the week. She isn't much for homework, but she says she tries to squeeze in some during the school day because she doesn't have time to waste. "Now you can see why I be so tired."

❧

During her pregnancy, Makela chose to go to school at a special program for pregnant teenagers in the Minneapolis Public Schools. It's called PACE, short for Pregnant Adolescents Continuing Education, and it's located in Northeast Junior High School.

Rebecca Strandlund, the coordinator of PACE when Makela was there, said, "Pregnancy used to happen to regular kids," many of whom now are abstaining from sex, using birth control or having abortions. "Now more and more of the pregnant girls have heavy problems." She listed them: poverty, poor school attendance, dysfunctional families, attempted suicides, sexual abuse, alcoholism, boyfriends whose interest in them is waning, drug abuse, depression, extreme youth. Strandlund has worked with 12-year-olds who wanted to keep their babies; one was pregnant by a 25-year-old boyfriend.

"They come here for help. They don't know what to do about the pregnancy or the baby," Strandlund said. Also, the pregnant girls come to PACE to escape the boy-girl intrigue at regular schools, where they hate the stares and the stairs. (All of PACE is on one floor of the school.)

PACE provides a basic education — math, science, English, typing, physical education, sewing and social studies. The girls' scholastic ability is limited. Thirty-two percent of the girls, ages 12 to 20, read at the third-grade level or below; only 20 percent can read at the ninth-grade level.

Instruction is individualized. For example, the math teacher handles everything from third-grade multiplication tables to 12th-grade algebra. The program offers nothing fancy. No fourth-year French; in fact, no foreign languages. PACE does have something not standard to most schools, though: parenting classes.

Most of the girls are from other Minneapolis junior highs and high schools. Some are from private schools, parochial schools and residential treatment programs for teens with emotional and family problems. About 75 percent of the PACE girls are minority members and many are poor. Of the 87 girls enrolled when Makela was, 80 were eligible for free lunch.

The PACE girls are just a speck in the statistics. Each day in 1986 (the year Makela got pregnant), an average of eight or nine Minnesota girls under 18 conceived a child. Of those 3,186 reported conceptions, about half (1,626) resulted in live births. Another 1,545 were aborted. Fifteen were fetal deaths.

In Minneapolis, about 10 percent of adolescent girls get pregnant. Yet as serious as the problem is here, Minnesota has the lowest teen birthrate in the nation, in part because the abortion rate for pregnant teens is higher than in other states.

❦

It was Strandlund and the PACE teachers who recommended that Makela be the one chosen as the subject of this article.

Not that she was typical. She was *better off* than most PACE girls. She had relatively good school attendance and supportive parents. While her folks never married each other and haven't lived together since before Makela was born, she has frequent contact with both. Her mother, an alcoholic, had celebrated a year of sobriety.

More mature and sophisticated than many of the girls, Makela, when she wanted, could be articulate, good with adults, charismatic, serious, polite and assertive. She wasn't alcoholic or otherwise chemically dependent, she wasn't hampered by shyness, she wasn't suicidal, she wasn't being physically abused at home or by the boyfriend who came around only occasionally.

Most important, her spirit wasn't broken; her hope wasn't gone.

Makela strongly wanted to finish high school. The odds were against her making it. Over a three-year period, half the PACE girls quit school by the end of the academic year in which they gave birth.

Of the 205 babies born to PACE students in the previous academic year, nine were placed for adoption at birth, the rest kept by their mothers. A few girls gave up the babies some months after the births, giving such reasons as, "That screaming baby drove me crazy!"

The girls need lots of understanding at PACE, Strandlund said. Most don't get it elsewhere.

Math teacher: "Don't you feel well?"
PACE student: "I have stomach problems. There's something growing in there."

Part of the message at PACE is that unwanted pregnancy need not happen. The girls are instructed in family planning and parenting, and most stop with one child born in their high school years. But some are at PACE for a second time. Staff members cringe when they recall a few girls who had their third child while in PACE. The reasons behind the pregnancies are complex.

Take Makela as an example. She said she asked her doctor from Pilot City, a county-operated clinic on the North Side, for birth control pills when she was 13 because she wanted to prove she was responsible. But because she had nausea and mid-cycle bleeding, she took herself off the pill. Besides, she was jealous of her Aunt Nada and her cousin Kelley, both two years older than she and new mothers. "I felt kind of left out. They were getting all the attention."

The jealousy didn't go away after she conceived. Makela's 36-year-old mother, Rita Carroll, cared for her older son's illegitimate infant, Thomas, and Makela admitted that she resented the attention little Thomas got. Rita doted on that baby, but she told Makela that she had room in her heart for two grandbabies: "There won't be no difference because they'll both be mine."

Living in a one-bedroom apartment in south Minneapolis were Rita, two of her three children (Makela and 11-year-old Cecil) and her grandson, Thomas. Seventeen-year-old Sibussis—Makela's brother and Thomas' father—was sometimes with them at the apartment while he waited to be sentenced for burglary.

As she warmed a bottle for Thomas, Makela said that early in her pregnancy she had felt guilty. No more. "Why should I be ashamed?"

Ashamed, no. Anxious, yes. She wondered aloud how her delivery would go. One day the girls in the parenting class were looking through books about childbirth. Makela said, "I ain't gonna be up in no stirrups." She looked sick when she saw a photograph of an episiotomy and said, "Oh yuck!" A classmate said, "I don't want that. I want a Caesarian."

As much as the teachers and staff tried to give a realistic idea of what childbirth would be like, the girls got much of their information from each other. Makela asked a PACE girl who had given birth three weeks before: "How's it like not to be pregnant anymore?"

"Good."

"Boy or girl?"

"Boy."

"Natural childbirth?"

"Yeh."

"Did it hurt?"

"Yeh."

"A lot?"

"Yeh. I'm OK now."

"First baby?"

"Yeh."

❧

A PACE student is having trouble working out a word problem in math class. The teacher stands at her desk, talking through it. "Well, how many weeks in a year?" the teacher coaxes. "Seven," says the girl. "No," says the teacher. "Five," the girl says, obviously reduced to guessing. The teacher, remaining calm, responds, "No. Does anybody know how many weeks in a year?" Makela volunteers, "360-some." "No." Eventually the teacher has to tell the girls that the answer is 52 and to continue shepherding them through the word problem.

❧

Makela often fretted about not being bright enough to satisfy herself, or her child. "I'm not the smartest person on earth. I mean, I'm not even the smartest person in school. I'm OK, but I want my baby to be smarter." How smart? "Smart enough to be a lawyer." Boy or a girl, she wanted it to be a lawyer.

"I suppose I could be a lawyer if I set my mind to it. I'm headed in the right direction. I want to finish school and go to be a RN." She had seen her aunt graduate from North High, stepping so nicely across the stage. Makela could just see herself taking that walk to "Pomp and Circumstance," strutting dignified, coolly picking up her diploma.

Yet she admitted she had done little toward her goals that day. She had gotten up at 9 o'clock, sat around the apartment and watched TV all day. Among PACE girls, conversation often is about the plots of "The Young and the Restless," "All My Children" and "General Hospital."

One day in social studies class, Makela slammed her book down. "It's too hard. It's stuff I don't need to know about." She should have been on Chapter 14; she was on Chapter 4. Easily distracted, she was pulled into a discussion about hair styles. She knew she and the others were misbehaving, and she said shamefully that the teacher was going to "get mad at us because we ain't working." The teacher told the students to get down to business. Makela was peeved and said, "I don't know nothing about the Roman Empire, and I don't see why I should."

Some of the PACE teachers try to make school work relevant to girls who are street-wise but classroom-deficient. The math teacher handed out a mimeographed sheet with such problems as: "Lisa buys a video recorder which costs $816. If she makes 12 equal payments, how much is each payment?"

The social studies teacher one day realized that a student had no idea who Rudy Perpich was. Once the girls learned that he was the governor, they couldn't care less. Makela said, "I ain't ever gonna vote. I don't think it's important." So the teacher fabricated an example of garbage piling up in a neighbor's yard and discussed how a person could get the authorities to take action. Makela said, "Neighbor's problem. Not mine." Another girl added, "Don't bother me none. Gonna stay inside."

Because most of these girls lack most measures of self-esteem, PACE praises accomplishments and hands out lots of awards. A prize went to a friend of Makela for the girl's "super attitude." The girl was nearly bursting with pride, but she began to crab that her name was misspelled on the certificate. The teacher jumped in: "See how important spelling is."

❧

"I be looking in the mirror at myself, and I see I'm tipping over my stomach already. I never expected to be this far out."

❧

Snippy and sassy sometimes, sullen others, Makela was known for her moodiness. In January 1987, she was in trouble at home and at school. She wouldn't say why. Told by the reporter and photographer who had been chronicling her pregnancy that they would have to find another subject if she continued to refuse communicating much longer, she began to sob. She couldn't stand the rejection. She said this was like the times when no one came to her sixth-grade graduation or to her choir concert. "It hurted so bad. I felt I wasn't important enough."

Her current troubles came spilling out. Her baby was due Feb. 7, and the doctors had told her that her pelvic structure might require a Caesarian section. She was short on cash, partly because she could no longer lift patients and had had to quit her nursing home job. Her mother was scheduled for major surgery—a weight-loss treatment known as a stomach stapling. The family had to move, partly because their lease was up, partly because inspectors had found high levels of lead paint. She hadn't heard from the baby's father in weeks.

Makela's hands were swollen, her feet hurt, her face was breaking out, her bladder always seemed full. She felt unloved. "I try to be positive, but then things happen and I have to go away and think."

Abortion may have been the wiser solution, she said. She had thought about that early in the pregnancy, "but then I heard about an older lady, 25 or so, who couldn't have a baby." This might be her only chance, Makela decided.

Sleep came hard to Makela during the last month of her pregnancy: "I be tossing and turning. I be hot and I can't get to sleep. I always wake up sweating. I got a clock and it be 3 o'clock when I get up to go the bathroom. I just lay there and try to doze off."

Her hands resting on her bulging belly, she said her only joy was thinking about her child. "I want my baby to have a better life than I did, to have things I never had." Love is the key, she said. She would love that child. She tried to prepare herself for parenting, practicing her crocheting. She asked her mom for a baby book, "so I can write down when he crawls, when he gets teeth."

She picked out names: Nakunda for a girl, Makevlin for a boy. Her Aunt Nada Jones, whose pregnancy had made Makela yearn for her own, made up the boy's name. "She was sleeping one night and dreamed the name. She woke up and wrote it down." Makevlin is good, Makela said. It's kind of like her name, but macho.

Nada is also her best friend, Makela said, and she feels she can "say stuff" to her. Just lately Makela had been asking Nada, "What do contractions feel like? How will I know when I'm having the baby?" Nada told her, "You'll know, you'll know."

Makela timed her contractions one night. False labor, the doctor said. Drat. She was wanting to get this baby out of her.

❧

To pregnant teenagers at PACE, maternity slacks aren't cool. The only ones who wear them are the Hmong girls, and most of them are married. Makela has two pairs, but usually she stuffs herself into sweat pants or regular jeans. "I can't wait to have this baby because I can't zip up my Calvin Kleins." Like the other PACE girls, she wears them unzipped and tugs a sweater over the opening.

❧

Rebecca Strandlund, the head of PACE, said that she winces when she hears the girls talk about their relationships with males. Most are willing to accept a great deal of what many women consider abuse—physical and mental. Sometimes she wants to shout, "Why do you put up with that? Be a strong woman!" Then she reminds herself that such talk is much easier for an adult with a job and self-confidence. "Here we have a little 16- or 14-year-old who's pregnant and getting at least some attention from someone."

(Makela, meanwhile, wasn't getting any attention from men. She was wearing a ring on the third finger, left hand: "Mom gave it to me. Bill wouldn't get me one.")

With all the strikes against the girls in her program, Strandlund said, "I think it's kind of a miracle they're in school." Makela was absent nine of 60 days in the first trimester. "As our kids go, that's real good. We get kids in here who have two, three, four credits for the whole year," instead of the 15 they should earn.

Even keeping middle-class, much-loved kids motivated for school and life is a tough task, Strandlund said. She noted that her own children, who have every reason to excel, still need a kick in the fanny some mornings to get them moving toward school.

So she could understand why pregnant teenagers with little family support and a history of failure don't take much interest in academics or in lining up day care for their soon-to-be-born children or in straightening out their love lives. She could understand, but sometimes it drove her nuts.

❧

Makela, broom in hand, says she is tired of the mess in her family's apartment. When she has her own place, she swears, it will be tidy.

❧

With her baby due in 10 days, Makela was a basket case. She was supposed to be taking it easy because her blood pressure was high. Toxemia was a possibility. Her doctors instructed her to get a balanced diet, to spend time resting and to lie on her left side in order to increase the blood supply to the baby. "I can't bother with all that," she said at suppertime. "I haven't been down since I got up at 7 this morning."

When her mother was in the hospital for the stomach stapling, Makela was in charge of her little brother, Cecil, and was supposed to find a new apartment for the family. She skipped a doctor's appointment that week, even though her uncle came with his car to get her. She had him take her grocery shopping instead. She wanted to get hot dogs and beans for Cecil to cook for himself after soccer practice. He could pick up potato chips on his way home.

Angry that she was getting stuck taking care of Cecil and often Thomas, too, she said she was tired of being the responsible one.

Besides all that, there was a big lump in her heart. Bill had been living in Iowa for a while and now she said she suspected that he was back in town, living with another woman. Her voice choking, she said, "It's gonna be hard. I don't know where I went wrong."

❧

The day before her baby was born, she swept out her room, put a Santabear in the infant seat, stacked up stuffed toys in the crib and talked at length about her hopes for the child.

"I want *everything* for it, most of the things I never got to have: a good family environment, responsibility, a good place to live. Not fancy. I don't mean fancy. A place he can come home to and talk to his mom whenever he has a problem."

Does that take money? "I care about money to a certain extent, but it's not everything. You don't have to come from a rich family." What's important? Education? "I ain't gonna force him to go to college if he don't want to." Discipline? "I'll be a little strict. Strict in a way a parent is supposed to be. I won't stand for a kid talking back or hitting a parent.

"Most, I want that if he want to go after something he can go after it and not be afraid."

She paused, then said it out loud. "I get afraid."

❦

Her mother tells her she's a natural with babies. When her brother Cecil was born, Makela was 5 years old. The family story is that Makela stood at the nursery window at the old county General Hospital and said to perfect strangers, "No, no, don't look at that baby! Come here and look at MY baby!"

❦

Makela was sleeping over at her Aunt Nada's apartment when she woke herself up with her own moaning at 4:30 a.m. Feb. 6, 1987. Labor was beginning. She called her mom at 6:45 a.m. to meet her at Fairview-Riverside Hospital. Rita called a cab to get herself and baby Thomas there. Nada's boyfriend got Makela to the hospital. By 9 a.m. Makela was alternately vomiting and watching cartoons on the TV in her room, which was also to be the delivery room if all went well. Her doctor, Tom Seasly, predicted birth sometime in the afternoon. The family tried guessing during which TV show the baby would come.

During "Oprah Winfrey," "All My Children" and "One Life to Live," Makela tried to sleep between contractions.

Her family drifted in and out. Nada left for two hours—she took a bus downtown and bought curtains—but still there was no baby when she got back at mid-afternoon. She tried to rib Makela about how long this birthing was taking, but Makela ignored her. Makela was totally uninterested in what was going on around her, except when she heard a woman yelling from a room down the hall. Her eyes got big. "Is that someone screaming?"

Her nephew, Thomas, 5 months old, spent the day being passed around to various admiring family members and hospital staffers. Grandma Rita joked that they ought to put the 16-pounder in the nursery to scare new mothers.

By 4:45, when "People's Court" was on the tube, Makela was in hard labor. "I'm dying, I'm dying," was about all she could say. Her mom responded, "You're not dying. You just feel like you are."

During the evening news—Liberace dying of AIDS; a rehash of the America's Cup—Makela was insisting, "It's coming, it's coming." Dr. Seasly said, "Well, you're close. You're about 9 centimeters. Another 10 minutes and you can start pushing." Makela said, "I want to push now." "Can you wait a few more minutes?" "No," she snapped, all patience gone.

Nada was eating a plate of spaghetti at bedside. Makela gave her a dirty look. "I wish I could have this baby. I'm hungry." The doctor laughed and said, "Me, too. I feel the same way. Take some slow, deep breaths, Makela. That's it. Slow and deep. Slow and deep." With her mother rubbing her back, Makela announced at 6:20, "I ain't having no more

The Last of the Tearoom Ladies ❦ 161

babies." Five minutes later, "I'll be so glad when this is over. Please God! Tell the doctor I got to push."

She got permission to push at 6:30. "Makela," said the doctor, "try to make that yell go down and help push." Makela said emphatically, "I never want to go through this again." Seasly told her, "I wish I had a dollar for every time I've heard that. If that would be the case, the human race would be extinct."

The delivery nurse started giving a steady stream of instructions: "Makela, put your chin on your chest and push. No noise!" "I can't do it!" "Yes you can, put all that energy into pushing. I want you to grab your knees and push like you're rowing a boat. Push it though, Makela. Good job!"

Rita said, "The baby's coming! He's got hair."

It was during "Hollywood Squares" (6:50 p.m.) that the baby's head emerged. "It's a boy, I just know it's a boy," Makela said. The left shoulder popped out. An arm. The other shoulder. The trunk. "It's a boy," said the doctor. Makela, sobbing, said, "Oh, give him to me." She studied him from a foot away and proclaimed gravely, "He looks just like Bill."

Rita cut the cord and announced with satisfaction, "Yeh, I've got me another grandson." On President Reagan's birthday, she noted.

After a few stitches for the new mother and a medical examination of the baby, Makela got to hold him. This time she wasn't so approving. "It's got a squished head."

Makevlin weighed in at 6 pounds, 2½ ounces. He was the sixth of nine babies born at Fairview-Riverside that day. No other moms were teenagers. Makela asked.

🐾

The day after the delivery, Makela lovingly strokes her son's face and says into the telephone to a girlfriend: "Guess where I am. . . . At the hospital. Yeh. I had a baby last night. A boy. . . . It didn't hurt that much. Just felt like bad cramps. . . . My stomach's still big, but it's going to go down. . . . No, he don't know. I had the baby when Bill was out of town."

🐾

Makela was back in her blue jeans, zipped, six days after Makevlin was born. "I had to lay on the bed to zip them up."

She decided to breast-feed her baby for a few weeks, until she would go back to high school. The first days at home, she spent hours staring at him, pushing his hair into a part like his daddy's, cooing, "My baby," loving him up. But once when he was fussing, she told him sharply, "Shut up, boy."

🐾

A week after the birth, Makela writes a letter: "Grandmother, I am so glad I had my baby. He is so little to me. I have my hands full now. His dad left me all alone to raise him by myself. I was so in love with him and I steel care. I don't quite know how to get him off my mind."

❧

Makela had missed school for so long — more than five weeks — that she had forgotten her locker combination when she got back to PACE. She said she was glad to be back; she had missed her friends.

She pulled out Polaroids that Nada took the day the baby was born and asked her friend Mary, "Do you want to see pictures of my baby?" The math teacher said, "Yes, we do, but not now. Don't you have a break coming up?" The girls pretended to settle down to rounding off numbers, but they sneaked the photos around. Someone got caught and was reprimanded. The girl protested, "Miss Heise, it won't take but two minutes to look at them baby pictures." The girl became so impudent that she was kicked out of class. Makela grinned at the distraction her baby's photos had created.

Between classes, Makela was surrounded by girls eager to examine the pictures of the birth:

"Mine weighed bigger than yours."

"You look rough in them pictures."

"Oh, is that blood on the baby?"

"Is that all you? Your stomach's flat now."

As do most of the teenage mothers, Makela minimized the pain and trauma of the pregnancy and delivery. "The only thing that hurted was the contractions," Makela said.

PACE staffers told the story of another girl, a 12-year-old sixth-grader, who slid off the delivery table and tried to run away when her labor grew intense. Three weeks later she was telling her school friends that delivery was no big deal.

Nor was it a big deal for Makela to leave her baby while she was in school, she said. "I be home soon to see my sweetie pie." She had planned to have her mother watch him while she finished out her sophomore year of school. She didn't like the idea of her mother raising Makevlin, but she had no choice, she thought.

Then she got a break. Another young mother didn't show up for a special program at South High for students with babies. Makela could go to South and have her baby in a day-care center right in the school. But she didn't express any excitement about the chance. Later she admitted that she was troubled about leaving her son with strangers. What should she do? she asked earnestly. It was hitting home that now she had to make decisions for two.

❧

A poster at PACE reads, "Oversleeping is a mighty poor way to make your dreams come true." But Makela has been up since the baby started crying at 4 a.m.

PACE social worker Jeri Gort said she doesn't believe in abortion, "even after working here. What bums me out is that they don't believe in adoption." Low-income white families and minority families don't accept the idea of giving up their babies, she said. "The sad ones are those who are fourth-generation welfare." She talks to lots of them, she said. So many of the girls plan to have illegitimate children that sometimes she hears, "I *waited* until I was 16 to have my baby." Having sex and having babies are among the few joys these girls have, Gort speculated. "We have the neediest population in the school district."

More than 90 percent of the PACE girls live with only one parent. Many have only one parent living. That's bad, but what's worse is that some of the girls lost that young parent to a knife wound or a shotgun blast. Partly because the parent mortality rate is so high, Gort routinely holds grief classes.

Despite all their problems, she likes these kids, she said. They're open and easy to talk to. They respond so eagerly to the slightest bit of attention from an adult. Example: The PACE staff realized that the girls' birthdays tend to pass unrecognized. So the school makes a small effort to make the girls feel special on their birthdays. Gort said, "We give them a sucker, sing happy birthday, put up a poster. That's it. And the kids are ecstatic." One young mother-to-be said she couldn't remember anyone ever wishing her a happy birthday.

The small class size at PACE helps the girls, Gort said. The enrollment is probably 25 in a class, but the actual number of girls per class is more like 15. That's because many are absent each day for morning sickness, bed rest, child care after the babies are born and any of the reasons nonpregnant teenagers skip school. PACE teachers get tired of being teased about what an easy load they have. Preparing makeup lessons for 10 kids or more every day is no snap.

❧

When she registered for classes at South High on March 3, Makela was overwhelmed. There were so many students, so much activity. Her poor scholastic record once again became a concern. She hadn't passed her benchmark tests in math or writing and had barely passed reading. As an 11th-grader, she read at about the fifth-grade level. She was told she had better buckle down. In addition to being a mom, she would be taking home schoolwork.

Also, she was scared to death that a stranger would steal her baby from day care at South, even though she was shown that the doors were locked and security was tight.

She brushed aside the possibility that the baby's father might try to take him. But she did tell a story of what he had told her when she was pregnant—that he would take a son to his mother to raise. "And if you have a girl," she said he told her, "you can keep her."

"He don't scare me," she said. "He couldn't stand the crying and the diapers, not even long enough to get down to Iowa."

Bill saw his baby for the first time in late March, when Makevlin was about 6 weeks old. Makela reported afterward that she had dressed up the baby in a new gray jumpsuit and a little white shirt. By putting the baby in Bill's arms and walking away, she made Bill hold him. The infant smiled at his dad, she said. Cried, too. Bill said nervously, "What do I do? What do I do?" Makela laughed and showed him how to comfort his son.

Bill told Makela he wanted her back, she said later. He told her he'd be mad if he saw her with another man. He told her, "Stand up and turn around and let me see how you look." Looks good, he said. But still, she wasn't so sure she wanted him back. Part of her was happy to see him; part of her wanted to tell him off, which she did some. He stayed an hour and said he wished he could stay longer. She said, "Another time, maybe." She wouldn't have let him take the baby away.

Makevlin has been with his dad only one other time in his life, when he was about 6 months old.

❧

Is she happy she has the baby? Sometimes yes, sometimes no. Feel trapped? No, she says, she can go out and leave the baby with her mom. Then what's the problem? "Ain't got no problems." Why did she say "sometimes no." "Don't know." She clams up completely.

❧

MICE (Mother Infant Care Education) is available at three Minneapolis High Schools—North, Southwest and South. The mothers go to regular classes plus parenting class while the children (ages 6 weeks to 2½ years) are in day care. The goal is to keep the girls in school and to teach them parenting skills, while the babies are helped to grow socially, emotionally and intellectually. At South, the maximum enrollment is 15 mothers. The waiting list has been as long as 85.

One day when Makevlin was 2 months old, it was an even bet who would fall asleep first in the rocking chair at South High—Makela or Makevlin. He had been waking up every night from about 1 to 3 a.m. She had to be up at 5 a.m. because the MICE school bus came for them at 6:30. The word she most associated with motherhood, she said, was "tired."

Like most of the teenage mothers, she and her child were dressed sharp nearly every day. The girls might not have done their homework, but their makeup was perfect. They looked like the other high-schoolers. The best way to pick out the teenage mothers is by the wet spots of baby drool on their shoulders.

Sue Ryan-Nelson, MICE coordinator, said all the young mothers have problems—boyfriend problems, trouble finding a new man, no time for homework, depression, threats of kidnapping the child from the father or grandparents (that issue arises in MICE two or three times a year, and security is increased even further). She said she wouldn't classify Makela as one of the better-off MICE students. Makela, she said, had a full plate of trouble.

Ryan-Nelson said she thinks that most of the MICE girls eventually get GED certificates showing high school equivalency, but she doesn't know for sure; there's no money for a follow-up program. Some of the new mothers are ninth- and 10th-graders, so they're out of the two-year MICE program by the time they would graduate. Since MICE was begun at South in 1977, 223 students have participated. Hennepin County pays $65,000 a year for the day-care program and the school district pays $85,000—that's $150,000 for 15 mothers.

"A lot cheaper," Ryan-Nelson said, "than having the mothers stay on welfare for lack of education."

As for Makela, she was doing well in the program, Ryan-Nelson said. She was bonding well with her baby and learning how to treat him. Makevlin was settling in well, too.

Makela got extra help in learning to raise her boy. Each Tuesday that she could work up the energy, she went to the after-school Young Parent Program at Lutheran Social Service. It taught basic parenting skills—how to hold the child, play patty-cake, toilet train, sing children's songs, control tempers.

Marie Mellgren, coordinator of the program, said many young mothers need help in learning to discipline their children so they don't repeat abusive patterns they had learned as youngsters. The program also tosses in big doses of self-esteem for the mothers. Said Mellgren, "We help young mothers keep their heads above water." Said Makela, "We go for a free meal and lots of gossip."

❧

By early March, Makela and her mother weren't getting along well at all. Makela moved out in a huff, and she and her baby moved in with her new boyfriend and his mother. Mitch, the boyfriend, was a student at the Work Opportunity Center, a Minneapolis school for students who are having trouble adapting in a regular high school. He also worked on a Sears loading dock.

Once again, Makela's problems touched various aspects of her life:

Makevlin was spitting up, and Makela decided his formula was too strong and began diluting it with extra water. The school nurse determined that was not what the baby's doctor wanted. MICE people were trying to get it through her head that she wasn't giving him enough nourishment.

Makela was hauled into an assistant principal's office because of a surplus of unexcused absences. Of 37 school days, she missed 12 and had excuses for only four. Not so unusual, Ryan-Nelson said. "I don't see a cross-section of pregnant teenagers, but she's a typical kid in the MICE program. Attendance is a problem. They're not responsible for themselves." Many have low skills and emotional problems and troubled home lives. Ryan-Nelson summed up, "What's going on at home is so overwhelming that they don't have their act together at school."

She has had girls not come to school because they don't have the "right" clothes for the baby. The physical appearance of the children tends to be of much more interest to the mothers than the emotional development. They dress the kids like little dolls and get upset if the clothes become dirty or torn.

❧

Makela knows she's failing history. She's not interested in it and won't study.

Assistant principal Sue Thomas: "Let me give you the bad news."

Makela: "I know. I have to pass that to graduate."

Thomas: "True. Do you have too many problems at home to think of school? So many it would be easy to give up?"

Makela: "Yes."

Her back is up. She refuses to write a note explaining why she wasn't in class. She refuses to discuss her predicament with school officials. "I don't want to talk to nobody about my problems. It ain't anybody's business."

Thomas: "That's true. But yours is a heavy load for a 16-year-old. There are adults who couldn't handle this. There are people you could talk to in strict confidence. . . . You may be carrying a lot of guilt that isn't yours."

But Makela won't talk.

❧

Makevlin had a physical in April, including his first shot and oral polio vaccination. Other than a little skin rash, "he looks real good," Dr. Tom Seasly said. They talked about the baby's "outie" belly button, which the doctor said many black babies have, for reasons he didn't know. Makela to'd him that she had taped a 50-cent piece on the navel for a while. Didn't do a thing, she complained.

The doctor and Makela had a long discussion about birth control, and eventually they decided on a low-dose birth control pill. He requested a urine sample for a pregnancy test; he wouldn't want her on the pill if she were pregnant. She wasn't.

In May, convinced she had to live away from her mother, Makela went to welfare, asking for an apartment of her own. "I got 15 bucks to my name, and my baby got no diapers," she pleaded. She was told that she could get a place to live, but she couldn't get an Aid to Families with Dependent Children check for May because her mother already had gotten one covering Makela, Makevlin and Cecil.

Makela's wrath was directed at her mother: "She ain't going to see me. I'm going to give her my keys, and I'm going to walk out of her life forever." Makela was furious that after 18 months of sobriety, her mother resumed drinking.

It became clear, little by little, that Makela was feeling cheated because motherhood wasn't turning out as she had expected. The baby wasn't great company for her. She felt drained. Money didn't stretch. She seemed humiliated that she didn't have life by the tail.

By middle-class standards, her 3-month-old baby was lacking. She bought him a brand-new crib (used wouldn't do), but he had no car seat for when they got rides in friends' cars and no playpen and no colorful mobiles. Even when he turned 1, he had only one book, a preschooler's version of "Winnie the Pooh."

❧

After eight months of cooperating with a photographer and reporter, Makela started asking for more than the rides around town she had begged before. She wanted clothes for the baby—preferably new, used might be OK. Her hints escalated to demands for cash for participating in this article. Ethics of journalism meant nothing to a 16-year-old who wanted for herself and her baby. She didn't want to hear that acceding to her demands would change the story the newspaper wanted to tell and that press people don't pay the subjects of their articles.

By Mother's Day she began to break appointments and wouldn't return phone calls. Her earlier wish to tell her story to the world didn't count anymore. She had one more reason to seethe with anger.

❧

Not until September did she consent to resume the newspaper project. "Look, I'm a moody person," she explained then. "I told you that at the beginning. I was in the thinking stage this summer. I just wanted to be left alone."

And by fall, she was pleased with her lot in life. "Look how far I've come," she bragged. "Things are going good for me; '87 is the place to be." She was ecstatic that she no longer was staying with her mother or her grandmother, with whom she had lived on and off before her pregnancy. She had a place of her own. She had a baby to love. She was back to part-time work at the nursing home. Her boyfriend, Mitch, was good to her—much better than the baby's father, she said, whose only contact was to call a few times from Iowa. Mitch liked her baby, she said; indeed, he was good at playing with Makevlin. He even changed a diaper now and again without being asked.

She was paying $310 for a south Minneapolis apartment, plus utilities. The money came from her $437 welfare check. Welfare also gave her a $340 voucher to buy furniture; she got a couch, a chair and a dining-room table. She also received food stamps. "We eat. I go grocery shopping. We do fine," she said.

She's on a roll. When things go well for Makela, she reaffirms her intention to get an education. "Years ago, when I was little, I was always told something by my daddy: 'If you don't know much, you can't do much.' That and, 'Do something. Use the sense God gave you.' "

❦

Makela soured again and cut off communication with most people, including those from the newspaper. What got her back in touch in February was Makevlin's first birthday. She wanted people to come to his party.

They were living in a different south Minneapolis apartment, a two-bedroom. (In the 21 months that the reporter and photographer knew her, she lived in six places.) She had broken up with Mitch and found Bobby. She had mixed feelings about her mother—pride that she had lost more than 120 pounds in the year since her stomach stapling, and embarrassment that her speech was slurred when she was drinking. Makela didn't want to think about her mother's problems, because they detracted from her baby's first birthday.

Makela dressed up her son for his party. She bought him red plaid pants and matching bow tie from Sears. He quickly figured out how to pull off the tie and suck on it. As the assembled guests sang "Happy Birthday," he helped himself to a handful of frosting from his cake and grinned a sweet smile. He was his usual cheerful self throughout the party. Makevlin was a good child—cuddly, full of energy, aware that a sharp voice meant he was about to get himself into trouble.

Invited to his birthday party for hot dogs, chips, punch (fruit juice and 7-Up) and cake were Grandma Rita, Grandpa (who didn't show up for the party, much to Makela's disappointment), three girls from the MICE program, their babies, and Makela's new man, Bobby, a 31-year-old accounting student. One of the guests asked, "Is he Makevlin's father or not?" Makela shook her head no.

She was so head-over-heels about Bobby that she had taken down from the living-room wall a studio photograph of herself, Makevlin and Mitch, her old boyfriend. The empty photo mat still hung on the wall. She explained about Mitch, "We was already having problems, and then I find him with someone else. Mitch kind of broke my heart."

The conversation among the teenage mothers at Makevlin's party centered on how lucky Makela was to have a place all to herself and her baby. Many of the MICE girls lived with their families and longed for freedom. Makela issued a warning: "I don't think half of them will make it. 'Cause it's hard."

Hard to do homework when a kid is whining, she said. Hard to keep a constant eye on a toddler: "I look up and he be gone. He be splashing in the toilet." Hard to do all for the baby that she knows she should: "I should be reading to him more but I be too tired." Hard to see him sick:

"He just had an ear infection and a temperature of 104, and I was all nervous and everything." Hard to have a moment to herself: "As soon as he knows I have something to do, he bugs me. You're eating something and you have to give him some."

Makela sometimes cooked up a storm. On an April Sunday she prepared for six family members what she called "a real Sunday dinner": meatloaf, canned corn, mashed potatoes, and macaroni and cheese from a box. Ordinarily, though, she and Makevlin existed on junk food, eaten in front of the TV. Chips were a staple. He had his bottle, she her Pepsi.

The best part of mothering, she said, was seeing Makevlin take his first steps. Just before Christmas, when he was 10 months old, she screamed in joy, "My baby can walk. He can walk! *He can walk!!*" She moved the little Christmas tree to the top of the TV.

Her dad and his girlfriend took Makevlin for a weekend so that she could have a break. She missed her baby so bad, she said.

❧

About homework: "I need a break after school. If I study too hard, I don't remember nothing."

❧

She said she was being a good mother and it was easier than she had anticipated. "For my age I'm doing pretty good. Not many girls my age want to live alone, raise a baby and go to school. A lot of people don't have the advantages I do."

Like Section 8 housing. Most of her $365 rent was paid for by the federal subsidized-housing program. She chipped in $16 a month. On March 1 Makela got a check for $437 from Hennepin County for AFDC. One dollar went to the bank for cashing her check, about $30 for the phone, $25 for lights, $50 for natural gas. She also got $111 a month in food stamps.

"Lots of people wouldn't have thought I'd be doing so good. If I hadn't had the baby, I wouldn't have this house. I wouldn't have Section 8. I'd be at my grandma's house. I don't even know if I'd be in school.

"In a way, I'm glad I had him. I've got it out of the way. I've got this part of my life over. I'll get a career and then decide if I want another baby."

❧

"I thought I wouldn't be lonesome after I had a baby. I found you still can be lonely. You just have someone to depend on you. Now I have Bobby, and I'm not lonesome." The telephone rings. Like most teenage girls, she lets it ring twice before she reaches for it. Her grin and the tone of her voice show it's Bobby calling.

❧

One school day in March, Makela and the other MICE girls were morose. The baby of a former classmate had died of encephalitis. During parent group interaction, Sue Ryan-Nelson told them, "Remember, it's OK to cry at a funeral. And afterward." She meant the advice for herself, too. This was her fourth baby funeral. In the years she has worked with programs for teenage mothers, two babies died after being born very ill and one child was killed by its mother.

The South High morning announcements came over the PA system—girls' track, the national math competition, armed services testing. The MICE girls paid absolutely no attention. There was no announcement that touched their lives.

That day, one of Makela's classmates read a report in parenting class about teenage suicide. She focused it on a friend who blew his brains out. Makela asked her, "Are you suicidal?" The girl answered, "I was from 13 to 15." Ryan-Nelson asked, "Is that when you were being abused?"

In the same class period, another student casually asked Ryan-Nelson, "Do you know much about schizophrenia?" Enough to know that more than a textbook definition was called for. After a few sensitive questions, she got the girl talking.

❧

With warmer weather, love was in the air, or, at least, hopes for love. Makela no longer was mopey and feeling cheated that other teenagers were hanging out in the park every afternoon when she had to take her son home. Her thoughts were turning to the South High spring prom at International Market Square, and she was going to go. Bobby had said yes.

She found the perfect dress. It was pictured in the Christmas Sears catalog. "Black, all-over lace dress," was the description. "Sparkles with sequins on the front bodice for a look that's enriched with elegance." $69. Perfect.

Problems: The catalog was old and the dress was no longer available. Plus Bobby said she didn't dare spend $69 for a dress to wear only one night. "It doesn't fit in the budget," he told her firmly. He was studying accounting at Minneapolis Community College and knew how to handle money. When Bobby said no, Makela gave up.

"Want to see the dress I'm going to wear?" she said to visitors, beaming. She went to her closet to find the white prom dress she had worn two years earlier, before she was pregnant. "I don't want to wear it, but I have to. This dude bought it for me to go to his senior prom, when I was in ninth grade." She still had the price tags: $100 for the dress, jewelry for $19.08, shoes, $35. She put on the white three-inch heels, and practiced walking like Miss America.

She tried on the dress. It was tight. Real tight. "My hips are bigger," she noticed. "It fitted me better then than it does now."

Even spreading hips didn't put her into a foul mood, now that she had Bobby. She would lose weight, she said cheerfully. She had almost two months. She peeled an orange to start her diet. Or maybe she would sew a dress. She could do that. Hey, no problem.

❧

Note on the dining room table, left for Bobby:
"Bobbie, I went over to a friend house to help her because she need someone to talk to because her baby got took."
What had happened was that authorities believed that one of Makela's school friends was severely depressed and unstable. They removed her baby from the home and took the mother for help. That night Makela loses some sleep, wondering if her baby could be taken away.

❧

The last week of April, Makela's life was disrupted once again. Makela and Bobby split up; she said it was because he was trying to choose her friends and run her life. Meanwhile, she went to Chicago for a weekend with an aunt, leaving the baby with her grandmother in north Minneapolis. She came home smitten with a new man, Cardell. He liked her, too, and soon he showed up in Minneapolis to see her and look for work.

She hadn't heard from Mitch, the man she lived with when the baby was little—not unless he was the originator of the crank phone calls she was getting, as she speculated. She hadn't heard from Bill, Makevlin's father, much either, but once he made a powerful impact. He called to say he loved her. She spoke of "that hold he has on me." Nonetheless, she "got hard" and started legal procedures to get Bill to help financially support their son " 'cause it's his responsibility, too." She wouldn't get more money if Bill helped; the state would simply pay less.

❧

Trying to be a good mother, she tries in April to teach colors to Makevlin. "Red," she says patiently, liltingly, as she holds up a red toy for the 14-month-old. He smiles happily, glad for the attention. "Red," she says again, "red, red, red, red, red." He, of course, is too young to say the word. She gets bored and stares back at the TV.

❧

Prom night, 1988. No prom at International Market Square for Makela. She and Cordell, who came up from Chicago to visit, spent the evening at her place, watching the tube, eating pizza, dealing with her son who hadn't had a nap all day and was racing furiously through the apartment and flinging himself onto laps.

Makela was nervous, moody, in need of affection from her mother, her boyfriend, her son, her cousin. Usually she doesn't drink, but that night she had a wine cooler. "Hey, it's prom night," she said. "Let's celebrate."

She didn't go to the prom for several reasons. No $30 for two prom tickets, to begin with. She had lent some of her welfare money to relatives and hadn't been paid back.

For another thing, "After what happened here, I didn't really feel like going," she said, tenderly stroking Makevlin's head.

What had happened was that she was raped 10 days before. The brother of an acquaintance of hers, she said, had introduced himself and talked his way into her apartment. They chatted, exchanged names and phone numbers. He left for a few minutes and when he came back, he slapped handcuffs on her wrists and flashed open a switchblade. He raped her. Then he raped her again. Makevlin watched and cried. She pleaded, "Don't hurt my son, please don't hurt my son!" She said she thought the man was going to kill her. When he left, she called police.

They picked up a suspect. He's being held in the Hennepin County jail. She said she doesn't fear testifying against him. She wants to. She wants him to rot in jail.

Prom night was the first time she had stayed in her apartment since the rape. Her mom, her cousin, her man were all there to protect her, to try to take her mind off the rape. "I see flashbacks," she said.

For diversion, she talked about why she had opened up her life to newspaper people for parts of two years. The first reason was practical: "I get a bunch of pictures of my baby."

The second was to teach a lesson:

"Anybody who read the article can see that some teen parents can make it."

Makela was absent 12 of the first 13 school days in May. Last week she mentioned the possibility of "going where the wheels take me" this summer and leaving Makevlin behind with someone—she doesn't know who. She daydreams of "adventures." She can't guess where she'll be in five years.

❧

More babies? Not for a long time, Makela says. "I won't have no more babies 'til I got a ring on my finger and I hear some man say, 'I do.' "

Makela did graduate from South High and is following her dream of becoming a nurse. She is studying to be an LPN. Makevlin is 3 years old. Makela's rapist was convicted. She is still planning to wait for marriage and more children.

Nina Draxten

Actress Ingenue at 85

October 3, 1988

❧

At age 81, Nina Draxten wanted a new career. She was feeling a bit lonely and unfocused. Acting appealed to her. Not that she'd ever done more than a smidgen. But why not give it a try, she told herself.

Armed with Polaroids that she'd had her nephew shoot of her, she took a bus downtown to a modeling agency and threw herself into the role of a lively old lady, not a difficult role for her.

That was four years ago. Her first major motion picture will be released next month.

Draxten was cast by Sam Shepard as Jessica Lange's 100-year-old grandmother in "Far North." Only 85, Draxten had to really act to play the part of an older, crotchety, confused, sputtering woman in a wheelchair.

In real life, Nina Draxten is refined but forceful, a retired high-school and college English teacher. She is stooped with osteoporosis, but she says it doesn't cause her pain. She didn't marry and lives in the north Minneapolis house that her grandfather, a Norwegian-born carpenter, built the year after she was born. Until last year she shoveled her walks. She walks to the public library, "six blocks away — and uphill."

Her second book was published this year. Reviewers called it "carefully researched" and "a fascinating account." It's called "The Testing of M. Falk Gjertsen" (Norwegian-American Historical Association, $12) and is the biography of a Minneapolis Lutheran minister who was the subject of a messy love scandal at the turn of the century. Her earlier book, "Kristofer Janson in America" (Norwegian-American Historical Association, $12) is about a man who in the 1880s came to Minneapolis to start Unitarian churches among the Norwegians in the Midwest, a startling idea for the time.

"I never like to write about someone who says their prayers, pays their bills and dies in bed," Draxten said. "It has to be someone of interest!"

That's why she likes "Far North." It's got some bite to it. Sam Shepard, who made his film-directing debut with "Far North," told the cast to say only that it's a movie about four generations. Draxten couldn't help but expand on that: "I would think that anyone in a literature class would say it's about social change, especially the role of the sexes." She hoped she didn't go too far with that. "You see, the play raises the question that if women get more power, will they pick up some of the habits of men, even the vices?" Oh dear, was she saying too much?

Anyway, she continued, Shepard is a very brilliant man, and Jessica Lange is prettier in person than on the screen, and Charles Durning and Tess Harper are fascinating. She said that during the filming in Duluth a year ago, "The actors had plenty of opportunity to pull rank on me because I was new, right off the street. They didn't. They treated me almost as if I were porcelain."

She said she had no trouble memorizing her lines; she had been an English teacher back in the days when people memorized things. She had no trouble acting, either. Her agent, Dee Ulsaker of the Eleanor Moore Agency, called her "a natural. When she first came to us, we noticed a certain flair, a spunkiness."

Shepard got such a kick out of her that he had her name — spelled incorrectly, unfortunately — printed on the canvas for the back of a director's chair and presented it to her. She doesn't have a director's chair. Doesn't care to get one. So the canvas is propped up on the spindles of a straight-backed chair in the dining room.

Now, about that name of hers. It's "Nine-ah," rhyming with Dinah, not Knee-nah. That's important because she was born on the ninth day of the ninth month at 9 p.m., a block away from the house where she has spent most of her life. Her parents were born in Norway. Her father was the founder and first president of the Sons of Norway and her mother was a mover and shaker in the Daughters of Norway. She said she must have been 7 or 8 years old before she realized the earth didn't revolve around Norwegian fraternal societies.

After she studied history and English at the University of Minnesota, she taught in high schools: Lester Prairie, Adrian, St. Croix Falls, Willmar and St. Louis Park. At Moorhead State Teachers College she supervised students who wanted to teach high-school English. After her father became ill and she needed to return to Minneapolis, she joined the University of Minnesota faculty. For most of her 23 years there, she was an assistant professor, teaching English in the General College.

She never finished her doctorate and it occurs to her she could now. But last year she stopped at the university library after the General College Christmas party, and she noticed that the library doors were so heavy she could hardly get them open. "I don't suppose the doors are any heavier than when I taught there."

As a high-school teacher during the Depression, she directed scores of student plays. But her acting was limited to an occasional small role in little plays put on informally by university graduate students. It would not stretch the point, she said, to say that she started acting when she was 81.

Her first acting job was in a training film for bank employees, who were being encouraged to be good to old people. She played the part of a loquacious woman who wanted to chat about her grandson. The teller scarcely listened, gave her cash and said, without feeling, "Have a nice day."

(Nina Draxten doesn't have the problem that her character did. People listen to her. "Or perhaps I'm insensitive, and I don't notice when they're not listening.")

Her big time in advertising was for a Burger King ad. She played the part of the former teacher of "Herb," supposedly the only person in America who had never been to Burger King. Draxten got to be ornery on film. She pounded the table and said sternly, "Herbert, pay attention!" For that shoot she went to New York several times, was fed well, treated like a big shot and paid "generously."

She'd like to point out to any creepy readers out there that she isn't rich — even after "Far North" — and she keeps only a few dollars — if that — around the house and it wouldn't be worth your while to break into her simple home. Besides, she isn't alone. Her tenants, a married couple much younger than she, recently became ill and had to move to nursing homes, but their big, brutish grandson has moved in.

Draxten said she stays healthy by eating an apple and a carrot every day. She'll have one cocktail when she's out for dinner but not at home. For protein, she eats fish. She starts out the morning with a cup of tea and uses the same tea bag all day to keep down the caffeine level.

But she wasn't always so pure: She smoked for 40 years and ate hamburger. It was after her brother died four years ago that she decided to mend her ways. They had lived together in the old family house since he came back after World War II, and his death sent her on a tailspin. It was then she decided she needed something to keep herself busy and tried acting.

Somebody from Johnny Carson's staff recently called her about being on the "Tonight Show" and kept asking her why she never married. "Maybe I lost out in fair competition," she explained. That wasn't good enough. "Well, I was a bridesmaid three times." No good. Now she's peeved. "They have to reduce everything to a joke. Marriage is not that big an issue with me. Johnny Carson was married and divorced half a dozen times and I don't care, that's his business."

She has not, needless to say, been on the Tonight Show.

Draxten is not old-fashioned on the divorce issue. If two personalities aren't meshing well, "sometimes it may be better to shake hands and to say goodbye. That's easier now than it used to be. Every change in society isn't bad, you know."

Nor is modern life all good: "I lived through the Depression but never have I seen a time as bad as this. All the homeless!" Even though now she carries an AFTRA card, she despairs that people in sports and other entertainment fields make so much money and so many other people are poor and without hope.

For all she knows, her acting career may be over. The phone hasn't been ringing off the hook with job offers. "Who knows," she said. "Maybe they're afraid I won't last through the shooting session."

Miss Draxten is well and happy but unemployed. "Far North" has been her only major film. If you have acting work available, please give her a call.

Nelson Aldrich

The Ins and Outs of a Doorman
January 30, 1988
❧

A few years ago, Karen Engen became terribly ill at work. She vaguely remembers that the doorman of her office building was being his usual helpful self as she was loaded into an ambulance. Several days later she got a get-well card in the hospital, signed Nelson Aldrich. Nelson Aldrich, she mused. Who in the world is Nelson Aldrich?

When she finally got back to work, the doorman came to her office to check on her and to say, "I'm so glad you're all right." He wore his name tag: Nelson Aldrich. Aha.

"I hadn't been the observant person he was," she said. "I should have known the name of the man whose smile makes so many of us feel we're kind of special."

Nelson Aldrich has been the doorman at the Medical Arts Building in Minneapolis for only three years, but he's becoming well known downtown as a kind, decent man. He gets a lot of chances every day.

The building has 160 tenants — almost all of them medical and dental offices — with several thousand employees. And thousands more patients are in and out of the building each day.

You may have seen Aldrich in action at the 9th St. door, just east of the Nicollet Mall. He's the pleasant man in the spiffy blue suit who springs to open the door and offers an arm to anyone who's frail.

He flags down taxis and chases away nervy people who try to park in the handicapped zone. He calls a person by name if he knows it, "sir" or "ma'am" if he doesn't. And often he's the first to hear what the doctor diagnosed.

Aldrich views his job as public relations for the Towle Real Estate Co., which manages the building. He firmly believes that a pleasant doorman can change a person's outlook on life: "A nice 'Hi' and a smile can go a long way."

He doesn't do a whole lot of self-promoting, so it's fortunate he has vocal fans. One is John Hein, 81 and blind. Whenever Hein is downtown,

The Last of the Tearoom Ladies ❧ 179

he makes it a point to stop at the Medical Arts Building to get an encouraging word from Aldrich. Hein said, "He's a good man, very helpful. They've had others around here, and I say he's the best."

There's a mink-wrapped elderly woman, who didn't want her name published, who appreciates Aldrich telling her, "You go inside and stay warm and when the cab gets here, we'll come get you." No, she has never tipped him, she said, but "One of these days I'll put a $10 bill in his hand."

There's Milo Skeate, a cab driver for 31 years who delivers lots of people to Aldrich's hands: "I don't see anybody help more people than he does."

There's Dr. Malcolm McCannel, a 71-year-old eye doctor whose patients include many older people and who compliments Aldrich on his kindnesses to them. He said of Aldrich, "It takes us out of the bush league to have a good, uniformed doorman. He's terrific. He's got a sweet personality and a sense of humor." McCannel remembers the cold, blustery day when Aldrich was stamping his feet in the snow to stay warm and joked, "Hard to stay inside on a nice day like this."

McCannel's associate, Dr. Donald Le Win, summed up Aldrich's job this way, "Doorman could be kind of a drudgy position, but Nelson doesn't treat it that way."

The Medical Arts Building had doormen from the time it was built in the 1920s to about the mid 1970s. In 1984, the building's doctors decided they wanted to add a position to create a little warmth, a bit of uniqueness. They thought about hiring an elevator starter but decided it would be better to find someone to help handicapped people get in and out of the building. Towle hired a young doorman, but his personality wasn't suited to the job. Word was spread to find a replacement.They wanted someone caring, conscientious, and who wouldn't take more than a half-hour lunch break.

"I know just the right man," said Ken Cornelius, a jewelry designer in the building. He recommended Nelson Aldrich, the chief usher from his church, Valley Baptist, in Golden Valley. Bob Rohrback, building superintendent, said Aldrich has been perfect: "You can ask anyone in the building, and they'll say he's friendly and helpful."

Aldrich's only problem is he's too responsible, Rohrback said. When the temperature dropped to 14 below zero and the wind chill was 46 below in early January, Aldrich continued his pattern of spending most of his time outside. Rohrback lectured him, "Stand in the vestibule. The job is important, but your health is also very important."

Aldrich is healthy, thank you. He's seen Dr. Ankner in No. 1020 for varicose veins and Dr. Norman in No. 401 for his eyes, but that's all.

Towle officials didn't want to get specific, but having a doorman costs them less than $20,000 a year. That includes salary, benefits and uniforms. Aldrich loves those uniforms, especially the ones with the gold trim on the cuffs. "I feel like a king."

Aldrich gets other perks. Scarcely a day goes by when he doesn't get a tip, he says. (He reports all tips to Towle — you can bet it's each and every quarter — and they keep track for the IRS.) At Christmastime, patients hand him notes of thanks, food baskets and cans of mixed nuts. The owner of the Arts Cafeteria and Deli gives him free coffee and sometimes lunch. Some people write to Towle to compliment his service. He got a free eye exam from McCannel. One of the nicest gestures came from a gentleman who told him, "When I see you here, I know I'm safe." Boy, did that make Aldrich feel good.

That's partly because of an incident that Aldrich and lots of other Medical Arts people talk about frequently. It shows how accountable Aldrich holds himself. He was helping a man into a cab and lost hold of him. The man fell. He wasn't injured, but Aldrich was mortified. Each time the man comes to the doctor now, he reminds Aldrich that he botched the job and won't let Aldrich come near him. When he pulls up, you can almost feel a collective shudder from the Medical Arts Building.

Otherwise, Aldrich's job is wonderful, he said. "I thank God every day for the job. I like people, and I like to be of service."

People show up at his door with canes, walkers, wheelchairs, neck braces, Seeing Eye dogs, face masks, casts and medical contraptions that look like torture devices. They arrive in wheelchairs, medi-vans and stretchers; some have to be carried in. He sees sick babies and dying old people. He knows who recently has lost a spouse and who is getting chemotherapy. He helps a quadriplegic who uses his tongue to control his wheelchair.

The parade of the ill is enough to dishearten anyone, including Aldrich. He says he has had to get more callous over his three-year tenure. He can't let things get to him like they used to.

He remembers an early encounter with a 5-year-old named Timothy whose legs were in braces and whose arms were supported by crutches.

"He was as high as this table top. Handsome boy, blond. I helped him in and he said to me, 'Thank you,' and I went outside and tears came down."

He celebrates with patients too. A man walked up to him the other day and said, "See, I don't have a wheelchair now."

Most people treat Aldrich well, but a few clunkers stick in his mind.

"Need a wheelchair, sir?" he asked one.

"No, I need a coffin," the man growled.

He sees a good share of celebrities. He regularly exchanges hellos with Channel 4's Marcia Fluer, Dave Nimmer and Little Markie Rosen. He's opened a door for Kirby Puckett of the Twins, former Gov. Wendell Anderson and Police Chief Tony Bouza. (Bouza, he said, didn't bother to say thanks.)

Not that fame or money mean a whole lot to Aldrich. He knows the names of more patients than doctors, and the worst thing he can call anyone is arrogant. "You speak to them nicely and they look right through you or make some sarcastic remark. I have to hold my temper. Minneapolis isn't as bad as New York, but people could work on better outlooks on life." Jerks, though, are few and far between, he said.

Aldrich has a bachelor's degree in animal husbandry from the University of Rhode Island and doesn't find it amusing that anyone would think his job is comparable to herding cattle. He came to Minnesota in 1962, partly because he liked the scenery and partly because he liked "a little Norwegian girl." She didn't end up being his wife, he said. Instead, he married a woman named Nellie: "She has a fabulous personality and loves the Lord, too." She came with a ready-made family of five children. Now they have 13 grandchildren and five great-grandchildren.

He was a room clerk at the Nicollet Hotel and sold men's clothes at Powers. He filled drug orders for Physicians and Hospital Supply Co. for 17 years, until new owners laid him off. He had a few other jobs before he got the doorman job he'd always wanted.

He's 51 and says that if the good Lord's willing and the creek don't rise, he'll open doors until he has to retire. Other jobs have paid him better, he said, but "at my age, it's hard to find work. Especially good work, like this." He frets some that the skyway being put into the building will rob him of customers, but he realizes he'll still have plenty.

Anyone with a temporary bout of depression is welcome to join him for a shift from 8:30 a.m. to 5 p.m. "Then they won't complain of a broken finger or a lost dollar or something. Some of these sick people put you to shame, such positive attitudes and so cheerful."

For his own positive attitude, he credits his parents and the Lord. Whenever he is complimented on his sweet nature, he says, "Give God the credit, not me. He gave me the gift."

Nelson Aldrich still is happy as a doorman.

Hulda Staples

A Poet's Heartbreak
December 6, 1988
❧

Hulda Staples paid $9,800 to have her book of poetry published, and she got exactly one book for her money. For all she knows, it's the only copy in existence.

More than two years ago, her husband took out a second mortgage on their small, unassuming house in New Hope to finish paying the publisher. She thought then she would see her book in stores. She didn't.

"In July (of 1988) they told me to get ready for interviews from the press," she said. "Nothing come of it. Not even the books. I've been taken."

The problem of naive writers being taken by publishers is so pervasive that "60 Minutes" has done a major piece on it.

Staples, 75, believes the world is waiting for her light verse. She recognizes that her work is simple. ("I didn't get much of an education, but I wore out four dictionaries," she said.) Her childhood education ended in the seventh grade. In recent years, she worked as a housecleaner and passed her G.E.D. to earn a high-school diploma. Then she took courses in basic English and creative writing at community colleges. She thought she learned enough to make her poems salable.

She writes of everyday things: the seasons, sweaters, growing old, faith. An example is this one, titled "To My Daughters":

> *How glad your message made me*
> *How happy I'm to know*
> *That you my children are concerned*
> *And worry about me so.*
> *I'm always glad to hear your voice*
> *And wonder how you are*
> *I'm looking for a letter now*
> *To learn how you do fare.*

In the early 1980s, Staples started sending her manuscript to publish-ers. It repeatedly came bouncing back to New Hope, unopened — except the times when she didn't want to make it easy to return and did not enclose postage; then she never heard from the publishers or saw the typed pages again.

A dozen or more rejections later, she saw an ad in the "Writer's Di-gest" yearbook for Todd & Honeywell, a New York publishing house. She sent her poems and was ecstatic when the firm agreed to print and publi-cize her book, which she called "Slices of Life."

In most publishing agreements, the author pays no fee. The publisher provides the money to print and launch the book, and the author's ad-vances or royalties are compensation for the labor. But little by little, Hulda Staples came to understand she would have to pay to have her book published.

Her husband, Marshall Staples, wrote a check for $2,200 in March 1986 and then made three monthly payments of $300 to Todd & Honey-well in Great Neck, N.Y. At that rate, they would have another 21 months of payments to meet the entire $9,400 charge, so he got a second mort-gage on their tiny home at 17 percent and paid off the fee in July 1986. They paid another $400 when she wanted a poem added to the book.

According to Hulda Staples and her family, the company repeatedly has promised to produce and promote the book. When? "Soon" is what they answer, she said, or "next month."

Staples wants the 125 copies she says she was told she could keep. She yearns to see her book in stores. She hopes Jergen Nash of WCCO Radio will read her poems on the air and interview her. "He reads poems so well," she said. And she needs the $4.78 for each copy sold (40 percent of the $11.95 retail price) that her contract entitles her to. She's always been a nervous type, but the big loan is wrecking her mind and her life, she said.

Part of her problem is that while she signed a contract provided by Todd & Honeywell, she does not have a copy signed by the company. Her friends and family members tell her to get a lawyer. She protests, "They have our money now. What am I going to pay a lawyer with? We're broke. Broke! I hope some of our friends will take us in if we lose everything."

Contacted by the Star Tribune, a representative of Todd & Honeywell said Staples' book "is just about ready for release." Pressed to answer when it will be released, creative director Hank Krell said 4,000 copies are being printed. He said they will be ready "the end of December, early January."

However, information supplied by Todd & Honeywell to "Books in Print" indicates that "Slices of Life" was published in 1987. Staples said the latest promise Todd & Honeywell made to her was that she would get books by last September.

She trusted Todd & Honeywell until last summer, she said, when she went to B. Dalton at Brookdale. "I asked them if my book was on the shelf—

'Slices of Life' by me, Hulda Staples.'' The assistant manager checked and told her it was not a title B. Dalton carries. "That's when my heart broke," she said.

She said she repeatedly calls Todd & Honeywell. "The girl says, 'Who is it?' so sweet, and nobody ever takes my call. They never call back either."

Staples grew up on a farm near Comfrey in southwestern Minnesota. Her family spoke only German at home, and she didn't learn English until she went to school. Her mother died when Hulda was 13, and she had to drop out of school to work on the farm. "But believe me, I learned a lot more than seventh-graders do today." She loved to read, especially farm journals and Zane Grey westerns. (She and a younger sister memorized a whole chapter.)

She married at 18. Her husband died of tuberculosis seven years later. She was left with a 6-year-old daughter, a 3-year-old daughter and 4-month-old twins. She remarried after eight years: "I was a happy girl with him, but he couldn't adjust to my children. He was too old." By the time he died 15 years later at 79, she had had two daughters by him.

In 1965 she married carpenter Marshall Staples. "I tell everybody he's a builder," she said. "Money always seems to elude him, but all my children love him." He's a hunter and fisherman and doesn't care much for poetry. All the more reason that she appreciates his going heavily into debt to finance her book, she said.

Hulda Staples has written poetry since she was a teenager and a boyfriend jilted her. She got more serious about writing in the 1930s, when one of her daughters was assigned to recite a poem for a Sunday school Christmas program — "about Santa Claus, of all things! I sat down and wrote a poem about Jesus for her. It's in my book." She picked up her one and only copy and read aloud:

> *I like to learn of Jesus*
> *Upon a starry night*
> *So very many years ago*
> *This star was shining bright.*
> *It led the wisemen from afar*
> *To where the baby lay*
> *They brought their gifts rejoicing*
> *To this Babe upon the hay . . .*

For decades she has written every day, filling notebook after notebook with her poetry. If her house were ever to catch fire, she said, she would run to her desk drawer to save the notebooks. When she's invited to a wedding shower or birthday party, she writes a special poem and tucks it in with her gift. Now that she has told everyone a publisher has accepted her work, her family and friends keep asking for it. Why, just a year ago, at the funeral of her sister in Windom, Minn., her nephew asked when he could get a copy.

In the publishing business, firms such as Todd & Honeywell are known as "vanity" publishers or "subsidy" publishers. For anywhere from about $5,000 to $20,000, a vanity publisher will edit a manuscript, design the jacket, manufacture the books and provide a limited amount of publicity and advertising. (In Hulda Staples' case, the poems were not edited and the cover illustration was done by her niece.) Only a small percentage of vanity authors break even on their investments. Few bookstores carry vanity books, and even fewer newspapers review them. Vanity publishers don't employ salespeople, relying instead on direct mail. The publishing industry says fewer than one in 10 authors will recover their money after their books are published.

Vanity publishers frequently point out that some of their products have made the big time or become regarded as important books. They include books by university professors unable to persuade scholarly presses to publish their work. Some people turn to vanity presses to publish their autobiographies, family histories or self-help books. Time may be a factor; vanity presses can turn out a book faster than trade publishers. Control is another reason to seek a vanity press; some authors felt they lost control of their work when they sold it to a mainstream commercial press.

Sylvia Burak, editor of The Writer magazine, told the Christian Science Monitor she advises authors never to publish with a vanity house. "We don't accept vanity ads, because we don't feel there is a way to protect writers from the shoddy practices that really go on," she said. "You see, they purport to be publishers, but really what they come down to is very, very expensive printers."

Most books produced by vanity publishers have little or no sales potential beyond the author's circle of friends and relatives. Rather than lay out thousands of dollars to a vanity press, Burak and other observers of the publishing industry tell authors, it is far cheaper for the author to arrange with a local printer to have a few hundred books manufactured and then try to place them in a local bookstore on a consignment basis.

Hulda Staples didn't know all that. Todd & Honeywell, she said, "didn't come across at first as a vanity press. I didn't want a vanity press. I didn't think I was going that way. I want my money back. Where do we go from here?"

Publishing experts predict that Staples eventually will get the 125 books promised her. Some copies of her "Slices of Life" may be mailed to reviewers.

The book is not likely to sell well, in which case her publisher might inform her it has stacks of books it cannot sell, and ask if she wants to pay for storage in New York or have the books trucked to her. Either way is expensive.

The Staples' loan is paid off, but they never got more than one book for their $9,800.

Karl Neumeier

A Report on 97½ Years

October 5, 1986

ह

Karl Neumeier would like a paragraph in the newspaper to tell his old friends he's still alive at 97½.

There you have it, Mr. Neumeier.

And if there's room for another sentence, he would like it noted that Pauline is still kicking too. She's his 98-year-old wife whom he refers to as "a much older woman" and "my first wife."

We heard about Pauline and Karl Neumeier from a friend of the family. Pauline, we learned, is a classy, quiet woman who studied music in Italy when she was young, reared three children and wrote poetry later in life. Karl was a Stillwater lawyer who retired at age 88. He also was a Republican state senator from 1935 to 1950, chairman of the Senate Tax Committee and a University of Minnesota regent in the 1950s.

Unlike his wife, he loves being the center of attention. The report was they've been married 71 years and still like each other.

That was intriguing enough to take a jaunt to Somerset, Wis., where the Neumeiers live on 160 acres of wooded land that Karl said he bought "dirt cheap" 62 years ago.

He wasn't much interested in talking about his career or old age or the meaning of life. Most especially, he didn't want to sit down to talk. He wanted a reporter to stroll his land with him for a bit, which turned out to be a delightful hour. His wife doesn't walk much anymore, he said slyly, and he likes to get into the gardens and among the trees with a woman now and again.

"These are my dahlias," he said. "I have them every year by the thousands. You take this one. Then people will know you've been here."

Gardening is his job, he continued. We learned later that he spends three or four hours at it every day, much of the time on his knees. "I've got more damn garden. See those? Beautiful white flowers. I can't remember the names anymore. Just when you get to the point of having a lot to remember, you don't."

Walking at a decent pace, Karl Neumeier gave the grand tour: the fish ponds that he had stocked with trout; the tennis court; the shuffleboard court from which he had swept leaves only the day before and here they are, "more damn leaves"; the homes of his son and two daughters, right next door to his; the family's hangar for an ultralight airplane; the fireplace in his basement that he built himself from fieldstone; the bluff overlooking the St. Croix River, and the forest tinged red with sumac and yellow with poplar.

His step hesitated only when he had to negotiate a narrow, slippery, slanted path from a shed. "Here I come, if I don't fall down," he shouted gaily.

In a more somber moment, he said, "I wish I were 40 again. I was pretty damn active when I was young. One year we went to Greece on the university plane and saw all the statues, you know. We went all over the whole damn Europe, too. I was head of the law firm so I could go when I wanted."

Pushed to reminisce, he talked about his father, F.G. Neumeier, who came to the United States at 17 and ran a German-language newspaper in Stillwater, and Pauline's father, E.L. Hostes, a prominent Stillwater lumberman.

And how did Karl meet Pauline?

"Couldn't help it. Small town."

He went to law school, had a fine family, served his state, saw the world. "I think I did just about everything I wanted." Any regrets? "Sure. I'm getting old. I regret it. But really, we're both pretty lucky. We're both alive."

How have they managed that?

"Well, we never drink any liquor."

He paused, looking devilish, then finished his sentence: "Until it's offered."

Cocktail hour is held every afternoon at 5:30. The Neumeiers, their children ("Hard to call them children when they're all retired," he said) and whoever else is around (there usually are guests) gather on the lawn for libations, he explained. "It's a good life. Although sometimes things turn out peculiarly."

After a while, the reporter's questions began to irritate him. Of course, he's glad he became a lawyer, he said sharply. "Do you think I'd want to be a nurse, carrying around bed pans?" No, he doesn't know offhand how many grandchildren and great-grandchildren he has. "I don't know a grandchild from a great-grandchild; got so many of them."

But then he remembered a definitive way of figuring out the number of his descendants. "I can show you my checkbook and show you how many damn Christmas presents I have to buy." The answer is eight grandchildren and 15 great-grandchildren.

During the basement tour of his house, we passed a wall of plaques, certificates of appreciation and photos of him as a regent, senator and bank director. An award from the university referred to him as "distinguished senator, eminent lawyer and citizen who has deeply enriched the life of his community."

He grinned. "Wrote that myself."

What he is most proud of, he said, is that he is the only living founder of the Stillwater Lions Club. He emphasized the "living," not the "founder."

Upstairs in the dining room, he pointed out the sign, "The Lord giveth, the government taketh away," and a thank-you-for-the-contribution card from the Republicans with a photograph of President Reagan. "My wife, she's crazy about him." And what does he think of Mr. Reagan? "I'm surprised he's done so well."

Finally, we got to meet Mrs. Neumeier, who was in a comfortable chair, a shawl over her shoulders, a book with regular-size type in her hand. She was as gracious as promised. Modest too. Her family sings her praises. For her 95th birthday, for example, her family printed a booklet of her poetry called "Painting with Words" and gave copies to 500 relatives and friends.

Asked for her secret to a long, happy life, she said, "We've had quite an outdoor life."

Her husband interjected, "We traveled a lot, you mean."

"No," she corrected. "I'm talking outdoors."

"Traveling around," he insisted.

"No, Karl," she said firmly. "I mean, we've been outdoors a lot. That keeps a person healthy, without a doubt." This winter, for example, the Neumeiers are going to Maui, as they have every January, February and March for about 15 years. She said, "I think he does better in a warmer place. It doesn't affect me, I don't think."

Their son, Karl, confirmed that each year they travel to Hawaii, without escort. He said, "We put them on a plane and tell the stewardess, 'Good luck!'" The Neumeier clan is not the fretting type.

"No use worrying," said the younger Karl Neumeier. "Just enjoy the continuity of life."

With a little snooping around, we found out some things to which the elder Neumeiers and others credit their longevity. They eat lots of fish ("brain food; I need it," he said), fresh fruits and vegetables. They don't nibble between meals. They laugh a lot. She uses half-and-half in her tea, and that makes her happy.

One of their household helpers, Robbie Hokenson, said they are wonderful employers. "They never tell you what to do. They don't tell you which day to do the laundry, what to cook, how to clean."

Karl Neumeier explained, "That's all due to ignorance, not manners. Besides, doesn't matter to us. We don't do a damn thing around here anyway."

While their children were children, Karl was Sunday school superintendent at an Episcopal church, but now that he has given up driving, they're not much in the way of church-goers. He said, "Sometimes I think God doesn't know what he's doing. Don't put that in the paper, for God's sake. Oh I don't give a damn what you put in the paper.

"Just say it was a pleasant visit."

It was a most pleasant visit, Attorney and Mrs. Neumeier.

Karl and Pauline Neumeier are alive and doing well at 101. They're living in their own home, with the help of their family and housekeepers.

Denny Ganley

A Tough Guy Who Cares About Kids
February 18, 1990
❧

"**L**et's go get the little darlings," said Denny Ganley, punctuating his sarcasm by kicking the metal desk with his sharp-toed cowboy boot. He likes to make noise.

His "little darlings" are some of the nastiest juveniles ever to make their way through Hennepin County's juvenile courts — armed robbers, crack dealers, burglars, car thieves, gang members, chronic truants. The murderers aren't his; they get sent away. But kids who are in other kinds of big trouble and who abuse drugs are sent to him.

Ganley is not a cop, not a social worker. He's an ex-con, a former junkie, a recovering alcoholic, a street-wise guy who still has friends at the fringes of society, but who has moved up to a $125,000 house in Apple Valley. He likes the tough kids — some, anyway — and he understands what they're going through. But sympathize? Not much.

He has one overriding message for teenagers in trouble: Stop whining. Take responsibility.

He recognizes that most of the kids in his program come from lousy families and haven't known the sweetness of success and are sick of being poor and, perhaps justifiably, feel picked on. They've been physically abused, emotionally neglected, scholastically embarrassed.

Doesn't matter. His childhood was rough, too. It included a father he didn't know until he was 15; polio in kindergarten; a stepdad he couldn't get along with; trouble in school, and stays in reformatories. As a young man in the Army, he was a safecracker and an armed robber. He was hooked on alcohol and barbiturates and used lots of marijuana, speed and morphine. He served time in Southern penitentiaries and to this day winces when he describes his whippings by guards.

But one day in the joint he said to himself, "This ain't working. This is going nowhere. I can't do no more time." He straightened out. So can kids today.

❧

Ganley to a young man who was insisting he wasn't using many drugs: "Come on, quit the bullshit. I was a junkie for 15 years. You ain't talking to no social worker. If you're smoking shit, you're getting high. When you gonna do something with your life?"

❧

Ganley runs a program called Rainbow Bridge. Judges send teenage boys and girls there when they don't know what else to do with them. At any one time, Ganley has about 30 kids he's supposed to help go straight. Most of them have served time, been through chemical treatment, gotten thrown out of school and placed in special classrooms. Nothing has worked. The noose of the juvenile-justice system gets tighter and tighter around their young necks.

He has an average of eight months to turn a kid around. One hour each weekday, he meets with his group in a conference room at the Hennepin County Juvenile Justice Center in downtown Minneapolis.

He cajoles, teases, begs, talks slowly and rationally, cusses, praises, rewards, dares and explodes. The scariest moments are when he screams. He puts his face half an inch from a kid's and bellows. Even the cockiest delinquent has a wobbly lower lip by the time Ganley backs off.

"You got to yell first," he explained. "Gives me a headache, all that yelling."

❧

To a boy who feebly protested that he was "trying" to quit drugs: "The reality is, young man, you're about 50 yards from jail. I'm not going to wrap you in a warm blanket and tell you it's going to be all right. You're full of bullshit, and you're getting loaded. You're making a dismal attempt in school. Why don't you knock off the bullshit? You're either using or you're not. There's no in-between, no trying. Quit bullshitting yourself."

❧

Some county officials think the world of Ganley. Allen Oleisky, a veteran Hennepin County juvenile-court judge who has has known Ganley for more than a decade, calls him "a tough guy who's been there and knows every excuse. Deep-down, he knows these kids and really cares about them. The type of kids we're giving Dennis are fairly sophisticated street kids, likely to carry weapons, becoming involved in serious crime. There aren't many people who could deal with them."

Some of Ganley's kids, especially the boys, don't look all that tough. They seem more like scruffy choir boys — you think you could take them home, scrub them up and treat them right, and they'd turn into regular teenagers. Ganley snorts at such naivete.

Besides scaring them with tough talk, Ganley has a host of persuasion techniques. He isn't allowed to lay a hand on the kids, but he can slap on the handcuffs that he carries at the waist. He makes spot checks to be sure they're telling him the truth about their activities; he calls their teachers, parents, grandparents, anyone they respect even a tad. He uses a variety of county cars to trail them; they're good at spotting authorities and their vehicles. He insists on good manners. ("Feet off them chairs. Sit up. Thank you.") He encourages decent appearance. ("Anybody can be poor. Nobody has to be dirty." "I can't see your eyes. I'm going to put your hair in a barrette, wise guy, if you don't get a haircut.")

Because he knows that runaways sometimes sell their blood for cash, he routinely checks out plasma centers for kids missing from his program. He kicks out of his program those kids out who are showing no signs of reform; probation officers and judges don't take it well when they hear a client was tossed out of Rainbow Bridge. Ganley gives kids doing well a few days away from the program as encouragement. If they behave, the leash gets longer.

Intent on proving that he's just as street-smart as they, he keeps up on jargon, on street drugs, on what's cool and what's not.

❦

Boy in big trouble, to Ganley: "Why are you so upset about my curfew? I stole that car before 10 o'clock."

Ganley, hitting the roof: "Don't come in and play that gangster role with me. I spent lots of time in prison. I'm one bad dude and you ain't."

❦

As bad as he was, times were different when he was a kid. Ganley, now 46, says that drugs and gangs have made life in the Twin Cities much harder for young people on the edge. "No question about it, the cocaine, the 'ice' that creates so much violent behavior, the gang influence — it's just a plague. Spend some time walking the streets at night, and then go see a psychiatrist for being crazy enough to do it. It's dangerous out there. Why don't we deal with cleaning up this city? We're going at it ass-backwards. Why spend money to beautify the city, build bridges, make everything pretty, build a big convention center, when the crud is taking over?"

These days, there's a certain romanticism with being a crook, he said. It's a badge of honor. Very few delinquents are embarrassed by it. When he was a teenager, there was a stigma associated with growing up in trouble. "He's been in Red Wing!" was a shocking thing to hear. Now it's easy for tough kids to find each other.

❦

Ganley: "How do you intend to stay out of trouble?"
Kid: "Stay away from friends who do drugs."
"Do you have any friends who don't do drugs?"
"No."

The Last of the Tearoom Ladies ❦ 195

❧

"Just say no" isn't the kind of argument that works with Rainbow Bridge participants. Ganley would like them to at least tell the truth about their drug use. They tend not to. What uncovers the lies are frequent tests of their urine. With highly sophisticated equipment, Ganley and his partner, Butch Hargraves, can determine with a great deal of accuracy what the kids are using, how often and how much. They run tests on about 100 people a month — including former and current Rainbow Bridge kids, plus other people whom county officials have under their wing and suspect are using drugs.

Ganley takes his title — senior chemical dependency worker — from that part of his job; he doesn't have a college degree so he can't be called a social worker. And, he added, "Guy Who Screams at Kids" doesn't seem bureaucratic enough.

In teenage years, Ganley often says, kids' minds leave their bodies. Drug use makes that worse. Kids in trouble don't stand a chance while they're abusing drugs or alcohol. Yet, Minnesota is much too liberal in accepting addiction as a reason for behavior against society and self, Ganley said. "You can get treatment for hangnails here. Over-eating, over-shopping, over-gambling, sexual addiction. It's crap. A person has to take responsibility for their actions." Programs can help sometimes, but the decision to shape up comes from within oneself, he preaches.

❧

Ganley: "Can you quit drugs?"
Kid: "Sure."
"How long?"
"I bet for a month or so."
"Then you can't quit."
"Well, you know. A party comes along."
"Yeah, that's like saying my car won't start so I had to get drunk. Believe me, I know the excitement. I never got sick of getting high. I got sick of doing time. Big deal you can quit for a month. I can stand on my head for nearly a month. A month ain't nothing."

❧

With his office work, his group sessions and his barrage of phone calls at his home on nights and weekends from teenagers and their parents, Ganley figures he gives the county about 55 hours a week for his approximately $35,000 a year. "Everybody wants a 8-to-4 job, but human services ain't one of them. That's why you burn out. If you're going to be effective with these kids, you've got to help them. They already know I'll kick their ass. They also need to understand I'll go to bat for them if I think they need my help."

Ganley usually shows up at the Juvenile Detention Center at mid-morning, wearing jeans and a casual shirt. One winter day was different. He left home before 7 a.m., all dressed up in suit and tie, to drive a young man named Anthony to court in St. Paul for an 8:30 a.m. pretrial hearing. Ganley wasn't required to shepherd the boy through the hearing, but he remembered from his own boyhood how rough it was to be hauled into court alone. He figured that Anthony could use some support: "He don't say nothing, but I'm sure he appreciates it."

While Ganley doesn't believe every excuse the kids in his program present, he thought maybe Anthony got squeezed in a bad situation. The teenager had been picking up his possessions at the place he stayed temporarily, after his mother had moved to Atlanta. The cops had swarmed all over him at a residence that supposedly was a crack house. Anthony was charged with intent to distribute cocaine.

So Ganley put in about three extra hours of work time for Anthony (getting no extra pay for his efforts); used his own money to take the hungry kid to a cafe afterwards for breakfast (scrambled eggs, sausage, toast, pancakes, juice and coffee); kept a finger on the case for weeks, and gave Anthony an occasional good word.

To what result? Anthony flew the coop. He wasn't heard from in months. "Too bad," Ganley said. "I think he would have gotten off." Ganley vowed that if the cops picked up Anthony, he would have no time for him. He would rather help the kids who are trying to go straight.

ૐ

Ganley: "Your old man still assaulting you?"
Boy: "No, I'm just staying away from him."
"One thing you can do. You got my home number? He lays a hand on you, you call me. Got that?"

ૐ

Success is hard to gauge. Ganley believes the program helps turn around lots of the kids. How? He said some are intimidated by the power he has, some appreciate the attention, some appreciate his working to alleviate their problems, some like to hear his war stories, some like the fact that he doesn't play cop. "And a few over the years have genuinely liked me."

He said he can make good guesses about which Rainbow Bridge kids will succeed and which ones won't. Reviewing a list, he said, "This kid will make it someday, I'd bet you anything. This guy probably will but I worry about him — a sniffer, abused at home. That girl will be OK; she just comes from a family that loves attention. This guy may or may not. This girl is having some attitude problems but she'll make it. This one is sitting in detention and he's going back to Red Wing. Nasty kid."

Peter Albrecht, a Juvenile Court judge for five years until he went to the District Court two years ago, praised Ganley as effective in getting the job done. "Sometimes an Edina kid gets thrown in by mistake, and their mothers are upset by the language and the no-nonsense approach." Suburban kids can get a healthy dose of shock value, Albrecht said; "It's like throwing a middle-class drunk driver in jail for a couple of days." Ganley is a good role model for less fortunate kids, according to Albrecht: "A white, middle-aged judge has had a much different life than what these kids are going through."

Ganley does have his detractors, most of whom cite civil liberties issues for Rainbow Bridge participants. Barbara Isaacman, a Hennepin County assistant public defender, said it troubles her that Ganley can impose punishment without going to court. He can order a misbehaving kid to spend Saturdays on the work squad, doing such chores as cleaning graveyards or raking lawns for senior citizens. Isaacman said, "They require kids to be open about their problems, and if they admit they're using drugs, for example, they can be punished."

Another issue she pointed to is that poorer kids end up in Rainbow Bridge. Most people with money get their wayward teenagers into insurance-paid treatment programs.

❦

Kid from a family with money: "I pulled $1,000 braces off my teeth 'cause I was mad at my mom and dad."

Ganley: "Very bright. Next time, plunge a knife into your heart. That would really piss them off. I mean, why do you harm yourself when you're mad at somebody? Have you ever thought of that?"

❦

Ganley was born in 1943 in Minneapolis. His father never came back from war service in the Air Corps. Eventually he was adopted by his mother's second husband, whom he described as a hard-working, hard-drinking Irishman. The family didn't have much, but neither did most others in north Minneapolis. By age 12, Denny was in trouble. He ran away frequently, once as far as to New Orleans, and he was sent away to Glen Lake and Red Wing reformatories. Authorities there thought he was crazy so he was hospitalized for mental illness at Glenwood Hills in Golden Valley.

As a condition of getting out of a reformatory at age 17, he was forced to join the Army. He and a buddy at Fort Campbell, Ky., lived off base and got into burglarizing safes, usually not getting a dime but sometimes putting their hands on $10,000 for a night's work. They got busted. Ganley was convicted for his work on safes (he never got caught for his armed robberies), and while waiting to be taken to prison, he escaped. He served time in a Tennessee penitentiary, where the standard fare was hog-head stew and fried okra. Meat was served once a week (pork steak on Thursdays), and chicken only on Christmas. Instant coffee in the cells was contraband.

Prisoners who broke rules were beaten by guards; "You'd lay on a mattress and get yourself a mouth full of mattress and then they'd hit you so hard they'd flip you over."

And what made him go straight in the joint? "Picking cotton. That's for real."

❦

Ganley to teenager: "Just how much loss of freedom can you stand? Walking around prison in paper clothes? Would that make you think?"

❦

Living the straight life didn't come easily for Ganley. He went through treatment several times, had a bad marriage and got divorced and remarried the same woman and was divorced again, went through a string of marginal jobs and sold some hot televisions and guns. On Jan. 1, 1971, recovering from a New Year's bender, he realized he was too sick and too tired to continue with drugs and alcohol. He's been clean since.

By the mid-1970s he was volunteering with a program that helped delinquent kids. The woman who ran it, Karen Stolz, offered him a job in 1978. He offered her a wedding ring in 1981. "I married the boss and then I got rid of her so I could run the program," he joked.

Now the Ganleys live in a four-bedroom home in Apple Valley with dogs, cats, a big-screen television, weight-lifting equipment to keep him at a lean, mean 150 pounds, "all the whistles and toys." Of their five children — three his, two hers — only his youngest son, 12, is left at home.

His 26-year-old son, he said, has gotten his fifth citation for driving while intoxicated. Ganley helped him through chemical treatment twice last year. "He's the smartest of the kids, but he's a gutter drunk. I never listened to my first kid. I do it different now."

❦

Girl: "My mom's been nice lately. I don't understand it."
Ganley: "I don't either. She seems like a loser. But that doesn't mean you'll have to be."

❦

Ganley has a sign in his office that reads, "It's better to build children than to repair men." He said he thinks America will suffer for allowing so many children to go wayward. "These kids are as much victims as perpetrators. We have to take a hard line to get them out their mess. Society's got to change, got to take a different approach."

❦

Ganley: "My advice to you is to stay squeaky clean. You're doing good. Getting high is not gonna do you any good. It's not worth the price you have to pay."
Kid: "Yeh. I know it."

A few of Ganley's kids

Derrick

Despite Ganley's best efforts, Derrick, 17, saw no reason to shape up. The boy admitted to spending most of his time lying around his folks' couch and smoking dope, even though he had been through chemical treatment at age 14. He got his girlfriend pregnant and turned down a job at McDonald's because he thought he could do better.

Ganley started an interrogation quietly, thoughtfully: "What's going to happen to you? How are you going to support a woman and kid? Sweeping out American Legion clubs?" Derrick got surly and said he was plenty happy with his life. He figured he could get a $16-an-hour job in a steel factory, a vague possibility his uncle had mentioned.

Seeing little chance for Derrick after six months in group, Ganley grew fierce. "You ain't going to stop smoking dope, despite all your problems. You've got no money, no future, no skills and all you're saying is, 'Hey, far out!' There's nothing anybody could say that would ignite some pride in you. Tonight's the last night you have to come here, Derrick. I'm done with you. I feel bad for you. Five, six, seven years from now, you'll be sitting in treatment and you'll have a kid who isn't properly cared for.

"I'm going to let you go, not because I think you're going to make it but because there's nothing I can do for you. It's pitiful, that's all I can say."

Derrick's reaction: "He's pretty cool but he can be harsh sometimes."

The young man called Ganley weeks later, essentially asking him to lie to help him get back into school. Ganley refused. That's the last he's heard from Derrick.

Charles

Formerly a car thief, Charles, 17, got into a big argument with his mother. She ordered him out of the house in north Minneapolis. In the cold of November, the only clothes he had were his shorts. Not knowing what to do (other than not to beat up his mother), he called Denny Ganley, who had counseled him at Rainbow Bridge and had helped him get a job and into special classes.

Ganley found out he could get Charles into a group home, but not that night. It would take a day or two. He considered taking him home to his house in Apple Valley; both Ganley and his wife, Karen, who also works in the field of chemical abuse, have taken in kids temporarily. But the logistics weren't right that night, and Ganley had Charles admitted to the juvenile detention center. At least the jail cell was warm.

Charles was appreciative: "He's helped me a lot. He understands. You tell him the truth, he tells you to face up. 'Are you prepared for the consequences?' he says. Instead of throwing a chair or kicking a car last night, I called Denny. He don't just see us as pieces of paper. He's been there."

❧

Stephanie

She easily was caught in a lie. Stephanie had called her mother to report that she and some friends had stolen a car and were in the St. Cloud area. Ganley asked the mother if it had been a collect call. No. Then she's still in the Twin Cities, he said. He's never heard of a teenager who called long-distance by plugging a phone full of quarters.

A few days later Stephanie showed up again at her parents' suburban house. Ganley went to arrest her for running away. He said that he could tell by her slow reaction time and by the fresh hickies on her neck that the night before had been a boozy, romantic evening.

After he put handcuffs on her and put her in the back of a county van, a reporter asked her what she thinks of him. "He's nice," she said. Even if he's about to lock you up? "Yeh." Why? " 'Cause he understands you."

Ray Neuman

Biking for Jesus

October 8, 1988

❦

There's this preacher up in north Minneapolis who likes riding motorcycles almost as much as he likes saving souls.

Every time Ray Neuman can get out of his polyester Salvation Army uniform and into denim and leather, he's roaring up Lyndale Av. to Chopper City for bike parts or off on the highway with his biker buddies or in his garage tearing down his Harley-Davidson.

Yeah, a Harley. A big, tough Harley. From the time he was a kid, he had a string of wimpier bikes, but he noticed that the hard-core bikers, the ones he would eventually like to tell about Jesus, never would talk to him on the streets.

One day he prayed about that. "That's when God brought Gabriel into my life," he explained.

Not Gabriel, the angel. Gabriel, the motorcycle. A '74 Harley Sportster.

It seems kind of strange to hear a minister say that he rebuilt Gabriel's engine last summer or that he's thinking of painting Gabriel black with blue-pearl overlay, but if you hang around Neuman you get used to mixed Bible and motorcycle images. He's a "Jesus and the Art of Motorcycle Maintenance" kind of guy.

Gabriel, he explained, is named for the chief among God's seraphim angels, a mighty battler, and "if you're going into the dens of iniquity, you'd better have a good fighter with you."

Neuman can be tough himself. He has a gold belt — that's a middle rank — in the kick-boxing martial arts form called tae kwan do. The skill has proved useful when he's told the kids in the neighborhood of 29th and Lyndale Avs. N. that he'll knock their heads off if they touch Gabriel or break into his church again. His predecessor suffered seven break-ins at the church, parsonage and garage. So far, so good for Neuman.

He hasn't gone for the complete biker image. He doesn't have tattoos — "yet." He hasn't picked up cuss words. He won't go in to bars, even for a Diet Coke. True, he has hidden around his house a few copies of Biker magazine, which features seminude women, but he has the magazines for the bike ads and vocabulary. "Besides," he said, "you've got to know the enemy."

Most bikers, Neuman insisted, are clean-cut people — bankers, lawyers, secretaries, house painters. Bikers like to say of themselves that 99 percent are straight, law-abiding people, and some of them are in Neuman's flock. But he feels a special call to reach out to the others, known as the "one percenters." They're the alcoholics, addicts, thieves, bums, the bottom crust of society. Converting the one-percenters is frustrating and slow, Neuman said. He has to wait for them to ask about God: "Jesus never walked up to someone and said, 'Hey, you're going to hell.' "

Sometimes Neuman thinks he's making progress and then the bikers "veer off and go back to their old life." If he can help one in 10 North Side bikers, he'll be doing good, he said. The neighborhood could stand the Lord's influence; he speaks of crack houses, gang fights, rapes in the park, gunfights and murders down the block.

Minneapolis Police Lt. Garry Frazier confirms Neuman's judgment of the neighborhood. "Rough? Yeah, it's rough." Not as rough as some other sections of town, he said, and most people are able to live there safely and comfortably, but "it's tough, active and what happens depends on who's renting this month."

Neuman claims three or four successes for the Lord. "The jury is still out on another dozen," he said.

The successes include Chuck West, 6 feet, 320 pounds, tattoos up one arm and down the other. He rides a '48 Harley Panhead. West has been off drugs for five years and alcohol for 18 months. He was getting interested in becoming a Christian before he met Neuman, and his faith has been strengthened since he has moved in temporarily with the preacher's family. West is taking classes to become a soldier (member) of the Salvation Army, and he's a substitute Sunday School teacher. He's crazy about the church: "They make you feel wanted and loved, not just on the spiritual aspect, but the human aspect too."

And there's P.J. Manson, not a regular church-goer but Neuman's friend now. Said Manson of the minister: "He kind of befriended me. When you quit drinking, you need friends. And he needed information from me. 'What part would fit here?' 'How do I fix this?' 'How do I get at that?' He's one of my friends now. I can talk to him about anything — looking for a job, the girlfriend, trouble making mortgage payments. Anything."

Neuman yearns and prays for more ways to make his message heard. God told him to organize bike rallies.

❧

For weeks, Neuman and his wife, Carol, also a Salvation Army minister, spread the word about the rally to be held last Saturday. They telephoned some hundred bikers, who promised to show up and bring friends. The Neumans got notices up in bike shops, persuaded bottling companies to donate 5,000 cans of pop, hired a band for $500, got a city permit to block off the street and spent $150 in Salvation Army funds for hot dogs, buns, ketchup and ice.

The idea was that the bikers — 300, maybe 500 of them — would meet at the church, contribute $5 and canned goods toward the Salvation Army's efforts to help poor people on the North Side, ride in a long string of bikes to Forest Lake and back, eat hot dogs, listen to '50s and '60s rock, have fun, see that the church doors were open and not get preached at.

"I just wanna rub shoulders with some of these guys," Neuman said. That was the plan.

What happened was that only three bikers showed up. Worse, that included Neuman and a friend, the biking brother of a church member. The only stranger looked uncomfortable.

Carol Neuman smelled failure. She called for prayer. She gathered the four Neuman kids and a few Salvation Army volunteers who were supposed to have been kept busy registering bikers. Hands linked in a circle near the garage, they prayed for bikers to show up. "Lord, we've done our work," she implored. "We ask you to bring us people. . . . In your name, we believe this will happen."

The Lord works in mysterious ways. He didn't send more participants. And the stranger dropped out of the bike run after three blocks, never to be heard from again.

Just to rub salt in the wound, old Gabriel — one of two bikes in the rally — broke down. She was popping out of gear in third. The problem was bad enough that Neuman would have to tear her down for the winter. He wouldn't even have his bike to console him about the rally being a bust.

Neuman admitted he was "very disappointed" about the day. His wife and his friends tried to buck him up. Remember Sturgis, they said. The bike rally in Sturgis, S.D., that attracted some 70,000 bikers this year started in 1940 with six participants. Maybe Neuman will have better attendance next year. . . . Maybe if he didn't hold the rally at the church. . . . Maybe if it had been in spring or early summer, not fall. . . .

But he put on his best face and announced that the bike rally was now open to the neighborhood and church members. He encouraged little kids hanging around to enjoy the band belting out "Johnny B. Goode" and "I Saw Her Standing There" and to run home for a dollar so they could eat all the wieners and chips they could hold. Friends of the church kicked in extra money. Eventually the party contributions were $111.63 and four boxes of canned goods. "It isn't what we wanted, but I suppose it's better than it could have been," Neuman said mournfully.

ᘒ

The next morning, he was spiffed up for 11 o'clock holiness meeting at his Parkview Salvation Army Corps Community Center. He wore a navy blue Salvation Army uniform, a crisp white shirt, black tie, shiny black shoes. Somehow even the woolly beard of the day before had been tamed. He looked cherubic, playing the guitar as his wife led the congregation in singing "To God Be the Glory."

Then he began what he says he does best, what the Lord wants him to do. "I feel more comfortable in jeans, but I'm prepared and called and built to preach."

For 25 minutes, he preached about Jonah going to the wicked city of Nineveh and warning the people that it would be destroyed in 40 days. Neuman was an orator. Sometimes he boomed, sometimes he whispered. He waved his arms. He paced. He told some simple stories that even the children could understand. When he spoke of the ordinary happenings in a day, he threw in names of neighborhood landmarks — the Camden Pharmacy and Monroe's grocery store. He got in some laughs. He had the congregation shouting up answers to his questions. He uttered an occasional "Brother, praise the Lord." He even got in some motorcycle references, such as urging his listeners to repent all sins — untruths, adultery, murder and, especially, stealing Harley parts.

He did whatever he could to tell people that they could walk out of church alive in Christ or dead unto themselves.

Neuman was born a Catholic 32 years ago. He was raised in Green Bay, Wis., and when he talks to the bikers the "dese" and "dose" of his childhood come bounding out. He turned Methodist to marry Carol. He always had an itch to be a preacher, but pushed that aside to go to college and raise a family. One day in February 1981, the Lord spoke to both of them, she in the bathtub, he on the road driving truck for a living. "I want you to be an officer," the Lord said. They didn't even know what an officer was.

They found out that the Salvation Army had ministers called officers. They sold everything and moved to Madison, Wis., to be assistant ministers at a Salvation Army church, and then to Chicago to study for the ministry. After a year's stint in Rochester, Minn., they were transferred to Minneapolis, where they've served for three years.

It's been a prime area for converting bikers, he said. The streets of the Twin Cities are full of bikers who need the Lord but don't know it. "There aren't many biker outlaws in places like Willmar," he said.

Neuman reports he has four bikers attending his church, maybe not every Sunday, but now and again.

Sandra Merwin

She Took a Golf Club to the Courts

May 4, 1985

❦

All she wanted was an apology. She hoped someone from the country club would say, "We're real sorry, Sandra. Come and have a drink on us. Let's talk about it. Change comes slowly in a place like this."

She says now, "One glass of club soda, and they could have bought me off. My goal is to play golf."

But there was no apology, she says; she barely got a response. She got no indication that the club's rules will be changed. So Sandra Merwin, a 35-year-old Deephaven businesswoman and self-proclaimed yuppie, filed action this week in Hennepin County District Court, charging the Minnetonka Country Club with sex discrimination.

She has gotten a favorable ruling from the Minnesota Department of Human Rights, which concluded that male members of the club get better treatment than women in such matters as open-golf times. Because she decided to sue in court, she has to drop action through the human rights department.

The Minnetonka Country Club declined this week to give its side of the story to a reporter. However, in a January letter to the Department of Human Rights, its president, Bodhan Witrak, wrote, "We are a private country club, not open to the general public, and as such are not regulated by the statutes stated in Sandra Merwin's complaint." (The human rights department rejected that claim. It concluded that the club is a public accommodation because it is unselective in soliciting members through such means as newspaper and radio advertisement.)

The Minnetonka club also noted that its regulations were formulated by the members themselves, both men and women, and said that the club provides more "women only" schedules than found in other golf clubs.

But Sandra Merwin says she doesn't want "women only" time; she doesn't want to play on a female foursome. She wants to golf with her husband and her clients, most of whom are men. "No one told us golf is such an archaic sport that men and women don't play together," she says.

According to Merwin, the club discriminates by giving the best open-golf times to men. For example, men have open play on Saturdays and Sundays; women may not golf before noon on Saturdays and 10 a.m. on Sundays. Wednesday afternoon open play is limited to men. Merwin contends there is no rational basis for saying women can't play when men are on the links.

Sometimes, Merwin says, she would just as soon toss her golf bag in the closet and forget about legal action. She'd rather not fight the system. She dresses for success, she knows the right people, she makes good money (she expects to gross more than $60,000 this year) and now she's suing a club of rich and powerful people. She wonders if her action will lose clients for herself — a writer and training specialist — and for her husband, Andrew Merwin — an insurance agent.

"It's a gutsy move," says her lawyer, Stewart Perry. "Women in these clubs are second-class citizens and can't say anything because they're half of a husband-wife team. If they rock the boat, the husband hears about it."

In fact, Andrew Merwin is already hearing about it. He said he got a call Thursday from a man who identified himself by name and implied he was a member of the club. According to Andrew Merwin, the caller said something like, "I want you to know there's a ground swell of golfers who will not insure with you or will cancel their insurance with you because of what your wife is doing to the Minnetonka Country Club."

Nonetheless, Sandra Merwin is riled up enough to take action. Never before that warm June day last year, she says, had she experienced what she calls "that back-of-the-bus feeling." She says she thought discrimination was a word that belonged to the 1950s or 1960s: "I believed I was born free and had earned my respect. After all, I owned my business and had clients such as IBM and 3M. I traveled first-class and people listened when I spoke and my money bought me passage in this brave new desegregated world."

Merwin runs a business called Professional Training Services. She develops and writes training programs for business, industry, government and education. She also is the author of a book called "Not a Victim," which advocates what she calls "preventative defense." She says she found books on what to do after a person is raped or victimized, but very little on what to do to prevent becoming a victim. That advice is intended for people (particularly women) who have not had training in self-defense, although Merwin herself has a brown belt in karate. The book is dedicated, "To the victims — may it never happen again."

She says she joined the Minnetonka Country Club a year ago for two purposes: to play golf for relaxation with her husband, and to entertain clients on the links and in the clubhouse. The Merwins bought a joint membership, and she paid the $1,000 initial fee with her check. She says, "I was led to believe that I was a full member of the country club and therefore had full membership privileges."

There were a few clues, though, that things would not go well for her, she says. She wanted the membership in her name. "I got a song and dance about how that's not how we do it here." She gave in, under protest; she was registered as Andrew Merwin's wife. And when she asked for a rule book, she says, she got a reply that it was being rewritten and temporarily unavailable.

Her next disappointment was the day she invited a client to play golf, intending to wrap up some business transactions at the club house. They arrived at 3:45 p.m. on a Wednesday. After she put on her golf shoes and checked in at the golf pro's desk, she was told by a club employee that she was not allowed on the course. Her client was allowed. He's a man.

"I remember wanting to cry," she says. "I felt vulnerable and hurt, yet it seemed paramount to maintain a facade of calm and poise. I didn't want anyone to know the depth of my genetic shame. Somehow I felt the whole situation was my fault. I was so smooth, though. I graciously thanked the 'voice' for letting me know the rules. I persuaded my guest to play without me."

While he was waiting to tee off, they watched two boys and their father tee off. In a letter of protest to the club, she wrote, "I find it interesting that I pay for a full membership but I am not allowed on the course, and yet my guest and junior golfers are free to use the course at their discretion."

She said those boys, by the way, were lousy golfers. When the second one missed the ball entirely, she walked away in disgust.

(Meanwhile, her game was improving. She's a natural athlete, she says, and learned fast. She played her first nine holes of her life at the Minnetonka Club and scored 120. By the end of the year she was breaking 100 on 18 holes. "Respectable," she says. "I'm not the best golfer, but I improved dramatically." Male club members were asking her to play, she said. She said she wouldn't mind if the club segregated poor players from good ones, but that doesn't necessarily break down along male/female lines.)

Her next problem was several months later, when the club offered a free Sunday brunch to the guests of golfers. She wanted to invite an IBM client from Rochester to join her for golf and brunch at the club, which Merwin calls the best brunch in town. When she tried to sign up, she was told women were not allowed on the course then.

Merwin wanted her $1,000 back.

In September she wrote to the club, "I should have been informed that I would not receive full membership privileges when I joined. Perhaps you need to have an associate membership which limits the privileges and of course does not have the same membership fee.

"When I travel on business I pay for first class. I do not expect to pay for a first-class ticket, and then be seated in second class during part of the flight because I am female. I cannot in good conscience pay for first-class membership at the Minnetonka Country Club and be treated to second-class privileges."

The Last of the Tearoom Ladies 🐇 209

She says the club's only response was to send a bill with the notation, "Dues liable for the year."

She said she doesn't relish the lawsuit and resulting publicity. "But I have to do it. It'll probably be painful. But when discriminated against, someone has to say, 'Hey, this isn't right.' How many times can you lie down and take it and still respect yourself?"

Sandra Merwin settled out of court with the Minnetonka Country Club. She received an apology, the refunding of her dues and an undisclosed amount of money. She said recently that she rarely plays golf: "I don't enjoy it any more."

Albert Joseph Alexander-Fryc

The Blind Bicyclist
August 24, 1985
❧

Al, the blind guy who runs a bike shop on E. Hennepin Av., has a neighborhood kid hanging around this summer to be his eyes. In exchange for free bike parts and an unpaid apprenticeship, 12-year-old Nuch Bashiri fetches handlebars, retrieves gizmos that roll under the workbench and answers Al's question of "Is that a customer up front?"

Al doesn't need a whole lot of help, so Nuch and a buddy had time one day to perfect the fine art of chewing gum and crunching sour cream 'n' onion potato chips. Simultaneously. The boys, whose fingers were as greasy as the master's, stared at Al at work. They were more interested in what Al can deftly do with a rim squeezer and a wrench than the fact that Al fixes bikes by feeling and hearing.

After Al adjusted a bike's brakes, he spun the front wheel to be sure the rim was true. Puppy-like, he cocked his head, then put his ear a few inches from the wheel. His fingers delicately felt for bulges in the tire. He fiddled and fussed and philosophized, and when he and the boys agreed the bike was in good order, his Popeye forearms bulged and he hoisted the bike up to the hook on the wall and pulled down another.

And just how did he know that was the bike he wanted?

"It's the tallest bike in the bunch. I know it stuck out from the wall more. It's been there two weeks; I *oughta* know where it is."

Albert Joseph Alexander-Fryc is legally blind, but not totally blind. "I call it hard of seeing." He has a tad of peripheral vision and with thick glasses can see at 20 feet what a normally sighted person can see at 1,000 feet. He sees only vague forms. When he tries to read a word or two, his eyes are so close to the paper that his crazy eyebrows almost brush it.

With his vision steadily failing, he relies more and more on his other senses to run his bike-repair business, Wheel Works at 320 E. Hennepin Av., Minneapolis. He "writes down" phone numbers on his abacus, moving the beads to correspond to digits. He speaks into a little tape recorder all day to make a list of parts he needs to order. He measures with his fingers. He can almost smell where hundreds of parts are stored.

Some things he can't do. Bookkeeping, for one. The fact that he doesn't even try pleases his part-time accountant, he said. Cleaning is another. A customer used the grungy bathroom under the basement steps and reported to Al, "There's evidence of a little rodent life. I stood up in a hurry." To which Al responded, "Where can I rent a cat?"

He has a good reputation in the biking community, not only for his bike-repair skills and his strange and wonderful inventory, but also for his gentle nature and crummy jokes, few of which are suitable for a family newspaper.

Al's blindness is affecting his biking more than his business, he said. "I ride slow now. I've gotten slower and slower. I used to ride *fast* and got hurt now and again. I'm married now, and my darling wife wants me alive."

Fast means fast. He loves to whiz down a hill on a bike at 40 miles an hour. He keeps his hair in a long, Ben Franklin style so the wind can whip through it as he bikes. His idea of an ideal weekend is biking to Taylors Falls with his wife. He bikes to work, sometimes with a guide, sometimes alone, mostly on side streets. ("I stop for a lot of green lights. If I'm not sure, I stop.") He bikes in the winter. He builds and rides tandems, and he's getting used to the idea that his biking may someday be limited to the back of a tandem.

When he skis downhill he wears a vest ("orange, I think") that proclaims BLIND SKIER, but he doesn't have an equivalent for biking. Sometimes in races (like the Grape Nuts race, which he calls the Great Nuts race), he wears a helmet with a flashing light on the back, but mostly he relies on a biking partner to shout "Stop sign ahead" and "Hole on the right." He and his biking friends call obstacles "Al traps." He's hit his share. But what the heck, he says. Anything to stay on a bike.

He's not as afraid of losing what little sight he has as he is of the government someday prohibiting blind people from biking.

❧

Now meet Al's darling wife. Sue Ann Alexander-Fryc is a librarian at the Northeast Public Library. They recently celebrated the 10-year anniversary of knowing each other and the six-month anniversary of their wedding. She's 53; he's 38. They've gotten relatively little guff about the age gap, the most notable from Al's dad who told her, "He looks older than you do."

When she got Al, she got bikes, too. Never before had she seriously biked. "I started last year and fell off six times," she said. "I've got good bones and a big fanny so I can bounce well. I'm an optimist, though. One trip around Lake Harriet and I thought I could race."

He doesn't care how she bikes, she said. He cares if she's having fun.

She is, especially when he's along, but she has to remind herself that he's legally blind. Sometimes she forgets to warn him of Al traps.

She married him, she said, not for his vision but for his "delicious laugh" and his humor and his sense of adventure. They'd known each other for years, but after their previous marriages broke up, they went out. On their second date she said to him, "I'd like to declare my intentions." She intended to keep him around. A few months afterward she told him in the shop, "Our love is very sacred and I think it's time for some vows." He didn't react, but he didn't walk out the door and she figured that was a good sign. Soon after, a friend told her that Al was spreading the word they were getting married.

In her wedding vows, she promised her dance-hungry man to love him, give him loyalty and Lindy with him the rest of her life. They danced a Polish polka down the aisle, saying aloud, *"One,* two, three, *one,* two, three."

She's a recovering alcoholic. His eyes are going to pot. But worry? Them? No. She said, "My dad died of cancer. My other relatives died of horrible things. I could have died of alcoholism.

"We celebrate each day. It's wonderful to sleep spoon-fashion again. We have birds in the back yard; he listens to their songs, and I glory in their colors. We love to touch. We *like* each other.

"It's such a kick to live with someone I adore."

❧

Al Fryc was born in 1947 in Germany to Polish parents. His father had been in a concentration camp in World War II and weighed 85 pounds when liberated. A man who owned a Brainerd, Minn., creamery sponsored the family's move to Minnesota in 1951, when Al was 4. His mother promised him a tricycle when they got to America. Their second day here, she went out and, not knowing a word of English, managed to buy him a trike. The Frycs settled in Cloquet, Minn. (Al, an unstoppable lyric writer, sang one of his few songs that is printable: "Oh Cloquet, where the smell will get you miles away.")

Al inherited his mother's vision problem; his brothers did not. Hers is not nearly so bad a case of retina pigmentosa. He has "always" had glasses, but had no idea he would lose his sight. His eyes kept him from pursuing baseball, "and I used to have a fastball that would jump and go up as it reached the plate. What a rush!"

From his mother he also inherited a good dose of religion, and he spent three years in a Wisconsin monastery, studying to be a Franciscan brother. He dropped out and went to vo-tech schools.

Biking evolved as the major passion of his life. (Now that he's a happy newlywed, he has relegated biking to the No. 2 spot.) His work became increasingly tactile. One night years ago he performed an experiment at a shop where he put together new bikes. He turned off the lights and found he was slowed only two minutes per bike.

He started his own shop three years ago. He rents 800 square feet. Many of his customers are there for the usual stuff — brake jobs and bike horns, rims and chains. But people know he has things few stores do — brake systems for old Schwinns, tires with good traction for winter biking, parts for commuter bikes, rims for English bikes. He has gotten more and more into supplying parts for wheelchair racing; he hopes to put together a catalog of lightweight, tough handrails, wheels and other wheelchair parts.

Usually there's someone hanging out at the Wheel Works. If not little kids, there's an adult biker or two yapping away. A few are yuppies, escaped from Riverplace three blocks away. More are aging hippies talking about how bikes don't wreck the environment, or the laws of physics as applied to bicycling. The conversation is varied and good. As Al said, "Bicycling people are more than willing to give their views." He calls the place a spoke-easy, "and we don't even need booze."

Musicians hang around, too, at least when Al isn't practicing his dulcimer. A classic example of a biking musician is 21-year-old Gregory Carr, who plays four bare bike frames suspended from his basement ceiling. One is so well-constructed, Carr said, that it sounds like a church bell; another sounds like a cow bell.

Al says his customers are first-class, for the most part. "Most are good people. Some are at their most vulnerable. People who are usually real strong and tough come in and say pathetically, 'I can't fix my bike!' They're panicking. And they want the work done yesterday. But for real nice folks you're more than happy to do extra work for them."

He spouted off some about people with "Ridgedale Consciousness," which he defines as the quest for bucks without responsibility for the environment or for other human beings. Rich he's not. He says he's lucky if he clears $3 an hour. The tedium and stress of the business haven't caught up with him yet. "I can still eat pizza and not get acid indigestion."

Usually he can find his way around his shop like a cat in the dark, but at one point he banged into a bike which hit another which hit a third. As he righted the bikes he said blind people are *supposed* to have grace and courage and super ability. He'd rather not think about all that. "I'd just as soon be another bozo on the bus." Actually, on the bike.

Will his eyes get worse?

"Probably. Everybody says, 'But aren't the doctors doing great things now?' Maybe, but I'm not holding my breath. I don't need lung problems."

Al's bike business went belly-up. He's back in school, studying music and English at Metropolitan Community College. His dream is to someday teach philosophy. Meanwhile, he's teaching bike repair. His eyes are worse so he's cramming Braille and restricting his bike-riding to tandems.

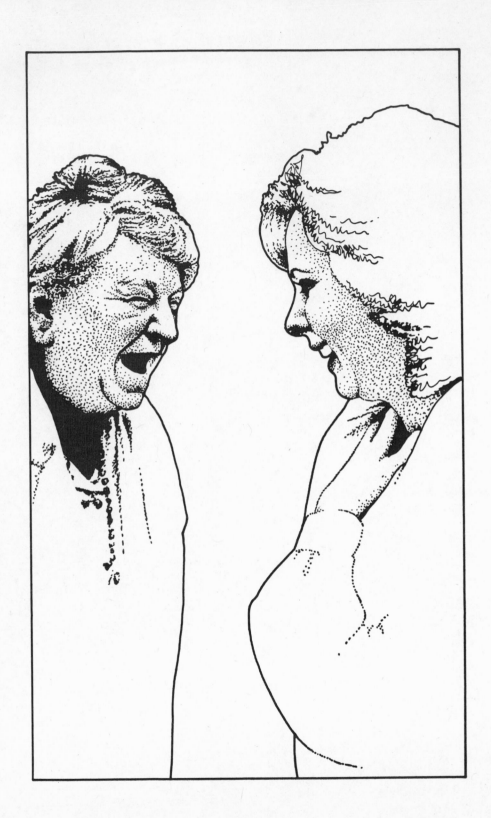

Nursing Home Opera Fans

The Song is Love

February 16, 1988

❧

The famous opera singer was running on New York City Time. The Minneapolis nursing-home residents were operating on Old People's Time. That meant residents starting showing up at 2:45 p.m. for the 4 o'clock concert, and it meant that soprano Judith Blegen didn't get to Luther/Field Hall until 4:30. A rebellion was brewing.

"This is ridiculous," said Ina Larson, who's 88. "Nobody does things the way they're planned anymore."

The situation was calmed when Meryl Kothlow, a volunteer at the Ebenezer Society home, offered to lead the group in some good old-fashioned songs, such as "Let Me Call You Sweetheart" and "How Great Thou Art." Staff members went around patting residents' hands and telling them, "It won't take long; you might as well stay now" and "I'll get you some water" and "Yes, I'm sure it will be worth the wait."

Just when wheelchairs were beginning to point toward the door, it was announced that Miss Blegen was downstairs, warming up her voice, and it wouldn't be very long at all now.

It wasn't. And once she started singing at 4:40, all was forgiven.

The Metropolitan Opera star sang Mendelssohn and Handel, Grieg and Strauss. She explained each song in an informative manner; never was she condescending. She looked deep into the eyes of the 70 or so old ladies and the several old men. Faces beamed. Heads nodded with her music. Eyes were teary, and not from sadness. One woman waved her handkerchief as a bravo. Afterward the residents talked about how each one felt Blegen was singing "just for me."

The best-received selection was "Vilia, O Vilia" from Franz Lehar's "The Merry Widow." Several women sang quietly with Blegen — in tune, lovingly. They liked the part that goes "burning with love and desire." As Blegen's high notes nearly knocked the stained glass from the chapel window in the nursing home, hands went to ears to adjust hearing aids. A startled Dagmar Leikvold, born in 1893, said, "I've never heard such a thing!"

There was no fussing afterward about the show starting late. "Not many places get a Met opera star for free," said Millie Spanish, whose father used to put her on his knee and tell her how he loved Enrico Caruso.

Judith Blegen was in the Twin Cities for a Friday evening concert at the Ordway Theatre. She volunteered to perform at Luther/Field Hall, because her great-aunt, Anne Blegen, lives there.

Now 46, Judith Blegen grew up in Montana and remembers visiting Minneapolis three or four times as a child. Her first escalator ride was at Dayton's. She had her first restaurant luncheon here — a cream-cheese-and-black-olive sandwich. She remembers her first visit to a hairdresser, at the Leamington Hotel where her grandmother lived; the child wondered if her hairdo would last until she got home to Montana.

Anne Blegen was teaching French at Macalester College in those days, and Judith would go with her and Anne's sister, Martha, to Minneha-ha Falls and other very important places. Their brother, Theodore Blegen, now deceased, was a University of Minnesota historian and dean of the graduate school.

Judith said last week of Anne, "She was a lovely lady, a very, very refined lady, and she still is."

Anne is 88 now, and she was ever so pleased to greet her great-niece at the nursing home. "Judy," she said simply, opening her arms. "It's so much fun to see you."

After some endearments were exchanged, Judith apologized. "I'm sorry I'm so late."

"It's wonderful you're here," said Anne.

"Why don't I go back with you to your chair. I'm ready to start singing."

Some members of the audience know opera. Several mentioned they revere the name Texaco for its sponsorship of Saturday afternoon opera on the radio. Helen Winter, who's 91, used to go to Northrop Auditorium every spring when the Met was here, "but as a public health nurse I couldn't afford to go more than two times" during each of the Met's visits. Paul Weinandy, 84, grew up in Germany in a family of opera buffs who knew Clara Schumann, wife of composer Robert Schumann. Orma Adam, 95, had not had the opportunity to hear live opera before, but has been to Orchestra Hall many times. "I don't get out much any more," so it was nice, she said, that the nursing home brought opera to her.

Other residents responded as Maude Gunnell, 93, did: "They said if you went to a regular showing of her, it would be $50. I've never seen an opera recital before, but I heard she was coming and what a beautiful singer she is."

After her half-hour performance, Blegen chatted with well-wishers. She accepted thanks spoken in German by Elfriede Gerlach, 82, who lives in a senior-citizens complex in New Hope and got her daughter, Ramborg Johnson, to drive her to Minneapolis for the little concert. Blegen had a long chat with Hagbarth Bue, who's 100, and told him she looked forward to seeing him the next time she visits her aunt in Minneapolis.

The aunt, by the way, made this critical assessment of her great-niece's performance: "Remarkably fine."

Judith Blegen sang at Ebenezer in November 1985 and asked a family friend, Karen Bruce, to set up another recital for Saturday afternoon.

Blegen is known for bringing opera to the masses. For example, she's been on the Johnny Carson show dozens of times. She likes people — opera aficionados, newcomers to opera, elegant people, plain people, young, old.

"Sometimes I ask myself why I feel so deeply for elderly people," she told a reporter. "I wonder if it's because my own parents died so early." Her father, a physician, died at 48; her mother in her 50s. "I'm sorry I didn't get to enjoy them in their later years."

After Saturday's concert, she listened closely to the stories of the old people. She said, "There's so much to learn from them. After all, the world didn't begin when I was born. I hope my descendants will be interested in my life."

And no, of course, she doesn't find it at all depressing to be at a nursing home. "Quite the contrary. I feel far too little attention is paid to the elderly in this country, and too little respect is given them. It's a privilege for me to sing for them."

She didn't try to come up with a glossy excuse for being late. "It took me a while to get going today," she said. "I have to work on budgeting my time."

Privately pleading exhaustion, she didn't hint to the old people that she would like to get away to rest up. She stayed at Luther/Field Hall as long as people had something to tell her. That was after 6 p.m.

Early, by New York City Time. But well past suppertime, by Minneapolis Old Peoples' Time.

Teenage Nightingales

Boys 'Aide' Handicapped Neighbors

October 9, 1986

❦

"**I**t's a great scheme," said Tony Rogers, a high school sophomore, rubbing his hands together and pretending to be a money-grubber. "I get six of us guys together, and we party, and I get paid for it. Not bad, huh?"

Strangely enough, his employers, Ken and Rosemary Ashmore, agree. They are victims of polio and have had recurring problems in finding sleep-over attendants who have "old-fashioned values" and don't smoke, drink, bring women around or charge a fortune. They have found they can depend on a group of teenage boys from their neighborhood.

These are boys to whom polio is as antiquated a notion as the black plague. When one was telling the others about the iron lung Ken used for six months in 1952, the teenager called it a "still lung."

Ordinarily, the Ashmores have just one boy at a time at their south Minneapolis home. But a few weeks ago the kids had made plans to be together on a Saturday night and no one was willing to give up a good time with the gang.

Ken Ashmore, desperate, suggested they all sleep over and he would pay one of them regular wages. So Tony Rogers got $8 for the night shift and, meanwhile, the six boys ordered three pizzas (paid for from their pockets), set the radio blaring, kept the microwave busy, busted up a few pillows they had brought from home and watched cable television for hours. All this was upstairs in the Ashmores' bungalow, in a remarkably soundproof room. That's lucky, Rosemary said, "because these boys aren't the quiet type. You feel you're being invaded."

About 3:30 a.m., the Ashmores had good reason to believe they were being invaded. Their sophisticated security system started screaming like crazy and automatically notified police. What had happened, it quickly was discovered, was that 15-year-old John Krook had been rolling around on the floor upstairs in a gale of laughter and had triggered the alarm.

Neighbors a block away heard it. By the time the house quieted again, it was 5 a.m., only two hours to wake-up time.

The Ashmores usually have a series of live-in adult helpers. But when the attendant has time off, they need someone on call. They were without adult help for several months this summer and fully depended on the neighborhood crew.

Ken Ashmore, 50, was left a quadriplegic from the polio he had at age 17. Of his limbs, he has only partial use of one arm; he can feed himself and hold a book or pencil, but needs help with such tasks as shampooing, getting in and out of bed and changing clothes. His breathing muscles were damaged and he needs a respirator at night. Rosemary, also 50, was 13 when she was struck by polio. She can't use her legs, and her arms are weak.

Of necessity, they insist that the boy on duty stick to business. One time, the boy had to leave for a bit and got a substitute. But the substitute wandered off. When Ken needed someone in a hurry, he found himself alone. He docked the boys' wages and delivered a good scolding.

He says stern things such as, "they're connivers" and "I tell them if they break anything, they pay," but it's obvious he's fond of the kids and their commotion. Out of their earshot, he calls them "exceptional kids."

For their part, they say they like Ken because he has a knack for spotting good-looking girls for them. Tony Rogers said, "We're pushing him around somewhere and he sees a girl and he said, 'Wow! Look at that!' He knows our taste."

More seriously, Chris Kos, 14, said, "My dad always says we're learning something here."

Like what? "Like his way of life and how he has to live and the stuff he does," Tony said. "He gets around more than it looks like."

"They don't slow down," Chris said.

True. Ken Ashmore has an accounting business in the house. His wife helps him prepare tax returns. "I never thought I'd sit around and collect welfare," she said. "I expected to go out and earn a living just like my sister." She also does the laundry and housecleaning. Tony said of the attendant's room upstairs, "They keep the place spotless where they can see it. Up here is a different story."

The boys marvel that Rosemary rarely asks for assistance. One time she was sick with the flu and was exhausted. She asked one of the boys to help her fold sheets, and that was so out of character that the story spread like wildfire.

Rosemary drives but needs help in getting in and out of the car. Whenever the Ashmores need to get to a business meeting, the grocery store, a wedding or a picnic, one of the neighborhood boys is with them. Chris Kos even got an all-expense paid trip to Moorhead and Fargo for an anniversary celebration.

The trouble with needing someone around much of the day is the Ashmores can't even squabble in private. "Yeh," she said. "We have referees. Teenage referees."

Handicapped people, she said, are out and about so much more now than when she first was in a wheelchair in the early 1950s. People would stare at her, and sometimes in aggravation she'd stick out her tongue at them. People have gotten kinder; she's gotten mellower.

The Ashmores pay the boy on duty $7 for the 11 a.m. to 9 p.m. shift and $8 for the 9 p.m. to 11 a.m. shift. (The night work involves getting Ken in and out of bed.) Monday is payroll day, and the boys line up at the back door. If they went through a nursing agency, the care would cost up to $60 a shift, they said. The Ashmores have to deduct for Social Security and pay workers' compensation and unemployment. "On 13-year-old kids, I think it's ridiculous," she said.

The boys say their pay is pretty good for not much work, and they hope other kids "don't move in on us here," Tony said. Still, they look forward to the time when they can get "real jobs."

Ken Ashmore has lived in the same south Minneapolis house for 30 years. He and his first wife, Ramona, also a polio patient, lived there with his parents. After she died of cancer, he married Rosemary. His parents moved to a condominium two years ago, and Ken and Rosemary had to hire help to replace what the elder Ashmores had done. They had the kitchen remodeled, a new garage built and a bedroom added. They also put in an upstairs bathroom.

The boys are intrigued by the technological gadgets around the Ashmore house, and they seem proud of Ken and Rosemary's accomplishments. John Krook's mother, Joyce, said the boys enjoy being useful. "In fact, I think they're more eager to work here than at home," she said in mock surprise.

They already are concerned with who will take over the work when they move on. Luckily 13-year-old Matt Engen has two little brothers, only 3 and 5, who'll be ready in another decade. The work is good for kids, Tony Rogers said: It "makes you realize being healthy and able to do what you want is pretty important."

It also makes them realize that accountants have a good business. Tony and Chris are trying to cut a deal that they'll hang around the house for free if the Ashmores teach them how to do taxes.

The boys are doing well in high school and college. Ken and Rosemary Ashmore were divorced a year after this article ran. He has remarried and is running his accounting business. Rosemary is going to college.

Harry Leonard

A Nonretiring Storyteller
June 15, 1985
❧

Here's a story 86-year-old Harry Leonard told on himself the other day:

After he enjoyed a glass of Italian Swiss Colony port at a socially acceptable time (after noon; 12:05 p.m., to be specific), he worked in the raspberry patch. He got a tad sleepy and took a nap on the couch. When he woke up, he checked his watch and shouted his favorite expletive: "Holy potatoes!" It was 6:30, and he had to be at work at 7 a.m. (Yep, he still works every day.) He made himself a gourmet breakfast (Special K) and jumped (OK, eased himself) into his car (a cute little VW Rabbit) and drove lickety-split (undoubtedly the truth) through northeast Minneapolis. Half way to work, he said to himself, "For the love of God, the sun, instead of coming up, is going down! It must be 7 at night!" It was. He turned around and went home.

That gives you a few clues about Harry Leonard. He told the tale without blaming his slip-up on his age, and then he had a good laugh. A natural storyteller, he's called the "Mark Twain of Northeast Minneapolis" because of more than his wild white hair.

He's got stories to tell about every period of his life except one: when he tried to retire as a labor leader. "The worst four months of my life were when I wasn't doing anything." That was in 1964, when he was 65. His buddies from the International Brotherhood of Electrical Workers gave him a 2-foot blue spruce as a retirement gift. The tree now towers over his house. He's been working a job or two ever since.

Leonard works mornings as a maintenance man at the Northeast Neighborhood House. The people there say he earns his keep; he's no charity case. He works hard from 7 to 11, and then flirts with the women before he goes home.

"I've been around here so damn long, nobody pays much attention to Harry except to say, 'Hi Harry,' " he said. Not so, say his colleagues. How can you ignore somebody who signs notes "The D.O.M." (Dirty Old Man) and who volunteers for dunk-tank duty for the annual fund-raiser at the neighborhood house?

"He's not like the rest of us, who sit up there in swimsuits," said Neva DeLong, an agency employee. "He comes in costume. One time he dressed up as an old lady — big hat, lady's dress, cane — and got soaking wet."

He's a little wobblier than he used to be, and his knees bother him. His boss, Keith Schwender, would like to limit his tasks. "But it's impossible," Schwender said. "I can't keep him off a ladder. He did take a bad spill off a 14-foot ladder in the boiler room a year ago, and we had a heck of a time to get him to go to the hospital." Turned out Leonard didn't break a thing but bruised himself badly. The next day he was sailing on Lake Minnetonka with his daughter and son-in-law, bouncing around in 4-foot waves. "It was so much fun. I wasn't feeling any pain," he said.

People ask him, "You still drive? You're 86!" and he says, "Sure. You've just got to use your head a little bit. If someone gets in your way, let 'em have it."

Those your own teeth? "They should be. I paid for 'em."

That your own hair? "I wouldn't be a damn bit surprised. It hurts like hell when I pull on it." He said he had a crew-cut most of his life, and his wife, now deceased, once told him, "You look like a jackass coming down the road, with your great big ears and that tiny little face between them." Now he likes to avoid the barber: "Think of the money I've saved."

And speaking of hair, he said, the other week he was at the University of Minnesota Hospitals getting a post-cancer checkup. (He's passed the five-year mark. And the 40-year mark. Back to that later.) Anyway, along came "this young chick, I'd say about 60 or 65" who ran her fingers through his hair. "When I saw that head of hair of yours," she told him, "I thought of Mark Twain and I couldn't keep my hands off you." Quite all right, ma'am, he replied.

Harry Leonard still mows the lawn on the three city lots he owns. He takes down the boiler at work every summer. Goes elk hunting in the mountains of Colorado. Gardens. Rents out a farm in Big Stone County. Enjoys books; he had 600 labels to put in his books last week and ran short of labels. Runs his snow blower. Passes around a lot of kindnesses. Lends money to kids around the neighborhood house. Listens to everybody's troubles.

Sure, his aging has forced him to cut back somewhat. He hasn't flown an airplane for about eight years. "But one of these days I'm going to go down and rent a plane and get the owner to fly co-pilot with me. You know, so he don't have to worry about his crate."

We said we were getting an idea of why he is famous in Northeast, and he said, "Famous? Famous! Listen, I cut down most of my trees, but I got two left. I think you're barking up the wrong one. Go write about somebody else, somebody interesting."

Judge for yourself.

Harry Leonard was born March 5, 1899, a war baby. His dad was off fighting the Spanish-American war — "off in Cubie." (He loves to play around with words: Democrats are "Demos," The Fidelity bank is the "Fiddle Lady." Doctors are "croakers" because they croak as many people as they cure.) He grew up in Little Falls, Minn., and used to play with Charlie Lindbergh. The two graduated from Little Falls High School in 1918. Leonard remembers of Lindbergh, "He was a pretty serious kid who didn't mix much. He had engineering going through his head most of the time." (One of Leonard's favorite possessions is a letter from Lindbergh saying he could not attend the 55th class reunion in 1973.)

A hair over 18, Leonard went off to World War I and came back safe and sound, he said, mostly because he never got out of Ohio. He spent three days in Little Falls, got bored, moved to Minneapolis and found a job digging ditches for sewers. "In those days, you dug dirt with a shovel, by hand. It was a good job, I'd say, but then I never had to smell myself."

He learned to fly a plane and in 1932 bought himself a 1928 Waco biplane for $800. He made some cash by flying low to the ground and using a Speed Graphic camera to shoot pictures of farms: "I should have been killed 40 times." He tries to talk people into learning to fly: "Buy yourself about 10 hours of time and it'll make your life completely different, baby doll."

When he was 42 his parents were beginning to wonder if he would ever marry. "I wasn't going to get hooked into anything like that," not until he went to his home town and met Louise Neumann. She was younger by 16 years and they were happy together, he said. "She was the greatest. She did a beautiful job of raising those two little gals of mine."

He found work as an operator at Northern States Power Co. and became active in his union, Local 160 of the International Brotherhood of Electrical Workers, AFL-CIO. He worked his way up the union ladder and became business agent (he calls it "busy agent") in 1947.

He was a heck of a good one, his contemporaries say. One of the people he served, Al Thielen, said last week, "Can I tell you how good he was? Drive up to 25th and Marshall, next to Tony Jaros' there, and look at the union hall — the Harry E. Leonard Union Hall. That's how much we think of him."

Thielen said Harry Leonard hobnobbed with big shots in his day — Hubert Humphrey, Orville Freeman — but he never wanted fame for himself. "He always was for the little guy. He never forgot the janitor or the new kid on the job or the guy working his way up. He tried not to be noticed. If anything, he's a little on the shy side."

Except for 1952, when someone beat him out in a union election, he served as business agent continuously until 1964, when the bylaws forced him to retire.

That's the period he went nuts at home. He was saved by the nurses, he said. The Minnesota Nurses Association sent a representative over one day and asked if he'd be interested in working for them. "Doing what?" he said. "Dealing on wages and conditions," was the answer. "Lead me to it," Leonard said.

Nurses' wages and conditions is a favorite topic of Harry Leonard. "They were getting damn sick and tired of the slavery that they was bound into. I've never seen such slavery! *Horrendous* working conditions. They were making less money than the lower labor classification in any of the labor contracts around and most of them had college degrees or the equivalent. They worked double shifts and got burned out. I became dedicated in a hurry. Things have changed; they're a hell of a lot better for the nurses now."

It was about in the early 1940s — maybe earlier, he can't remember — that Leonard read about a cancer detection program at the University of Minnesota Hospitals. "It was 10 bucks to go through there. Ten bucks. What's 10 bucks?" He was examined, and, "Sure enough. I was cancerous." His lower colon was removed and he claims to have lost only a day of work. "Wasn't much of an operation, I didn't think."

His wife was a Christian Scientist, and so was his mother, and Leonard agreed with them that it does nobody any good to stand around and think about health problems. He said last week, "It's all within yourself. Your mind is very powerful. If a person says, 'Oh geez, I feel lousy today,' then he will. If you get interested in other things, you don't think about it and you aren't sick."

That explains his reactions the night he wrecked his hand. He was awfully tired and was working in his shop in the garage when a 10-inch bench saw caught a string on his new work gloves and, zip, there went two fingers. He was dripping quite a bit of blood on the kitchen floor as he tried to bind himself up with a rag, so he thought he should get some help from his wife. "What happened to you?" she said. "Just a little cut," he said. "What?" "Yeh, I cut off a couple fingers, but nothing serious."

She went out like a light, he reported, and he had to wrap the hand a little tighter while he waited for her to come to. Then he asked a neighbor to drive him to an emergency room, which the neighbor did, at roughly 70 miles an hour.

But back to religion, he said he took more after his dad, a railroad man. "He didn't have any religion. He believed in doing what in his opinion was right." Harry Leonard was never much of a churchgoer. "'Course, when you're generating power, there's no relief. We didn't have many Sundays off. When somebody wants light on a Sunday morning, they don't want you in church, they want you at the power plant."

He misses his wife. "Louise died Dec. 5. Two o'clock in the morning. Cardiac." For company, he has a dog, "but there are lonesome hours."

❧

Harry Leonard's views of politics: Fighting in Vietnam was a mistake:

"I don't believe it was our business to look after tribal difficulties." World War II was different: "With a guy like Hitler, what else could we do?" Politics: "I could be nothing but a Demo." President Reagan: "No matter what he feels, he puts on a nice face. He's an actor. I haven't seen much to make me think labor was wrong about him."

The meaning of life: "Personally, the way I feel is, don't be a fast operator. Don't try to get the better of someone financially. If you don't have the regard of people, your friends and neighbors and business associates, then what's the use of living? And something that really throws me is the trust little kids place in you. Don't betray that trust. Remember when you were little? Someone you liked, you respected — that name will stick with you always."

Aging: "There's a lot of contentment in being old. A lot of the wonderings you used to have about this girl and that girl are past. They caused you some worry. As long as you don't have to worry about where your bread and butter are coming from, being old is a nice period."

Harry Leonard died in December 1988 at age 89. His daughter said that late in his life he thought his actual age didn't seem important enough so he sometimes called himself 95 or 97.

Back of the Bus Bunch

The Route to Lasting Friendships
December 12, 1987

❧

Jo Fridlund vividly remembers the first time she rode the 35N. It was her first bus ride. Her husband had been transferred to the Twin Cities area by Republic Airlines, and they desperately missed Arizona. He had driven her downtown in the morning, and she was going to try to take the bus home at 5 p.m. At the bus stop, she grabbed the sleeve of a kindly looking stranger, Janet Blad, and asked for help.

Which bus? Where? How much? When? Blad's den mother instincts took over, and Fridlund had a great time on the bus. Three years later, she now is a member in good standing of the Back of the Bus Bunch.

"This group has made Minnesota tolerable," Fridlund said. "Otherwise, my husband would be a single parent. I'd be home."

The regulars on the 35N express line — 19 miles from Burnsville to downtown Minneapolis in the morning and 19 miles home again in the evening — have developed a reputation for frivolity.

"Friendly and fun" is the way they like to think of themselves. "Loud and obnoxious" is what they overhear others say, including their least-favorite driver, The Twit.

The bus bunchers have become so fond of one another and think themselves so funny that they get together about three times a year on non-bus time for a whopper of a bash. They gather at Blad's house in Burnsville to do what they do best — party and tell old bus stories.

Blad loves to party. She loves to yak. She's the glue of the bus bunch. But even before she became a 35N regular nine years ago, there was something special about the commuters from Burnsville.

At the Christmas party last Saturday night, the bunch was joking about the occasional poor unsuspecting rider who makes the mistake of taking a seat at the back.

"They only do that once," said Pat Shade, dropping his voice and looking his meanest. "That's how we get new members. If they can take our noise and needling, they're in. If not, they go up to the front."

Paul Wallace, the MTC's manager of operations, said he has not heard complaints about 35N riders. He said that loud talk and fun at the back of the bus are fine, unless riders become disruptive to other passengers or driver. Gambling and drinking, he said, are prohibited on the bus.

The 35N riders spend so much time together — 35 minutes one way under the best of conditions, more than an hour some winter days — that they have time for lots of jokes, an occasional champagne party (don't tell the bus company), card games organized by Donna McMillen and remembered for their ungracious winners, book swapping, long discussions of personal problems, complaints about work and one-sided marriage counseling.

They joke that the bunch has voted down spouse swapping; Blad says the riders agree "most of us can't handle the one we have."

Spouses are invited to all parties, including the quickly organized ones. Someone will say, "Friday is going to be a Bulrushes night" and a dozen or so riders and spouses meet at Bulrushes in Burnsville for a few hours of levity.

Rita Butler, whose husband, Chuck, is a rider, said he's cheerful and relaxed when he steps off the 35N at the end of the day. He's got a few new jokes. He's passed around the family snapshots he picked up downtown. He's let off steam about work. She said, "The tensions are gone by the time he gets to the door."

So strong is the sense of solidarity that some riders have thought hard about accepting new jobs that meant ending their commuting. The bus bunch, an understanding lot, confers alumni status and continues to invite them to parties.

Last August, alumnus Jean Hovey came back from Winter Park, Fla., and Janet Blad used the visit as an excuse to get the bunch together for a party that lasted until 3 a.m. or so. At last week's party, they fulfilled Hovey's mailed request and all signed a birthday card for her husband, Bruce, who will turn 40 on Jan. 25.

The youngest alumna of the bus bunch is Annie Adelman, 8½ months, who rode 35N until a week before she was born. She rode one time afterward, when she was six weeks old, so that her mom, Nancy, could pass her around for inspection and thank everyone for the baby gift of $30.

The bunch has gotten so large and so many work schedules have changed over the years that they don't all ride the same bus anymore. Some get the 6:45 a.m. bus, some go as late as 7:45. To get home, many take what they call the 5:11 bus, which they say the bus company calls the 5:10 and which really goes at 5:20. (The nastier riders say that Northwest Airlines is the bus company's mentor.)

The riders have little in common but the bus ride. They know where the others work downtown, but they don't have a good idea of position or income. Somebody said the bunch includes everyone from clerical workers to a senior vice president, but others weren't very interested in con-

The Last of the Tearoom Ladies ❦ 230

firming that. A few of them get together for lunch every once in a while, but mostly they're known only for their bus personalities. For years, they've known each other by first names.

"These people are not pretentious," said Roger Merritt, one of the bunch. "Nobody's selling anything. Nobody's hustling. You can do as you want. You can sit and read the paper if you want, but if you choose to do that every day you might choose to sit somewhere else.

"Our common goal is to get from Burnsville to downtown and home again at night, to laugh and have fun. That's all."

That, and maybe provide a new circle of friends. Roger and Carol Merritt have lived for years about six houses away from Gary and ImoJean Ovick. The couples knew each other only by sight, and they learned names last week at the bus bunch party.

The bunch has more elaborate identities worked out for the drivers, most of whom are very good drivers and very nice, they say. Their favorite was Herbie, who hasn't been seen on the 35N lately.

Nonetheless, it's the rotten drivers who get the nicknames and merit the stories:

The Twit pulled the bus over one day. The Back of the Bus Bunch assumed the bus had broken down and they waited patiently, as patiently as they could, for repairs. Twenty minutes later, they saw a Metropolitan Transit Commission (MTC) worker arrive with a bottle of Windex and a rag. It seems The Twit wouldn't move until he had a nice, clean windshield.

The Speeder makes the bunch shudder when they board and has them think their obituaries will say they died on a bus.

The Sleeper jerks herself awake. That's enough to keep the bunch from snoozing.

The Driver Who Will Not Change Lanes has an aversion to crossing the dotted line, even when his lane is clogged and others are freer. The bunch has suggested a lane change, but the driver wasn't interested. "I'm a professional driver," he said, "and I don't have to listen to you."

The "Deliverance" Look Alikes are the women drivers who look a bit on the rough side.

The all-time classic story is about the morning Dick Dishneau had his usual five quarters for the bus, but the driver wanted 85 cents at the beginning of the ride and 40 cents at the end.

Dishneau volunteered to put the whole $1.25 in the fare box at the beginning. That wasn't acceptable to the driver. He didn't even want Dishneau to get change from a friend. When he got the bus downtown, he pulled over. Two waiting policemen boarded. The driver had telephoned ahead that a passenger refused to pay. After much discussion, an officer said to Dishneau, "So if you had change, you'd pay?" Of course. The policeman gave him change for a quarter and left. The bunch views it as a major victory, worthy of an epic poem.

Or maybe a mural in Janet Blad's basement. See, they are plain-talking folks, these 35N-ers. Most people with a party room complete with video games, a jukebox, bar, old barber chairs, good sound system, slot machine, Jacuzzi in the bathtub, etc., would call it something fancier than basement. It took Janet Blad's husband, Roger, some eight years to build it himself and they use it a lot. They hope that if a tornado comes along, it'll take the first floor of their rambler and leave the basement.

After two or three bus parties a year since 1983 at the Blads, she no longer sends out invitations. It's word of mouth: Saturday in the Blads' basement. The bunch knows to bring a bottle and something for the food table.

This time the Blads provided gifts: MTC Rider Rags, which Roger Blad made from flour sacks. They came with a sheet of suggested uses, such as "To flag down another bus when yours breaks down" and "to conceal identity when ragging on driver or fellow rider."

The Back of the Bus Bunch occasionally hears of other bus groups that have fun together. But mostly they hear of dull rides. People say, "They don't talk on my bus."

Pat Shade experienced bus dullness for himself last summer. Highway construction forced him to take the 35M, another Burnsville-to-downtown Minneapolis express, "and let me tell you, 35M people are dead. It was the most boring-est time I ever had. Nobody would talk to you. It was just like they were stiffs."

Maybe the unpleasant rides had an element in his recent decision to quit working downtown, after 11 years. He misses the bunch.

The Children and
the Princess

A Charming Visit Over Tea and M&Ms

September 18, 1985

❦

Once upon a time there was a beautiful princess named Alexandra, who loved children. Whenever she went visiting other kingdoms, she went to grown-up teas and balls and concerts. And then she would ask, please, to see the children.

So it was that when the princess went to St. Paul, she accepted with pleasure an invitation to visit the Children's Museum at a place called Bandana Square. There were no children's museums in her land; only big people had museums, and sometimes they took their children there, but that wasn't much fun for children, and the wise princess knew it.

Waiting for the princess were 70 5th- and 6th-graders from Longfellow School in Minneapolis, who had been studying her land and its customs. They learned that commoners do not ask a princess questions and that they must address her as "your royal highness" and that they are never, ever rude or smart-alecky to a princess. The children wrote down some nice questions to ask the princess, and they practiced and practiced. "What is it like where you live?" Molly Trettel would ask her. "What is the national pastime?" Kevin La Fond would say.

On the big day (Tuesday, to be exact) the children put on their best clothes (so good that the bus driver for the field trip asked if their school had a dress code), and the girls practiced their curtsying (Beth Hand was ever so graceful and lovely in her white dress and white patent-leather shoes), and they told each other not to say naughty things (like "shut up") within earshot of royalty. Their teachers were proud of the children, and a little nervous, too. "I hope they can contain themselves when the time actually comes," said Juanita Morgan.

And as it happened, things were not quite as the children had expected. They hoped for great formality and pomp. They wanted the princess to wear a tiara and ride in a glass carriage and have diamond rings so heavy

The Last of the Tearoom Ladies ❦ 233

that her servants would have to support her hands. What they did not know was that the princess had plenty of pomp in her life and that sometimes she liked to talk to real people, especially children.

So when the princess arrived in a car and wore regular-sized rings and had no crown, the children asked among themselves, "Is she *really* the princess?"

But she and her husband, the Honorable Angus Ogilvie, were very kind to the children and amused themselves greatly. When Cathleen Nyman presented them with snack foods that she and other Minnesota children enjoy, such as M&Ms and chips, he said, "Corn chips? Can we eat them now? I *love* corn chips!" And so they saw him gobble down corn chips.

The children showed the princess the railroad engine and big crane and the pretend dentist's chair and the Legos room. She loved everything, especially the Legos creation Brian Edgar had made and named a "flight pod."

They tried to be good, but sometimes they forgot the rules, or misinterpreted them. They pulled on her jacket to get her attention. Some spoke directly to her, instead of waiting for her to speak first. "Hi, your royal majesty," said William Shaver, who's 12. She said "hi" back. When asked by a reporter if he had used proper protocol, William said, "Sure. Our school just said not to go up to her and say, 'What's up?' "

The princess asked the children about their school and their teachers and if they liked writing essays (they don't) and what they've learned about England (lots) and if they will visit her land (they will). She asked the teachers about team teaching and classroom size and other serious things.

Her husband was less serious. He liked to play with the personal computers and he enjoyed the make-believe castle. He said to Jason Jensen, who wore a red jacket and played the part of a sentry, "You have to do the buttons up and stand straight for two hours at a time. I had to do it. I was a soldier once, a long time ago." And he said to two children who sat on thrones and played a king and queen, "But you should have crowns!" Darris Larkin asked him, "Do you have a crown?" No, he said, and added, pointing to the princess, "She does. But not a proper crown. Just the king and queen have proper crowns."

Because the princess and her husband were so pleasant, the children became more and more bold. "Do you like your fame?" Tony Kujawa asked her. She said she's hardly famous but has a nice, happy life. "Over in London, what time does it get dark?" someone else asked, and the princess said something about "after the sun sets," which in her kingdom, she said varies according to the season. (She did *not* say anything about the sun never setting over the British empire.)

And then came the best part of all. The princess was asked if she would like to see where the children were to have tea. She did, and she was most impressed. She saw the silver teapots (rented for the occasion) and the nice china (ditto) and the children (not rented) using their best manners. They put their linen napkins on their laps. They did not grab for the scones or shortbread.

When the princess asked if she could sit with them, the children could not contain themselves and became quite boisterous. They tugged at her and said, "Sit by me! Sit by me!"

So the very important princess sat at the head of the table and poured some herbal tea for Chuck Cox and Jason Jensen and several other children. She was 20 minutes behind schedule, and her servants let her know — politely, of course — that it was time to leave for a grown-up gathering, but the princess said she was in no hurry. "When she enjoys herself, she stays," the royal bodyguard said. She chatted with the children and thanked them for a wonderful party, and they shouted "Bye! Bye!" to her.

They were very proud of their good manners, and the princess's lady attendant whispered that the princess had a wonderful time — maybe the best time of any part of her visit. And when she left, the princess asked Kate Murray from the Children's Museum to thank them for a very special treat. M&Ms, the princess said, are her favorite snack.

And so the children found they could be themselves and still have the princess like them very much.

THE END

And they all lived happily ever after, we hope.

Index

240 ❦

Brian A. Cravens, compositor
Jim Freitag, illustrator
Linda James, indexer
Jarrett Smith, designer
Ingrid Sundstrom, editor